CANNES : THE NOVEL

Elizabeth stared out into the snow, her gaze unfocused by her own thoughts.

'Is a memory something we have, or something we've lost?' he asked.

She turned slowly to him and fixed him with a stare, as if she were trying to find the solution in his eyes. 'That's an intriguing question.'

'Not mine,' Robert acknowledged. 'I think it comes from a Woody Allen film.'

'And what's the answer?'

He shrugged his shoulders. 'There is no answer. It's a pure conundrum.'

'You're wrong,' she corrected him with assertive certainty. 'A memory is something we have. It can never be taken from us, it can be more precious than the present.'

'Do you really believe that?'

'More precious than my present –' she began, but as she spoke the chair jerked forward and the lift started to move again.

It was as if the spell of those few stationary moments had been abruptly broken and Robert sensed that their shared intimacy was over.

For Jack

IAIN JOHNSTONE

CANNES:
The Novel

Mandarin

A Mandarin Paperback
CANNES : THE NOVEL

First published in Great Britain 1990
by Chatto & Windus Ltd
This edition published 1991
Reprinted 1991
by Mandarin Paperbacks
Michelin House, 81 Fulham Road, London SW3 6RB

Mandarin is an imprint of the Octopus Publishing Group,
a division of Reed International Books Limited.

Copyright © Iain Johnstone 1990

Iain Johnstone has asserted his right to be
identified as the author of this work.

A CIP catalogue record for this title
is available from the British Library

ISBN 0 7493 0923 7

Printed and bound in Great Britain
by Cox and Wyman Ltd, Reading, Berks

CHAPTER 1

Thursday 23rd January 1997

Pinewood, England

'Quite, quite beautiful. Wonderful. Wonderful and beautiful. Could we try it just one more time, though?'

'What was wrong?' Elizabeth's voice was clear-cut and direct, heightened by more than a tinge of annoyance.

'I just have an instinct,' the director replied – he found instincts easier to have than reasons – 'that the inner melody, the one that is playing deep, deep inside you, should perhaps find a resonant chord of compassion at this moment.'

Tim was rarely able to express exactly what he wanted – usually because he rarely knew what he wanted – but when he did and could, the musical metaphor was seldom very far away.

'You want it harsher?' Elizabeth suggested wilfully.

'On the contrary, I want it softer. Just as soft as you can possibly be. This is the moment when you could be beginning to fall in love with him.'

'It.'

'If you think it's an it, you'll never find the right note.'

'You just called it an it yourself,' she pointed out with glee.

'No, I didn't. If I did it was a mistake.'

'I think it's a fairly big mistake myself.' Elizabeth's irritation was growing. She thought the take had been perfectly satisfactory.

Douglas raised his blue head from her lap in indignation. 'I'm not an it. If my agent hears that I'm an it, the whole contract is going to have to be renegotiated. An it would be an entirely separate deal.'

'You are not an it, lovey,' Tim reassured him, readjusting

1

the flamboyant scarlet scarf round his neck, something he was in the habit of doing when he felt uncomfortable. 'Never have been. Now maybe to you *we* are its.'

'Oh, God,' said Derek, the first assistant director, in a muffled aside to the crew. 'Don't let's complicate the whole fucking thing.'

'Yes, Derek? Some problem?' Tim might not be considered smart but he could certainly be sharp, especially when pulling rank. The thing he had always prided himself on was his leadership. An agency had once sent him on a week-end course to learn about this. As he cast a decisive eye over the two hundred people ranged across the vast shooting stage – electricians, carpenters, extras, stunt men, grips, riggers, wardrobe, prop men, actors and assistant directors – Tim knew that, whatever they thought of him, they were there to respond to his every whim. He regretted the passing of the days when British crews habitually referred to their director as 'sir'.

'I just thought,' Derek ad libbed, backing down, 'that maybe we could spray a bit of blue blood on his scales. Heighten the sense of tragedy.'

'He doesn't bleed,' Tim whipped back.

'How do you know?' demanded Elizabeth, beginning to enjoy the fray.

'Because it's not in the script,' announced the director definitively.

'When I worked with Kubrick we used to improvise all the time.' Douglas was warming to the idea. 'He would see something you did in a take and like it, and he would want to make it better. But he knew if he told you what it was, you might never find it so naturally again. So he would keep shooting, more and more takes, nearly a hundred sometimes just for that . . . moment.'

'I hardly think we need a hundred takes, Doug. Just get Ray there to spread a bit of blue jelly along one of your cracks.' Derek raised his megaphone to his lips. 'Ray, make-up,' he boomed.

'No, no, Ray. No make-up. No blood!' Tim was happy to have found a decisive moment. 'Douglas does not bleed. He is free to bleed in as many of Mr Kubrick's takes as he wishes but not here.'

Douglas became warily penitent. 'I only meant that it might be possible, just on occasion, to interpret the script – '

'You've wounded him,' interjected Elizabeth mischievously.

'I have not. I merely wanted to respect the sanctity of the – what's so funny?' Tim looked round at the grinning faces of the crew.

'Nothing, guv.' Derek came to his aid. 'Better get this shot in. We've got fifty-four of the buggers ready in make-up for the net shot.'

'Next shot?'

'*Net* shot. In the tank. The sailors lower it and the Jus scramble up the side of the ship.'

'But is it next?'

Derek raised the megaphone once more. 'Dolly!'

'Put that thing away.' The reprimand came from a small grey-haired lady on a stool, covering her ears. Dolly was continuity, as old, some said, as the studio itself. 'Yes, it's next.' She glanced at her script. 'First after lunch. Second after lunch if we don't get this bleedin' scene finished.'

'There is *no* bleeding,' screamed Tim. 'He is ethereal. Let us go again. This time, Elizabeth, darling, cradle its head in your arms and feel the pain.'

'His,' said Elizabeth.

'No, sweetie, *your* pain.'

'*His* head,' she pointed out, 'not its.'

'Quiet, everybody. Hold the noise.' Derek at last had use for his megaphoned authority, although the only real noise was coming from him. To reassert himself he continued. 'Ray, make-up, a dab of sweat for her brow.'

'Perspiration for ladies,' corrected Ray as he nimbly weaved his way towards Elizabeth and, having dabbed, trotted back even more nimbly – a mini-performance in itself.

The scene was now set. Cruise liner interior. The surgery. Evening. Nurse Florence has crept back in to comfort the alien leader who has been lying lifelessly on the operating table. His blue scales glow in the low light, his skinny legs and arms flop over the side, like a dog asleep, and his crustaceously human head rests forlornly on the pillow, with outsize eyes gazing at the ceiling.

'*Jupiter Landing*. Scene two hundred and four, take four,' yelled the clapper loader.

'And . . . action,' whispered Tim.

Elizabeth, her hair caught back in an austere bun, cautiously opened the surgery door and moved lightly across the room with a dancer's grace. Indeed she had the fresh and open looks of a member of the *corps de ballet*, and the starched severity of her white uniform only served to highlight her trim, supple figure. The natural lustre in her eyes was deliberately subdued as she stood and gazed at the creature, half in horror, half in sorrow.

'I think you've come a long way,' she said, 'a long, long way from home. I think I know what you feel. Perhaps, in that other world, you have a wife and maybe a daughter, too – like me.'

She knelt beside him, then reached out and took his shell-like head in her arms.

The creature gave an electric movement backwards, releasing itself from her caress. Although unnerved, she continued.

'There. No need to worry. You've fallen among friends. We mean you no harm.'

Again she tried to take him in her arms and this time no resistance was offered. The doleful eyes turned towards her and from within came a deep, lingering moan, like an antique foghorn across a distant bay.

'And cut. Perfect. Absolute perfection.' Tim stood up, demonstrably moved.

'Want to go again?' enquired Derek chirpily.

'No, print it.'

Dolly eagerly wrote the instruction down in her book, then closed it emphatically and began to fold away her canvas stool.

'Right, lunch everyone' – the megaphone was back in action. 'Green pea loop the loop and Duke of York in the canteen today for those of you with their own teeth. Back in an hour.'

'Tim, can I ask you something?' The creature rose from the table.

'Yes, Douglas.'

'My moan – was it all right?'

'It was music. It was the lost chord.'

'So you won't dub it over with some electronic effects.'

'Certainly not. I wouldn't dream of it – not unless Fyodor insists.'

4

'I worked on it for quite a long time. I went to the zoo and listened to the animals, searching for the ones I felt were in a similar situation. And do you know where I found it?'

'The wart-hogs?' suggested Elizabeth innocently.

'No, the sea lions. Go and listen for yourself. There's something in their bark that says "I want to go home".'

Tim was impressed. 'Poetry. I wondered where you found it. It was like a subdued version of the moan that Larry did in *Othello*.'

'Not too similar?'

'Similar, and yet original. I think we could be talking Oscars with a moan like that.' Tim was not joking. Or, at least, appeared not to be.

Pinewood Studios nestles in the lanes of bosky Buckinghamshire, seventeen miles to the north-west of London. It was built in 1936 by a property millionaire, Charles Boot, as Britain's answer to Hollywood. But, on this crisp January day in 1997, the studio commissary, as always, resembled the panelled dining-room of a once-great English public school. Indeed, like such an institution, Pinewood paraded its trophies with pride. An Oscar for *The Sound Barrier* occupied a prominent place in the trophy cabinet in the stately entrance hall, ornate with chiselled oak. Portraits of famous old boys – Dirk Bogarde, James Bond, Michael Caine, Superman and Batman – adorned the corridors. The well-tended, country-house gardens were familiar from their use in the *Carry On* films of the sixties – never a series that liked to venture too far from the bar for its locations.

Howard Cousins was already at the Jupiter Landing table when Elizabeth got there. He had artfully placed himself by the French window so that the subtle January sun would backlight his golden hair, sacrificially cut short for the benefit of the picture. He was not yet in costume. His deep-collared pink shirt needed no label to proclaim its Jermyn Street origin. As he raised a glass of mineral water to his lips, the four buttons on the cuff of his blazer led with military precision to the family signet ring on the small finger of his left hand which caught the sun with an expensive gleam. It was almost as if he had been rehearsing the movement in anticipation of her arrival, which, of course, he had.

'Good morning?' He rose to kiss her left cheek but, in the royal tradition, made sure his lips only brushed it.

'Good going on ghastly,' replied Elizabeth, sitting down. 'I think Tim knows a little less each day.'

'Then soon he will be down to nothing. What's his problem? It was only you and Douglas wasn't it? Communication still bad?'

Elizabeth grabbed a bread roll and started to break it up. 'It's not so much communication, it's the fact that he has nothing to communicate.'

Howard looked at her admiringly. He liked it when she was caustic and slightly enraged. It seemed to make her eyes even more threateningly beautiful. They were wide-set and had the deep, angular sparkle of Matisse eyes. People had been known to argue behind her back about what colour they were but it was not an argument that could be won since they changed with her mood and her surroundings. The deep brown centre of the pupil was encircled by jagged lights of white and rust and ochre bounded on the circumference by a steel-grey that could turn to sapphire. It was hard to look into those eyes and look away again, for they were disturbing and captivating and entirely rare.

In her grey sweater and blue jeans she looked like a student on an American campus. The image was reinforced by the white tennis headband that held back her shoulder-length blonde hair. Only a flicker of merriment stopped her lips from being too prim. Her nose was a little *retroussé*, a shade too small for perfection but, as Cecil Beaton had said of Grace Kelly's nose, if it had been any larger she wouldn't have photographed so well.

Elizabeth grimaced. 'Tim has no real understanding of actors. Douglas is milking it for all he can get. Today he wants to bleed, would you believe, doubtless so that he'll get another scene where I stitch him up, which will make a nice change from him stitching me up.'

'Very good,' applauded Howard, hoping, incorrectly, that he might find a path to her affections by being a constantly appreciative audience.

'And bloody Tim, instead of saying "yes, brilliant idea" and all that shit and letting him down gently, starts to lose his bottle and scream "it's not in the script", as if we were shooting *Timon of Athens*.'

'That would make a good movie,' said Howard, approving her every word. 'The trouble with Tim is his pedigree. Twenty years of making sure the doggies go to the correct bowl and the child unravels the lavatory paper from left to right only prepares you for twenty more years of doing the same.'

Elizabeth poured herself a glass of Moselle from the bottle in the ice bucket. 'The trouble with Tim,' she said, 'is that he's a wanker.'

'Howard, darling, why aren't you in costume?' Tim placed a large neat vodka in front of him as he sat down between them. 'You're in the first scene after lunch. It's the big one in the tank, you know. Very tricky.'

'You've only just got there, it'll take you an hour to set and light. But if you need me in drag for line-up I'll be only too happy to oblige.' Howard was always only too happy to oblige.

'You're right. Stay just as you are. We may have to ruffle those locks a little. This is, after all, a sea rescue.'

Howard looked marginally crestfallen. 'I thought I would wear my military cap – you know, with all the scrambled egg on it. One would, I think, when greeting the commander of an alien power.'

'You've been brushing up on it?' asked Elizabeth.

'You're not military,' Tim reminded him. 'You're the captain of a cruise liner.'

'Commodore. Senior captain of the fleet. So I still wear badges of rank. And war decorations,' Howard added eagerly.

'You're thirty-five years old. You were born in 1962. Which war did you fight in?'

'The Falklands?'

'That's fair enough.' Elizabeth came to Howard's aid. 'We watched videos of it at school during history lessons. He could have been in that.'

'Very well,' replied Tim, indicating to the waitress that he would welcome a refill, 'I shall make sure wardrobe puts a Falklands campaign medal on your costume.'

'No bravery?' pushed Howard.

'How about VC and bar?' Elizabeth had learnt her teasing at her father's knee.

'It's a long shot.' Tim's voice grew louder. 'You could be the most decorated hero in the history of sea warfare. You could be standing there with soup all down your tie. But still nobody would notice.'

Howard was by now definitely feeling hard done by. 'No close-ups? For the rescue? It's a central dramatic moment.'

'Yes, but it's the ordinary merchant seamen who are hauling them out of the water.'

'But I ordered it. I have taken the decision to put the crew and passengers at risk – "slow ahead" I say – to rescue these things. They could be killers. It's a close-up decision. I remember in your freeze-dried coffee commercial when the wife decides to give him instant instead of percolated, it was a close-up decision. This surely ranks as that important, if not more so.'

Appeals to his advertising past inevitably had a persuasive effect with Tim. He began to soften. 'I'll think about it. Look, there's hardly any queue, you coming?'

The traditional democracy of the Pinewood dining-room meant that even the most illustrious stars and dollar-laden producers still had to stand in line to get their food.

'I've eaten,' said Howard.

'I'm not really eating,' said Elizabeth, interrupting him with her daily plea as he got up, 'but could you bring me a plate of green vegetables?'

When Tim had gone, she turned to Howard. 'Well done. Polish up your Jack Hawkins look.'

He bathed in her congratulations. 'A sea rescue, with no reaction shot of the captain. Madness. Do you want to eat dinner?'

'Now?'

'Tonight, you duffer.'

'I'm bound to have a 6 a.m. make-up call.'

'I've booked at Stanage. They actually had a free table.'

She stretched a hand out to his expensive cuff, anxious not to upset him. 'Howie, I'd like to. But not tonight. Another night.'

'You promised. You solemnly promised. I need to talk. There are things I have to say – '

Any thought of revealing his hand further was interrupted by a new arrival. He was a short, almost stubby man in a blue double-breasted suit that went some way to concealing a potentially corpulent body. His pebble spectacles, once the preserve of the National Health Service but now expensively fashionable, and a shock of grey hair that would defy any barber, gave him the appearance of a schoolboy going on fifty. Carrying a lighted Gitane in front of him in the European fashion, he was not the sort of person who would necessarily merit a second glance were it not for the fact that he radiated the penetrating fragrance of power. This was Fyodor Lasky, their producer. Elizabeth nervously withdrew her hand, but too late.

'Elizabeth, Howard – such a pleasure to see my two stars getting on so well. You would be surprised how rarely that happens. Normally jealousy stays the hand of friendship between leading players, especially if they have an on-screen romance.'

Fyodor's conversation, when he was not talking to bankers and even sometimes when he was, consisted of pronouncements dressed and delivered to sound like philosophy, a style of speech enhanced by his gravelly accent.

He sat down in the seat vacated by Tim. A waitress appeared from nowhere to place a half-full bottle of claret in front of him. He removed the cork and poured himself a glass.

'Howard, you'll try a little?'

'No, no thanks. Close-ups this afternoon. Wine only reddens the complexion.'

'I was under the impression we had a make-up department to take care of that.'

'But still . . . my timing.'

'You're wise. An actor must think first of himself, and then of the rest of the universe. I mean no disrespect. If you ask a writer if it is hot outside, he will tell you, yes or no, maybe even come up with a simile to indicate how hot. If you ask an actor, he will reply, "it didn't worry me, I was only wearing a vest and shorts and I spent the morning in the shade."'

'Are you implying that we're selfish?' asked Elizabeth defensively.

'No more so than anyone else. It is merely that where the writer looks out and observes the world, the actor looks out and first sees himself, then through himself the world. It starts as part of his training and ends as part of his art. Ah, Tim, I've stolen your place.'

'No problem, I'll sit over here.' Tim put Elizabeth's vegetables in front of her and walked round to the empty place.

'Spoiling her, are you, Tim? You'll create a monster, that's how they begin. Today a plate of vegetables, tomorrow a clause in their contract that spare ribs must be flown in from New York every third day.'

'Got to keep the crew happy,' came the nervous reply. 'Wet work this afternoon. Never easy in the tank.'

Fyodor managed simultaneously to brush aside and pick up from his remark. 'They once built Alexandria harbour in this studio – before the 007 stage – and filled it with a million gallons of water. I doubt if you remember the movie.'

He glanced quickly round the table but saw, to his satisfaction, that nobody knew. '*Cleopatra*,' he said.

'The one with Elizabeth Taylor?' asked Howard.

His producer nodded. The actor dared to correct him. 'I think you've got that wrong – they shot it in Rome. The whole Burton thing, remember?'

Fyodor lit another Gitane. 'The only thing any producer remembers about *Cleopatra* is that it went out of control, the biggest overspend in movie history if you translate it into today's prices. And part of the reason was that they built Rome here. They even had five thousand extras on call one day. Peter Finch was Caesar and Stephen Boyd was Mark Antony. And when Miss Taylor fell ill do you know who was put on stand-by to take her part?'

'Joan Collins,' put in Elizabeth quickly.

'Very good, my dear.' Fyodor's admiring glance made her blush and feel childishly uncomfortable.

'Who knows how her life might have changed?' he went on. 'And Taylor's. She might never have met Burton. But Fox pulled the plug on the movie here and the new male stars and the director waited to fight another day in Rome. The history of movies is the story of small men taking big decisions. So eat up your greens.'

'Madness,' observed Tim, crunching his pork crackling.

'In its fashion. But they generated more publicity than any movie since *Gone With the Wind*. And they did attempt to tell a classic story. Just as we are with the curious blue aliens from Jupiter. Yesterday's rushes were rather good, as a matter of fact. I like the bit where Lu Xun is carried into the surgery. Do you think we should have him bleed a little, just a spoor of blue blood, to make us think he is going to die?'

Tim swallowed a Brussels sprout. 'Excellent idea. I'll shoot an insert later.'

'The art in such films as these,' continued Fyodor, 'is to make the audience bleed a little as well. An unknown alien can be just as moving as an ancient Roman. After all, we've never actually encountered either. At least I haven't.'

Derek swept by their table on the way back from the bar. 'Good afternoon, sir. Coming to watch the rescue?'

'Most certainly. As a matter of fact I'm bringing two of our bankers who are in town. It's funny how they tend to turn up on the days when the big money's being spent.'

'I thought you wanted a closed set – nobody to see what the creatures look like till the picture's released.' Tim was demonstrably anxious.

'Precisely. That's what makes it such a treat for them. Something to tell their wives. And their boards.'

The 007 stage, so named because it had been the home of many of the major set-piece action sequences in the James Bond films over the years, housed one of the biggest indoor tanks in the film world. It looked as if a whole section of a disused dockyard had been shipped to Pinewood and was now sequestered within this mammoth aircraft hangar. Today the words '*Jupiter Landing*. Strictly No Admittance Without Official Permission' had been posted on every door. Inside, at the far end of the tank, a life-size forward section of an ocean liner loomed out of the water. It was actually on rollers so that teams of four stagehands at each end could manoeuvre it to simulate its rise and fall with the swell of the South China Sea. In the middle of the tank the remains of the

Jupiter spacecraft, an incongruous blue carbon-fibre fuselage and charred Perspex dome, bobbed gently on the choppy waters. On the upper deck of the ship cruise passengers in swimming costumes and sun clothes peered down at the craft. The merchant officers, immaculate in white, were ranked below them, with ordinary seamen, considerably grubbier in blue, standing by on the sea-level deck to effect the rescue.

Tim, surrounded in turn by his crew, was on a platform at the other end of the tank. They were looking intently at a television monitor which was playing back the long shot of a real ship, filmed by the second unit in the English Channel a month earlier.

'Force 8, it looks to me,' he suggested to Derek. The latter shook his head.

'Nothing like, guvnor. Just a bit choppy. Besides if we overdo it in that tank we'll have more dead than the Titanic.'

'I think I'll start from Howard's point of view,' said the director. 'Observe the rescue through the eyes of those on board and then we can shoot it the other way round.'

Derek made a clicking noise with his tongue. It was a sign, although he himself was unaware of it, that he was about to contradict somebody, usually Tim. 'If you do it that way, you're going to get the ship and everyone covered in muck and water without seeing them. Best to start on the ship – doesn't matter what the Jus look like, they're going to be soaking anyway.'

'Don't call them that. They are Aliens.' Tim at least had the satisfaction of reprimanding his first assistant. 'Right everybody, we'll shoot this way first, towards the ship. Down goes the net and up come the Aliens. Ready, Terry?'

An elderly man in a baseball cap peered up at him. 'I'd lit it for the other way first – like you said.'

'Change of plan. We can make do with the same lights, can't we?'

The lighting cameraman gave Tim a resigned look. 'I've got my lights all over the side of the ship. They're going to go right up your lens. I need to re-key them.'

'Can you make it snappy? We've got an audience this afternoon.'

'I thought this was a closed set.' Terry muttered.

'The money,' replied his director and, on cue, Fyodor accompanied by two strangers appeared at the studio door. Both men were taller than the producer. One was heavily tanned and almost entirely bald; the other had close-cropped grey hair. They wore expensively cut dark suits, light blue shirts, and anonymous business ties. Their calfskin briefcases were the kind that bulged if they contained more than a couple of documents. The grey-haired man had a compact portable phone dangling from his wrist.

Derek rose to the occasion. The megaphone was at his lips. 'Very nice, everybody, very nice. Now we're going to take a slightly different angle, so just relax and check your clothing. Thank you.'

The unexpected politeness turned most heads towards the new arrivals. Even those extras who had no idea who Fyodor was or what he looked like could recognise an undoubted figure of authority.

'Take a seat,' suggested Tim as the three men climbed onto his dais. 'I just want to alter the mood a little. A subtle lighting change, but sufficient to heighten the tension.'

'My director, Mr Lawrence,' smiled Fyodor. 'May I introduce Monsieur Godfree and Herr Katz.'

Tim felt at home in such company as he shook their hands. Buttering up the client was the first skill he had acquired back at the advertising agency. 'You've come on a good day. Plenty of action.'

'Not at the moment,' observed Herr Katz with the air of a man who had come to mind his money.

'That's film-making' – Tim was unperturbed – 'ten per cent inspiration, ten per cent perspiration and eighty per cent waiting about.'

'And a hundred per cent financing,' added his new adversary.

Fyodor interrupted. 'Tim, why not put us in the picture?'

His director grabbed the opportunity with relief. He had told this tale before, many times. He clenched his right hand into a fist and held it up in the air. 'The planet Jupiter. Not quite round, about seven thousand miles less in its polar diameter than its equatorial diameter. But the biggest object to circumnavigate the sun, something that it does every twelve years. Scientists always thought it was incapable of sustaining life as we know it. It seemed to be made of liquid hydrogen, although they acknowledged there was something hard – probably rocks – in the interior. But there's always been an air of mystery about it. In the middle there is an unfathomed energy reservoir, intense radiation, strange multiple radio waves, those sorts of things. What our boffins who have been monitoring and scrutinising the planet failed to realise was the crucial fact – central to this drama – that those very waves were spying on us, summing us up.'

'Boffins?' enquired Monsieur Godfree.

'Another word for scientists, slightly pejorative. And rightly so. They have no idea what has been happening for the past ten years. The mind controlling the energy – Mr Jupiter himself, if you like – has been creating a new race of people who will be able to exist on the planet Earth. That's the reason for all the radioactivity coming from there. It's like a monster spy satellite watching over us. So the Jupiterians create these near-human aliens, making one cardinal error. They assume since seventy per cent of the Earth's surface is water they will have to swim much of the time – hence the scales and fins. They may have spotted our boats but since there is no water on Jupiter they are unable to fathom them – if you follow my pun.'

The blank stares indicated that they didn't. But he still had them, for the time being, in the palm of his clenched hand.

'So they build a craft that will take them on a five-year journey to Earth. But they have no idea of buoyancy – the thing is made of their rock which might just as well be marble – and when it hits our sea they are in major and unforeseen trouble. Now they may be aliens but they come as friends. From their monitoring they have realised that the largest nation on earth is China and they have actually been in touch with Beijing, negotiating the details of their arrival. Their leaders speak fluent Mandarin and Cantonese because they suppose that everyone else in the world will then be able to understand them.'

'If they're in contact with the Chinese, how come they don't know about buoyancy and boats?' Herr Katz enquired tartly.

'Ah . . . well,' Tim looked to Fyodor for help. 'There you'd have to talk to the script writers . . .'

'You're taking it too seriously, Willy.' Fyodor laid a reassuring hand on the banker's arm. 'It's only a movie. But you see how incredibly persuasive it's going to be. It will have an effect on people like Orson Welles's *War of the Worlds*. People ran out of their houses with towels over their heads, they were so convinced that the Martians had arrived. Nobody who sees *Jupiter Landing* will ever be the same again – a good slogan, don't you think, Tim?'

'Excellent. Dolly, make a note of it.'

'What happens next?' Godfree was clearly enraptured. 'Do the coffins make contact with them?'

'Boffins,' said Tim. 'No, there's a bit of a snarl-up. They land slightly off-course in the South China Sea several hundred kilometres away from the Chinese naval flotilla that is waiting for the secret rendezvous. But they're spotted by an English cruise ship which turns around and goes to their rescue – very much in the British tradition,' he added, staring pointedly at Herr Katz.

Thinking he had been invited to speak, Katz remarked clinically, 'there is a love interest, I hope, and sex.'

'Not with the Aliens, no.' Tim shook his head. 'Market research indicates that the audience won't wear that. But love, yes. That's what this film is all about. Sister Florence has been having a steaming affair with the captain – wait till you see the rushes, you'll never believe how much can be done in a bunk.'

'Will we get a "12" certificate if there is a steaming bonk?' Godfree looked worried. 'Our investment is dependent on a "12" certificate. We need that audience.'

'No need to worry,' said Tim. 'Plenty of tits and a bit of male bum, all within the rules.'

Godfree's brow remained furrowed. 'Why must it be a nun who makes this love? I do not think people will like that.'

'No, she's a medical sister,' Tim reassured him. 'All the uniform but none of the vows. Anyway the head Alien, who is programmed to call himself Lu Xun – after a Chinese writer – falls in love with her, and agrees that they should be secretly shipped back to Britain. There the Foreign Office makes a deal with them taking Jupiter into the British Commonwealth, even giving them British passports, and the whole international balance of power is altered by this alliance, with the West gaining access to the vital extra-terrestrial know-how that the Chinese thought they were going to get. All for the love of a pretty girl.'

'Would it not be better to make it the European Community?' suggested Godfree. 'Fyodor tells me he wants to take it to the Cannes Festival. I think that might help sales.'

'It's too late now – ' Tim began, but Fyodor interrupted him.

'What a brilliant idea. That will be a perfect plot for the sequel, *Jupiter Landing II*.'

'Got a bit of light on the scene now, guv,' interrupted Derek. 'Want to give it a twirl?'

'Let's get cracking.' Tim's narrative skills had given him a new confidence. He had always been much happier pitching the client with the copy.

Derek raised the megaphone to his lips. 'Right, get those Jus into the water.'

Both bankers straightened with a jerk, as if pulled by a mutual string.

'I told you not to call them that,' snarled Tim through his teeth. 'They are Aliens.'

'Sorry, guv.' The first assistant turned back to the set. 'All Aliens in the drink, passengers and crew to the rails and anyone who isn't an Alien or on the ship get right back or we'll never get this fucking shot done.'

Fyodor diplomatically ushered his guests to a platform behind the camera.

'He's a marvellous first,' he whispered to them, 'keeps the thing right on time and undercuts all the artistic bullshit that the director comes up with when he thinks he's Britain's Bertolucci.'

Tim chose this moment to address his principals. 'Howard, darling, we'll do your close-up after the extras have gone but I still want a full performance from you. You wonder "what have I done?" You look at these creatures swimming towards you and for all you know they may be hostile. So this is a cathartic moment, an inner crisis which you must hide from the passengers but communicate to us. The only person who really knows what you are going through is Florence and I want you to look at him, Elizabeth, not at the Aliens, and we will sense his dilemma refracted through your tremulous face. You see, you can show all the emotions that he must hide.'

'But my head is going to be about the size of an aspirin in this shot, isn't it, Derek?' Standing around rarely improved Elizabeth's mood.

'Slightly smaller, love, and out of focus.'

'Nevertheless' – Tim looked witheringly at him – 'I need to feel that emotion even if we don't see it. You're fearful that Howard might go as far as jumping into the ocean as a peace offering to Douglas.'

'But I can't swim!' Howard's anxious look had rarely appeared so plausible.

'No, lovey, you don't jump. But you lean right over, craning to see just who these creatures are. And Douglas – where is Douglas?'

'Just about drowning and I can swim. How much longer do we have to tread water before you turn over?'

'Patience. You're meant to look tired. You've come a long way. Jupiter is five light years – '

'I know how fucking far away Jupiter is! What I *want* to know is how long it's going to be before you start shooting or do you want us to shrivel up first?'

'You're turning blue with cold,' Elizabeth remarked.

'Enough,' Tim reprimanded her. 'I just want Douglas to carry the voyage with him. Think of Shackleton, Scott, imagine their faces at the end of the journey. Drained with fatigue but sustained by knowing that the goal is in sight.'

'But if I'm swimming towards the boat you'll be on the back of my head.'

'It'll show in your swimming. Let your body tell the story –'

'Guv,' Derek interjected, 'I think we should get going. The sea's beginning to turn blue.'

Tim eyed him patronisingly. 'Correct me if I'm wrong, Derek, but I think it's meant to be that colour.'

'Not in little blue patches. The dye's coming off.'

'Can't we pretend it's blood?' Douglas suggested.

'Okay, let's go.' Even Tim's relish for procrastination did not extend to reopening that wound. 'Stand by.'

'Red light,' called Derek. 'Very quiet everywhere, and front board.'

'*Jupiter Landing*, 188 take one, A and B cameras,' the loader called out as he snapped the slate.

'B camera?' Tim queried.

'On the gantry,' indicated Derek, 'making a back-up master in case we don't get it again.'

'Because of what?'

'Oh, if Douglas has a heart attack.'

'I heard that,' came the voice of the leading Alien. 'And I'm not far off it. I'm starting to get pickled.'

'Stand-by then, everybody.' Derek looked up at his director.

'Don't forget, Aliens, desperation and hope. And those on board, horror and exhortation.'

'What's exhortation?' asked the woman standing next to Elizabeth.

'Don't worry,' she replied. 'Just do the horror.'

'And action.'

The shoal of Aliens wriggled across the 007 stage tank, bizarre, ethereal tadpoles leaving twirling clouds of blue ink in their wake. On cue, two Goan members of the crew lowered a large net, as if they were going to fish for them. The passengers on deck jumped up and down with agitation, like anxious parents at a school sports day.

Howard adjusted the peak of his hat to make sure that it wasn't putting his eyes in shadow and then cupped his right hand to his mouth. 'Do you come in peace?' he yelled in a rich Barbican baritone.

'*Ah tung yang*,' Douglas gurgled back.

'Make yourself clear.' Howard stood on tiptoe and leant far out over the railing, as if the extra foot gained would help him to hear. 'Do you come in . . . faaaaa . . . uck!'

The entire railing had worked itself loose and began to give way. There was a sickly creak as it slid out of its socket. Instinctively Howard grabbed hold of it but it was of less use than a straw to a drowning man. His hat went first and he followed after, the weight of the bar causing him to perform a slow-motion somersault as he plummeted forty feet into the dark waters of the tank below.

'Five point seven,' Ray whispered to Dolly.

'Quickly, somebody, cut,' screamed Tim.

'Keep running,' Derek countermanded him, 'we may use it. Get the divers in.'

But the frogmen were located at the opposite end of the tank from the liner and had a fifty-yard swim in order to get to him. Howard came to the surface and emitted a scream higher in tone and more blood-curdling than any extra-terrestrial could ever imagine. Then he disappeared flailing into the dark waters.

Suddenly a swatch of white came flying towards him. Elizabeth had grabbed hold of the rope dangling from the lifeboat in front of her on the upper deck and swung into the water. In one graceful unbroken arc she grabbed Howard round the waist with her spare arm and managed to keep him from going under again.

'Scene stealer,' she said breathlessly.

In seconds the divers reached them and they were helped back to the edge of the stage. Wardrobe came running round with blankets. Tim rapidly made his way down to them, followed by a concerned Fyodor.

'Are you two okay?' asked the producer.

Howard tried to stop gasping and regain his composure. 'Sorry to have ruined the shot. It was nobody's fault but mine. I shouldn't have leant so hard.'

'It was marvellous,' said Fyodor. 'Did we get it, Derek?'

'Gantry camera zoomed right in, sir.'

'Wonderful. We can cut to a reverse angle of you actually saving Douglas's life. It is the first time he sees a human being from Earth and this spontaneous gesture makes him your friend for life.'

'I'm not going back in there,' whimpered Howard.

'Don't worry, we can shoot from behind you, use a double. Can't we, Tim?'

'Exactly what I was thinking,' came the unconvincing reply.

Howard turned to Elizabeth and hugged her.

'Lizzie, my darling, you did it for me.' He paused to catch his breath. 'How on earth did you do it?'

Elizabeth stood dripping before him. Her soaking uniform had become transparent, revealing a body that was lithe and fit and full-breasted.

19

'Oh, some silly boy-friend I had at school,' she replied, pulling a towel round her shoulders. 'We jumped off a suspension bridge once. He had these sort of elastic ropes – like you launch gliders with. I gave my word to Mummy I wouldn't do it again. Promise not to tell.'

The general laughter was interrupted by the financial concern of Herr Katz.

'The insurance will pay for this take, no?'

'No,' said Fyodor. 'It is an act of God which may pave the way to some great acting. Look out – behind you.'

Katz turned quickly and let loose a frightened yelp as a dripping blue creature, its fins crumpled and flopping from spending too long in the water, climbed out of the tank.

'Was I all right?' asked Douglas. 'I gave a sort of inward gulp of apprehension, something I saw Ralph Richardson once do in a Pinter play. I think it may carry the scene.'

CHAPTER 2

Thursday 23rd January 1997

New York

Things were going from bad to worse. The enemy had regrouped around the castle and there appeared to be reinforcements inside, thousands of them. Massive cannons thundered from the battlements, blasting craters in the desert sand, killing some men immediately and causing others to tumble into them. As the soldiers fell to their deaths not only did they let loose embittered, harrowing screams of agony, but some had time to shout farewell messages to their loved ones. 'For God's sake look after my wife and children' or 'Bless the King and grant him victory.'

The sun was beginning to set now behind the castle, making their task doubly difficult. It seemed madness to continue the assault. The leading sergeant threw himself to the ground and Robert automatically followed suit, his rusty armour jangling as he did so. A shell exploded noisily in front of them, showering them with stones and sand and fish.

The sergeant picked up a fish – it was still alive and wriggling – and bit off its head. 'We must be getting near the moat,' he said. 'One final push and we'll make it. Can you see her?'

Robert looked up. He *could* see her. They were startlingly close. She was standing at the highest point of the battlements, her simple white robe rimmed in red by the setting sun. Although she had the hood up he could easily distinguish her face, pale and frightened. Her lips spelt out the words 'come quickly' and, to his surprise, he could hear them quite clearly across the ringing noise of battle.

He stood up and caught hold of the sergeant by the arm,

tugging him along. 'Hurry up,' he screamed. 'Can't you see her? We've got to get there.'

The older man refused to budge. 'I want to finish my fish,' he said. 'I'm starving. I haven't eaten in three days.'

'There's no time for that,' cried Robert, 'Come on, come on, come on. "Dauntless the slug-horn to his lips he set and blew 'Childe Roland to the Dark Tower came.'"'

He fell on his back on the sand, his head moving uncontrollably from side to side, desperately willing his body to get up and continue. His face was burning and his chest clammy with sweat.

'Calm down,' said a voice beside him. 'I told you you should have taken a pill.'

A dark brown arm slipped across his body and a tongue began to lick his neck.

'I love the taste of your sweat,' she said. 'Mixed up with that Calvin Klein stuff. They should market it as an aphrodisiac.'

He looked at the green neon letters on the digital clock. Six thirty-two. No sense in trying to go back to sleep. 'I've got to get up. God, that dream.'

'Crusaders, again?'

'And fish.'

'Am I in it? Neris could be a Saracen name. My father said we originally came from Egypt, way back.'

'No, you're not in it. You should be thankful for that.'

Tanya caught sight of the book that was open face down on the side of his pillow and tried to make out the title. '*Philip Augustus and the Siege of Acre 1191*' she read, letting loose an artificial snore. 'They're dead, Robert. It's all over. They're not recruiting crusaders any longer. It was probably a lousy life, anyway.'

'Mmmm,' he agreed sleepily. 'But you didn't notice the discomfort if you were committed to the cause. Nice to have such a clear-cut purpose in life.'

'Not much sex on the crusades, I guess,' she suggested as she moved closer to him, attacking his neck more furiously with her tongue, licking and kissing him and making as if to devour him. Her body seemed as cool as marble in contrast to his as she gently tickled his rib-cage with her breasts. She put her leg across his, rubbing the top of his thigh with the soft inside of hers. Her hand worked its way down his stomach and began to fondle him.

'I love you,' she said.

'I love you too.'

'No, you don't.'

'I do.'

'If you love me, make love to me.'

'I can't.'

'There.'

'There what?'

'You don't love me.'

'You can't blackmail me,' said Robert. 'I have to get going.'

He kissed her on the cheek and, with a regretful glance at her limber black body draped enticingly across his crumpled white linen sheets, reluctantly made his way across the bedroom to the shower.

'– it looks like spring weather, plenty of sunshine scheduled, a nil chance of precipitation and an expected high of 64 degrees in midtown Manhattan and for you ski-bums sadly still no snow at Stowe – '

I wonder who invented the waterproof shower television, Robert mused, as the gushing jet of steaming water brought him slowly back into reality. Was it a byproduct of the Mars probe? Did they get an award? Perhaps we should do an item on it.

Not for the first morning in his life he cursed the devil inside him that had made him take that final glass of Amaretto, and the one after that, and the one after that. There was something in the air at the Pantheon which induced irresponsibility. He relished the semi-showbusiness atmosphere of the restaurant – the founders were two Englishmen who had once been on or near the stage – and he enjoyed being seen there with Tanya. People looked at them when they came in, the first glance still reflecting the fleeting double-take of seeing a white man with a black woman and the second glance either wondering whether this athletically curved girl in a clinging silk dress was a pop star they should have heard of, or where they had seen the man before. He loved being with her on nights such as that, but on mornings such as this the recurring problem came back to haunt him that every time he told her he loved her he knew more certainly that he did not.

His thoughts were abruptly terminated. Another body was with him in the shower. 'Hello, this is Norman Bates,' whispered a voice, 'and I have come to fuck you dead.'

Her breasts were already hard as she rubbed them up and down his moist back. She had the soap in her hand and began to massage his stomach with it. Her tongue flickered around the back of his neck and then deep into his ear.

'That tickles,' he remonstrated as he turned to her. She kissed him, hungry for a response which was not slow in coming. Deftly she put him inside her and wrapped both her legs around his waist.

'Now,' said Tanya, 'you're mine.' And he was.

An hour later, at the morning meeting of *Arts Action*, they could have been taken for total strangers. One or two of the production team sensed that there might be a passing friendship – indeed Jim Hurley, the senior producer, had once encountered them in the queue for a Bertrand Blier flim at an upper East Side cinema – but they did not in any way resemble a couple. Robert Barrett looked more like a Wall Street lawyer than an entertainment reporter. His darkening sandy hair was cut short and neat, and his resolute mouth hinted at the determination of a young army officer until it broke, as it frequently did, into a smile that could charm his way past many a negative publicist. He looked his age, which was thirty-three. His light grey suit, blue button-down shirt and boldly striped tie came, as did all his clothes, from Brooks Brothers – a shop that his mother had taken him to as a child and one to which he had been continuously faithful, as if he had sworn an unspoken masonic oath of loyalty. He dressed in a style that had changed from preppy to yuppie a decade earlier and was now back to preppy again.

'Why do you have to dress like Clark Kent?' Tanya had chided him, half joking, half annoyed. 'It saves having to worry about clothes,' he had explained, 'you don't buy new ones, you just replace the old ones when they wear out. Besides, I don't wear glasses – yet.' Her own style was a bomber jacket and skin-tight leather trousers.

She had started it all, almost three months ago. They had been dispatched – she as producer, he as reporter – to Deer Lake, Pennsylvania, the former training camp of Muhammad Ali, to make a retrospective look at his career on his fifty-fifth birthday. Navigation was not a talent Robert had acquired at Princeton and, two-and-a-half hours after setting out by car from New York, they were in deepest nowhere. To a married couple this would probably have been the cause of a tearing row but they had just sat there and laughed, heady with the sense of adventure. Out of the dark gleamed the dubious welcoming neon sign of the Dusselfink Motel. Tanya took the initiative at the desk. 'We need a double room for the night,' she told the clerk, without bothering to consult Robert.

'Why me?' he had asked, as he lay detumescently beside her some hours later.

'I used to look at you every morning in those terrible clothes,' she had replied, 'and I just wanted to take them off.'

Hurley called the meeting to order. Burly Hurley he was known to one and all, his heavyweight frame and large slightly boozy, Irish face, giving him the air of an off-duty cop. 'Okay. LA is handling this new television detective – what's his name, er, Fusco? – anyway the one that's facing the coke charge and the sponsor wants to drop from the series.'

'Is it Pepsi?' asked Jessica, a thickset scriptwriter in her late forties. It was her habit to make her presence felt with barbed interventions. In her thinner days a lover had once told her that she looked like Dorothy Parker.

'Very good,' continued Hurley, passing over her remark with familiar nonchalance, 'and they've got that story of the Warner senior vice-president who took his family on holiday in their executive jet.'

'What's so unusual about that?' Robert enquired.

'What's unusual is that the IRS doesn't usually get to hear about it. Jack wondered if we could twin it with another angle on executive perks from this end. Any ideas?'

'Show me a movie and I'll show you a fistful of executive perks,' stated a thin, scholarly man at the back of the office. 'I mean, every producer expects to live off his film. It's standard. I reckon we're going to rub a lot of contacts up the wrong way if we start pushing that one too hard.'

'Something else, then?' asked Hurley, looking around.

Robert avoided his eyes. He had no immediate ideas. His head was still fogged and the sight of the drab office didn't make it feel any better. In contrast to the high-tech set, dubbed 'air traffic control' by Jessica, which the *Arts Action* viewers saw, the production office was a tawdry collection of desks, most of them piled high with videos and magazines. Bunches of old-fashioned television sets hung from the ceiling and vast, ungainly planning charts decorated the walls like official graffiti. He gazed sleepily out of the window. The few skaters on the ice rink in Rockefeller Plaza were carving deliberate and cautious turns. A couple, probably in their late sixties – she in a mini-skirt and with a permanent smile which she seemed to have applied with her lipstick, he in long white trousers and a dolefully distant expression – danced in a slow, robotic fashion. The desire to show off and be noticed was endemic in this city, thought Robert, and it didn't disappear with age.

Tanya looked up from doodling on her clipboard. 'How about product placement? You mentioned Coke and Pepsi, they're obvious. But nearly everything you see in movies nowadays is part of a placement deal, from the Armani suits to the Nike shoes.'

'Nothing wrong in that,' countered a bald man in a tartan shirt. 'It's all part of good producing.'

'Okay, they're fine,' she agreed. 'But I heard that the production designers on *The Bloomie Murders* were getting six-figure kickbacks for using Sage Airline planes in their JFK sequence. The money's going straight into their pockets.'

Hurley was interested. 'Can you prove it?' he asked.

'Not sure that I can. I haven't followed it up yet. But my contact said there might be a couple of disgruntled airline employees who are prepared to talk.'

'Disgruntled because they didn't get a slice of the action,' interjected Jessica.

'Doesn't matter,' insisted Hurley. 'If we can get them to open up it's a good story. Tanya, take Ed Butler – we'll come live from JFK if it stands up.'

Ed, one of the anchors – a lean, black man with designer glasses and a style of dressing that changed with each month's *GQ* – almost managed to cover his look of alarm. 'We *will* have a writer as well?' he queried.

'Don't worry,' Hurley reassured him, 'Tanya will do the questions, just look frank and fearless.'

Robert shifted uncomfortably in his seat. The unspoken hostility between anchors and reporters – the former got all the fame and usually did little more than read their autocues – was inflamed by the feeling that a meaty story had passed him by, especially one unearthed by Tanya. He threw a glance at the senior producer.

Hurley had already anticipated it. 'We need you for the opening night, Robert. We'll have a live link there, too, if we can.'

'What's opening?'

'That musical, *Wimbledon*, the one that seems to have been in preview for the past six months. I hear the *Times* hates it. It's rumoured they're only opening it to close it.'

'Seems more like a funeral than a first night.'

'Why not take that line, with the money men at least. But go for the glitter, there should be enough names there this evening to give us a glitzy package. We've got access to the final stagger-through with songs this afternoon, so you can make up your own mind about the show.'

'I thought *I* was employed as the critic.' The nasal whine that emerged from behind a well-thumbed copy of *People* magazine certainly sounded as if it had been criticising things since birth. Raymond Rainier ('no relation', he would always assure people, modestly but truthfully, since the surname was borrowed) lowered the magazine to reveal the sort of gaudy bow tie that is the hallmark of television personalities in search of an identity.

'Don't worry,' said Hurley. 'You can have a bite at it on Monday. They only agreed to let us come live from the foyer if we didn't do a proper review till after the week-end.'

'I saw it in preview.' Rainier seemed determined to give his review now. 'I loved it. The bit where those two Swedish boys have just been cudgelling each other to death on the centre court and then sing mournfully like brothers in the shower for their native homes on the fiords just melted me.'

'Get some footage of the Swedish boys to keep for the

Rainier Review,' Hurley instructed Robert. 'Right, let's get going. And let's put it across LA.'

The rivalry between the New York and Los Angeles ends of the show was keener than that between *Arts Action* and any of the competing entertainment news magazines and accounted for much of its success. As people drifted back to their desks, Hurley called Robert over. 'Stick in your opinion on *Wimbledon* – I have no objection. I'll deal with Rainier if it gives him a hot flush.'

As he was leaving, Tanya contrived to walk out of the room at the same time as he did.

'Why didn't you tell me about the Bloomies piece?' he whispered.

Her face registered wronged innocence. 'Don't want to mix business and pleasure. I might devour you in front of camera.' She squeezed his elbow. 'I'll be round at nine. Be prepared.'

Charley O's at lunchtime was as chaotic as a rush-hour train. New Yorkers seemed to need a place more frenetic than a commodity trading floor to keep their adrenalin pumping. The beef sandwiches grew thicker by the day; no human mouth could possibly get round them. They must be designed, Robert mused as he savoured the punch of his Bloody Mary, for visitors arriving from another planet, a happening of which only Charley O himself had foreknowledge.

Robert had telephoned his friend, Hutton Craig, from the office and they had managed to find a spare table, the raucous din ensuring the privacy of any conversation that was not shouted. Hutton felt obliged to explain away his Perrier.

'I've got to see the foreign editor this afternoon. Rio's coming free – the guy's resigned to write a book or something – and they want someone who speaks the lingo.'

'Spanish?' asked Robert.

'Well, they won't be sending you – even if you worked for the *Times*. Portuguese, they've been there for five hundred years. Ask me any question about Rio – anything.'

'How easy is it to get laid?'

'Boy or girl? The former comes easier nowadays. Just go to the right spot on Copacabana. You know, people meet in pre-ordained areas on the beach' – he mapped it out on the table with his fork – 'architects here, then journalists, then financiers, people in the fashion trade and gays at the far end, just by Ipanema. If you happen to be a gay architect you have to keep sprinting backwards and forwards between your peer groups. Now, what did you want to know?'

Fourteen years previously the two men had been put in rooms together at Princeton. At first there had been a mutual suspicion of each other. Hutton came from wealthier parents, had his own convertible Camaro and seemed to have a ready-made society of friends from his school, Phillips Academy. Robert was aware that he was on a much tighter budget. His mother had gone back to her job as a secretary in a law firm after her divorce and it was only thanks to his uncle and a series of student loans that he was at university at all.

But a wary respect had slowly grown up between them and Hutton gradually introduced Robert to his circle. Those days at Princeton, especially the summers, had seemed the best and the brightest in Robert's life. But he had repaid his friend's generosity in the most graceless fashion by falling intractably in love with his girl-friend, Lynne. She had known Hutton since childhood, their families had holiday homes near each other on Martha's Vineyard, and it had always been assumed by all who knew them that the two would eventually marry.

What made it even worse was the fact that in their final semester Lynne had reciprocated Robert's affection. Hutton had closeted himself in his parents' Boston home in order to revise and the other two began to see more and more of each other, sharing meals and often going to late movies at the Garden Cinema. One day, out of the blue, she had told him she was fed up with the pre-ordained path of dating Hutton and was desperate to assert herself. That night they made love by the bridge over Lake Carnegie, an illicit location for what they both knew to be an illicit act. After their final exams Lynne went abroad. She wrote him long and wistful letters from the South of France throughout the summer which he read and re-read to while away the tedious hours of his temporary job as an NBC page in New York. And then, in September, she came home and married Hutton, as if nothing had happened.

They invited Robert to the wedding and, after much soul-searching, he went. And by that gesture his friendship with Hutton had resumed, stronger than before, with neither of them ever mentioning the lost summer. Now Lynne was the mother of Hutton's two daughters. Robert envied him her and them and he also envied him his job. The *New York Times* was a prestigious paper to work for, a far remove from *Arts Action*.

'I need to know about *Wimbledon*,' said Robert.

Hutton put down his Perrier assertively. 'London SW19. Home of the world's premier tennis tournament until they dug up their grass courts last year. Founded 1877 so they'll be celebrating 120 years this summer.'

'I meant the musical.'

'How do you think I know all that stuff? I had to write a backgrounder on it. You can find it all in the programme notes as a matter of fact.'

'I'm covering the opening tonight. But it's likely to be the closing as well – which seems strange since I hear it's quite good. Even that atrophied poseur who passes for our critic liked it.'

'So did Kew in the *Times*.'

'That's not what I heard. I understood he was going to pan it.'

Hutton shook his head. 'No. I spoke to him about it. He saw it quite early in preview. In fact, he was going to mention it in a Sunday piece but they asked him not to – said they were cutting some of the songs.'

Robert looked quizzical. 'So his review tomorrow is favourable?'

'More than that. Not a rave but not far off.' Hutton paused. 'Wait a minute, though. It won't be his review – Kew's in Europe. Sheila will be doing it.'

'What's she likely to say?'

'No idea. But it should be in the computer by now. Ring me at five and I'll tell you. Why does it matter so much? Afraid of being out of step with the opinion leaders?'

Robert smiled. 'No, just digging around the subject. It still seems strange that one critic can make or break a show. Doesn't happen in the movies. You can read a whole slew of raves for some new director from Burkina Faso or some place and when you get to the cinema there are eight other people there.'

'Doesn't *always* happen in the theatre,' Hutton pointed out. 'Those Lloyd Webber musicals in the eighties were critic proof. I still remember Frank Rich's review of *Song and Dance* in the *Times* – "grating, monotonous and empty". People still went, though. But you don't want to be a critic?'

Robert stirred the ice in his drink with his finger. 'I'm not sure. I've got to get out. Do you know what the sum total of my journalism is? I counted it once. About six hundred words a week if I'm lucky. At least they named a theatre after a critic like Brooks Atkinson. I doubt if they'd name a dog's lavatory after a television reporter.'

Hutton laughed. 'They still send you out to cover the opening of a book, do they?'

'Books are too intellectual for us. Just the closing of a musical.'

'You take it all too seriously, Rob, you always did. You've got it made. You could end up like me covering some guerrilla war in South America with only your press pass to stave off the bullets.'

Robert finished his drink. 'I don't think I could handle that. Besides, I thought Rio was all beaches and carnivals.'

'It's quite a hairy place. People used to get robbed in their cars at stop lights and when there was a public uproar about it the mayor of Rio said it was the drivers' fault for stopping. So now nobody ever does. You're more likely to be run over than murdered.'

'Still auditioning for the job,' Robert observed good-naturedly, gathering up his coat. 'Hey, listen – good luck, you'll get it. And I'd really like to hear Sheila Wilson's review. I'll ring you.'

*

'Forty, love? It isn't true
You know I'm stuck on thirty, too.'

'Thirty all, I couldn't care,
We're a deuce, a perfect pair.'

The sexy duet between the two bronzed females, the stocky

31

one in pigtails and white shorts, her taller, skinnier partner in a low-cut tennis dress and wearing an Indian headband, was accompanied by a very Gilbert and Sullivan ladies' chorus, making choreographed motions behind the pair with their tennis racquets.

It was cute and camp, and Robert enjoyed it. This came as a surprise: he had not really expected to. But the show succeeded in sending up the tennis world while at the same time bringing out the history of Wimbledon. He made notes of the more absorbing details. The third Wimbledon champion, the Reverend J. T. Hartley, actually returned to his church in the north of England to take the service in the middle Sunday of the championships and, in an ironic triumph of good over evil, the man he subsequently beat in the final, V. St Leger Gould, was later found guilty of murder. In 1939 the Wimbledon Committee with a very British respect for international law believed the trumped-up criminal charges of homosexuality levelled by the Nazis against the likely winner, Baron Siegfried von Cramm, and refused to let him play. So along came the outsider, the American Bobby Riggs, who proceeded to bet on himself at 1000-1 to win the men's singles, the men's doubles and the mixed doubles, and then did just that.

'Okay, take fifteen,' called the director. True to the spirit of the musical he was wearing a shiny green Agassi track suit and thick Chang training shoes. He towelled himself down as he came across to Robert.

'They should know it by now,' he remarked as he slumped beside him in the front row of the stalls. 'We've been previewing for almost twelve weeks. We should have opened a month ago.'

'Why didn't you?' Robert asked.

'I guess they were waiting for perfection, in which case 1998 would have been too soon.'

'It seems good.'

'You like it?'

'Yes, I really do – as far as you can judge from a stagger-through. It's clever, catchy music, especially when it seems almost to be in time with the shots.'

'It's the other way round, actually,' the director laughed. 'The press office said you wanted to do an interview.'

'Would now be okay?'

'Now would be about the only time.'

They went up on the stage which had been converted into part of the stadium for the next scene and sat in the Royal Box. The crew had already set up a camera position there and, with a nod from Robert, were ready to roll. He always started with a few soft questions and Gerry Allen, the director, seemed content to reply with the traditional superlatives about the writers and music and cast. Realising these would be of little use, Robert decided to push him on the issue of the opening date.

'A lot of people feel this show is in danger of becoming stale before it even opens. Why the delay?'

'No, we had the opportunity to work hard on it and we just wanted it to be perfect.'

'But you will agree that it was in prime shape almost a month ago?'

'There's always room for improvements. Tonight's the night and we'll just have to see if people like it.'

'What are the advance bookings like?'

Quite suddenly Gerry Allen's showbusiness bonhomie dropped and he began to look flustered. 'I don't know.'

Robert leant forward intently. He knew he was onto something. 'You mean you're directing this musical and you don't know the box-office take?'

Allen wiped his face with the towel that was round his neck. 'This is a confidential area. And it's not relevant to the artistic side of the show – which *is* my concern.'

'But you are a focal part of the team putting this on. It's costing three and a half million dollars. You must have some idea of the potential audience interest, even before the reviews.'

'I . . . I'm er . . . I'm not allowed.' Allen held up his hand. 'Listen, will you stop the camera, please.'

'Why?' Robert enquired, as politely as he could.

'This interview is terminated. I'm here to talk about the artistic side, not the business. And I have to go.'

Gerry Allen pulled off his microphone, rose from his chair and, without another word, disappeared into the wings like a disgruntled loser.

'Opening night nerves,' suggested the sound recordist as he removed Robert's microphone.

'I don't think so,' Robert replied. 'Something's wrong. Listen, Pete, can you write on the Betacam box that the editors are to use *all* of the end of that, from where I ask him about the advance sales, him saying stop the camera, the walk-out, the lot. I'll confirm by phone. But I've another call to make first.'

'She hates it.' Hutton's voice sounded less jovial than usual. 'Absolutely hates it. Says people will be fighting to get out of the theatre.'

'Is it the dykey bit that puts her off. Is Sheila – ?'

'Probably. Not the most married person on the staff, tends to smoke a pipe at conference. No, I'm only joking. Who knows? It's just wall-to-wall bad. Looks like rain stops play, I'm afraid.'

'Hutton, thanks, you're a friend.'

'I'm likely to be more interested in Roland Garros than Wimbledon, by the way.'

'Who's he?'

'You really *are* on the ball. Paris. It's a tennis stadium. It's where they play the French championships.'

'Why there?'

'I've been posted to Paris as number two. No Rio. They say I need a couple of years' foreign training first. I'd rather be running an office but I suppose Lynne will love it.'

'Hey, so will you. Congratulations. I'll buy you a drink. Better brush up your Italian.'

'They speak Fren–' But Robert clicked off before Hutton could realise he was being sent up.

His suspicions confirmed, Robert moved to a more secluded part of the stalls where he was certain he could not be overheard talking into his mobile telephone. He called information to get the number of Broadway Exclusive, the largest group booking agency. Up to seventy per cent of the sales on any major show went through companies like this. Ladies in specially acquired hats and humanely killed mink coats would come in coach parties to go to the theatre, usually stopping at Pier 54 or some such place for a preliminary meal first.

'Hello, Broadway Exclusive?' – he put on a deep, responsible voice. 'This is the Rockaway Inner Wheel Club. We would like to know the seat availability on *Wimbledon* at the 46th Street Theatre. We're looking for thirty seats together.'

There was a pause. '*Wimbledon*? Can you hold?' He did, for nearly a minute. The woman came back on the line. 'I'm sorry, I can't help you on *Wimbledon* at this moment in time.'

'Surely it isn't sold out?'

'No, it's not sold out. We just have a hold on bookings. Now I may be able to do something for you on *Phantom* – first time in nine years we're at last able to get seats for the same month.'

'I'm not interested in *Phantom*,' Robert's voice sharpened. 'Who's put the block on *Wimbledon*?'

'Our instructions come from the theatre management. If they don't want advance sales, we can't make them.'

'I see. That's fine.'

'Thank you for calling Broadway Exclusive and enjoy the show.'

Her pre-programmed farewell took no account of the fact he had bought nothing. But she had provided him with something more valuable than a ticket. The pieces were almost in place. He just needed some inside facts and figures. In a small office, directly below the dressing-rooms, he found what he was looking for: an old lady doing the books. She, like most people in the business, was conversant with *Arts Action* and happy to put her pen aside to talk about the show. After he had told her what Ed Butler was really like in the flesh, not even adding the bit about halitosis which he did if he was feeling mischievous, he skilfully drained the information he needed from her.

'I'll be watching,' she shouted after him as he sped down the steps back to his crew. The run-through had started again. Two blond men were stripping off in the changing room.

'Listen,' he told the cameraman. 'I've got to get back to the office. Make sure we get a prime position outside the theatre tonight, will you?' Glancing at the stage he added, 'and cover those Swedes – Rainier thinks they're adorable.'

The chairs at the rear of the control-room were filling up with researchers and producers, as well as one or two guests who observed the increasing chaos with bewilderment. Jim Hurley sat in a high chair, the small cigar in his mouth dropping ash onto the yellow script he was attacking with a thick black marker pen as he called out last-minute cuts, both to the people in the gallery and on the phone to his opposite number in Los Angeles. Although the main management of *Arts Action* was over there, on nights when the East Coast input was greater Hurley had responsibility for the running order. The show had anchor-people in both cities, usually Ed Butler in New York and Terry Hall on the other side of the continent.

In front of Jim two young women with stop-watches and scripts were yelling instructions into microphones, standing by video inserts, opening titles, remote cameras and giving last-minute running times to the director, Harry Hudson, who sat hunched over the desk, nervously unwrapping a piece of gum as he gazed at the three banks of television monitors in front of him.

'Thirty seconds, everyone, and we're coming to you first, LA,' Harry's voice rang out with edgy confidence. 'You're looking lovely, Terry, what's the weather like?'

'Fucking fog,' replied the exquisitely groomed blonde on the monitor, taking a final desperate pull on a long, mentholated cigarette.

'Then to you at JFK, Ed. Tell them to stop the planes while we're on the air, will you.' Harry liked to keep the dry patter going until the last minute.

'And five seconds, four, three . . .' counted the production assistant beside him.

'Cue titles and then Terry,' shouted Harry.

Just before the closing notes of the tinkling musical montage came to an end, Terry casually stubbed her cigarette out in an off-camera ashtray, coughed and smiled. 'Welcome to *Arts Action*. Here in Los Angeles we'll be dropping in on the wrap party of the latest Rob Lowe picture, *Divorce Malibu Style*, and we've got a report on a cop who's usually causing trouble for other people but in real life has brought some on himself with his drug habit. Good evening, Ed, you going somewhere?'

'Hello, Terry, and no, I'm not. But, as you can see, I'm here at John Fitzgerald Kennedy International Airport, a place once known as Idlewild, and we have a sad story about some airline employees who have been far from idle and made their co-workers more than wild. But first let's tread down to Broadway where it's another opening, another show. *Wimbledon*, for 120 years the showpiece of British tennis and now, who knows, the showpiece of the 46th Street Theatre. Robert Barrett has details.'

'Cue Robert and stand-by play-in seven,' Harry snapped his fingers. They had got off to a sprinting start.

Robert was positioned in front of a crowd of men and women, many in evening clothes, waiting to go into the theatre. He looked up and quoted from the programme in his hand. '"Girls in white dresses, and men in pullovers, racquets in presses, and green grass with clovers, rocketing services hit hard with strings, these are a few of my favourite things." Or they used to be. Tonight we turn the clock back to the golden age of tennis when men were sportsmen, and girls were girls.'

'Run video seven,' bellowed Harry. The two female players and their chorus of racquet-wavers temporarily filled the screen.

'That was a bit near the mark,' observed Jessica from the back of the control room.

'*Double entendre*, darling,' the director shouted over his shoulder.

'Double fault if you ask me.'

'Coming out of video in twenty seconds.' The assistant leant forward towards her monitor. 'Who's that he's got with him?'

'It looks like Lewis Klein,' Hurley's voice boomed authoritatively through the room.

Robert nodded. He could hear everything that was being said on his earpiece.

'Ask him about his *Macbeth*,' continued Hurley.

Robert gave a resigned look, indicating that he was hardly going to ask him about the price of cucumbers. The extract ended and he was once again on air.

'We're back live at 46th Street Theatre for the opening of the new musical, *Wimbledon* – that was one of the twelve original songs in the production – and with me is Lewis Klein whose *Macbeth* at the Public Theatre has been hailed as the definitive

37

performance of the nineties. What do you feel about that, Lewis?'

'I feel . . . I feel . . . gratified?'

'Even the British critics said your Scottish accent was terrific. Did you spend months in the Highlands working on it?'

'No, not at all . . . I modelled it on Sir Alec Guinness in a film called *Tunes of Glory*, as a matter of fact.'

'We don't often see you at first nights – what brings you down here?'

'I have some friends who put some money in the show and I said I'd keep an eye on it for them. And, more important, I have some friends who invested their talent. I dunno, I like the idea.'

'Lewis, thank you. We hear your Captain Hook in the new Peter Pan movie is really something.'

'No problems. I did it single handed. The crocodile's good, too.'

Klein gave the camera a wave and made his way into the foyer while Robert moved quickly towards a stout, olive-skinned man with dark, thinning hair who was just getting out of a stretch limousine.

'Who the hell is that?' said Hurley. 'Get him to hand over to Ed, we can come back to him when he's found someone interesting.'

'Get that, Robert?' yelled Harry.

Robert either didn't or ignored the voice in his earpiece. He seemed intent on talking to his new arrival. 'Mr Estes, I expect you have a special interest in this evening?'

The man looked considerably startled, but then straightened his mohair coat and made to walk past the camera with a throwaway remark. 'I'm looking forward to the show like anyone else. Thank you.'

'What the fuck – ? Get him off.' Hurley was shouting now.

But Robert managed to interpose his body between Estes and the entrance.

'Would I be correct in thinking that you're looking forward to the show closing?'

Estes blanched. 'That's nonsense. What are you saying?'

'I'm saying that you purchased this theatre earlier this week. Is that correct?'

'Listen, this is a night out. Speak to my accountant.'

'Coming to JFK, stand-by Ed, we'll crash out if we have to.' Harry was oblivious to what was unfolding on the screen.

But Hurley was now standing over him at the control panel. 'Hold it, hold it. Take your time, Bob, go for it!'

'You've bought this theatre, haven't you?' said Robert.

'No comment.' Estes tried to move away but his path was now blocked by the watching crowd.

'And your company,' Robert persisted, 'has exchanged contracts to start converting the theatre into a television studio next Monday morning.'

'Show them to me.' Estes became aggressive. 'Either put up or shut up.'

Robert ignored the challenge. 'There's no alternative theatre available at present to take the show so you're making quite sure it folds by the week-end.'

'You're in dangerous waters, my friend.' Estes had begun to redden. 'I can't close shows.'

'No, but you've ordered the staff to put a hold on advance bookings, especially the big agencies. And you've deliberately delayed the opening to avoid a favourable review from Kenneth Kew in the *Times* in the knowledge that it's going to be panned by Sheila Wilson, his second string.'

'You're talking shit. Slanderous shit.'

It was Robert's turn to go on the offensive. 'The people who are being slandered are the people who made this musical – people who'll be looking for another job when you announce that the box-office take is so low you intend to close the show.'

He thought Estes was going to hit him but the television camera over his shoulder served as a protective older brother.

'Listen, you schmuck,' Estes yelled at him. 'You'd better cut all this out of your tape or you're going to have to make these allegations stand up in a court of law.'

'No tape, Mr Estes, you're live on *Arts Action*. And maybe because of that the people who've been working for the past four months on this superb production won't be out of a job tomorrow.' Robert turned back to the camera. 'Now, over to Ed Butler at JFK.'

'A clean ace,' observed Jessica at the back of the control room. 'I just hope he hasn't foot-faulted.'

'Well, you showed up that fella all right then.'

'You saw it, did you?' The buzz of recognition usually pleased Robert, at the same time making him feel marginally uncomfortable.

'Sure, it's a rare thing if I miss it. I know when it's over it's time to get down here. That Testes is some slippery character. You caught him good and proper.'

'Estes. I'm just beginning to have my doubts. Maybe the place would be better off as a TV studio. There are too many dark theatres in New York. TV would give more steady jobs, things like that.'

'That's not the point. You could see there was something underhand about that guy. And we need theatres. When Broadway goes, we all go. They say it's the main reason people come to this city. Now – how about a Manhattan like you've never tasted before, on the house?'

'Sounds good to me,' replied Robert, partially relieved.

The attentive Irish barman, with a physique to withstand the Donegal weather and a fisherman's face to match – but who had probably spent most of his life in New York – measured the Jack Daniel's and vermouth into the heavily iced glass with deliberate excess. P. J. Clark's on Third Avenue was not one of Robert's favoured watering holes but a post-programme summons to a drink with Hurley there amounted to an order. They had not had time to talk after the show and he was apprehensive. Deliberately going solo on the story without consulting anyone was something of an irrational bid for death or glory.

The barman's remarks on the need for theatre to attract tourists seemed to have little application here. It was past the interval of most shows and the place was packed, with more people coming in all the time. It had the feeling of a club – most of the men were in suits and ties and the girls were city girls, confidently made up and pungently perfumed. Everyone seemed to know each other, or at least by their presence here were party to a tacit agreement that anybody could talk to anybody, even complete strangers, as if they were acquaintances. Nobody else noticed Robert, but there again few people had noticed Jacqueline Kennedy and Aristotle Onassis when they ate here during their courtship. He didn't have to eavesdrop on conversations, they came at him like intersecting radio stations on full volume. The most common topic seemed to be what people were going to do next, whether later that night or the following day or the next weekend. Living life by filling filofaxes, thought Robert.

'Jimmy, the usual?' The barman's tones would have carried across Galway Bay on a stormy night.

Hurley was wending his way towards him through the chattering masses.

'Bit empty tonight – where is everyone, Sean?'

The barman laughed and set a large glass of stout and a none-too-small glass of whiskey in front of him. 'Gone to catch that play your friend told us about before it closes.'

'I don't think they need hurry.' Hurley downed the whiskey and turned to Robert with the Guinness in his hand. 'Cheers. You're a fool, but a clever one.'

'What's happened?'

'Nothing as bad as what might have. The *Times* were on the phone before the programme was over. Sheila Wilson had rung in and offered to pull her review. So they're going to print Kew's original alongside hers and under their version of your story.'

'It's true. I wouldn't have gone with it otherwise.'

'Truth is rarely a defence against power and money. It's lucky the *Times* took the line they did. If they thought we were implying Wilson was in any way involved we could have been in deep shit. Anyway the Estes people have contacted them and us saying they're postponing the TV series and they'll run *Wimbledon*. They may not love you but they love this sort of publicity even less. Hey, look at that woman over there, the platinum one. Now *that* could be a night to remember.'

Robert was temporarily surprised by Hurley's abrupt change of subject. He had been beginning to expect a paean of gratitude. Instead he felt constrained to follow the turn in the conversation.

'Yes, though what you'll remember her for only highly skilled physicians can tell.'

Hurley laughed. 'Have another. Sean, more medicine. No, you did well. We can keep ahead of that story for another couple of days – useful for the ratings. LA aren't too thrilled, always a good sign. The one thing that always gets on their tits is that they have no real theatre there. Too much time spent at barbecues to listen to the bard. Besides, they like their tennis in the back garden with a ball machine and a pitcher of Pimms.'

He lifted a drink in either hand and moved across from the bar to what appeared to be his regular position by a ledge on the far wall. Robert followed him. 'I never feel comfortable there,' he said. 'The Beverly Hills scene doesn't seem part of the real America. We bought Alaska from the Russians. I sometimes think we bought California from another planet. Jupiter, maybe.'

'Do you really feel like that? I was going to send you across for the Oscars.'

'I did feel like that until I heard you were going to send me across for the Oscars. Are you serious? That's terrific. I heard Ed was marked down for the remote job on that with Terry in the studio.'

'We thought we might take a slightly more abrasive line this year – since ABC does the show itself we don't need to hype it for them. No, even before tonight this was in the works. And after tonight it's official. Cheers again.'

The platinum woman had wormed her way to Hurley's side.

'Have we met?' she broke in, slightly drunkenly.

'I don't think so – I would have remembered. What are you drinking?'

She finished off what looked like a gin and tonic. 'No, I'm doing the buying. I got promoted to the first-class cabin today so I guess the drinks are on me. What are you boys having?'

'I have to go,' said Robert. 'But congratulations on your appointment.'

Hurley eyed her hungrily. 'Anything that's wet,' he said.

'Guess that rules out dry martinis,' she muttered as she made her way back to the bar.

'Will you be all right on your own?' Robert teased him. 'We don't want you hijacked up, up and away.'

'Why not?' Hurley looked radiantly smug. 'It's not a bad life, is it? I feel alive when I'm in here. The people are alive.

Most of the world retreats to a room on their own or a wife they could do without and children who could do without them. But here, you don't know what the night might hold. You step into the future.'

'I don't think I have the constitution for it.' He squeezed Hurley's arm. 'Fasten your seat-belt,' he advised him. 'It's going to be a bumpy night.' As he apologised his way to the door through the thickening throng he glanced back to see his boss's new friend return with the drinks. Hurley had lit two cigarettes and was in the process of handing one to her.

He caught sight of Robert watching him and shouted: 'If the Oscars work out okay we're looking for someone to cover the Cannes Film Festival.'

I wonder if he's saying that to impress her or to impress me, Robert pondered as he stepped into the relative peace of Third Avenue.

Tanya was in bed, naked, thumbing through *Rolling Stone*.

'You're a shit,' she said.

Robert sat on the edge of the bed. 'I'm sorry. I had to see Hurley. I'd still be there drinking now if Miss Pan Am hadn't flown him away.'

'That Estes – why didn't you tell me? Jesus, I could really have done with a break with that. You didn't need it, it's not your job.'

'Slow down. I didn't even know about it this morning. You had *The Bloomie Murders*.'

'It didn't stand up. We needed time, you overran.'

He loosened his tie. 'Listen. I'm sorry. I didn't even mean –'

'It's okay,' she interrupted. 'I saw it on playback in the office. You got lucky. What did Hurley want?'

'Promises, promises.'

She put down her magazine. 'Like what?'

Robert sat on the bed beside her. 'The usual stuff – the Oscars, the Cannes Film Festival, the stars.'

Tanya put her arms around him from behind, pressing her cheek against his, and began to unbutton his shirt.

'I think you might get lucky for the second time today,' she whispered.

CHAPTER 3

Thursday 30th January 1997

Paris

The icy blast that coursed down the Champs Élysées bit like an angry adder. Paris still wore its colourless winter cape as Chantal Coutard crossed the Place de la Concorde, the wind eddying as threateningly as the traffic that swirled round the bleak open square. The Seine was full and fast, its murky brown waters straining to get out of the dismal city.

She regretted not having taken a taxi. She walked whenever possible. Paris is a city where you can go everywhere you want to on foot, Raoul had once persuaded her, and throughout their affair he insisted on demonstrating as much. He had been a policeman in the drug squad but knew the streets from his days on patrol. Their relationship had come to an end one snowy night on the way to La Coupole – a restaurant too far. But the habit lingered. She saw it as a form of exercise although today she wondered whether one had to freeze to be fit. She drew her billowing black cloak around her as she trotted along the Rue de Rivoli. It was only the sculpted styling of her Titian-red hair that stopped her from looking like a refugee from a holy order. With some relief she finally burst through the doors of W. H. Smith into the fussy warmth of the shop.

This was one of Paris's anachronisms, a little piece of England hiding on the doorstep of the Louvre. It lay across the street from the Jeu de Paume, which, until the mid-eighties, had been the temple of the Impressionists, now shipped to statelier splendour in the Musée d'Orsay. Smith's sold all things British, from magazines to marmalade, but it was the former that were Chantal's quest. She picked up copies of *The Economist*, *Time* and *Newsweek* in English, the London *Times*, the *Guardian*, the *Herald Tribune* and even found a six-day-old copy of the *New York Times*. She had a standing order for *Variety*, which the sales assistant produced from a shelf beneath the till.

Then, with a guilty glance around her to make sure that no one she knew was watching, she swiftly climbed the stairs to the tea room on the upper floor. As a child she had always sought out secret places where no parent or teacher would find her and now, at the age of twenty-five, this dimly lit room with its quaintly attired waitresses provided an adult refuge. Smith's had actually closed it down a few years previously but the outraged reaction, not from the English but from the French, had caused them to rescind their decision. Here she indulged her secret passion for muffins and Earl Grey tea, shrouding her identity by scrutinising the *New York Times*.

It was not that she was doing anything wrong; she was merely late for work. Besides, it was part of her duties, as the English Language Press Officer of the Cannes Film Festival, to collect the British and American papers on Tuesdays and Fridays. She was fluent in the language, having spent a year at Bristol University where her craving for muffins had been born – and where she discovered that the British perversely called them toasted teacakes, even when they ate them in the morning.

Wrestling with the paper, she turned automatically to the arts pages. Her attention was caught by the headline: 'Theater owner thwarted in attempt to avoid paying off cast.' It was the Estes story. The *Times* gave credit for the *coup* to a Robert Barrett, and there was a small photograph of him beside the article. Chantal scanned the item and was about to move on to the film reviews when, as an afterthought, she took a neat leather writing pad from her handbag and, with a miniature gold pen, noted down '*Arts Action*, US TV'. Beside it in brackets she put 'Robert Barrett'.

'Chantal, you're late. You're always late.'

Madame Rivette ran the press office with the autocracy of a village schoolmistress, a job she might well have ended up doing had she not, many years previously, been in the right bed at the right time. After the 1992 reshuffle of the Festival administration, many were amazed to find her still there, let alone promoted from shipping film prints to managing journalists.

'I was getting the English-language papers.'

'Others get them and they are not late. We've been waiting for half an hour.'

Chantal was unrepentant. 'For the papers? Nobody opens them for weeks – they're often thrown away unread.'

'That's not so. How do you know we don't read them while you're still on your way to work? Besides, we've got an emergency. We need the computer. It is a matter of great importance. The Director is demanding details of all the Australian films that are under consideration for *Un Certain Regard* this year. Immediately.'

Chantal's unique talent, more greatly valued than the calm that she brought to the intermittent hysteria which frequently blew up in the press office, was that she was the only person there who had mastered the revamped computer system. Cannes had resisted computerisation over the years, preferring instead the chaos of piles of documents that still cluttered the office shelves. But more and more people had pointed out that the Berlin Film Festival had been fully computerised for over fifteen years. At a touch of a button they could find out every detail about any delegate – where he or she came from, how long they were staying, which invitation lists they should be included on, what class of hospitality they merited and so on. Cannes had always considered this slightly vulgar and very German. Even though a computer system had been forcibly installed in their old premises further up the Faubourg St Honoré, it had always been an object of derision. Madame Rivette would have preferred quill pens.

But, as nobody needed to be reminded, this May would bring the Fiftieth Cannes Film Festival, the greatest anniversary so far of the most important movie event in the world. And computers, the Chairman of the Festival had insisted, were *de rigueur*. His diktat did not stop the old ways. Files were still kept on people, with their details haphazardly stowed in buff folders crowded into cardboard boxes which formed a tottering castle by the door. Articles by journalists about previous festivals were pinned to their requests for accreditation, with any adverse comments underlined in censorious red ink. No computer could match the impact of this and many a delegate failed to realise that the two days he spent with his accreditation missing or the shrug that greeted his request for an upgrade in his screening pass might well have a direct link to the number of red lines that decorated his file.

The press office was a law unto itself or, more precisely, unto Madame Rivette. She had no control over, nor much interest in, the selection of films, but she permitted her staff in the languorous months of the late summer and early autumn to assist the Festival Director, Renaud Callet, as he compiled early lists of potential entrants. Those which he liked but nevertheless deemed unworthy of the main selection fell into *Un Certain Regard*, an enigmatically untranslatable phrase which really meant all the films which, for reasons of quality or diplomacy, were seen to be near-misses for the competition.

Chantal sat at the screen with little idea of how she could access this file, save through the usual process of trial and error. But she had no intention of letting anyone else share these doubts. She typed the code CANNES 50 into the computer and followed it with a colon and then the word 'Australia'. A list of French names came up before her and as she scrolled further down them she came upon a second list beneath the underlined words 'not invited'. The home button brought her back to the top which had a date – 15th May 1996. What was the significance of that, she wondered. She rummaged in her desk drawer and pulled out her Festival diary for 1996. It was the night of the Australian party on the Carlton beach. When asked by the hosts, the Festival evidently had its own ideas of who merited invitations. This would doubtless be referred to in compiling this year's Australian reception so she found the correct alphabetical spot and entered her own name in the first list, hesitating and finally deciding not to delete that of Madame Rivette. That would be too obvious, but she mentally reserved the right to dispense further largesse to any friends who might be impressed.

'Chantal, Monsieur Callet's secretary is on the phone. Do you have the details?' Madame Rivette's shrill tone bounced back off the screen at her.

'Not yet. Why the hurry?'

'He is having lunch with the Australian ambassador, and he has to leave the office shortly. We do not want an international crisis.'

'They'll hardly break off diplomatic relations,' Chantal shrugged.

'We need results, not impudence.'

Chantal turned back to the computer. She punched in the word 'regard'. The negative response 'unfamiliar command' came up on the screen. 'Regard 97' proved more fruitful, itemising those films, three French, one Russian and one Chinese, that had been confirmed as selections for the category this year. None came from Australia. A small crisis loomed. On a hunch she typed 'Ausregard' and, to her amazement, two titles showed up: *Viennese Nights* and *Archduke Ferdinand – the inside story*. Somehow these did not sound all that Australian, but she was onto something. Her hacking hackles were rising. 'Regardaus' yielded nothing; neither did 'certainaus'. Somewhere, she felt, there must be an Australian sub-directory. She tried 'subaus'. At last, there it was. The fourth heading was 'regard' and a complacent glow of satisfaction spread through her as she called that up. Two films, *The Boat People – Twenty-Five Years On* and *Aboriginal Revenge*, were itemised as possible contenders for *Un Certain Regard*. Beneath each were brief summaries of the plots.

'I've got them,' she yelled in triumph.

'About time,' snapped Madame Rivette. 'Now, how do we print them out? It's no good. That man has still not mended the printer. I told them last week. Now it's a disaster.'

'There are only two films,' Chantal observed drily. 'Less than five hundred words in total. Somebody could copy them down.'

'Elise, do it now.' Madame was nothing if not fast to act on the obvious once it had been pointed out to her.

When Madame had left the room, proudly clasping the sheet of paper, Chantal inquisitively returned to the 'subaus' file. Her interest had been aroused by the fifth heading which carried the somewhat self-defeating title 'confid'. The contents intrigued her:

'The Director has now viewed the film *Aboriginal Revenge* and doubts its suitability for inclusion in *Un Certain Regard* this year. Although the first work of a promising Aborigine film director, it seems to do less than justice to the original inhabitants of the continent. The prolonged massacre scene of innocent white holidaymakers is both gory and offensive with implications of cannibalism which have no basis in fact.

'The Festival has yet to receive a viewing copy of *The Boat People – Twenty-Five Years On*. Evidently this deals with the plight of the Vietnamese, partly featuring two successful immigrants and their families who own popular Melbourne restaurants but primarily emphasising the lack of compassion from the Australian government for those still living in reduced circumstances. It comes highly recommended by the film board.

'As yet there is no potential Australian film of sufficient merit for entry in the main competition.'

'You choose the wine.'

The Australian Ambassador – a florid, heavily-built man – passed the list, padded like a valuable manuscript, to Renaud Callet. The *sommelier* looked on in anticipation, his medallion worn with the pride of a war decoration, as he waited to be consulted.

Callet was not unskilled himself in the art of diplomacy. He picked a Wolf Blass Cabernet Sauvignon '85, from South Australia. He was amazed that Florette's carried such a selection and the *sommelier* was further amazed that a Frenchman should select it.

'Your vines are challenging us from every quarter, Monsieur l'Ambassadeur,' he remarked, as he closed the weighty tome and passed it back to the *sommelier*, who managed to convey in his stiff bow what he thought of the choice.

'Dick,' said the Ambassador.

'I beg your pardon?'

'I'm Dick. Dick Lockwood. I'm beginning to suffocate in the formality of this country. I thought you had a revolution to do away with titles but I meet more barons here than I met lords when I was in St James's'.

'St James – a cathedral?'

'Sort of.' Dick took a slug of the substantial whisky that he had carried with him from the bar. 'London. The British always make simple things more complicated by hanging onto some element of their history. Maybe it's because it's all they've got.'

'You were Ambassador there? Paris is a promotion?'

'It's certainly more fun. No, I was first secretary. We don't actually have an Ambassador in London. He's called a High Commissioner. The British way of reminding us we were once a colony.'

The table was cleared to permit twelve oysters to be placed in the middle. A simple terrine of duck was set before the Director. Dick seized a Claire Number 2 and scooped it greedily off its shell into his mouth.

'Only two nations in the world understand oysters and we're the second. But ours are fatter and have less savour. Like our films.'

Callet smiled but did not disagree. He had started his career as a diplomat, graduating with honours from the École Militaire on a path that, at one stage, looked as if it were leading directly to the French Embassy in Washington and maybe beyond. But all his life he had been in love with films, and the chance to run the Cannes Festival seemed a gift from the gods. At fifty he was the same age as the Festival itself and his position required rather more diplomacy than most foreign service postings. Not that he looked fifty. Only recently had flecks of grey added some *gravitas* to his thick, charcoal hair which habitually looked as if he had combed it with his hands. In the ministry this had been seen as a statement of individuality; when he moved to the Film Festival in 1992 it seemed to go more naturally with the job. His dark, searching eyes played a persuasive role in his skill as a negotiator. With an angular, vulpine nose and lips which, even in repose, seemed slightly pursed he looked not unlike François Truffaut – even down to the tangled scarf that frequently girdled his neck. Indeed Callet would have loved to have been François Truffaut, but proximity to the mighty was an acceptable second best. He broke a little bread, tasted his terrine and waited. He sensed that he was about to receive a lecture. And he was right.

Dick had evidently rehearsed his speech, as any good diplomat would.

'Our wine, our oysters, our films. I know a little about the first two and a lot less about the third. My wife and I can't get out to the cinema. Too many receptions. Besides, we're not of an age to stand in queues.'

Renaud broke in: 'It can always be arranged. You only have to ring – '

But he was cut off. The Ambassador had embarked on a speech, not a conversation.

'However, I am instructed by my principals in Canberra that this year, your half-century as we would say in cricket, a time to tip the peak of the cap with the bat to a ripple of respectful applause, is an occasion to be commemorated. Mindful of the fact that seventeen short years ago it was your very Festival that gave such a fillip to our small but growing industry, especially our film, *Breaker . . . Breaker's Yard . . . Surf Breakers?'*

He was lost. The Director sensed that he might be permitted to speak. '*Breaker Morant?'*

'Thank you.' Dick had regained his carefully memorised place and his stride. '*Breaker Morant*, the sad story of three fine Australians who were court-martialled during the Boer War. A film which won the Best Actor prize for Jack Thompson – ' Renaud suppressed the desire to point out that he knew this already, wondering only how long Lockwood was going to go on – 'and in many ways launched our industry in the international market-place. You have been generous to Australia over the years and we would like to honour the Festival with a bursary of ten thousand Australian dollars a year which would enable a promising French film student to come to our country and study our industry, film and television. Before these ridiculous European quotas were introduced Australia provided Great Britain with some outstanding domestic television dramas. Anyway, we would like you, as Director of the Cannes Festival, to be trustee of this fund.'

Renaud raised his glass. 'An honour. You are most kind. I will have to consult my Chairman and my board but I am sure they will ratify my acceptance of such a generous gesture.'

The Wolf Blass had too much tannin and tasted acidic. Did Florette's, he wondered, deliberately stock bad years? He sensed that the Ambassador was now coming to the real point of the lunch.

'Have you made your selection of an Australian film for this year yet?'

'Nothing is finalised,' Renaud replied. 'There are so many countries in the world and room for only so many films. My staff are still reviewing all options.'

Dick swallowed his twelfth oyster. 'I understand completely. I am sure you feel as we do that with the eyes of the world – to say nothing of the television satellites – focusing on this historic anniversary, you would not wish to present a country like ours in an adverse light.'

Renaud opened his hands apologetically. 'Sometimes art and politics do not chime together,' he said enigmatically.

Lockwood looked unimpressed. 'If I were to mention a title like *Aboriginal Revenge* – not a film I have seen or have any intention of seeing, I hasten to add – would you think there was any danger of it gracing or disgracing your anniversary?'

'I am loath to discuss individual films but the scenes where the Aborigines arrive by boat at Drunk Island – '

'Dunk,' interrupted the Ambassador, happy to provide a point of information.

'Thank you,' Renaud smiled and went on: 'Anyway, the mass killing of the holidaymakers and the offensive scenes in the kitchen seem to be a matter of speculation, not history. We will not be showing it, no.'

Lockwood beamed with pleasure. 'What about *The Boat People*?' he asked.

'Really, Dick, you must not push me on this. That is said to be a film of considerable merit. Artistic integrity cannot be compromised.'

'Quite so. But you should know that many of them live in comfortable suburban houses.'

'Alas, films about comfortable suburban houses are not always the most stimulating ones.'

'I don't want to go into details. Canberra merely felt that it was important that you should come and see for yourself.' The Ambassador reached in his pocket and brought out an airline folder. He placed it by Renaud's glass. 'One first-class return ticket to Sydney. No conditions. We would just like to help in any way we can.'

He raised his glass and drained the remainder of the Wolf Bass. 'Now, let's forget about films and talk about something interesting. I have a confession to make: I prefer French wines.'

'Are you coming?'

Stephanie, who was responsible for French television and radio in the Festival office, removed her coat and scarf from a hanger by the door. She and Chantal had fallen into the habit of going shopping after work, usually finding time for a glass of wine before they finally went home.

'I want to stay for a bit,' Chantal replied as nonchalantly as she could, adding by way of explanation, 'I'd better make up for being late this morning.'

Stephanie shrugged her shoulders as she struggled with her coat. 'Why bother? Madame's gone. There's nobody left to see you.'

'All the same, there are a few things I have to do.'

'Okay. Don't forget to lock up. See you tomorrow.'

Stephanie put the keys back in Madame's drawer and gave a wave as she left.

Chantal felt an illicit thrill as she switched on the computer again. She had no specific quarry in mind; like a nervous sorcerer's apprentice she was merely intrigued to find out the extent of her new powers. The system had been programmed by a young American, spending a post-graduate year in France, who had departed overnight after what was termed a 'conflict of personalities' with Madame. Everybody had personality conflicts with Madame but most people just lived with them.

With the nervous hands of someone opening another person's diary Chantal experienced a slight *frisson* as she typed the word 'staff' into the system. There was a pause as the computer searched for information but the words 'file not found' eventually came up on the screen. A little lateral thinking, she muttered to herself and tried 'personnel'. This time it worked. There was a sub-heading 'press office' and calling this up she proceeded to write her own name 'Coutard, C.'. She held her breath.

Five seconds later her personal file unfolded before her: 'Chantal Coutard, 25, apartment 7, 61 Rue Jacob. Unmarried. She joined as a secretary in 1992 and for the past two years has been in charge of English-speaking press and television. Her popularity among the critics and correspondents makes up for a certain laek of respect towards some of the officers of the Festival.'

The hand of Madame was evident. Eagerly she read on. 'While she is well equipped to deal with the extra pressure of the half-centenary celebrations, it is arguable that she should subsequently be posted sideways to a job that has less contact and influence with foreign opinion-makers, especially in the light of her affair last year with a prominent British critic.'

'My God,' thought Chantal, 'how the hell do they know?'

'In addition her past relationship with Inspector Raoul Bazin, currently on suspension from the Paris drug squad and likely to face serious charges, could result in some unnecessary personal publicity which might reflect adversely on the Festival press office.'

'The bastards.' Chantal was outraged. She had to tell somebody but there was nobody there to tell. She took out her diary and looked up Raoul's number. When they had last spoken, at Christmas, he had been running a bar in Cannes.

She thought for half a minute and then dialled the number. A voice answered instantly.

'Raoul?' she asked.

'Who is it?' came the growled reply.

'I had to talk to you.'

'We're busy. The fishermen are in.'

'I had to talk to you.'

'Later.'

'How are things? Any news?'

'No charges, if that's what you mean. They still hope I'm going to resign peacefully.'

'Are you?'

'Perhaps.'

'Listen, I've just discovered my personal file. Your name is on it. They're going to try to use you as – '

Chantal broke off. She thought she could hear someone coming back.

'I'll ring you later,' she whispered.

'What is it?' he asked, less abrupt and more concerned than before. 'What's wrong?'

'Don't worry,' she said. 'I'll ring you in a moment.'

She put the receiver down and turned anxiously back to the screen. As she pressed the keys to get rid of her file, she sensed that there was somebody else in the room. Was it just guilt? She swivelled round in her chair but she could see no one.

'Yes, who is it?' she called out. There was no reply. She spoke more loudly. 'Can I help?'

Still nothing. But she was certain she had heard someone – or something. She got up and went towards the door. As she passed the high pile of cardboard boxes containing journalists' files a gloved hand shot out and covered her mouth before she had time even to scream. She reeled backwards but another hand stayed her fall, in a less than gentle fashion. She pulled herself away, lurching awkwardly against the mound of boxes which scattered as she hit the floor.

She looked up. Her assailant was a short, broadly built man, clad in a thick blue sweater with matching military trousers. He wore leather gloves on his hands and a knitted black balaclava on his head. He was accompanied by another man similarly attired who was now pointing a small pistol at her.

'Get out of here,' she yelled, stupidly and ineffectively.

The one with the gun approached her. 'Where do you keep your money? Quickly.' He spoke imperfect French with an English accent, but from their eyes both men looked like Arabs.

'There is no money here,' she said tremulously. 'This is the press office.'

'All offices have money,' he insisted, gesturing with his gun. 'Do you want a bullet in your leg to save a few francs?'

Fearfully she pointed towards Madame's desk, annoyed that her hand was shaking so obviously. 'There is petty cash in that drawer. But it is nothing.'

It was now apparent to Chantal that the man with the gun was in charge. He was taller and leaner than his partner. The dark skin around his eyes was damp, as if it had been oiled. He gestured to the stocky man to go and look. Then he took a threatening pace towards her.

'Take your clothes off,' he ordered, almost in a whisper.

'Why?'

'Take them off, or *we* take them off.'

She did as she was told, first unzipping her skirt and letting it fall to the floor. Then her silk shirt, although her fingers seemed to freeze and she could barely get a purchase on the buttons. She stood before them in her underwear, knowing that she was going to be raped and feeling she might prefer a bullet to what was about to come.

'There's nothing here,' called the man with the cash box. 'Two hundred francs, not enough for dinner.'

The first seemed uninterested. 'Go back and sit in your chair,' he told her.

She had no option but to obey. Something in his manner made him seem somehow more menacing than an ordinary burglar. He followed her closely. She mustered as much defiance as she could summon up but inside she felt as if she had fused, as if all control had gone out of her body. He put his hands on her shoulders and turned her round. Carefully he removed his gloves and she sat and shuddered as she watched him. Should she scream? There was no one in the building to hear and it might provoke him even more. His hand went down her back and undid her brassière. She held her breath, feeling she was about to vomit. He grabbed first one wrist, then the other, and with the undergarment tied her hands behind her back.

Chantal could control herself no longer. She screamed, loudly, venomously and unstoppingly. Almost immediately, the telephone began to ring on her desk, not quite drowning out cry but rendering it more futile. The tall man reacted nervously, clasping his now ungloved hand over her mouth. Looking down she could see it was dark. Maybe he was

Indian. She could feel the icy muzzle of his gun against her back. He was wearing a sweet musky after-shave or body-lotion, that smelled like saffron.

She sensed the tension in his voice. 'Leave the phone,' he insisted – as if she could do anything in her present position. 'If you make any noise or turn around we will kill you. But before we kill you, you may have an experience that you will regret even more. Do you understand?'

She nodded, mutely. The phone continued to ring.

He moved away and she could hear them both emptying drawers and searching through the scattered cardboard boxes. Like rats in a rubbish dump, she thought. They continued to converse in inaudible tones. After a time the noises that they were making became less and less audible. The phone stopped ringing and the sudden silence came as a shock. They must have gone to another room.

She sat shivering, half-paralysed with fear, and tried to collect her thoughts. She did not dare turn around, but bent slowly over the desk as if she were feeling faint. No reaction came from behind her. With her mouth she lifted a Bic pen from the broken coffee mug on the desk. Still no reaction. She half-glanced behind her and thought she spotted one of them on the other side of the filing cabinet. Nevertheless she deliberately leant forward over the keyboard of the computer and, with the pen in her mouth, pressed the key to return to the operating system. Then she laboriously typed in the word *'bavardez'*.

This activated the modem in the computer, joining it up to the phone line. A series of precise electronic blips acknowledged that she was connected. They seemed to ring out like a church bell across the room and she held her breath in terror. But there was no other sound, no reaction. In the old days she would occasionally send messages to Raoul's personal terminal at the headquarters of the drug squad. Thankfully the code remained fresh in her mind: 9377477. Laboriously she picked it out with the pen in her mouth. She looked pleadingly at the computer to see if she had made contact. She had. She gripped the pen more tightly in her teeth and typed in her name 'chantalchantalchantalchantal' in desperation across the screen.

'What are you doing?' Just her luck: the man had returned.

Chantal straightened herself up, dropping the pen from her mouth as she did so. She said nothing. She heard footsteps and felt a chill gun on her naked shoulder.

'Chantal, Chantal,' read the voice behind her. 'What is that? A cry for help? Is your typewriter going to arrest us?'

He let loose a bird-like giggle, definitely more Indian than Arab she found herself thinking.

A hand came down on her shoulder and he spun her round to face him. She turned her head away. His pupils were so brown as to be almost black with a gleaming white surround.

'Where are the keys to the Director's office?' he demanded.

'He takes them home with him.'

The gun was pressed into her stomach, as much a crude sexual gesture as one of proposed violence. Chantal now looked up into the man's eyes, determined that if she lived through this she would recognise him again.

'There are always spare keys,' he insisted.

She acquiesced. 'In that drawer where you found the money. In an envelope.'

Her tormentor signalled to his colleague to look for them and then reversed the pistol in his hand, holding it by the barrel.

Chantal flinched in fear, anticipating a blow to the head. But his upraised arm swung past her and crashed the handle of the revolver into the computer screen, which shattered stridently into fragments.

'There,' he said, with the same eerie laugh, 'he's dead.'

The shorter man had found the keys and the two of them headed for the door. But they were halted in their tracks by the piercing noise of the phone.

The man with the gun turned back to Chantal, a thin smile on his lips. 'Don't answer it,' he warned.

They were gone. She sat rigidly in her chair, her mind racing through the possibilities of what might happen next. She found it hard to believe that this was real and she was part of it. It was as if she were observing it happening to someone else.

She could no longer hear them. Five minutes had elapsed, maybe ten, maybe fifteen. She couldn't see her watch and in her bewildered state she found it hard to calculate the time. Perhaps they had left the building.

She became aware that her body temperature was dropping rapidly. The central heating had automatically switched itself off at six o'clock and she had heard on the radio earlier in the day that the Paris weather was due to drop to minus five that night. In her naked state she might freeze to death. It might almost be better if they came back.

Another ten minutes, maybe twenty. The cold was beginning to hurt. She decided to risk making a move and tried to get to her feet. But they were numb and she collapsed on the floor with the chair falling on top of her, digging deep into the calf of her left leg which started to run with blood. In desperation she tried to wriggle across to the door, leaving a gruesome red trail on the floor behind her. 'Madame will be annoyed,' she found herself thinking.

She had barely covered a couple of metres before she heard the men returning. The door burst open and somebody rushed in. Chantal buried her face in the carpet and held her breath. In trepidation she felt a wet glove on her shoulder.

'No, no, no,' she screamed.

'Chantal?' asked a voice, this time without an accent.

She looked up and saw, to her immense relief, a friendly face.

'Didier,' she cried. 'Thank God.'

The policeman bent over and undid her hands. He lifted her up and carried her to a sofa in the corner of the office. Removing his overcoat, he placed it on top of her and then picked up her silk shirt from the floor and wrapped it tightly around her bleeding leg.

Leaning forward he rummaged in the coat pocket and brought out a small flask which he offered to her.

'Cognac,' he smiled. 'An inferior brand. Police pay, you know.'

She sipped it gratefully.

He went to the phone. 'I'll call an ambulance.'

'You got my message?' she asked.

'I was just going home,' he replied. 'I tried ringing but there was no answer so I thought I'd better come by.'

Chantal knew him from her days with Raoul. Occasionally they would go to movies with Didier and his boyfriend.

'There were two men – ' she began.

'I think I may have seen them leaving. All muffled up. We'll put out an alert.'

'Didier, thank God,' she repeated, relieved to be alive. 'Have you heard from Raoul?'

He glanced solemnly across at her and shook his head. 'Things are not good there, Chantal. Not good at all. But don't worry about it. Not now.'

CHAPTER 4

Thursday 30th January 1997

Burbank.

Dusty heat, fuelled by the lingering rays of the late afternoon sun, hung around and above and below the familiar water tower that dominated Warner Bros' Burbank Studios. As Leland Walters gazed across at it from his air-conditioned office he could not feel the warmth but he could see it. The weather men said that January 1997 would go into the record books as Southern California's hottest.

Such thoughts did little to alleviate his apprehension about the forthcoming meeting. It was likely to be less than pleasant. To clear his brain and put matters in context, he let his mind slip out of gear and freely associate with whatever thoughts came unprompted. It was a technique he had learned on a weekend seminar in Santa Barbara and, although at the time it had seemed so much humbug, it had on many subsequent occasions provided an effective antidote to the pressures of being President of the studio. Earlier in his career he had always had colleagues with whom he could argue things through, but to hold down his present job he needed to present an outward front of oracular wisdom – a front that could be dangerously dented by confiding his doubts and moments of inadequacy to those who would be happy to fill his shoes.

He remembered the water tower from the first time he had set foot in Burbank in the spring of 1976, Bicentennial year. He was working as a lawyer for Paramount and had come with some contracts for the producer, Mike Frankovich, to sign on the set of *The Shootist*. His journey wasn't necessary; the contracts could easily have been sent by messenger. In truth he had come to look at John Wayne. Whatever title you might collect in the studio system, Leland reflected, you were always one notch down from a true star.

The rasping lilt of the familiar voice, inserting a break in a sentence where none grammatically existed – a clever trick to gain the audience's attention – reached Leland's ears before he turned the corner of the Western street which lay shabbily at the far end of the back lot. They were shooting in a barber's shop with Wayne playing a dying gunfighter. Sometimes cantankerous, sometimes full of bonhomie, the star undoubtedly ruled the set with the director, Don Seigel, judiciously accommodating his caprices. How different, thought Leland, from the dominating young Turks directing today who worship the camera and pay scant attention to the star. Maybe that was why so many actors took to directing.

Wayne was clearly ill. He had some chest complaint which continued to dog him, and he was desperate to finish the picture and take off for Acapulco where his converted minesweeper, *The Wild Goose*, was waiting. He wheezed and spluttered and cursed himself for wheezing and spluttering. And yet, when Leland was introduced to him, an instinctive courtesy and old-fashioned charm came immediately into play. The man respected his public and that message got through even to those millions who never met him. Leland remembered their meeting, more than twenty years ago, better than those he had had twenty minutes ago. As it happened, it was the last day John Wayne ever worked on a movie.

Leland had always regarded himself as the temporary custodian of a piece of American heritage. Unlike the brash, parvenu agents who claimed to run the new Hollywood, he believed that there was a tradition to be upheld. He loved to reminisce about the history of Warner Bros to visiting foreign bankers, as if he were talking about an ancient seat of learning. The studio even had a motto – 'combining good picture-making with good citizenship' – something to which, in its early decades, it had aspired, ever since the four Warner brothers, sons of a Jewish cobbler who escaped his Russian persecutors in Poland by cattle boat across the Atlantic, first experienced the American dream and immortalised it on celluloid.

Seventy years ago they'd gone further and changed the face of movies, with *The Jazz Singer*, the first talking picture. It had always seemed to Leland that Sam Warner must have been the brother with the initiative. It was he who had persuaded the others to put music on disc.

But, twenty-four hours before *The Jazz Singer* opened at the Warner Theatre in New York on October 6th 1927, Sam died. None of the Warners attended the premiere. They returned to California to bury their brother on the eve of Yom Kippur. Leland had always hoped he might have a son to name after him; in the event he had called his daughter Samantha.

The buzzer on Leland's intercom interrupted his reverie and brought him abruptly into the present. 'Mr Booker and Mr Schenck are here.'

'Two minutes,' he replied, adding, almost without thinking, 'I'm on a call to Rome.'

'Very well.' His secretary knew he wasn't on a call to Rome, Booker and Schenck would know he wasn't on a call to Rome but it was the Hollywood custom to appear to be seen to be delayed by something that was, by implication, more important than the scheduled meeting. Besides, it gave him further time to prepare himself. He moved across to the cabinet in the wall thinking to pour himself a fortifying drink. But his eye was caught, not for the first time, by the adjoining photographs of Humphrey Bogart and Ronald Reagan in the line up of studio stars of fifty years ago.

The studio had originally wanted Reagan to play the Bogart part in *Casablanca*. But Jack Warner switched horses, changing the fate of the company and the country, Leland mused. If Reagan had become a bigger star he would never have set out for that other casa blanca at 1600 Pennsylvania Avenue.

There was another prolonged buzz on the intercom. Janice was being leant on.

He snapped deliberately. 'Yes, Janice, what is it?'

'It's not Janice,' growled a laid-back voice, instantly identifiable as belonging to the most popular screen cop in America. 'It's me.'

'Bud,' acknowledged Leland. 'How are you?'

'Tired of waiting.'

'Well, come on in.'

63

The speed with which the door was thrown open indicated that Bud Booker had hardly waited for the invitation. In marched a tall, imposing man – one of those rare stars who looked, if anything, more impressive off the screen than on it. His simple chain-store T-shirt, blue jeans and white sneakers, the costume of a hundred million Americans, emphasised the well-toned body, blond hair combed into casual disarray and imperceptibly larger than life rectangular features that made him one in a hundred million. At the age of fifty-five he was still good for another decade of romantic leads. Following him came a small stick-like man in a business suit. Alopecia had unforgivingly removed every wisp of Barry Schenck's hair, making him look much older than his thirty-five years. At the age of twenty-nine, he had set up the Motivated Management Agency which represented all the talent that mattered in town. But only stars of Bud's magnitude merited Barry's personal attention.

Leland felt constrained to speak first. After all, it was his office even though Bud had requested the appointment. Besides, he was outnumbered two to one. It was standard Hollywood practice to match numbers at any potentially contentious meeting but Bud had pulled something of a fast one by indicating that he would come alone. It was always unwise to negotiate with an agent without the head of business affairs present, and preferably a lawyer as well. Lawyers played a different role in Hollywood from that which they played in the rest of the world. They were letter writers. Nobody in the industry dared to write one without them lest it be interpreted as a form of contract. So lawyers had become scribes, like the wise old men with typewriters in the streets of Calcutta who took dictation from the illiterate. Sometimes they used the knowledge gained to go on to become studio heads, as Leland had, only three years previously.

He opened his arms in a form of greeting. 'Bud, it's been too long. Barry, my lucky day.'

Bud threw himself down on the sofa. Schenck waited more politely until Leland indicated a chair. He sat himself on the edge of his desk, a minor advantage – they might be numerically stronger but he was physically higher.

'That's a pity about the nominations,' he said. 'I thought

we'd at least get a few hits in the technical categories.' Looking towards Bud, he added, 'they're going to have to give you a career Oscar like Cary Grant if they don't hurry up and nominate you. I guess you can't have it both ways in this town; it's either box-office or Oscars and I'm very happy with the former.'

'What are we at?' Bud asked idly.

Leland pulled a sheet of paper on the desk towards him. 'Should pass $100 million the week after next.'

'We'd be nearer $120 if we'd opened in as many cinemas as *Mountie Mac*.' Bert Schenck's look was rarely anything but sour. He thought it made him a more effective negotiator and he was right.

The new popularity of the Canadian cinema was confounding all the Hollywood pundits. For years the studios had been happy to use cheap facilities and labour in Toronto to make American movies but now an indigenous horseback hero in a red jacket, standing for 'the Canadian way', had proved the box-office hit of the mid-nineties.

Leland was nonplussed. '*Mountie Mac*'s a spent force. Just a transient phase. When he's finished, he'll be buried. Bud has a career curve that has its up and downs but within the same high parameters. We aim to preserve that for a very long time. Besides, *Black Cops Kill* is a much more violent film – it's not for kids. I'll tell you, I took my Samantha to *Mountie Mac* the other week. No blood, no bad language. He gives the truant schoolboy a Galaxy Bar and tells him not to do it again. She loved it. They're selling more than five hundred Galaxy Bars a performance. Something we should think about. Did you know that exhibitors in Mexico make more money from the candy counter than from the price of admission?'

'I don't think Bud's too interested in selling candy.' Schenck seemed about to reveal his hand. It was evident that he had been brought along to give the hard word.

'We don't feel that *Black Cops Kill* has been accorded the stature that it deserves,' the agent continued gravely. 'It's an important social statement for our time but that poster, for instance, with Bud pointing the gun out at you, it's just not representative of the film. He only ever shoots in self-defence.'

Leland feigned amazement. 'But, Barry, Bud okayed the campaign and that picture. It was taken by Bud's personal unit photographer. It's one of the main reasons we're up $100 million.'

'That's as may be,' Schenck retorted dismissively, 'but the critics all concentrated on the violent aspects without addressing themselves to what was a unique perspective on crime and the position of minority groups. *Black Cops Kill* exposed how a small vigilante group within the San Francisco Police Department was prepared to infiltrate Chinatown and deal with a crime wave that hitherto the white police had largely regarded as something for the community itself to deal with. There've been hundreds of these Tong murders and our police have done fuck all about most of them.'

'It hardly exposed it,' countered Leland. 'We have no evidence that it was happening. The film's popularity lay in part, I'm sorry to say, with black-skinned men killing yellow-skinned men for various felonies – .'

'The guys were running drugs, protection rackets, what do you mean felony?'

'Whatever they were doing, it hardly merited summary execution with minimal investigation.' Leland was slightly mystified by the turn the conversation was taking. Everyone in the room knew the best way to avoid the charge of exploitation in a killer cop movie was to have the hero come in and clean up the force – which, indeed, was Bud Booker's role here, with the celebrated line: 'This bullet doesn't know if it's aimed at a black man, a yellow man or a white man – it just knows it's going where I tell it.'

But Barry Schenck was anxious to establish his client's intellectual contribution to urban sociology – not a role that had overly concerned Bud when he was making his name in movies as the leader of a motorcycle gang.

'Bud directed this film because the subject mattered to him. And, as you probably know, he made major contributions to the script. It is quite extraordinary that someone of his eminence would take so much trouble with a problem that should be the concern of politicians and social workers and city officials themselves. He even had a researcher live in the Chinese community for a few weeks so that he could get the feel of it.'

Leland was still very unsure of what point Schenck intended finally to arrive at. Did Bud want a part in a Warner's movie for his new girl-friend, Carole Anne Spencer? Such decisions had been easier when the studio turned out thirty B-movies a year. But there were a couple of ten-million-dollar horror films due to roll in the fall that were really being made for the video market and would get a limited release for the publicity. Even Carole Anne could look horrified if a director showed her how. Or did he want the studio to back another of his wife's anti-nuclear homilies? They could afford it. Just. The last one, *Testament of Doom*, ran for all of three days in New York but – as Mary Booker never tired of pointing out – it got a very good review from the woman in the *Manhattan Guardian*. 'Mary Booker's art is in the right place,' was the phrase Warners had been obliged to append to twenty-five thousand ignored posters.

No, probably neither of those. It wasn't going to be that easy. Leland decided on a tactical diversion to make them come to the point. He crossed to the wall and picked a file from the bottom shelf.

'Our research actually shows that the favourite scene in *Black Cops* is where Bud shoots the driver of a mini-bus filled with Moonies and the whole thing goes up in flames. Apparently audiences cheer in seventy-eight per cent of urban cinemas at that moment.'

'It was in self-defence,' put in Schenck rapidly. 'The bus would have mown him down and killed him. He didn't know it was going to explode.'

No, thought Leland, except when he wrote it into the script with a view to a few more million at the box-office.

Schenck glanced respectfully but pointedly at Booker who got up from the sofa and strode purposefully across to the refrigerator. The warm-up act was over; it was the star's turn to come on. He poured himself a Perrier and, still holding centre stage, took it with him to the window where he gazed out across the lot. Then, without turning, in the unnatural fashion only ever used by characters in plays or films, he addressed Leland through the back of his head.

'Ever been to Cannes?'

Leland got the entire scenario immediately but decided to play the game for a little longer. 'The can? Sure. Three times a day. Just like mother taught me.'

At least he managed to make Bud swivel round.

'Not the, *le*,' the star explained, marginally irritated. '*Le Festival de la Film*.'

'*Du Film*,' Leland corrected him. 'The French regard it as a masculine activity. Sure, a couple of times. The asparagus takes some beating. Want to come? The Warner jet knows its way.'

'I thought it just took members of your publicity department on holiday,' Schenck remarked with point-scoring satisfaction.

'You heard?' Leland acknowledged with a grin. 'Not true, of course. We've issued a denial in the trade press. Even those TV guys on *Arts Action* were getting a sniff of it. Absolute lies. Rosenthal was on company business and had my personal permission to take along his wife and daughter – who was sick, by the way.'

'With what?' inquired Schenck.

'Leukaemia, brain tumour, chicken pox, a bad cough, you name it, she had it. The idiot. We're going to have to let him go after the fuss dies down.'

'Let's get back to Cannes.' Bud was not to be diverted.

Leland looked at the studio's most valuable property now silhouetted against the reddening sun. Like a four-hundred-pound gorilla, here was a creature who could do precisely what he wanted.

'You might enjoy it,' he said. 'I'm surprised you've never been. It's possible to have quite a good time there provided you don't mind ten thousand photographers.'

Bud looked him challengingly in the eye. 'I want to go and I want *Black Cops Kill* to come with me.'

Leland smiled reassuringly. 'I don't think that'll be a problem. Why not? A special showing and a big party. It'll give us a good launch in Europe – except with the Moonies.'

'So you can get it in the competition?' interposed Barry Schenck, anxious to tie up the details.

'Hey, wait a minute.' Leland could see they were over-bidding their hand. 'That I don't control. There are about twenty films in competition and the one thing they have in common is their ability to induce narcolepsy.'

The two looked at him questioningly but neither of them asked for an interpretation.

'They're festival films,' explained Leland. 'They rarely have anything to do with regular cinema-going. These are films from Czechoslovakia and Uruguay and Sierra Leone that are never seen outside of festivals. For the most part it's cinema for people who believe that film is something you write books about rather than enjoy.'

He had said the wrong thing.

'That's it, precisely.' Schenck tapped the arm of his chair emphatically with his finger. 'If *Black Cops Kill* is correctly appraised by *cinéastes*, if it's written about and Bud is acknowledged as an "auteur" then it will change the whole perception of his work. The time has come to do that.'

'But what if the reaction is adverse?' Leland asked.

'As you said' – Schenck spelt out the scenario – 'you give a big party. And Bud would like to meet selected foreign journalists for a series of small but extraordinarily exclusive dinners after which they walk away with the *Black Cops Kill* production notes in an individual Cartier attaché case also containing, shall we say, a forty-carat gold pen with which to write their reviews. I think we can, to a certain extent, anticipate the response. What else have you got a publicity department for – except to ride around in the company jet?'

Bud came over and sat down beside Leland. 'But we need to be in the competition. I'm relying on you for that, Leland. You've got some brownie points to be used down there, I'm sure. Square it for me and then we can finalise that three-picture deal.'

'Besides' – Schenck was anxious to underline the plan – 'they like movie stars in Cannes. Why else do all these photographers go there? Why are there TV crews from all over the world looking for stories? Not to analyse Finnish films where a man falls in love with a fiord.'

They all laughed without enthusiasm. Leland could see the logic of the scheme but he knew that the studio would be in for a quarter of a million dollars in costs, visible and invisible, to make it happen. His trained Hollywood instinct, however, was not to agree to a deal without a trade-off.

He turned to Bud. 'Okay. If I manage it – and at this stage it's a fairly major if – will you do something for the studio?'

Bud, happy to have obtained Leland's acquiescence with such relative ease, looked him closely in the eyes – as men do to each other only in movies – and promised.

'Anything.'

Leland drew his breath in. 'They very much want you as a presenter at the Oscars. I realize you said no after they failed to nominate *Black Cops*, but we have a couple of other pictures in there with healthy chances and it would help the studio a great deal in the build-up if you made the magnanimous gesture of appearing on the night.'

Bud looked at Barry and back at Leland.

'You have a deal,' he said, holding out his hand.

'Provided we also win a prize at Cannes,' added Barry Schenck.

This time, nobody laughed.

CHAPTER 5

Friday 14th February 1997

Pinewood

'The Foreign Secretary has asked me to let it be known to you both – Commodore Lewin and Sister Florence – what a debt the nation owes to your prompt action. Your bravery, Commodore, in personally diving into the dangerous waters of the South China Sea to rescue Lu Xun – now known as Lew Sun – was an example to your men, a single spontaneous gesture that made these foundlings from another star realise that the human race has an inner quality that none of their superior electronics could divine. I am referring to that of compassion. Something that you, Sister Florence, have displayed above and beyond the call of duty. I am authorised to announce that, for this, you have been made a member of the most excellent order of the British Empire.'

Florence made a semi-curtsey. 'I am most honoured.'

The junior minister, his already shiny face further glistening with a thick film of perspiration, continued to read the speech: 'And you, Commodore, for your outstanding valour are admitted to the same noble order as a Commander of the British Empire.'

The Commodore lowered his head in modesty then changed the gesture to a sharp military salute. The sprinkling of applause greeting the announcement would have been louder had not most of the guests in the ornate Foreign Office stateroom been holding cups of tea and, in some instances, plates with chicken sandwiches on them. It was a British tradition, practised at receptions down the ages, to make speeches to people who found themselves unable to applaud.

'And, finally, to Lew Sun and his crew, who leave

71

tomorrow for the long journey back to Jupiter, we say *bon voyage* and will ye no come back again.'

A rattling of teacups indicated the general approval, as well as a general movement towards the serving tables for refills.

Lu Xun came across to Florence. '*Bon voyage*? No come back? I thought I had mastered English. Does he want us never to return?'

'Oh no, he wants you to come back. We all do. He was speaking French and Scottish.'

The Alien guided her to a *chaise-longue* slightly away from the rising chatter that had broken out.

'A Commander of the British Empire?' he enquired. 'Does that mean the Commodore will find himself with military responsibilities, leading the Empire in time of war?'

She put a comforting arm around him and smiled. 'No, not at all. There is no Empire, not any more. And even if there were, I don't think he would be obliged to command anything. It's just a piece of history, a fantasy if you like.'

'So you have been made a member of an Empire that does not exist. That does not seem a very fair honour.'

'Oh, I get a badge for my uniform. And I expect I'll be invited to a garden party at Buckingham Palace.'

'With tea like this?' Lew Sun looked around, his distaste clearly registering.

Sister Florence giggled. 'Slightly worse, I'm told.'

'You have curious ways of honouring people on your planet. Does nobody think of giving you money?'

'Good Lord no, that would be bad form.'

'Well, I have my own reward for you. It is here, in this.'

Stretching under the chair, he pulled out a tapestry bag which he had strategically left there earlier and placed it on her knee.

She embraced him. 'Oh Lu, how lovely.'

'Why don't you open it?'

Florence glanced behind her to make sure no one was watching. The guests were gradually leaving and maids were clearing away the remains of the tea.

She undid the zip. It seemed that he had given her a goldfish bowl, or possibly a table lamp. She lifted the perspex globe out of the bag, only to find that it was attached to a metallic blue jump suit. At first she was slightly mystified. Then she realised.

'A space suit. What a wonderful, wonderful gift. Whenever I feel low, I shall put it on in the solitude of my room and dance around and think of you.'

Lu's large ultramarine eyes – as big as a cow's – stared earnestly into hers.

'It isn't for the solitude of your room. I would like you to wear it tomorrow.'

'For the blast-off? No, I think that might be too extravagant. Besides, I don't have a very good seat. You'd never see me in it. Too many bigwigs between me and the rocket.'

'Florence, I think you misunderstand me, and yet I am not speaking French or Scottish. I would like you to wear it tomorrow. There is a reason.'

'I love it. I love the blue. It's . . . it's so effervescent.'

She was playing for time, aware that the conversation had taken an uncomfortably serious turn but yet unable to fathom why. She confronted him.

'What reason?'

He gazed imploringly at her. 'There can only be one reason.'

Suddenly it dawned on her, as if she had swallowed a chunk of ice that was slowly slithering towards her stomach. She shivered and almost dropped the suit.

'You – ?' She cleared her throat but the words still stuck there. She picked up a cup and took a gulp of stone-cold tea.

'You want *me* to come?'

'You always said you would like to.'

'One day,' she reminded him.

'Tomorrow is one day. One day away.'

'Flo,' Commodore Lewin's voice carried authoritatively across the room, now virtually empty save for some ladies removing the table-cloths. 'We've got to go. I promised your mother we'd show her the engagement ring and then there are drinks at Victoria's.'

She raised her hand. 'One moment, darling.'

She peered wistfully down at the space helmet, as if it were a crystal ball that might tell her what the future would hold.

'I don't think I could live there, Lu. Not yet.'

'Physically you could,' he replied, a misty sentimental expression in his eyes. 'We know how to accommodate that.' He paused. 'Do you love him?'

'That's an unfair question.'

'I thought all was fair in love and war.'

'Very good, your English is more than perfect.'

Lu took her hand. 'Or if I were to stay. Would that work?'

Florence opened her mouth to speak, but instead took in a brief gasp of breath and remained silent. A small diamond tear appeared in the corner of her right eye.

Lu Xun himself was now perilously close to breaking down. 'It's the way I look, isn't it?'

She lowered her head into her hands. 'That's another unfair question.'

'Florence!' Lewin's voice had become angrily strident.

She clasped the space suit close to her body and stood up.

'I must go. And you must go. But there is one thing you must know. I've never felt such love for another, not so much, not ever.'

She leant over and kissed the top of Lu Xun's crustaceous head and her tears, now in full flood, seemed in danger of running copiously down her cheeks and onto him.

'Absolute statues everybody. Hold it. Thirty seconds. There's a music crescendo. I expect they'll freeze the frame in the labs but you never know. Opticals are expensive and Mr Lasky might run out of money. Stop breathing, Douglas, it's ruining the effect. And cut. Well done, ducky. Check the gate.' Derek's megaphoned voice brought the scene down to earth and the shooting to an end. He turned to Tim. 'What do you think, guv? Go again?'

Tim was unable to reply. He sat in his high director's chair, sucking his knuckle and looking as crestfallen as a child who has just lost a favourite toy. 'Marvellous, absolutely fucking m-marvellous,' he stuttered.

Ray of make-up offered him a tissue. He was already wiping his own face with another. 'I've never seen anything quite so tragic,' he said. 'She should have gone, started a new life on a new planet. It's not an opportunity that's open to many of us. What's she wasting herself on that sailor for?'

'What do you think, Dolly?' Tim turned to his continuity girl, hoping for some congratulation from the senior member of his crew.

'She transposed the first two sentences of her final speech.' Dolly put her finger down the script quite unmoved. 'It should be: "You must go. And I must go". Do you want to retake it?'

'Well, I suppose . . .' Tim began, but he was interrupted by a soft, deep Hungarian voice.

'Only so often in cinema do you find a moment of such magic. The spell is broken. No words can weave it again. So we leave it, yes? You have made my picture, Tim. I thank you.'

Tim put his arm round his producer. 'Not just me, Fyodor. But the best bloody crew I've ever worked with. I'd never have had the idea of doing that scene in one take without the agreement of a great lighting cameraman. We based it on that great Hitchcock film, *Rape*, didn't we, Terry?'

'*Rope*,' said Terry nonchalantly, rolling up a length of cable. He had never been able to drop the habits of his days as one of the sparks.

Tim became defensive. 'Are you sure?'

'Maybe the o was blurred in the book you read,' suggested Elizabeth generously. 'We don't want no aliens raping our womenfolk – not unless they look like Bud Booker.'

Fyodor smiled, admiring her ability to jump in and out of character as if it were a play-pen. Her unworldly looks masked a worldly insight.

'Sweetie, you were incredible.' Tim enveloped her in a hug. 'Somehow you seemed to be reaching inside you for an empathetic experience of your own. It showed. What were you thinking?'

Elizabeth shrugged. 'As a matter of fact, I was just trying to remember my lines. You and your never-ending takes.'

'But the tear. The tear in the right eye. So moving. Where did you find it from?'

'The script,' said Elizabeth. 'It was there in the script.'

Dolly looked up from her stool. 'In the script it says left eye.'

Elizabeth smiled at her. 'Silly me. Never could tell which hand held the knife.'

'Ray, darling, could I just have a touch more blue under the eyes. For my close-up.' Douglas knew every trick in the film actor's repertory but on this occasion he was unlucky.

'No close-up.' Tim was unusually affirmative. 'It was word perfect.'

'No close-up?' Douglas's gills almost went a lighter shade of blue. 'But the look I gave. The sense of this creature about to embark on a six-year journey home without the woman he loves. It's a unique look in the history of cinema. I think you'll find that audience sympathy at this point is very much with – '

But the whine of the megaphone terminated his plea. 'That's a wrap, ladies and gentlemen. Thank you very much,' intoned Derek, signing off with the phrase that had stood him in good stead in his last forty pictures. 'See you at the Oscars.'

In fact all of them were to see each other less than two hours later at the wrap party. This had elements of both a celebration and a wake. The film family that had worked, lived, argued, fought, teased, helped, hindered, created and, above all, survived together was to split up, never to be reunited in the same constituent parts again. But everybody knew that sooner or later, somewhere or other, they would meet again on another movie, maybe in another country. Nobody seemed concerned about the impending shadow of unemployment. There remained a buccaneer, gypsy mentality in film people; and on occasions like this they reassured themselves with nostalgic anecdotes from the past that similar cause for nostalgia lay waiting in the future.

' – and the problem is Superman doesn't sweat, so Chris has to spend all day holding this fuckin' fan under his armpits.'

' – anyway what Chuck doesn't know is that the cake's full of drugs and he leaps off the ladder yelling "I'm bleedin' dying". Sir Dickie was furious.'

' – she's already in the bed but Roger wants to finish his cigar and he says to her "you just get started without me, darling."'

' – Marlon's on more than a million a week but it's not enough to make him learn his lines and old Dick Donner has to run around holding 'em up beside the camera.'

' – so bloody old Horn can't be bothered to go home to his sister's in Kilburn and sleeps every night in his van on the Batman set. People used to write to him care of Gotham City.'

'Lizzie, can we talk?'

Howard, pink and sparkling fresh from the bath, his military blue blazer intentionally preserving a vestige of his film character, joined her just as she was giving Ray a traditional end of shooting present. It was a large bottle of cologne, wrapped in expensive blue paper.

'Don't open it until you're feeling really sexy,' she teased.

'Oh, what can it be?' Ray held the parcel up. 'An inflatable choir-boy, perhaps?'

'You're a horny old devil, did you know that?'

Ray gave her a kiss. 'And you're lovely. Stay away from married men and you'll be all right. I always do.'

He screamed at his own joke. Howard became more agitated.

'Can we talk?'

She turned to him. 'Yes. I was coming to see you anyway. I wouldn't have gone without saying goodbye.'

Howard became serious. 'That's what I wanted to talk to you about.'

Ray took his cue and left them. 'Don't forget to ask for me on your next picture. Somewhere exotic in the Far East if possible.'

Elizabeth smiled. 'I promise. 'Bye, Ray.'

Howard spoke in a loud whisper to combat the drunkenly deafening roar of the party. He decided to make a clean breast of it. 'I'm going in the other direction next week. New York. Want to come?'

'Well, that sounds intriguing.' Elizabeth had been anticipating an invitation of sorts, but not one as concrete as this. She was content to tolerate Howard's slightly pompous company, but despite his raffish, public-school looks, or maybe because of them, she found him sexually unappealing. There was little mystery in him; in some ways he seemed, not effeminate, but curiously feminine. 'What are you going to do?'

'Oh, just see some agents, catch up on a few plays – maybe if there's one that's right for me I could bring it back here.' His eyes brightened. 'You could do the same. No sense sitting at home waiting for your agent to ring.'

'There's a possibility. My cousin's there, I could stay with her. What day are you thinking of going?'

'Next week, any day really.' Howard took a gulp of his gin and tonic. 'But that's not really what I had in mind.'

'What isn't?'

'Staying with your cousin. My idea was that we should stay together. Forget about the plays and agents, that's really what I wanted. I mean we could go to Paris, it's nearer, quicker.'

Elizabeth knew that it was time to come clean. She took him by the hand and looked with open sincerity into his eyes.

'I'm sorry, Howard. It wouldn't work. Not from my side. Nor from yours, either, if you think about it.'

He was hurt and annoyed simultaneously.

'But you – you always indicated – when we were shooting, I felt there was a bond between us – I mean, wasn't there?'

'There was,' she reassured him. 'I felt it myself. A tremendous bond. I couldn't have done the part without it. I *needed* you.'

'And now you can dispense with me?'

'That's cruel. And not true. We're both actors. We draw from our real emotions to find our stage ones. But there's still a difference between the two.'

Howard shook his head. 'This time it was different. I don't want you to drop out of my life. I've come to rely on you. On having lunch with you. On talking to you. On just being with you.'

'We can still eat lunch. I'd like that.'

'In a way that's even more painful. Christ, Lizzie, you *must* see, I'm totally . . . you're absolutely . . .'

'Mind if I join you?' enquired Douglas, cheerfully joining them whether they minded or not. He had dispensed with his Alien costume but still retained a bizarre appearance, dressed from head to foot in jaundiced suede and puffing on a theatrically outsize briar pipe. 'There's only so much conversation you can have with a film crew. By the time they've discussed their overtime, the inadequacies of the director and who had most pints last night their vocabularies seem to be stretched to the end of the elastic. Isn't Tim perfectly hopeless, by the way? No sense of emphasis. God knows how he's going to cut this thing together, everything seems to have been taken in long shot to put the money on the screen for the bankers.'

'He's in the business of satisfying the clients,' Howard was almost relieved to agree. The battle for Elizabeth might seem temporarily to be lost but there was still a war to be waged. 'And this incessant appealing to the inner emotions,' he went on, 'when all I want is a decent reading of the line. That's the trouble with the new generation of British directors – hardly any of them have ever set foot in the theatre. All they know about directing is how to point a camera at a riot in Pakistan and then call the result a documentary.'

'Or at a biscuit tin.' Douglas was delighted to find a soul-mate with whom he could bitch.

'I think you're both being unfair,' Elizabeth stood her ground. 'Tim seems able to co-ordinate other people's ideas quite effectively.'

As if conjured up by their conversation, Tim, now radiant in a red cashmere sweater and intoxicated by the congratulations of the crew – anxious to work on his next film – moved in to join them. He, too, had reached the stage of rosy reminiscence. 'Now, I directed a football team once. It was a soap powder commercial, funnily enough, and the idea was that the wives would stop by the match on their way to the shops to determine how strong a detergent they would need to buy. So I had the entire field watered down until the mud came up to their knees . . .'

Elizabeth felt the urge to escape. The noise, the heat and, especially, the reproachful presence of Howard made her uncomfortable. She waved her hand, as if returning a greeting from across the room, although none had actually been sent.

'Excuse me for just a moment,' she muttered. 'There's someone . . .' She edged her way through the jovial, smoky throng. Nearly everybody had a kind word for her, several offering the confident prediction that this picture was going to make her a star. She had rarely experienced such a genuine surge of goodwill and when she reached the French windows that opened onto the patio, she found herself both uplifted and more than a little sad.

It was a raw February night. The hoar-frost was already on the ground but she did not feel the cold. The moon cast a spectral light on the neatly groomed gardens of Pinewood, making the bushes and trees seem artificial. She walked quickly, past the privet hedges, hoping not to be observed by anyone in the dining-room, down to the wooden bridge on the lake. The water was still and partially iced over. She hung over the narrow rail gazing at her faint reflection, wondering, as she sometimes did, whether Elizabeth Brown was real. There had been occasions when she had glanced at herself as she hurried past a shop window or the mirror of a changing room and thought she could see nobody there. The idea intrigued her. Since childhood she had often felt the need to be, if not invisible, something other than she was. If a stranger talked to her on a train she would, if she could be bothered, paint a portrait of herself that belonged to somebody else.

She wished she could do it now. Life had been seductively artificial for the duration of the film and she wasn't ready to return to reality. The Howard thing made her feel depressed and ashamed. It had been her fault, she knew. She had egged him on during shooting. Eating garlic to punish your co-star in love scenes might have been part of movie mythology but she had had an instinct that an off-screen flirtation would at least make their on-screen romance seem more plausible. Heavens above, there were few enough plausible features in the film. But she could have told him earlier. Or differently. Or at all. Or at least have spared him the ordeal of building up his hopes only to have them dashed to the ground.

She felt adrift and alone and fearful of freedom. She wanted the alarm to wake her at 4.30 the next day, for Danny to give her the latest gossip on the drive to Pinewood, for Ray to spoil her in make-up with buttered croissants and camomile tea. She needed the camaraderie of the set, vainglorious Douglas, Derek's advice and experience, even Tim's inner commands. She wanted to sit round their allotted lunch table and chew the fat and munch her greens and listen to Fyodor.

The moment she allowed his name to stray into her

thoughts, she realised how hard she had been trying to steer clear of it. He had left without saying goodbye. She had made excuses to herself to go over to C Block, ostensibly to take flowers to wardrobe but really to see if the light was still on in his office. And when she saw it wasn't, she had later pretended she wanted to collect some stills from the publicity department so she could find out if his car was still there. But it had gone.

She wanted to see him and – now she admitted it to herself for the first time – she wanted him. He had shown little interest in her, but that had only served to fuel her feeling. She had made a check-list in her mind of his shortcomings: he was overweight and over-opinionated and over-age. Entirely wrong for her in every way. But at lunch one day Fyodor had thrown a quotation from Freud into the conversation – something about every extreme personality trait having its origins in an unconscious attempt to conceal the opposite – and it had begun to dawn on her then that three wrongs might make a right. He intrigued her, as no other man before had done. His presence had a narcotic effect that might be hard to give up, she realised, and, in his cuddly fashion, she found him rather sexy.

The tapering noise of the party darted across the lake like a moonbeam towards her. This outburst of self-directed candour cast Elizabeth into a deeper depression and, wallowing indulgently in her sorrow, she reprised the final moments of her work on the film and started to weep – only, this time, for real.

'You're spoiling the sound of the night with that noise. I came out to listen to the silence.'

She could smell him before she saw him; the unmistakable aroma of the Gitane must have been there all the time, triggering her thoughts, but she had been too self-absorbed to scent it.

'Fyodor, I thought you had left. Your car had gone from its parking space.'

She immediately regretted being so obvious, but he appeared not to notice.

'You're most observant. I let the driver go. He takes his wife to bingo on Fridays. Besides, there are plenty of cars.'

She had moved to the edge of the bridge and could see him, his cigarette glowing fitfully in the dark. He was seated on a wooden bench by the sycamore tree.

'What are you doing?' she asked.

'I often come here. To sit and look at the sky. If you're making a film about Jupiter you may as well turn to it for inspiration.'

Elizabeth walked up the path and sat down beside him. 'But you can't see it.'

'Look up,' he said. 'Look through the curve of the moon – the star that seems like a part of the Turkish flag.'

'That's Jupiter?'

He nodded.

'I never knew.'

'You knew it was there. Just because you can't see something, it doesn't mean it doesn't exist. The galaxy, like movies, is just projected light – only in the case of the real stars it can take fifteen thousand million years before it reaches us. Worth the wait, though.'

'Why fifteen thousand million?'

'The age of the universe. And even then there's a horizon beyond which we shall never see. It's all up there: our future and our past.'

Elizabeth was afraid that he would get up and go and she wanted him to stay. 'You don't believe there are little men on Jupiter, do you?' she asked. 'Not little blue ones like Douglas.'

Fyodor gave a gruff guffaw. 'No, I don't. Nobody could survive there for one thing. They'd be fried alive. It gives out twice as much heat as it gets from the sun. But I respect Jupiter, it's a probable planet. Earth is the improbable one. We should never have happened. The combination of nitrogen and oxygen should have exploded us into smithereens. But we bucked the law of averages. We were no accident. Someone drew up a unique equation that gave rise to life.'

'Who did?'

He looked up and blew a whisper of smoke into the night air. 'God, I suppose.'

'Which one?'

'The one who did it. Aren't you cold?'

He made as if to get up and, emboldened, she tried to

provoke him into remaining. 'If you come here to have lofty thoughts about the nature of creation, how come you spend your days making crummy fantasy films?'

Fyodor was amused by her spirited impertinence. 'I don't think it's crummy and neither do you. But I agree it's a fantasy. We need fantasies. Without them daily life would be insupportable.' He held up his hands to dramatise his point. 'We need to gaze through our prison bars and think of what we might do, if only we had the freedom and the power.'

'You *have* freedom and power,' she insisted.

'Nobody has as much power as they appear to have. And few people have as much freedom. You are what you are.'

'And what are you?'

He smiled gently at her. 'I'm a familiar enough plant. *Tradescantia fluminensis*. Do you know what that is?'

'Should I?'

'The Wandering Jew. The man who told Christ to hurry up on his way to Calvary and was condemned to wander the earth until the second coming.'

'And where will you end up?' She knew the direct intimacy of her questions must be giving away more than she intended. But she felt reckless, and reluctant to restrain herself. And she could feel that Fyodor was responding to her as she always sensed he might.

'Who knows?' he shrugged. 'On the moon maybe. There's plenty of oxygen there, in the rocks. They think there may be hydrogen and even water in the dark polar craters where the sun never shines.'

'It would be pretty boring, all on your own.'

'On the contrary, on the dark side of the moon you could see sights that no human eye has ever witnessed before. You could see the edge of our universe. You could watch for the Big Crunch that, one day, is going to squeeze us out of existence.'

Elizabeth looked at him sceptically. 'You don't believe that, do you?'

He studied her eyes, almost luminous in the pale moonlight. 'What do you believe in, Elizabeth?'

She averted her gaze. 'Oh, nothing . . . nothing as cosmic as that.'

'You must believe in something.'

She had never told anybody – not her parents, not her closest friends – but there was something in his manner, partly avuncular, that led her on.

'I seek out goddesses. It sounds silly but I think they're safest. At the moment it's Kuan Yin. She was the daughter of a Cambodian prince. Bit like Cinderella, really. Sure you want to hear this?'

'I want nothing more,' he replied, still gazing at her.

Elizabeth felt immune to the outer cold but was chilled by an inner *frisson*. 'Kuan Yin had two sisters, both of whom married noblemen. Her father wanted her to do the same but she didn't. She joined a Buddhist convent – the White Sparrows. And her father was so angry that he ordered it to be burnt down. But she saved it by putting out the flames with her own blood. Then he ordered her to be beheaded – some father – but the executioner's sword broke into tiny pieces. So he told his men to strangle her, but a tiger descended from heaven and carried her to safety. However, she rejected paradise and came back to earth to help the suffering and protect the children. And me. Kuan Yin, Goddess of Mercy. Her birthday's on the nineteenth day of the Second Moon.'

'So the moon does come into it, after all,' Fyodor pointed out. 'Perhaps we're not so far apart as you think.'

'No,' Elizabeth replied, rising from the bench, 'I don't think we're far apart at all.'

He got up and followed her, quite naturally taking off his jacket and putting it round her. She stopped as he did so, wanting him to keep his hands on her shoulders.

'Elizabeth,' he said quietly.

'Yes?'

'Can you give me a lift home?'

'My home?' she asked, still not turning round.

'Yes, your home.'

CHAPTER 6

Thursday 6th March 1997

Hong Kong

Renaud fiddled with the small dial awkwardly located in the arm of his seat, searching slowly through the channels. An enthusiastic woman was giving instructions on how to do keep-fit exercises while sitting down, on another a doctor was lecturing on the inadvisability of having too much alcohol during the flight – a bit late in view of the cocktails, Pauillac and alluring liqueurs that had been served at lunch. He moved the dial again. A man had gone into a cheese shop to buy some cheese – there clearly wasn't any but, for some perverse reason, the proprietor was not prepared to admit this. A nation of small shopkeepers, thought Renaud, switching on to the next channel where he found what he was looking for: *Rigoletto*. Good, it was near the beginning. Sparafucile was offering his services to the hunchback jester, should he ever want anyone knocked off. Such a splendid name for a freelance assassin, he mused, Sparafucile.

He had worn his headphones throughout lunch although they had not been plugged in. Four years of travelling the world as Director of the Cannes Film Festival had taught him they were not primarily intended for listening to music or the film soundtrack, but were a cunning invention to stop your neighbour talking to you. A marketing genius should be able to adapt the idea for dinner parties, he thought, as he glanced at the sleeping salesman stretched out beside him. He normally travelled Business Class and, although the Australian ticket had upgraded him to First, he doubted if the conversation would have been any more stimulating.

'How like we are,' sang Rigoletto, 'the tongue is my

weapon and the dagger his. I have to make people laugh, he makes them weep.' It was an opera that never failed to move him – in more ways than Verdi intended. The day his mother had left home to live with a man in Algiers, his father had returned from the office with two tickets to see *Rigoletto* at the Paris Opéra. He had been fourteen at the time. In the final act he had no longer been able to control himself: tears ran unrestrainedly down his cheeks. When he glanced, surreptitiously, at his father he could see that he was in a similar state.

He never saw his mother again. From that time on his father had instinctively stepped into her role, cooking for him, ironing his shirts, smothering his son with affection. The old man's passion was rugby; there was nothing he liked more than to attend an international at the Parc des Princes. But he never insisted that Renaud should share his enthusiasm. On the contrary, he indulged the boy's lonely obsession with movies, driving him to the cinema when he wanted and even waiting outside to collect him on occasion.

Once he had accompanied him to see a film but they both knew it hadn't worked. This was Renaud's personal domain and his father respected his privacy. In the cinema the boy could set aside the problems of a lonely upbringing – he had no brothers or sisters – and escape into a more perfect world of his own choosing.

His father followed his career in the civil service with pride and when Renaud was appointed Director of the Cannes Festival was heard, on more than one occasion, telling his friends at the rugby club that his son was now a significant power in the French arts world. He never enquired into Renaud's private life, never asked why he didn't marry, never hinted that he might like grandchildren. It was accepted that Renaud had made his vows to the movies, like a novice entering a monastery.

Life in a Cathay Pacific First-Class seat, Renaud reflected, is possibly the most passive form of pleasure known to man. One is spoilt in a fashion not experienced since the nursery. Even in 1997 women's lib had failed to get any substantial purchase on the Orient. An ever-smiling stewardess, with the name Lolita on her badge, brought him everything from steaming hot towels to ice-cold champagne. After the high-lights from the opera finished – with the accursed jester crumpled over the murdered body of his own daughter -- he watched the news on satellite television and then flicked through the channels of the TV screen set into the back of the seat in front of him. Movies were too much of a busman's holiday so he settled for an Italian soccer game instead.

It was when the plane took off again after their stop in Bahrain that he made the earphone error. He had not noticed that there was a different occupant in the seat beside him. He was attempting to doze when the voice of the new arrival brought him back to wakefulness.

'It's impossible to sleep properly on a plane, did you know that?'

Renaud took in the calculator on the man's knee, the white shirt with a personal monogram and the sober glass of Perrier.

He attempted a smile. 'Well, I was trying to disprove that hypothesis.'

The man was oblivious to the irony. 'You're French, aren't you?'

Without waiting for the answer, he reached into his wallet for the obligatory card. 'Ronald Bunce, Press Relations. Computers mainly.'

Were computers now so conscious of their image that they needed PR men? wondered Renaud. He took the card and murmured, 'Renaud Callet – and, yes, I am.'

'What?' enquired his unwelcome companion.

'French,' replied Renaud, closing his eyes and indicating his desire to sleep.

'It's the white noise,' said Bunce.

Renaud opened his eyes with an exaggerated start. 'Where?' he asked, looking around.

'Everywhere. You think that the plane is nearly silent but there's white noise everywhere. And that's what stops any of us getting any real rest.'

Renaud stared at him. 'Only that?'

'It's actually a watered-down form of torture,' went on Bunce. 'The best way to disorientate a prisoner is to keep him awake with constant noise. If you were subjected to it long enough it could literally drive you mad.'

'Really?' said Renaud icily.

'Let's say you were to fly round the world,' continued Bunce, switching on his calculator as if to give a prepared lecture.

Perhaps it *was* prepared, thought Renaud. Perhaps Bunce was paid by rival airlines to fly on Cathay Pacific routes to drive passengers screaming into the arms of their competitors.

Renaud's hands tightened in despair. This man is going to torture me all the way to Hong Kong, he thought.

Bunce traced his finger down a mileage table in the magazine he had opened and punched the figure into his calculator. 'Right, let's begin with Bahrain – Hong Kong – '

Like a timely gift from the gods, a Filipino stewardess glided up to them. 'Mr Callet?'

'Yes?'

'There's a telephone call for you.'

'Thank God,' he cried rising from his seat. 'Where do I take it?'

'It's here,' she smiled, handing him a portable phone.

He put it to his ear. 'Hello?'

'Mr Callet, Mr Renaud Callet?'

'*Oui*, yes, sure.'

'Your office in Paris told us you were on this flight. I hope it would not inconvenience you to take a call from Mr Leland Walters, President of Warner Bros.'

Renaud glanced to his right. 'No, no inconvenience at all.'

'Would you hold on momentarily,' crackled the voice.

Bunce glanced across at him. 'Don't mind me,' he assured him. 'I've got some quite amazing statistics we can discuss when you're finished.'

'Renaud, Renaud. It's Leland. Long time. Up in the skies I hear. How're you getting on?'

The two men had never met before, but Renaud was sufficiently experienced in dealing with studio brass to know the tone adopted was that of the mutual camaraderie of men at the top. In truth, he was rather flattered by it.

'Leland, good to hear from you. I'm just fine.'

He was more than surprised to be receiving a call from the president. He rarely got past the vice-president of marketing and publicity when trying to elicit films from the American studios.

'Renaud, I'm ringing you with some very good news. It's our intention to have a substantial presence at your Festival this summer. Warner Bros salutes fifty glorious years. We're even thinking of hiring fifty planes to fly over the town – like the Salkinds did for *Superman* in the old days.'

God preserve us from that, thought Callet. People had been able to eat their lunch in peace ever since that cacophonous squadron had been grounded.

'Renaud, Renaud, can you hear me?' The voice at the other end sounded anxious for a reply.

'Not terribly well,' lied Renaud. 'Let me just move to a quieter spot.'

'It's quiet enough here,' chimed Bunce who had been listening to every word.

'I think I'm picking up the pilot,' Renaud went on, getting up and stepping over his travelling companion.

'I'm not interested in your sex life, I want to know what you think of our plans,' laughed the voice at the other end.

'They sound splendid. Can you elaborate?' Renaud continued, making his way forward to the toilet. It was vacant. He went in, locked the door and sat down on the lavatory seat.

'We want to have a gala, maybe on the second Saturday if that suits you. A Warner Bros day when we show some of our new product and there's a big dinner in the evening, perhaps in Les Ambassadeurs if it's free.'

Callet nodded his approval. 'It can be made free, I am sure.'

'And Renaud: I don't want this to get around – you're not being overheard, are you?'

Renaud looked about him. 'No, I'm in a private office.'

'Fine. I think I can persuade Bud Booker to attend. Maybe even make a speech.'

The Frenchman was pleased but nevertheless suspicious. People like Leland Walters didn't do favours unless there was a quid pro quo. He knew only too well that the Festival was dependent for its international kudos on a scattering of big Hollywood names.

'Leland, this is good news indeed. Now, is there anything I can do to help you?'

'Renaud, I think you can. Is your competition full up yet?'

'No, I am still considering films. You have a good one?'

'It isn't so much a good one. It's more an expedient one – something which we can base our whole celebration around. You see, Bud has directed himself in this story of urban conflict – '

'*Black Cops Kill* – the one where he slaughters anyone who isn't white?'

'You've seen it?' Leland's voice dropped.

'No, I have read about it. Not your *Mountie Mac*, I hear.'

'Very far from that. But it has its points. Renaud, I badly need you to play it.'

'*Hors compétition*? Perhaps.'

'What's that about whores?'

'I'm sorry. *Hors*, out of competition.'

'No, not *hors*. No *hors*. We need this one in the ring. I think I have to say that our plans are pretty well contingent on it. *Comprenez*?'

'I'm not sure how I can explain to my board – '

'Renaud, there'll be a print in Hong Kong tomorrow. Take a look and then call me. You can make cuts if you need to. We can discuss all that. But I'm sure there's a way round it.'

'I hope so.'

'That's wonderful. I'll come back to you on this. I've got to take a meeting right now so talk to you soon.'

The connection was severed. Renaud got up, looked in the mirror, combed his hair with his hands, and splashed some water on his face.

He was reluctant to return too speedily to the garrulous companion who awaited him. As he lingered in the aisle his eye was caught, not for the first time, by the occupant of seat 3B. Unlike most of the rest of the First-Class cabin the man was Chinese, or maybe part-Chinese. With his swept-back hair and urgent eyes he reminded Renaud of the young Alain Delon. He wore large reading glasses, like two tortoiseshell portholes, and although he was assiduously studying a business magazine, he appeared to sense that he was being observed but did not look up. When they had boarded the flight Renaud was certain he had seen the young man before and now he remembered where – it had been in the lobby of his apartment building in Paris.

'Is there anything I can do to help, sir?' asked a stewardess, making her way towards him.

'I wish there were,' he muttered. 'Wait – a large cognac. That's a start.'

The phone call might have created one dilemma but it had solved another. When he reached his seat he found Bunce firmly asleep, his mouth open and his calculator, fast asleep too, on his lap.

'May the white noise never wake you,' prayed Renaud as he silently sat down beside him.

When, six hours later, he set foot on British soil at Hong Kong's Kai Tak Airport, the Dependant Territory had only 116 days, 14 hours and 7 minutes left to live. It was due to be absorbed by mainland China at midnight on June 30th. When the British had signed the Treaty of Peking in 1898 and leased the 355 square miles of the New Territories from China, they had no idea that 99 years later their colonial successors would have to surrender one of the most thriving and vital trade centres in the world.

The customs officer who stamped Renaud's passport was Chinese but wore a royal insignia on his uniform and spoke perfect English. Until 1948, as a citizen of Hong Kong, someone in his job would have had the same common-law rights as any British subject. But in 1962 the mother country, fearful of being deluged by the great-grandsons and daughters of those who had made this colony prosper, passed the Commonwealth Immigration Act, depriving them of their right to live in the United Kingdom.

A girl in Renaud's research department had provided him with a briefing document on Hong Kong to help him avoid diplomatic pitfalls. The communist Chinese promised to preserve the Colony's capitalist system and lifestyle for at least fifty years. She seemed to think the capitalist part would work out successfully since China had long used Hong Kong as a trade conduit – most of its external investment came through the banks there. But she was less optimistic about the life-style. Hong Kong was to become a Special Administrative Region, just like Tibet half a century earlier. The Chinese had murdered more than a million Tibetans who had dared to speak up for religious freedom and the right to self-government.

There had been minimal protest in the West about this, unlike the killing, by the People's Liberation Army, of several hundred students in Tiananmen Square in 1989 which had attracted world-wide condemnation. The British Government had expressed concern about the fate of those British citizens who were going to be abandoned – but it had only agreed to offer sanctuary to a small proportion of them. The Shanghai Massacre six years later in 1995 indicated that the new government in China still preferred the old methods of maintaining law and order. In an emergency debate in the European Parliament in Strasbourg it was regretfully concluded that there was no room in the Community for any more refugees from Hong Kong.

Renaud had rarely seen a city so forcefully alive as he gazed out of the taxi window and sampled his first taste of Kowloon. Multi-coloured signs in English and Chinese festooned the streets giving it an air of continuous carnival. Every second shop seemed to be a restaurant, and the stores in between, goods overflowing onto the pavements, were brisk with business. The crush of people on the pavements was matched by the build-up of traffic on the street. Everyone seemed purposeful and in a hurry. As he looked up he could see old people sitting at the windows of the apartments above, many of them with caged birds for company. Was it his imagination or did those with the added sagacity of age and time for thought seem that much more melancholic than the huddled masses below?

'We can walk to the Star Ferry from here. The exercise will give us an appetite.'

'You don't look as if you've taken any exercise for the past five years.' Renaud eyed his old friend warmly.

'Nor in the fifty before that. It's always the fitness freaks who drop dead prematurely – it doesn't do to challenge nature in that way.'

Renaud had arranged to have lunch with Sheridan Kimber. They had met in 1968 when, as a student, he had been caught up in the Paris *événements* and Sheridan had been covering them for the *Washington Post*. Thanks to this contact the American had obtained useful inside information which frequently enabled him to steal a march on the more experienced older journalists. The two men had struck up a friendship and had continued to correspond when Sheridan left Paris, and the *Post*, in the mid-seventies to try his luck as a freelance writer in Hong Kong.

If appearances were anything to go by, he looked prosperous. His pendulous belly testified to a partiality for large Chinese meals and his ruddy complexion to a propensity for large Scotches. Nevertheless his chubby figure cut a distinctive dash. The cream suit looked as if it might once have been the uniform of a colonial administrator – indeed it could have been, since Sheridan had bought it in a second-hand clothes store – and his battered planter's hat and hickory cane were the trappings of an English gentleman of another age, although Kimber himself had been born in the Bronx.

They strolled through the imposing lobby of the Peninsula Hotel. The men and women taking a pre-lunch drink seemed mainly to be Chinese although their formal demeanour was undeniably European, an image underwritten by the string quartet up in the balcony that was playing selections from Noël Coward. Sheridan idly slipped a couple of boxes of the elegant hotel matches – as long as fingers – into his pocket. The doormen bowed low as they stepped out into the humid air, past the row of gleaming green Rolls-Royces, ready to collect hotel guests from the airport.

'Will those still be in use in four months' time?' asked Renaud.

'I should imagine our friends from Beijing will be riding around in them,' Sheridan smiled knowledgeably, 'just to show they're keeping up the capitalism.'

As they turned into Salisbury Road, Renaud could see a vast domed structure, curiously smooth and curved compared to the angular buildings which surrounded it.

'What's that?' he asked.

'The Space Museum. Looks like it landed from another planet, doesn't it? I think they show movies in there – you should check it out.'

The remark reminded Renaud of his unwelcome appointment with *Black Cops Kill*. 'I think I've got enough movies on my plate,' he replied.

'How's it going this year – got your dance card full yet?'

'No, that's why I'm here. You should come over to Cannes. It's our fiftieth anniversary – it might be fun.'

'It might be more fun here,' Sheridan remarked drily, 'it's *our* ninety-ninth anniversary. Well, up there it is, north of Boundary Road.' He waved his cane out to the right, just missing an elderly Japanese couple who ducked instinctively.

'Not down here?' Renaud was unable to remember any such demarcation in his researcher's notes.

Sheridan cleared his throat with an unhealthy wheeze, reminding Renaud of his penchant for turning conversations into verbal rehearsals for his articles. 'Nah, the Brits have got this bit and Hong Kong island for ever. They had to lease the extra territory above Boundary Road because they needed the space. Not that the Chinese ever recognised any of the treaties – said they were made under duress. But they knew the British and their alleged sense of honour so they just had to sit it out for a dynasty or two and it was game, set and match to Beijing. When you're bargaining with the world's oldest civilisation there's not much sense in dealing in short leases.'

There were many more European faces in Salisbury Road than Renaud had seen in his drive from the airport and the shops were tidier, with a definite tourist appeal. Jade and porcelain, designer clothes and stuffed yellow caterpillars adorned the windows. Frequent travel bureaux offered cut-price tickets to London.

'The end of empire,' Renaud observed. 'I feel a bit sorry for the British.'

'No need to,' sniffed his companion. 'They only came here as a band of drug dealers.'

'I know,' Renaud interjected, remembering his research. 'They blockaded Canton when the Emperor tried to stop their opium trading and the Chinese had to give them Hong Kong to buy them off.'

'What they gave them was a small fishing village on a desolate rock' – Sheridan indicated with his stick ahead of them – 'look what they're getting back.'

On the far side of Victoria Harbour lay a modern Manhattan lapped by the South China Sea. Wealth and yet more wealth was the message sent out from the mass of skyscrapers and hotels, iridescent in the midday sun. Dominating these upright worshippers of Mammon were the twin temples of the Hong Kong and Shanghai Bank and, higher still to the left, the communist-owned Bank of China.

'First class?' enquired Sheridan reaching into his pocket.

'What?' Renaud contemplated the clanking green and white hulk that was to take them the ten-minute ride across to Hong Kong island.

'Upper deck. It only costs twenty cents extra. Hangover from the Raj, I suppose. Until 1941 you had to be wearing a collar and tie and shoes to travel upstairs. There's no real difference now. Only on this deck I think you'll find the notice says you may not spit, and down below it says you must not spit. The sensible Chinese travel on the lower deck and get off first.'

They sat beside each other on a wooden slatted bench, watching the new shopping developments of Kowloon bumpily recede in their wake.

'There was a riot on this thing in 1967,' said Sheridan, persisting with his guided tour. 'Students complaining about an increase in the first-class fare. The irony was that none of them would have travelled first class anyway.'

The people packed next to them were involuntarily recruited to his audience. 'You've got to remember that the mainland Chinese despise the Brits. They have long memories. Any nation that puts up notices like 'no dogs or Chinese', as the English did in Shanghai, can hardly expect to be loved. It's the locals I feel sorry for.'

'They'll be all right, won't they?' Renaud tried to keep his voice lower than that of his friend.

Sheridan smiled. 'Just wait till they hold their first public execution at Happy Valley race track and you'll see how happy everybody is.'

The boat was skilfully docked at the pier on the Hong Kong side. An ageing Chinese deck hand swiftly undid the rope and lowered the wide gang-plank onto the landing stage. Clustered like runners at the start of a marathon the passengers poured out on to the shore. Despite his bulk, Sheridan joined them at a sprightly pace and Renaud had occasionally to break into a trot to keep up with him. The crowds seemed even more crammed together than they had been in Kowloon.

'Don't you ever get fed up with this constant sea of humanity, hanker after somewhere a little more tranquil?'

Sheridan turned round with a flush of boyish excitement on his face. 'This city's a narcotic. I'm hopelessly hooked.'

'At least the Commies know how to make good beer.' Sheridan drained his second glass and signalled to the waiter: 'Two more Tsing-tsao.'

The other diners in the Guangzhou Garden were primarily British. It seemed incongruous to Renaud to hear English voices chattering casually about share prices and rugby matches and cocktail parties, while the diners sipped their shark's fin soup and tucked into braised goose and steamed pomfret.

'It must be the water supply,' Sheridan stated, finishing off his beer. 'Although, come to think of it, it's the same as ours. We get our supplies from their reservoir in Guangdong. They could have cut us off and held us to ransom if they really wanted to. No Berlin airlift possible here. Look at this rice. The basic element in ten million meals a day eaten in this city. And it's all imported, mostly from China. There's hardly a paddy field left here now. In fact no one even knows how to use a plough. Try one of these.'

He handed Renaud a small, shrivelled egg. The Director unpeeled the flaky shell and tasted it.

'Some bird laid that even before the ninety-nine-year lease began. It's a delicacy. And do you know how they preserved it?'

Renaud shook his head.

'Arsenic.' Sheridan grinned as his friend's jaw slackened. 'Like the Sleeping Beauty. Not really poisoned, just put to sleep for a hundred years. Then along comes a prince and a kiss and everything is restored to its former glory. They all lived happily every after.'

'Are you going to stay on?' asked Renaud.

Sheridan's mouth was too full for him to reply. He nodded and munched more rapidly. 'Minced pigeon, exotic, wouldn't miss it for the world.'

'The pigeon?'

'That, too. No, the handover. I could write it now. You can see them taking down the "Royal" at the Hong Kong Jockey Club, the enclosures now open to all. I doubt if they'll retain first class on the ferry either. A noble exit by the Governor, Lord Brown, in his plumed hat. It's the best story in years.'

Back at the hotel there were three messages for Renaud. A car would be waiting for him at four o'clock to take him to the Tai Hang Tung studios to watch the last hour's shooting on the new Elvis Ho movie and then a meeting had been scheduled with the daredevil star. Warner Bros had arranged a seven o'clock screening of *Black Cops Kill* at the same studios. Somebody knows my schedule down to the nearest sneeze, he thought. And, even more remarkably, there was a specially delivered envelope from Government House. Lady Brown, the Governor's wife, appeared to know his timetable equally well. A handwritten note invited him to come to coffee and liqueurs after dinner that evening. What a snobbish nation the British were; only they could have devised so condescending an invitation which managed to avoid having him to dinner. Nevertheless he resolved to go.

Elvis Ho stood on the roof of the palace and bellowed: 'If you want us, you can gather up our corpses. Our souls belong to the Empress.'

He jumped nearly twenty feet down onto a balcony, ran along the edge of it and leapt off, seemingly to his death below, but actually managing to twist in the air and grab a flagpole that was protruding from the wall. Having steadied himself he dropped a further fifteen feet with pinpoint accuracy on to a window ledge no more than six inches wide. From there he began to abseil down a massive, winding creeper that snaked half-way up the front of the building. On cue, when he was about twelve feet from the ground, a riderless horse trotted beneath him and Ho landed precisely on its back. From either side of the building massed ranks of

Mongolian cavalry joined him, firing arrows ahead of them as he led them, brandishing his curved sword, into the fearsome fire of the French artillery.

Once past the first set of guns Ho turned and yelled to his troops. 'Okay, cut, cut, cut, cut. Hold it.' He rode up to the camera. 'Too much smoke, I think I have to go again.'

An old cameraman with a wispy beard held up his hands in disagreement. 'It was fine. We need the smoke. Without smoke, there is no fire.'

'But can they see me come down the building? Every step? I must check the video.'

He caught sight of Renaud, to whom he had been introduced earlier. 'Come and see,' he commanded. 'We will watch together.'

Renaud walked across to the television set, the screen protected from the bright sun by a metal hood temporarily bound on with gaffer tape.

'Some stunt,' he said in appreciation.

'You liked it? It is no more than my audience expects from me. First we work out the action, then we find a story to fit it. They have filmed the storming of the Summer Palace before, but never with such fantastic fighting have they shown the bravery of the Mongolian cavalry and their general, Xu Lang.' Ho dissolved into a fit of giggles. 'That is because he didn't exist. We made him up to give me a good part.'

'But the battle did happen.' Some of the information from Sheridan's lunchtime discourse had taken root in Renaud's memory. 'It followed the treaty giving Kowloon to the British, didn't it? I believe my fellow countrymen did not distinguish themselves by their fair play.'

Ho – a sturdy, compact man with limbs like girders and the cheeky smile of a six-year-old – looked up at him. 'So you know something about China. Very good, Mr Cannes.'

The playback of the scene looked, if anything, more terrifyingly dangerous than the real thing. The camera had stayed wide, always emphasising the perilous drop that Ho faced but still keeping him identifiable. Renaud had not noticed at the time how, when he climbed down the creeper, Elvis knowingly favoured the camera with his right profile lest anyone should think it was a stunt man and not the star.

Ho read his mind. 'No danger, no audience. That is what they want. No sense having safety nets and stand-ins like namby Rambo. No truth, no thrills.'

He nodded towards the cameraman. 'It's okay. We finish for today. Tomorrow, I kill ten Frenchmen.'

His giggle revebrated across the Tai Hang Tung back lot as the extras made their battle-weary way to the changing rooms. Renaud noticed that most of those playing British and French soldiers were Chinese. It was better that they did not display their profiles to the camera.

Ho slapped Callet on the back. It was meant to be playful but it felt to the Frenchman like the blade of a windmill. Perhaps the star was getting into practice for tomorrow.

'So, you like my film.'

'What I've seen, certainly.'

'No, the film for your festival. They tell me you have seen our rough-cut.'

'That one, yes, it's just what we want. It's most important that we have a Hong Kong film this year. Cheung Po Tsai is a remarkable historical character. You didn't make him up, as well?' he added cautiously.

'No, no. The only make-up is on the girls. We make him a little gooder than some people think he was, but that is how it must be for the heroes I play.'

Renaud had seen a print of the work in progress in Paris. Some years before the British annexed Hong Kong, Cheung Po Tsai had been the most famous pirate to rule the South China Seas.

'Do people here remember Cheung?' Renaud enquired out of politeness.

'We remember everything,' Ho responded proudly. 'On the eighth day of the fourth moon on the island of Cheung Chau we have a bun festival. It is to keep quiet the avenging spirits of the thousands of people he massacred. Even the dead can cause you trouble here, you know. Come, we have finished dubbing the first two reels. Great battles, very loud. You want to see?'

'That's why I'm here,' Renaud replied.

The lot was empty now with a lowering sun burnishing the ruins of the Summer Palace, almost making it look as if it were on fire, an impression reinforced by the still smouldering piles of car tyres that surrounded it. In the distance, across the harbour, the first lights were beginning to twinkle in the Hong Kong skyscrapers.

Elvis Ho stretched his arms out proudly, as if he were the proprietor of all that lay beyond him. 'The greatest city in the world. A place where every man is free, where anybody can do anything. You come with nothing, you leave with everything. I love it like my mother. I am Hong Kong. Hong Kong is me.'

Renaud stared at him, impressed. 'So, you're going to stay.'

Ho let his arms collapse by his sides. 'Stay? What for? The past? I know what will happen. For one year, maybe two they say "we must have more Elvis Ho movies" but then somebody gets jealous. Some students from the Beijing Film School who think they are being brave because they shake their little fists at the government. Pah!' He spat furiously into the ground. 'They have no audience, they do not know the people. One day they will come in and take over Tai Hang Tung studios. But they will be too late. Already we have land in British Columbia. We are going to move into Pornic Studios near Vancouver.' He grinned. 'Not porno – no porno for Ho – Pornic.'

'I know them,' Renaud assured him. 'They're named after a town in Brittany, just where the sea and the Loire unite.'

'We will build Tai Hang Tung there. But you must tell no one. After Cannes, Canada. We will never come back here.'

'It is a great shame.' Renaud could think of little else to say.

'It's the future,' countered Ho. 'Hong Kong teaches you to live in the future. Not like my mother. She clings to the past. Why you think she called me Elvis?'

'I assumed you made that up.'

'No, no. It is on my British birth certificate. My mother all shook up, you know.' He roared at his own joke. 'But I am real. Elvis Ho is real.'

Ho's dramatisation of the life of Cheung might have had a limited foothold in reality but it came across with thundering integrity. You knew where you were with pirates, Renaud conceded, as they sat in the darkened preview theatre, much more honest men in many ways than generals and politicians because they were open enough to admit that the only cause they served was themselves. No wonder young men flocked to Cheung, anxious to escape the shackles of their parents' history and find a way of life which made up in glamour and excitement for what it lacked in morality.

Renaud liked it. It was crude in parts and frequently simplistic but the sight of Ho trapezing through the rigging, a cross between Tarzan and Peter Pan, gave him a thrill that he had not experienced in films since he was a child. He thought about opening the Festival with it but in the back of his mind was the memory of the disastrous start to the thirty-ninth Festival with Roman Polanski's *Pirates*, starring Walter Matthau. It had sunk with all hands because the director, fatally, had tried to send up the pirate genre, failing to realise – as Ho had instinctively grasped – that it traditionally sent itself up, thereby making it immune from mockery. The only legacy of that costly venture was a six-million-dollar pirate ship which they sailed in to promote the movie and which remained for several years silhouetted in the Old Port, a landmark and a warning to any director who tried to parody parody.

He watched the freshly dubbed reels with renewed pleasure. The noise that now accompanied the sea battles sounded like a cross between a frenzied day on the Futures' Market and a scrambled Stravinsky symphony. This will wake the Festival up, he thought: Cannes needs a whiff of Chinese drama.

Ho sat beside him, urging his film self on like a football supporter. 'You see that jump, that one there, I broke two bones in my right foot. If you watch the rest of the movie carefully you see I always land on my left foot after that.'

Renaud leant back as the lights went up. 'I expect film semiologists will read all sorts of political meanings into that in years to come.'

'Semiologists?'

'People who analyse films down to the last detail, trying to work out exactly what statement the director was trying to make with every gesture.'

'Sometimes it is not me. If you work with a good team, they can get into your brain before you.'

'That's true,' Renaud acknowledged. 'Although I don't think believers in the *auteur* theory worry too much about teams. When you come to Cannes you can tell them how it happens. After each film we have a big press conference and the thing we learn most from it is how little the so-called experts know about the way films are actually made.'

'Best to keep them in the dark,' replied Ho, getting up to go. 'Everybody know, everybody do.'

'Not what you do,' laughed Renaud. 'I have to look at an American film in this theatre – Bud Booker. Do you want to stay?'

'Bud Booker very big in Hong Kong. But not with me. Too many close-ups, too much talk, too many stunt men standing in for him. I must go and write tomorrow's scene.'

Renaud looked at him in amazement. 'You don't have a completed script before you start?'

'We have an ending. But how do you know what will happen tomorrow until you finish today? If you do not create from day to day you will get a tired movie, all predictable. Like Bud Booker.'

An infectious giggle charted Elvis Ho's departing passage down the corridor. Renaud pressed the button on the console in front of him.

'Have you got a film in there called *Black Cops Kill*?'

'Sure have,' came the tinny voice of the projectionist. 'Bud Booker. Very good.'

'How do you know?'

'We run it as soon as it arrives. Bud sorts out these black killers. Good for Chinese.'

Well, there's one favourable review, thought Renaud as the lights dimmed and he settled back. In the first twenty minutes a gang of black vigilante policemen had entered the Mexican, Greek and, especially, the Chinese communities in San Francisco with forged orders to investigate indigenous crime. Their leader Errol delivered disturbed homilies on how the inhabitants had failed to become true Americans – there was no longer any such thing as a hyphenated American, he insisted. These people had left their native countries, now they should act American and talk American. But when the vigilantes found doors still closed to them and even the victims of the crimes unwilling to co-operate, the only language Errol and company were prepared to speak was hot lead. There was no need for the accused to master the language for their defence in an American court; the investigating force had already acted as judge and jury as the body count rose higher than a San Francisco heatwave.

Twenty years ago, Renaud reflected, it would not have been possible to cast blacks as villains. Then the bad guys would have been played by Southern rednecks with sneers. At least there was some variation here on the familiar theme. But the traditional hypocrisy of contriving to have your cake and eat it by revelling in the excessive, righteous violence used by the good guy survived intact. Enter Captain Bud Booker, who used precisely the same tactics as the renegade blacks to track them down and remove them from active service. The Moonie bus crash was a wholly gratuitous piece of crowd-pleasing, but even Renaud got a complicit sense of satisfaction when Bud pushed his gun into the ear of the black warden who was attaching a wheel clamp to his unmarked police car, and whispered, 'Remove it, or I'll remove you' – a phrase which had rippled across America.

It was wholly unsuitable for the competition at Cannes; indeed Renaud had grave doubts about whether to play it at all. Only the prospective presence of Bud Booker at the Festival permitted his mind to remain open. He would have to think carefully about it.

An appreciative cackle came across the intercom. Clearly the projectionist was equally amused the second time around. 'Can you pick up the phone on the desk,' he said. 'there's a call from you from Mr Kim Bell.'

Renaud was only temporarily mystified. It was Sheridan.

'Grab a taxi,' he insisted. 'Meet me in the Hung Hom bar on Ma Tau Wei Road. There's going to be some action there – better than the movies.'

There was. From the open second-floor window of the bar Sheridan pointed out a pair of Toyota Land Cruisers forcing a path through the evening traffic. They pulled up on the other side of the road. Led by two European officers, eight armed policemen in shorts jumped out and ran into the restaurant opposite. For a moment there was only the noise of the traffic and then above it came frenetic shouting and screaming.

'Drug raid,' explained Sheridan. 'They'll only pick up the small fish – plus a few packs of smack if they're in luck.'

'How did you know about it?' Renaud was impressed.

'Same way as they did – a tip-off. Only mine came from the cops.'

A crowd had gathered outside, drawn by the noise. The police at the restaurant door stopped them from entering. Eventually four young men in handcuffs were led out to the waiting vehicles.

'Triads,' said Sheridan, picking up his whisky. 'They used to escape to the Walled City just up the road. Amazing place. Full of unlicensed doctors and dentists – you could see them pulling teeth in old-fashioned barbers' shops on the perimeter. Mainland China always claimed sovereignty over it, but really it was a law unto itself.'

'Was?'

'It's all been knocked down now.'

'So where do the Triads go?'

Sheridan smiled. 'Everywhere – the Sui Fong started here in Kowloon, the Wo Sing Wo are over in the Western Districts and the big boys are the 14Ks who used to operate out of 14K Poh Wah Road – not that you'd find them there if you knocked on the door. But when the commies take over they'll all have to move house.'

Renaud failed to understand him. 'Why?'

'No more cosy British justice with a good chance of an acquittal and a tame sentence if you're not. A bullet in the back of the neck, more likely. That's why there are no Triads on the mainland. Exterminated.'

He downed his whisky. 'I'm going across to get some quotes from the cops. Coming?'

Renaud looked at his watch. 'I'd better get back. I had an invitation from Government House. How do you think they knew I was here?'

'They monitor who comes and goes. There's only one airport, Kai Tak. Let me see . . . Director of the Cannes Film Festival.' Sheridan thought for a moment. 'You should be good for a cocktail party.'

'Nearly right. Drinks after dinner. Tonight.'

'That's fast. Brown must want something. Price of retirement homes in Provence, perhaps.'

Freshly showered and clad in the most presentable clothes he
could find in his suitcase – a navy blazer, cream shirt and
slightly loud red and yellow striped tie – Renaud stepped off
the ferry at Chung Wan.

Statue Square was crammed with a series of public meetings. It reminded Renaud of Speakers' Corner in London,
only a hundred times busier. There were people of all ages but
mostly students. Since the various speeches were in Chinese
he was unable to understand them. But a young woman came
up to him with a clipboard and asked him to sign a peti-
tion.

'You must get your government to act,' she insisted. 'It's
not too late, even now.'

'Not my government, I'm afraid,' he replied taking her pen
and signing anyway. 'I'm French.'

He decided not to mention that he was about to have a
drink with the Governor but wished her well.

'*Au revoir*,' she shouted after him. 'Think of us.'

He passed through the open atrium of the Hong Kong and
Shanghai Bank and set a course, as Sheridan had instructed
him, for the Bank of China. It was a more cautious piece of
work by the Chinese-American architect, Ioh Ming Pei, than
his audacious glass pyramid in front of the Louvre. Renaud
turned up the hill but found himself at the terminus of an
ancient tram which made its perpendicular way up to the
Peak. He was lost. He wandered alongside the Botanical
Gardens but there was no sign of Government House, only
the tower of what appeared to be the Japanese Embassy.
Making for the gate lodge to try and get instructions, he
caught sight of a large gleaming Daimler in the drive with a
regal coronet instead of a number-plate. This must be the
place.

A Chinese servant, formally dressed in white bow tie and
tails, bowed low as he opened the double doors. He was late.
The smell of cigars and sound of satisfied laughter emanated
from the drawing room. A petite blonde woman in her fifties,

105

her deep tan boldly exhibited by a silver evening dress that clung to her still svelte figure, came into the hall.

'Monsieur Callet? I'm Nora Brown. I'm so glad you could come.'

She held out her hand and Renaud annoyed himself by involuntarily bowing his head, though not as deeply as the servant who had greeted him.

'I expect you had difficulty finding us. People do if we don't send a car. It looks like a set left over from a touring version of Madame Butterfly, doesn't it? Well, in a way it was, the 1941-45 tour of the Nipponese Imperial Ballet. Do come in.'

He followed her into the room, on his way accepting a brandy from a tray proffered by a servant.

Lady Brown steered him towards a solidly built woman who was adjusting her hair in the mirror. 'Now this is Bettina Kingsley. She was at Covent Garden with me and both our little girls were at RADA together. Monsieur Callet, the man from Cannes.'

The years had been less favourable to Bettina who weighed two or possibly three times as much as Lady Brown. As if she had been reading Renaud's thoughts she offered an immediate explanation.

'Nora was ballet, I was opera. That was in the days when there was a market there and the pubs opened at dawn. I used to stop for a Guinness on my way in to morning rehearsals. How do you like Hong Kong? You'd better be quick, there's so little left. The 1879 Hong Kong Club, the old Bank of China, the Supreme Court, the Repulse Bay Hotel, all bulldozed by the new money. Terrible, isn't it? But there's such a heady atmosphere, don't you find?'

'I've only been here a day – ' Renaud began.

'First thing tomorrow you must take the tram up to the Peak,' insisted Lady Brown. 'Marvellous view if it isn't stuck in cloud. Then you can walk in the Victoria Gardens. They used to belong to us. Previous Governors had a mountain lodge up there but the Japanese demolished it during the war. You can't trust some people to look after anything.'

'When you go, Nora,' asked her friend, ignoring Renaud, who appeared to have failed in his only chance to make an impression, 'what are you going to leave behind?'

Lady Brown's expression underwent a barometric change, as if a cold front had unexpectedly swept across her. 'Everything,' she said. 'Every damn thing. The drinks cabinet will be stocked, the vases overflowing with flowers, the new Harrods covers on the chairs, all the paintings on the walls – even the Hockney – the Daimler full of petrol and polished to perfection. Have you seen *The Bridge on the River Kwai*, Monsieur Callet?'

'It was written by a Frenchman,' he reminded her.

'Well, that is how we like to do things. When you drive out from Kowloon to the New Territories you pass by the Amah Rock. It's a woman with a child on her back who was told that her husband, a fisherman, had died at sea. But she refused to believe it. So there she stands. For ever. And it's my intention that even though the Union Flag no longer flies over this building, we shall remain, in spirit . . .'

She reached in her purse for a handkerchief. As she did so a lofty, balding man in a dinner jacket detached himself from his group and came quickly across to them.

'I'm so sorry,' she said. 'Ronnie, this is Monsieur Callet, from Cannes.'

'So glad you could make it,' he beamed. 'You all right, Nora?'

'Fine, darling. Why don't you two go and have your talk.'

Her husband, while looking at her compassionately, nevertheless managed to raise an imperceptible eyebrow of disapproval. Renaud caught it. So he had not been summoned here just for the cultural pleasure of his company.

Nora tried to cover herself. 'Darling, why not show him the azaleas. They've never been quite so tall, nor so fragrant. I doubt if they ever will be again.'

Lord Brown took his cue and ushered Renaud through the open French windows down to the lawn. There was indeed an aromatic tang in the peaceful garden, far removed from the turbulent throng of the city they could both hear in the distance.

The Governor put his whisky down on the edge of the terrace, took a few paces across the lawn and crouched down to pull a weed out of the grass. He twisted it in his hands.

'Funny old place. We're going to miss it. Nora takes things a little too much to heart. Always goes for the human side of every situation. See that tower, there? Built onto the house by the Japanese. The Foreign Office wanted to knock it down, but you've got to accept that things change. It's come in quite useful actually. Our daughter keeps a room there, filled with candles and little statues and things, and she can have her chums to stay when she comes to visit. Not that she'll be coming any more.' He took a pipe from the pocket of his dinner jacket and attempted to rekindle it. 'So: Cannes, eh?'

Renaud had no idea what he was meant to say, so he merely smiled in acknowledgement.

'Nora and I don't get out to the cinema too much ourselves.'

The Director broadened his smile. If he had a hundred-franc note for every occasion somebody had said that to him, his hundred-metre yacht would by now be bobbing on the Baie d'Antibes.

'But I gather from my people here that you're thinking of putting a Hong Kong film in your Festival this year.'

'It's a possibility,' Renaud acknowledged defensively. 'We are an international event. *The* international event.'

'Well, Ho's a popular chap in this town and can certainly hold his own. We had him up to the house for afternoon tea once. Funny little fellow. Climbed right up the outside of the Japanese tower there, no ladder, nothing.'

Ronnie Brown threw back his head and laughed, a practised diplomatic laugh that came not from the solar plexus but from accumulated years in the foreign service.

'But this film he's making, *The Storming of the Summer Palace*. I'm not sure that now is the time to reopen sores like that – especially at an international festival. Ho tends to fool around with the facts. The truth plays second fiddle to his deeds of derring-do. In any event the boys in Beijing might get a little tetchy.'

So that's it, Renaud thought. For somebody who doesn't go to the cinema you are extraordinarily well-briefed, not well enough, however, to be told that the film Ho was currently shooting would not be ready for Cannes – unlike *The Yellow Pirate*.

But he resented Brown's interference in his Festival and was damned if he was going to put the man in the true picture.

'I have diplomatic pressures from every country in the

world,' he informed the Governor. 'If Cannes gave way to politicians it would become a convention of international tourist board documentaries. I have yet to make a decision on this particular film – but, when I do, the art of cinema will be the sole deciding factor.'

'I see,' said the Governor, bending down to retrieve his drink. 'Well, I just hoped the matter could be solved at an informal level. I suspect London will be exchanging notes with Paris on this one.'

He straightened himself up to his full six foot five inches, ever the erect Englishman and anxious to remain courteous. 'Come inside and have another drink. By the way, is that an MCC tie you're wearing?'

CHAPTER 7

Thursday 6th March 1997

New York

'Jesus Christ, wait till you see this. You're never going to believe it. You'll never believe what I've found.'

Tanya Neris burst into the *Arts Action* office like an Olympic sprinter. She rushed up to Jim Hurley's desk and smacked down a compact black video cassette in the middle of his old-fashioned blotter. With feigned slow motion he lowered the copy of *Daily Variety* which he was reading and looked quizzically at her. 'What have you found?' he inquired. 'A television interview with Greta Garbo? Or just the Ark of the Covenant?'

Impatiently she took the cassette out of its box and thrust it into the video recorder by his desk. It wouldn't go in. There was already a cassette in there. She drummed impatiently on the television set while she waited for it to eject. By now she had attracted the attention of the others in the office and one or two got up from their desks to see what was happening.

'The suspense is too much,' observed Jessica, reaching for the sixteenth cigarette of the day.

'This is something you've never seen in your life before,' Tanya challenged her. There was little love lost between the two women.

'I've seen it all,' came the world-weary reply.

By now several people had gathered round the executive producer's desk to watch. Tanya fumbled the cassette into its slot and pressed the play button.

'Welcome to the Pantages Theater on rain-swept Hollywood Boulevard for the Twenty-fifth Annual Academy

Awards. The first time you at home will be able to join us live at this glittering ceremony.'

Tanya punched the pause button neurotically. 'Anybody know who that was? Anybody know?'

'A man with the same initials as me.' Raymond Rainier was incapable of stating anything other than in a roundabout way – a hallmark of his frequently confusing reviews.

'No, it – Jesus, yes it is! How the hell did you know?' Tanya glared at him, annoyed that he had got it right.

Rainier looked nonchalantly out of the window. 'Everybody knows that Ronald Reagan did the off-screen narration for the first televised Oscars. At least everybody who's read their television history – as I presume we all have.'

'Wait a minute,' interrupted Hurley. 'You've got film of the 1952 Oscars? The first televised ceremony? It doesn't exist.'

Tanya shook her fists in delight. 'It does now. Not everything. Just the highlights.'

Hurley was impressed. 'How did you find it?'

Her words tripped over each other in her excitement. 'The son of an NBC video editor. He lives right here in the city. The Museum of Modern Art put me on to him. His father had rooms full of stuff, 35-mill, 16-mill, 2-inch, 1-inch tapes, all sorts of cassettes. The old guy was a collector. Just like stamps. It took me two days to go through it all. They may have let NBC televise it but they sure as hell hated television then – just you look at Bob Hope.'

She restarted the tape. The familiar face of the comedian came on the screen. 'Welcome to *Suspense*. This is television's most exciting giveaway show. Television? That's where movies go when they die,' quipped Hope. 'You know what Jack Warner called it – furniture that stares back at you.'

Still, the furniture managed to bring to a movie-hungry nation shots of the rarely-to-be-heard-of-again Shirley Booth winning Best Actress for *Come Back Little Sheba*, John Ford getting the Best Director Oscar for *The Quiet Man* and Cecil B. de Mille and Henry Wilcoxon accepting their Best Picture Oscars for *The Greatest Show on Earth*.

'Greatest shit on earth,' observed Rainier derisively. 'You know what should have won that year? *High Noon*. Too close to the knuckle, though. Lone sheriff, apathetic society?'

'Why should that stop it?' Ed Butler was genuinely intrigued.

Rainier was pleased to have found an audience. His views – and reviews – were usually ignored by the other members of staff.

'Think back, pilgrim,' he said patronisingly. '1952. UnAmerican Activities. People were paranoid about the picture. They wouldn't even give Foreman his producer credit. When he won his Oscar for *River Kwai* he wasn't allowed to collect it. Went to some goddam Frog.'

'UnAmerican what?' inquired Tanya. At the same time Jessica butted in: 'Pierre Boulle. He did write the book, you know, and at least he wasn't a Communist.'

'Neither was Foreman,' insisted Rainier. 'Those guys just didn't want to be fucked about by Washington. Fifth Amendment Communists they were called.'

'But why was –' began Tanya. But Hurley, to save her from any embarrassment, put a comforting arm round her shoulder. 'You did well, kid. Now haven't we got a show or something on tonight? Raymond, are you reviewing the new Woody Allen?'

'That is my penance.'

'No good? I thought you liked him.'

'I adore him. He's about the most original film-maker this city's produced. But every five films or so he becomes Ingmar Allen with a cast of actors competing for the character with the longest face award, to remind us that the human condition sucks. And we don't need reminding.'

'Will he do an interview for us? Did we put in a bid?'

'He only talks to Europeans. They appreciate the gloomy ones more than we do.'

Jim shrugged and turned to Ed. 'How's the *Hair – thirty years on* special coming along?'

'Bald,' interposed Jessica.

'It's looking good,' Ed assured him. 'Jerome Ragni's tracked down the girl who gave him the original idea for Frank Mills. And we've already got Joe Papp in the can. Can we show naked breasts?'

'Only from behind,' replied Jim with a straight face.

'Isn't that amazing. Thirty years ago the whole cast

undressed in one of the biggest theatres on Broadway. And still television won't let us see a single tit.'

'It's just furniture that stares back at you, remember?' Jessica had added another piece of ammunition to her cynical armoury. Pleased with the acquisition she returned to her desk singing 'this is the drowning of the age of Aquarius'.

Tanya began to remove the cassette from the machine but Jim gently restrained her.

'That's some nice stuff. I wouldn't mind taking a look at this guy's loft. Did you give him anything?'

'Only a couple of hundred bucks. He's a fan of the show. I think he likes the idea of getting involved.'

'Maybe we could build an archive slot around him. Get the lawyers to check the copyright on this. I'm prepared to pay anything. It's great. By the way, I thought you didn't work Thursdays?'

Her lips curved into a sheepish smile. 'I don't. This isn't my story. I was helping Robert out.'

Jim gave her a collusive glance. 'I had heard.'

He liked Tanya. Everything was upfront with her. She was so anxious to please and to succeed that the fact that she knew relatively little about the history of the business rarely stood in her way. It was just another hurdle to be jumped and she took a professional delight in the race. Keeping up with Bob Barrett, Hurley sensed, was going to be a more daunting marathon.

Tanya pressed both palms down on the desk and leaned defiantly towards her boss. 'Listen, Jim. I want to go to the Coast with him. I can make things happen. Those dodos out there are fast asleep on the job most of the time.'

'Have you discussed it with him?'

'Sure.' She paused, clicked her tongue and gave him her little-girl look. 'Okay no, not yet. But it would sure make the discussion easier if you wanted me to go.'

'It's not a bad idea. I'll sound out LA. You sound out Bob.'

'You've got a deal.' Tanya grabbed him in a bear hug and kissed him noisily.

'Office romance,' sounded a disconsolate voice from the far recesses of the room.

Robert rarely enjoyed having lunch with movie agents. There were two reasons: they always turned up late and, even if it was their invitation, they usually managed to leave you with the bill. Today was to be no exception. At least he had been taken to the Robert Benchley table at 21; Homer still had clout in these quarters. The place had the trappings of a club but the inhabitants of a fast-food restaurant. The fact that the management asked you to wear a tie did not instantly endow the bearer with either good manners or taste.

During the dark, dry days of Prohibition, 21 West 52nd Street had obtained widespread notoriety as Jack and Charlie's Speakeasy and even now, when the wine flowed freely – expensively but freely – it still retained a quasi-exclusive air. Many of the occupants were men who as small boys had stood in the street beside the diminutive plaster jockeys and watched the long silent limousines dropping the diners, vowing that one day they, too, would be knowingly greeted by the maître d.

Robert waved aside the waiter's assumption that he would want a dry Martini and ordered a Budweiser instead. Paradoxically the incessant babble gave him the chance to think, something he had not been able to do at the office nor at home over recent weeks. He was beginning to fear he had lost control of whatever rudder was steering his life – there was an increasing sensation of being adrift. At first he had thought that it was simply Manhattan getting to him. To have a fast-paced job in a fast-paced city was outwardly attractive, but the recipe for inner despair. It was as if pace itself had become a substitute for any more meaningful way of life. He was not alone; he could see it in his colleagues. The frantic desire to get the daily programme on the air and then, afterwards, the desperate need to celebrate, go out, 'enjoy' as the waiters said. Very few of them seemed to be running their own lives; many were running away from them.

'Go and see a shrink,' Tanya had advised, when he voiced his disquiet to her. 'It worked for me.' Had it? The layer of zappy bravado that covered her niggling insecurity was perilously thin. She had made it. She had come from a middle-class black family and now she was the outward embodiment of a mid-town girl. She had progressed from secretary to researcher to producer faster than any other woman in the office, spurred on by a desire to succeed that verged on the hysterical. What was she trying to prove? And to whom? She had been like that long before she became involved with Robert. In truth it was one of the things that initially drew him to her. That, and the fact that she approached sex with equally excessive ardour.

The mere thought of her aroused him. He took a sip of his beer as if to calm himself. The anomaly was that she could find a total life within *Arts Action* – she was likely to be tried out as on-screen talent if the progression continued – whereas Robert began to sense, a little more certainly each day, that if he didn't escape from the suffocating atmosphere of show business, he would begin to confuse it with the real world. The Oscars were going to be a fresh challenge; he had never been before and he was looking forward to them. But nagging within him was the uncomfortable thought that one day he might start hyperventilating, live on air, as he conducted yet another interview with a soap star who had nothing to say to him and to whom he had even less to say.

He looked at his reflection in the Benchley plaque and pushed back his hair. '1889–1945. Humorist.' There, he thought, was a renaissance man, an essayist, a drama critic for *Life* and the *New Yorker*, someone who dabbled in films. Such an existence seemed infinitely more adult and creative than the picayune hurdy-gurdy of television. What had gone wrong? Was it Robert or merely the age he lived in? Although he envied Hutton his *New York Times* posting to Paris, such a job hinted of anachronism in the age of the television satellite. You were only telling people tomorrow what they had learnt yesterday, although admittedly in greater depth. Maybe he would go and stay with Hutton to sort himself out. Maybe he would chuck in *Arts Action*; there were other jobs, other programmes. Maybe he would give up Manhattan for a while and find out whether he was capable of life without the nightly fix of adrenalin that the programme gave him.

Deep down, he knew he had no need to go to a shrink. Who was it who said that a psychiatrist was someone you told your phobias to and he told you what you were afraid of? He had already diagnosed the underlying cause of his dissatisfaction yet he was afraid to confess it, even to himself. His affair with Tanya had been a mistake, pretty well from the beginning. He was not in love with her and never would be. In the past he could have sustained a relationship on that basis; indeed, apart from that one short summer with Lynne, he had never known a relationship on any other basis. But now, at the age of thirty-three, he harboured this disconcerting fear that life – and that included love – was being lived somewhere else. Somewhere, not necessarily in Manhattan, maybe not in America even, there must be a girl who could enter his life and change it and quell his central restlessness. He was certain that every day and every night he spent with Tanya robbed him of the opportunity to fill this deepening emotional vacuum.

'Who invented the telephone?'

Robert looked up. 'Alexander Graham Bell. Or the Chinese. Depends who you want to believe.'

'Well, fuck 'em both,' announced Homer Mangold, sitting down. A chunkily built man, he affected an English country check suit and an oddly contrasting crew-cut that made him look like a military veteran, something he was not. But he needed to utter no words of command for a Martini with two green olives to be placed in front of him.

'I need this. I've just had a call from Daniel in London. The British have no idea of the meaning of money. I got him three million and points to match in the new John Milius picture and he wants to read the script. Actors do not need to read a script with an offer like that and full studio financing. And he says he may not be able to do it even if he likes it. He's interested in a play at the Royal Court. That's a theatre where even the cast pay to go in.'

Robert had forgotten what agreeable company Homer was. 'They still have some standards over there, you know,' he suggested.

'Remember when Spielberg wanted Tom Stoppard to get started on *Empire of the Sun* and Stoppard said he had to finish something for the BBC? So a VP from Warners rang him in a panic and asked him why he was messing about with television when he had the hottest offer in Hollywood, and Stoppard said: "What do you mean television? I'm writing for BBC radio."'

Homer laughed politely. 'But he did the movie as well. Even great artists find it hard to turn their back on Hollywood money. Look at Robert Benchley there – they always give me his table if it's free – made the first talking picture.'

'I thought that was *The Jazz Singer*,' Robert countered.

'No, five or six years before that he made *The Treasurer's Report* – it was a sort of monologue he used to do. And he won an Oscar for some cartoon picture called *How To Sleep*.'

Robert took out a pen and noted this down on the back of his *Times* as Homer congratulated himself on his knowledge by swallowing the rest of his Martini. He could see Robert was worried about something.

'You look a bit down in the mouth. What's the problem? Not paying you enough on that show of yours. If they want you, you can always squeeze them for twenty-five per cent more, and if they don't want you, you may as well walk now. Who's your agent?'

'I don't have one. They're too expensive.'

'You're kidding me. I'll talk to our television division. You won't notice their percentage with the money they'll get you.'

'It's not so much the money,' Robert confessed. 'I'm not too sure I want to spend very much longer at the wrong end of show business. I need a change.'

'Write,' counselled Homer. 'Good money there. Look at Stoppard.'

'I don't know if I can.'

'That doesn't matter.' Homer raised his eyes to the Benchley plaque. 'Remember what the other Robert said? "It took me fifteen years to discover that I had no talent for writing, but I couldn't give it up because by then I was famous." Now why did you ask me to lunch? To discuss your career?'

'*You* asked *me*.'

'I did? Are you sure? What do you think I wanted?'

'Hash browns with an egg on top,' smiled Robert. 'The waiter told me your order.'

'That's why I come here. I have to make enough decisions every day without having to pick my way through menus. I know what it was: Oscars. You're going to cover the Academy Awards.'

'Nothing's been announced.' Robert quietly registered his surprise as the waiter brought their lunch.

'My job,' said Homer, his delight evenly allocated between his scoop and the juicy nursery meal in front of him, 'is to know things before they're announced. What do eggs benedict and a blow job have in common?'

Robert had heard the joke but obligingly replied that he had no idea.

'You don't get either of them at home.' Homer chuckled. 'Well, maybe you do. I've heard that Tanya Neris is a hell of a good cook.' The chuckle transformed into a crude laugh. 'Excuse me, I just happen to have a friend in your management. He comes to our Friday night gatherings.'

Here Robert was the possessor of some incidental intelligence. Homer had parties on many nights of the week, especially if a leading client was in town, but Friday night was gay night.

'It's true. I probably will cover the Oscars. One of a team I should think.' Robert abruptly turned the conversation away from this intrusion into his private airspace.

Homer failed to notice – or appeared not to. 'I have a friend with a restaurant, Le Moulin de l'Abbaye – you've heard of it – and ever since Swifty gave up Spago's' – for innumerable years the veteran literary agent, Swifty Lazar, had hosted a party for those too aged, infirm or famous to make their way downtown to the actual ceremony, a gathering to which admission after the awards was either by private invitation or the possession of an Oscar – 'he's been trying to establish an occasion of similar stature. I shall be flying across myself and you are most cordially invited . . .'

Robert waited for the proviso. It wasn't long in coming.

'. . . to come along with the *Arts Action* crew and make it one of the major locations for the night. We're going to have a lot of big names there.'

Robert took his pen out again. 'Like who?'

Homer put his fork to his mouth. A drop of egg yolk dribbled onto the handle. '*Shtum.* For the moment. You won't go empty-handed.'

The bait was taken. 'But I need some names. They're not going to send a mini-cam and dish for me to talk to the chef.'

'He's quite a guy. Used to have a restaurant of the same name in Brantôme in the Dordogne.'

'Even so, he's unlikely to win any Oscars – unless they're giving one for best truffles this year.'

Homer leant forward conspiratorially. 'The Oscar winners are no problem. They're available for everybody. What you need on that night are some good stories with star names and I have one for you. I am going to say to you two words but you must forget immediately that they ever came from me.' His voice dropped almost to the inaudible. 'Bud Booker,' he whispered.

A waiter was hovering by the table. 'Mr Mangold, your office called. Your two-thirty meeting has been brought forward to two-fifteen.'

Homer glanced ostentatiously at his watch. 'I'm sorry. I've got to go. Don't tell anyone. Trust me. Absolute *shtum*.'

He squeezed Robert over-affectionately on the shoulder and, managing only fleetingly to work a couple of the tables on his way, made for the door. Then, as if he had forgotten something, he stopped and called back.

'By the way, thanks for lunch.'

Long before he reached the door the heavy FM thud of rock music informed him that Tanya was in the apartment. He stopped for a moment before inserting his key, afraid that even if he said nothing his demeanour might betray his unspoken thoughts about their relationship. He didn't want a confrontation, not yet.

She was sitting in the middle of the floor, an open book on her knees. Other half-read paperbacks and magazines were scattered around her. Robert turned off the booming radio.

'We interrupt this broadcast to bring you the following warning. Any attempt to use the brain while subjecting it to the sounds we are currently transmitting could result in it exploding all over the walls and ceiling.'

She looked slightly guilty, as if she had been caught doing something wrong. 'I always listen to music when I read. I always did. Everyone did at college. Reading needs background music.

He slumped down on to the sofa. 'I had lunch with Homer

Mangold today. Guess who paid the bill? This is a multiple-choice question. Was it: a) me, b) on the house, or c) given to someone who made the mistake of joining us?'

She ignored the question. 'Did you know that *High Noon* was a communist attack on the government?'

'It wasn't,' he replied without thinking.

'It says here it was.' Tanya indicated the book on her knees.

Robert shook his head. 'It showed a strong individual in a weak community but that doesn't make it communist, rather the reverse. People read into it what they wanted. It was President Eisenhower's favourite film; he used to show it to dinner guests at the White House. And it got a bad review in *Pravda*. The Russians criticised it for the glorification of the individual.'

'Well, how come the writer guy,' – she looked down at the page – 'Carl Foreman, was exiled to Britain for being a communist?'

'He wasn't. He was just blacklisted so he couldn't get any work under his own name. He produced a film about Winston Churchill that looked like it could've been made by the press office of the British Conservative Party – hardly the work of a communist.'

'Was Gary Cooper a communist then?'

'You've got to be joking. He told the House Committee he turned down scripts because they were tinged with what he called communistic ideas.'

Robert stood up and made a lame attempt to mimic the actor. 'I could never take any of this pinko mouthing very seriously because I didn't think it was on the level.'

Tanya was not amused. 'One final question.'

Robert looked breezily expectant. 'Yes?'

'How come you're such a fucking know-all?'

It stopped him in his tracks and he sat down again. 'I studied up on the period for my paper on Nixon – Eisenhower's Vice-President, remember? – while you were doing needlework at the BU School of Public Communication.'

Even as it fell from his lips, he wished he could have taken the last remark back. Tanya lifted the book from her knees and slammed it closed.

'We studied practical matters – broadcast news, lighting – you have no idea what a key light or a kicker is, you admitted it yourself.' She started to itemise things on her fingers: 'Camera-work, editing, documentary, programme construction, things you'll never understand because you can't just memorise them from a lot of lousy books.'

'So what are you upset about?'

'I'm not upset. I'm just interested. Why was Hollywood so communist?'

'It wasn't. It was just a label they pinned on anyone left-wing. All the real hysteria happened during the Cold War when Russia was a big bad place. It was okay to make pro-Russian movies during the Second World War when we were on the same side. Metro had *Song of Russia*, Warners produced *Mission to Moscow*. Then, in front of the House Committee, Jack Warner recanted, said he wouldn't have any commies in his studio, that he had cut out insidious propaganda from scripts and that the Communist Party should be an illegal organisation.'

'I think it should,' said Tanya.

'Really? In Russia as well? They're the good guys now, remember?'

'Don't patronise me. I think the Committee was right. Why should Hollywood make movies knocking America?'

Something inside Robert exploded. He turned on Tanya, ostensibly to attack her ignorance, but really to vent his pent-up frustration. 'The Committee were a load of prejudiced neanderthals – somebody said their session with Bertolt Brecht was like a zoologist being cross-examined by a bunch of apes. What they didn't like were Jews. Congressman Ranking read out the Hollywood names like the admissions officer at Auschwitz: Danny Kaye, real name David Daniel Kaminsky, Eddie Cantor, real name Edward Israel Iskowitz, Melvyn Douglas, real name Melvyn Hesselberg. He even accused them of interfering with the Committee's right to save America from the horrible fate the communists had brought to the unfortunate Christian people of Europe. Note the word – Christian.'

Tanya shrugged. 'Doesn't it make *you* suspicious that they were all Jews?'

Robert pointed his finger accusingly at her. 'You see, you're just as blinkered as the rest of them. Just because you're black doesn't mean you can't be prejudiced.'

'Why do you have to bring my colour into it? We're not talking about me. We're talking about communists. And I don't care if they're in Russia or China or Israel or Beverly Hills, it's a system that stinks. My dad said so and I know so.'

'You know nothing,' Robert yelled at her. 'What's the difference between Communism and Confucianism in China? Very little. They both believe in same thing – sharing land, the power of the peasants. Corruption lies in leaders, not creeds.'

'You know-all motherfucker,' screamed Tanya. She threw the book she was holding violently against the wall and ran tearfully into the bedroom, slamming the door with a crash.

Not for the first time, Robert had tried to humiliate her and succeeded. But he knew he had humiliated himself more. It was a cheap debating tactic to manoeuvre the conversation into areas where he had some knowledge and could make her look foolish.

And yet, at times, her ignorance appeared to him to be almost wilful. She seemed to have opinions about everything and knowledge of virtually nothing. It was no hindrance to her job in television where the ability to thumb through *People* magazine and consume the front and back pages of *U S A Today* provided more than the required wisdom. What was eating into him was the fact that this was true for him, too. Whereas previously he had been able to escape from a world that he managed to adore and despise simultaneously, now he was forced to confront it at home as well with all the routes of escape squarely blocked by signs marked Tanya.

He knew he had been selfish, and unfair to her. The relationship had had its own destruction in sight even as it began. But he was hooked on the narcotic of her sensuality. She tantalised him with her absolute abandon. Sex with her had no boundaries, it was reinvented every night, delivering new excitement by trading in utter freedom. She had made a commitment to him and he had betrayed her by enjoying this intimacy while only deceptively returning it. He wanted both to have her and not to have her, yet he knew that this was not an option on offer.

He picked up the book she had thrown and knocked on the bedroom door.

'Fuck off. Get out. Go back to China.'

'I've never been there. I'm sorry.'

'So are they.'

'I'm sorry about just now. Verbal abuse. I'll get twenty years one day. I love you.'

'You say that. But it's just more of your words. You probably read them in a book.'

'Probably. I certainly didn't learn them at home.'

Her voice changed to a lighter tone. 'Ah, poor Bobby. Mummy scrimped and saved to send him off to school but forgot to say she loved him.'

He attempted to humour her by playing along. 'I know, I'm all fucked up. Can I come in? Then you can be all fucked up?'

'That's all you want from me. I'm just a black blow job.'

He opened the door. It wasn't locked. She was lying on the bed clutching the pillow like a fretful child. Robert sat down beside her.

'How did we get into all this anyway?' he asked.

She sat up, wiping her eyes. 'I was trying to help you. I had some time and I thought I could get some material on the Oscars. I lucked out – there's a tape of the first show, the first one they televised, anyway. Then Jim and Raymond started talking about the blacklist and – I'd vaguely heard of it but . . . you're going to sneer at me . . .'

'Never again.' His empty promise floated across to her like a dummy pass on a football field.

'I thought blacklisting was to do with blacks in Hollywood. I'd never really taken on board who the Hollywood Ten or the Unfriendly Ten or whatever were.'

'Neither had most people,' Robert reassured her. 'Billy Wilder said that only two had any talent and the rest were just unfriendly.'

She managed a wan smile. 'Anyway, after feeling so good finding that tape, I just felt small and humiliated. So I came home to look at your books.'

'What tape?' he asked.

'The '52 Oscars. It's sensational. I showed them at the office. I just wanted to help you with your research.'

He leant across and kissed her on the cheek. 'I don't deserve you.'

She took the book from him. 'There's a great story there about Robert Rich. I bet you've never heard of him.'

He shook his head. 'Truthfully, no.'

'He won the Oscar in 1956 for writing *The Brave One*. It was about a little boy and his bull – sounds a real turkey. But nobody could find him. So the Academy just held onto the award. And lots of people wrote to them saying "I'm Robert Rich and I claim my Oscar." And it wasn't until 1959 when they finally let communists win Oscars –'

'People who took the Fifth – communist or not.'

'Don't start off again. It was only in 1959 that this guy' – she looked down at the page – 'Dalton Trumbo revealed he was Robert Rich. Didn't get his Oscar till 1975, though.'

He lay down on the bed beside her. 'I didn't know that. Seriously. It's a good story. That's just the material that might come in very handy for the Oscar coverage.'

He placed both his hands round the back of her neck to make her face him. 'What can I do to thank you?'

'Who are you?' she asked. 'Are you Robert Rich or just Robert Poor?'

'I'm poor Robert. Horny Robert, too.'

He attempted to kiss her but she turned away her head. 'I want to finish reading this book. You interrupted me.'

She wanted him, even more than he wanted her. But she was satisfied to see from the expression on his face how contrite he became when he was physically rejected.

CHAPTER 8

Thursday 6th March 1997

London

Fyodor was dripping with sweat. It spread in widening rivulets across his brow, staunched only by his blue cotton headband, and discoloured substantial areas of his short-sleeved white shirt. His face, puce and puffy, sat dispro-portionately large on top of his stubby body. A lifestyle that regularly embraced the most acclaimed restaurants in Europe and America was not the best diet in the world and his stomach muscles had long since surrendered to the unequal challenge.

'Not a pretty sight,' Elizabeth thought as she looked down from the balcony of the indoor tennis court. Yet she had slept with him the previous night, as she had done as often as he had been able to get away from his wife in the three weeks since the evening of the wrap party.

It had not been her intention. She had frequently asked herself why she had invited him home that night and the answer was always the same: she didn't really know. It was nothing she had calculated or planned. Throughout the shooting of the film he had always treated her with an almost condescending politeness, light-years away from any obvious form of flirtation. Indeed he adopted a role that seemed to be, if anything, *in loco parentis*. It had certainly been a relationship that was more natural than the one they had now since she was twenty-two and he, she had worked out, must have passed his fiftieth birthday. Subconsciously, she realised now, she had probably been striving for his attention during the final weeks of the picture. The more overbearing Howard Cousins had become, the more desperately she had sent out distress signals to Fyodor. Yet he had studiously ignored them; he had even seemed to encourage Howard's advances. For the good of the movie? How could she be sure? And then, at the eleventh hour, he had managed to be in the right place at the right time. Or maybe the wrong place at the wrong time. All she knew for certain was that she had been anxious to preserve his companionship after the shooting stopped and, to her, one of the most important things about their affair was that it achieved precisely that.

She had been an only child, and frequently a lonely one. With a father in the diplomatic service the family had spent long tours of duty abroad interspersed with shorter periods back in London. She had never really felt settled anywhere. As soon as she made friends they usually turned into pen-pals when she and her parents took off for another country. So Elizabeth found a more permanent friend in her own imagination and at her boarding school at Sussex, with her golden hair and striking eyes, was given prominent roles in school plays which led to a genuine aptitude for acting. Younger girls formed undisguised crushes on her and she secretly enjoyed that.

She set her heart on going to the Royal Academy of Dramatic Art and, at the second attempt, she succeeded. It was there that she met young men, and became aware that they could have crushes too – although most of the drama students were infinitely more interested in themselves than anybody else.

But in her final year she started to live with another member of her class, Tony Miller. Inevitably they had met when rehearsing a play. He had been an acclaimed Jimmy Porter in a student production of *Look Back in Anger* while she had got the part of his wife, Alison, only when the actress originally chosen fell ill with glandular fever. Tony had brought much of himself to the part and even more of the part to himself. He was happy to abuse Elizabeth's upper-middle-class background and happier still to move into the flat her parents bought her in Notting Hill Gate. She was more than a little in awe of him, flattered that he had chosen her, attracted by the paradoxical manner in which he sought the praise of his fellow students and at the same time was dismissive of them for according it to him.

Tony needed to be an actor; he knew the only role he could satisfactorily play in life was a life playing roles. His ambition, relentless as a downhill racer, enabled him to face the mounting rejections and humiliations as he unsuccessfully auditioned for parts. He seemed certain that there existed a form of divine thespian justice that would reward his talent with the fame that destiny was keeping in store for him, and he chided Elizabeth for what seemed to him her amateur approach to the profession.

When her agent put her name forward for commercials, he reacted sneeringly. As she cooked him dinner, he would drink more and more cheap wine and sermonise on the integrity of the profession. But their answering machine recorded the swing of the pendulum as she received frequent call-backs and he an indifferent silence. She began to realise she could no longer live with his increasingly jealous ego, and when he was eventually offered a small role in a fringe production at the Edinburgh Festival, she surprised herself by suggesting that their parting should be permanent. She was even more surprised when he broke down and told her that he loved her, not an emotion that had ever been mentioned in their eight months together. She had assumed that it had been a reciprocal bond of friendship and said so. After he left, she remained in doubt as to whether his departing declarations were from the genuine Tony or were just another histrionic performance for an audience of one. He stayed on in Edinburgh when the festival finished, informing her by postcard that he had moved in with a girl called Sally who owned a bookshop. He intended to work there as an assistant until the right part came his way.

She had expected to be lonely but instead felt exhilarated, as if she had been released on probation for having had the guts to speak her mind. London was blessed with an Indian summer that September and, for the first time in her life, she had the giddy sense of being a liberated adult unaccountable to anyone in the city. Almost immediately she landed a part in a television commercial for animal insurance. The director was Tim and her display of lip-biting grief when her dachshund was run over, bringing her emotional state to the perimeter of tears without ever letting one break – a technique that Tony had taught her – led directly to her successful audition for *Jupiter Landing*.

'Did you see that? Such shots are not man-made, they come from heaven.'

'Very good.' She applauded politely.

'You're a liar,' laughed Fyodor. 'You're weren't even watching. I glanced up. I can spot RADA lying you know. It's the sincere look that gives you away. Where were you? You were looking so sad.'

She leant over the balcony. 'How can you play tennis and gaze into my thoughts at the same time? Those are not compatible activities. I'll watch now. My mind is clear.'

'And your conscience?'

She ducked the question. 'Get on with the game. I said I'd watch.'

One of the four men on the neighbouring court gave her a withering look that suggested their conversation was interfering with his match. Elizabeth smiled at him apologetically which embarrassed him into smiling back. The four indoor courts at the Queen's Club in West London were all occupied by middle-aged men who approached the game with a fervour not always matched by talent. Yet Fyodor, despite his weight, occasionally played strokes with a fluency that hinted at a superior command of the game in his younger, leaner years. Now, when the ball came naturally to him, he dispatched it with style and cunning, but when he was forced to run wide into the tramlines or forward for a stop volley no half-remembered technique was able to compensate for his present lack of fitness. He was playing a younger man who, Elizabeth noticed, was decent enough on some occasions to cater to Fyodor's shortcomings.

Fyodor finished the set with a cross-court backhand that left his opponent stranded in the wrong corner.

'No more, Alex,' he insisted. 'I want to live to fight another day.'

Elizabeth waited for him on the verandah overlooking the immaculate square of grass courts, still two months away from their annual christening in May. It was a warm March lunchtime but Fyodor, being rich and foreign and a movie producer, chose to play indoors at this time of year as a hedge against the weather.

He came and joined her, giving off a strong spicy tang of recently applied cologne, his thick hair still wet from the shower. He lit a Gitane and the familiar, intertwining aromas enveloped her and made her feel secure.

'This place is like a superannuated public school,' he remarked. 'I just passed a door with a notice on it that said "out of bounds". They use this lingua franca so that members may retain their eternal youth.'

'You're too fat,' she said provocatively.

'I have watched the great Jaroslav Drobny play here,' he replied, managing effectively to ignore and twist her insult, 'and he was like a woman about to give birth the following day' – he outlined his stomach with his hands – 'but he could beat any opponent of the same age, a half or even a quarter of his weight. It is a question of concentration and spin and, above all, experience. But I agree. I still need to shed a few pounds.'

Elizabeth snuggled close to him. 'I thought you played with great artistry. I like watching you move. It excites me.'

'It's all fake, imitation. I have sat here in this very seat and watched the true artists. I have seen Jimmy Connors play a perfect backhand that no ordinary mortal could reach, or Boris Becker deliver serves that came with the strength of Wotan, or' – he shook his head in disbelief at the recollection of it – 'John McEnroe, in his prime, volleying as if his racquet were a magician's wand.'

Elizabeth felt curiously warmed by the heat of his enthusiasm. Just when she was beginning to harbour doubts about whether she should continue to see him, he would deliver such reminders of the compelling *joie de vivre* that made his companionship seductive.

As if sensing her unspoken response, he indicated the tall Victorian houses, now sub-divided into flats, that overlooked the grass courts on the far side of the grounds.

'On summer evenings I will always try and book court six, between six o'clock and seven-fifteen. When we sit down, in between sets, I watch people arriving home from work. And, through the windows, I can tell by their body language – no need for words, no need at all – what sort of an evening they're anticipating. The secretary, maybe in her mid-forties, moving slowly and methodically. She has been to Marks & Spencer and unloads her bag precisely, everything goes to its allotted place, nothing may be disturbed. Plants are watered, ornaments are adjusted. She is the squirrel, back in her nest, safe and comfortable but alone. And then you see, in the apartment below her, the young couple whose marriage is not going well. They contrive to come home at different times and barely acknowledge each other. She is in the kitchen, the radio turned up loudly – Radio 4 usually, a quiz programme at six-thirty which she appears to laugh at with the exaggerated response of the studio audience – and he sits in the other room with his feet up and the evening paper and a drink.'

'That could also be a relationship that was working well,' Elizabeth responded, thinking of such nights with Tony.

'If so, it will not be for long. But wait, best of all, on a fragrant June evening when the courts have been cut and the smell of freshly mown grass is so delicious that you sniff the ball before you serve, you sometimes catch a young girl, a girl like you in a light pink summer frock, come out onto the top balcony with a glass of wine in her hand, kick off her shoes, flop into a wicker chair and converse excitedly with her girlfriends on a white portable phone. And then, at seven o'clock, when the line is free, she will get a call from the man she loves and her tinkling laughter will spread across these courts –'

Elizabeth punched him playfully in the ribs. 'You,' she pronounced, 'are a romantic voyeur. But it might have the makings of a good movie.'

'Too late.' Fyodor leant forward and took her hand. 'Hitchcock already did it in *Rear Window*. I wanted to make a film about a man who comes back to one of these flats – an insurance salesman, who hates tennis with deep-grained vehemence, maybe his wife was stolen by a tennis-player. But he bought the apartment one night in winter and had no idea where it was situated. And when the summer comes he lays plans to machine-gun all the players. But first, he decides to take out insurance policies on their lives, so he has to find out who they are. It's only half an idea.'

'Why not remake *Rear Window*?' she suggested, trying to be helpful.

'Why forge a Vermeer? There's no director any more with an eye like that.'

'No?' She eyed him, unconvinced.

Fyodor lit another cigarette; he liked to exhale his philosophy with smoke. 'They don't have the chance. Hitch used to write the dialogue cards for silent movies – the first ten films he directed were silent. So he knew the language of pure cinema is not that of words. He knew his Pudovkin, his juxtaposition.' Fyodor formed a bowl with his hands. 'You take an actor's face – utterly expressionless. You cut to a plate of soup and back to him and he looks hungry. You cut to a sick child and he looks sad. But the expression has never changed. It's all there in *Rear Window*. But today . . . today they learn by selling rock groups and cornflakes – it is the same technique in both, the wall-to-wall sound-track covers up the random assembly of the pictures. They don't direct, they illustrate scripts.'

For a moment he stared mournfully into the past, then looked at his watch to bring himself back into the present. 'The car should be here by now. We're going out to Pinewood to see how well Tim has illustrated his.'

The film editor, like a surgeon about to perform an operation, donned a pair of white linen gloves, lifted a coil of celluloid from its can and threaded it through the gates of the Steenbeck viewing machine. His assistant deferentially passed him two brown rolls of sound-track which were laid on the adjoining circular plates and then synchronised with a bleep when the number 3 showed up on the leader.

Tim hovered nervously at the back of the cutting room. 'I think we've got the dissident scene down to about twelve minutes. Maybe it could lose another couple, but I can't see where.'

Fyodor did not respond but pulled his chair into the central position, where he could see the small screen most clearly, and shook a Gitane out of its packet. Elizabeth had been aware that Tim and the editors had not expected to see her. Fyodor had said nothing by way of explanation, but there had been something proprietorial in the manner in which he had escorted her in, which let the others know their relationship was more than that of producer and actress. Besides, she wasn't even in the scene they were about to look at. Fyodor had only told her at the last minute that they were going to Pinewood and there was, in the pit of her stomach, an uncomfortable feeling at being there at all. She sat on a high swivel chair by the door of the small room and fixed her eyes on the screen with unnatural intensity.

It was a scene that was entirely dependent on audience credulity. By now they must accept the Jupiterians not as a light-hearted piece of science fiction, but as an alien tribe. Some of their number, unknown to Lu Xun, have requested an independent meeting with the British Foreign Secretary. They inform him that they are dissidents, opposed to the ruling government of their planet, who have been sent on this mission to carry out any dangerous tasks where loss of life is expedient. Now they are safe, they do not wish to go back to their home where certain imprisonment awaits them, but want to set up an independent colony here on earth. He listens to their request with a sympathetic ear but, after they have left, contacts Lu Xun who insists that all must return. A Cabinet meeting is called to discuss the matter of sanctuary but the majority decision is that diplomatic relations with the planet must prevail over human – or even Jupiterian – rights. The dissidents are informed. The following day their dead bodies are discovered in the boarding-school which has been their temporary home in England; they have all committed suicide.

The editor punched a red button to stop the machine and the lights automatically switched on. There was an uneasy silence, nobody daring to proffer an opinion before Fyodor spoke. Surprisingly he turned to Elizabeth.

'What do you think, Lizzie?' he asked – a name he had never called her in public before.

She blushed. 'I was moved. It works. Sir Albert brings much more sympathy to the Foreign Secretary than there was in the script. It gives his dilemma an edge.'

The silence having been broken, Tim was anxious to assert himself. 'Yes, I had long discussions with him on that. We wanted to involve the audience in his impossible choice between politics and compassion.'

Fyodor looked at him and slowly shook his head. 'There is too much. It is a stage performance. If they want to see Sir Albert deliver graceful lines, they can go to the National Theatre.'

He turned to the controls and rewound the film. Then, spinning it forward again, he waved an admonitory finger at the screen. 'Too much, too much, too much. I need only three expressions from Sir Albert and the story is told. Look, there,' He stopped the Steenbeck on a freeze frame. 'There, compassion. But do we believe him?' He moved the film forward. 'And now, no need for words. You see, when he makes the phone call and Lu Xun answers. That is enough. We can tell from his face he has betrayed them. And the final Cabinet meeting. We have two, maybe three close-ups of ministers shaking their heads and we close with a shot when Sir Albert is thinking nothing. You will have one, won't you, Johnny?' He turned to the film editor with a complicit smile. 'Usually that expression before the slate when they are trying to remember their lines.'

'Yeah, plenty of those on Albert,' nodded the grey-haired veteran. 'Get us down can 20a, will you, Chris? We made up a little assembly of them for you to select from, sir,' he added with a knowing grin.

Tim was unable to disguise the undoubted fact that this came as news to him.

It caused their first row. Fyodor had sent the driver home and Elizabeth went to wait in the car while he finished some letters in his office. When he got in, she did not greet him and remained deliberately silent. At first he chose to ignore her, looking straight ahead at the traffic as he talked about staggered release patterns and upfront sales guarantees – matters, he knew, that did not interest her.

Then, abruptly, he swung the solid green Mercedes into a lay-by, occupied only by heavy trucks.

He turned to her 'Want a tea? They serve the best brew in Britain here.'

She was taken by surprise and just nodded mutely.

'Two sugars, yes?' he muttered as he got out of the car.

He came back with two steaming half-pint mugs. 'Fyodor' was printed on his in bold red capitals.

'How on earth did you get that?' she exclaimed, involuntarily breaking her silence.

'Oh, they have one for every name. Unfortunately "Elizabeth" was out; apparently she's driving that sixteen-wheeler behind us.'

She turned to look. There was no vehicle behind them, he was teasing her. She scowled at him.

'Some of my best thinking is done in this place,' he went on. 'And some of my most private phone calls. I come here a lot. They know me. Every Christmas I give them some money, enough to make sure they will still be here the following year. Last year they gave me this mug, with my name on it. It's always ready, nobody else is given it. But if you start talking to me again I may have them add your name underneath mine and then you can use it, too.'

'I don't want it, thank you very much,' she replied coolly.

Now it was his turn to remain silent.

'If you can be so generous to some gypsy serving tea from a caravan, how come you treat your director so fucking shabbily?'

'They're not gypsies,' Fyodor assured her. 'She's an old woman who used to do the trolley round at the studios. Only she was made redundant in the cut-backs. Now she operates this tea van with her husband. He was injured in the war so she's always supported him. And don't swear. It sours your face.'

'You can't control my language. Nor me for that matter.'

'Why are you rushing to protect Tim? He's done his job, done it rather well within the confines of his imagination. But now he is only slowing down the cutting room. Johnny has edited my last four films. He knows what I want, and his time and my money are wasted by Mr Dogfood and his servile flattery of Sir Albert. Do the car workers in Detroit want to listen to a declamatory speech about British foreign policy?'

'But it was in the bloody script.' This time she swore with measured deliberation.

'How else do you expect me to engage a knight of the

English stage? By giving him a script with a few grunts and glances that look like Bobby De Niro's leftovers?'

'That's so devious. No wonder they say that nobody works for you twice.'

'But they walk away rich the first time. Albert's agent got him three points – two more than I wanted to give. That'll give him a million dollars and more if the box office is what I expect.'

'Okay. But why do it to Tim? If you're so certain of everything why not direct the damn thing yourself?'

Fyodor drained the remainder of his tea. 'Too boring. Directing is just standing around waiting. For the weather, for the art department, for lights, for make-up, for the stars – especially the stars.'

His voice became more guttural and more insistent. '*I* make my pictures. Nobody else does. I read this bilge in the press and in movie magazines that says "this director did this" or "that director did that". They have no idea how the decisions are made. I decide on the script. I decide on the casting. I go through the sets with the production designer and tell him exactly how much money he can have. I decide on the final cut. In between I engage a man to stand all day on the studio floor and supervise what goes through the camera lens – and if I don't like it at rushes the next day, I tell him what I want instead. And when my films come out I have to read all this bullshit from so-called film critics who set out to interpret the director's motivation as if the film was something that came out of his brain like a dream every morning. Wait and see what they make of that dissident scene. Tim Lawrence will be praised for his understatement.'

'It does come out of some director's brains every morning,' she countered defiantly.

'About one per cent of the directors in the world. But people apply the *auteur* theory to every film they see because it is easier to pin every decision on the director rather than actually work out who might have done what.'

She refused to concede her ground. 'Okay, so Tim doesn't happen to be an *auteur*, but that's no reason to treat him like shit in front of other people.'

'Did I?'

'Yes, you did. He looked like a kid who had failed an exam.'

'Then I will apologise to him. But on one condition.'

'There you go again. You always have to make a deal. Nothing is straight with you.' She turned away from him and looked out of the car window. 'What condition?'

'That you kiss me.'

Elizabeth slowly brought her eyes round to look at him and shook her head. For the first time since she had known him his confidence seemed to take a step backwards. Satisfied, she moved closer to him and took the mug from his hand, placing it on the dashboard. She drew his head towards her and from the moment their lips met she left him in no doubt as to what she wanted.

'Where did you learn to make films?' she asked as they joined the motorway on the drive back to London.

'At my father's knee, in Budapest. He had a studio there, over forty years ago – nothing as big as Pinewood, more of a family business. He made good films, though. And after we had to get out in '56, and we came to England, he got it into his head that he wanted to film the complete works of Dostoyevsky. How do you think I got my name?' He held up his mug triumphantly. 'He was going to begin with *Notes from the Underground*. He wrote the screenplay himself but before he had completed it, he clasped his hands to his heart and fell to the floor. He died within the hour. Perhaps he knew he would never make the movie. How many Dostoyevsky videos do you see in the corner store?'

'You could still make it,' Elizabeth suggested. 'You owe it to him.'

'You're right. But today people do not make films, they make money. That's what I'm doing. And when I have enough, then I will make something that matters to me.'

'When will that be? How many millions away? Two? Ten? Twenty?'

'When my responsibilities are less and I can afford to indulge myself,' he said more gently.

They had come off the flyover and were driving east along Holland Park Avenue. Instead of turning left towards Elizabeth's apartment. Fyodor guided the car south into Kensington. It surprised her. The kiss had been a clear enough indication of how they might spend the rest of the afternoon and the speed with which he had tackled the M40 had seemed an equal affirmation of his intentions.

They drew up in a green and shady cul-de-sac just off Campden Hill. A sense of foreboding assailed Elizabeth for the second time that afternoon: she had been here before. A small group of women – the young ones in jeans and gaudy sweaters, the older more heavily made-up and competitively groomed, some holding little children by their hands, others leaning on prams – were assembled on the pavement by a wrought-iron gate.

Fyodor got out. Elizabeth tried to stay in the car but he came round to her door and opened it, taking her arm. Two of the women began to stare at them so she had no option but to join him on the footpath.

'Why have you brought me here?' she whispered.

'The time was right. I wanted you to learn that I didn't just count my life in millions.'

'But what about your wife?'

'It's all right. I telephoned her.'

'And what did you tell her?'

But before he could answer her question, a bell rang and the gate was eagerly opened. The infectious sound of children's laughter replaced the subdued murmurings of the mothers and nannies who moved forward towards the entrance. A joyful stream of small, ebullient girls – none much older than ten – spilled out onto the pavement. They wore matching dark green winter coats and scarves, although the day was mild.

One of them, a little shorter than the rest, with inky black hair and a gap in her front teeth, ran laughing towards Fyodor.

'I knew you were here, Daddy. You can't fool me. Mrs Starnes looks out from transition window and tells us who's come.'

Fyodor lifted her up in his arms and feigned sadness. 'And I wanted it to be a surprise. Mrs Starnes is a spoil-sport. She can never have been young herself.'

'Yes, she was,' insisted the child innocently. 'She was born in 1969, she told us. On the day the man landed on the moon.'

'That makes her ancient. Now, I've brought a younger friend to meet you. This is Miss Brown. She's an actress and she is in my new film. Elizabeth, this is Pola.'

The child loosened herself from her father's arms and made a modest bob as she took Elizabeth's hand.

Elizabeth was still slightly stunned. 'What did you do today?' she asked. She could think of nothing else to say.

'We had sums and spelling and we went on a nature walk in Hyde Park and, do you know, Miss Parker bought us all a lollipop at the ice-cream van – only you're not supposed to tell anyone.'

'I won't,' promised Elizabeth. 'But I knew already.'

'How?' asked Pola, and her father's look of surprise mirrored the child's question.

'On sunny days she used to do the same for us. I went to school here myself, not so many years ago.'

As she said the words Elizabeth could see herself in her school coat, carrying a muddy hockey stick and waiting for her nanny to come and collect her. It made her feel fraudulent and unreal standing beside Fyodor, as if her cashmere wrap and calfskin handbag and Jourdan shoes were somehow a costume for a school play. She resented the trick he had played on her in bringing her here. It betrayed the privacy of their affair and deepened the sense of unease about it that had never been very far from the surface of her emotions all day.

CHAPTER 9

Monday 10th March 1997

Sydney

'It's not even a feature film. It's a television programme. And a pretty lousy television programme at that. The research is shabbily selective, in fact it's bloody biased. I can point out half a dozen allegations the bastards make that the government has already dealt with – to the satisfaction of their community leaders, I might add. And it shows the true people of Australia as mean-minded and prejudiced. Where are the beaches? Where's the outback? Where's the cricket?'

Don Lugg, the Australian Minister of Information – known in the press as the Scarlet Pimpernel due to the waves of red hair that surfed off his brow – was also in charge of national film policy. He closed the file in front of him wih a sufficiently flamboyant flourish to indicate that there should be no further discussion of *The Boat People – Twenty Years On*.

'The Vietnamese don't play cricket,' pointed out Jenny Bates. She had no intention of being bullied into silent acquiescence. In fact she felt stimulated by the stormy approach of her federal adversary. The Director of the Australian Film Board was a dark-eyed woman in her mid-forties, her figure now as solid as her convictions. The natural tendency she had to dominate men had made both her marriages short-lived but her affairs all the more exciting. She had no family but she defended her films with the ferocity of a mother protecting her offspring.

'That's exactly one of their fucking problems, not that you'd know it from the film. You'd think Australia had become a chopstick society. We're talking about less than thirty-five thousand inhabitants of this city to whom we, as a caring society, offered the chance of a new life.'

As he spoke the Minister gestured with his arm towards the framed panoramic window of the Film Board offices. Seventy-two floors below them, on the ultramarine carpet of the south Pacific, rusting green ferries that bore the names of the wives of bygone British governors chugged between Circular Quay and Cremorne, Taronga Park Zoo and Kirribilli. The hump of the Harbour Bridge, like some prehistoric skeleton crouched in prayer, stretched out towards the Nordic helmets of Sydney Opera House.

The sight was too familiar, however, to have any beneficial effect on the minister's mood. He waved his finger accusingly at Jenny, annoyed that she should have chosen to challenge him in front of the rest of the assembled board of the great, the good and, especially, the rich. Lugg usually sent a civil servant to these meetings but, having been informed that the Cannes Festival Director, Renaud Callet, was about to arrive to finalise his selection, he had on this occasion decided to drive home the government line personally.

'What I want to see at the Fiftieth Cannes Film Festival – and our man in Paris has already had significant talks with their authorities on the subject – is something that represents the splendours, past and present, of this nation. What we need is another *Crocodile Dundee*. Not a bunch of people who turned up here ten minutes ago on a raft. And certainly not a crowd of koories on the rampage.'

'Koories?' inquired a nervous lady in a grey silk blouse, its high neck circled by three rows of pearls.

'Aborigines,' explained Jenny. Although she had no intention of endorsing *Aboriginal Revenge*, with its gory massacre of innocent white tourists on Dunk Island, she still had principles to protect. 'The ones who had been here for sixty thousand years when we arrived chained to our rafts. We used to lease our land from them, remember?'

'The ones we didn't even include in our census thirty years ago.' A bearded young man in an open-necked shirt with defiant wire glasses rallied to Jenny's cause. 'They used to be counted in with the marsupials: wallabies, kangas and koories.'

'They get special privileges,' the lady with the pearls was prepared to nail her colours to the mast now she knew what they were talking about. 'There are government handouts.'

'Handouts!' Jenny reiterated sarcastically. 'They are a wholly exploited people. They have no rights. Do you know that some of them still suffer from leprosy in this allegedly civilised country? No wonder you end up with a film like *Aboriginal Revenge*.'

The Minister decided to change his tack, fearful that Jenny might actually be serious about espousing the movie. He and his colleagues had seen it and all had agreed that not even the lefties on the Film Board would let this blood-bath be shown at Cannes.

'None of us round this table wants to wash our dirty linen in a foreign country – let alone at an international film festival,' he pleaded. 'It's an internal matter. That dingo movie did our system of justice no good at all. The government is anxious to give as much support as possible, providing you guys come up with a film worth supporting. We're not exercising censorship – that would be an un-Australian thing to do. We merely don't want to look like a lorryload of larrikins over there in Europe.'

'There's not a lot any of us can do about that,' Jenny pointed out. 'The French make their own selection in the end.'

Don Lugg, gradually succumbing to the realisation that he was not going to bluster his opponent into submission, tried a final flattering appeal to her patriotic sensibility.

'Listen, Jenny darling, I've been in politics long enough –and I'll be very surprised if I don't see you working in Canberra before your hair turns grey – to know that the French need only to be seen to make their own decision. We can guide them. Can I rely on you to make sure that I don't have to face the Prime Minister to explain why a pile of Australian arsewipe is on display in Cannes in two months' time?'

The Director of the Film Board composed her features thoughtfully for a moment and then relaxed them into a victorious grin. 'No worries, Don,' she smiled.

There was one message which Renaud Callet did not want to find waiting for him when he checked into the Bellevue Hotel in Sydney's Double Bay and it was presented to him at reception. 'Ring Lee and Waters, President of Warner Bros,' it read. 'Urgent.'

His annoyance was sufficient to make him oblivious to the status that the call had bestowed on him. The staff of the Bellevue were used to transient soap stars, rising pop singers and fading British television personalities, but the president of a Hollywood Studio – the emperor of an international court to which they had only recently gained a tenuous admittance – meant that Callet must be more than a mere Frenchman. Accordingly, added to the standard basket of fruit in Renaud's room, were two bottles of Hunter Valley Cabernet Sauvignon and a note of greeting from the manager.

He knew he had to deal with Burbank straight away. Before he left Hong Kong, a discreet call to the Chairman of the Festival in Paris and another to the foreign ministry had given him a base from which to negotiate. He lifted the phone and asked for the Burbank number, quite unprepared for the casual Australian mateyness of the operator.

'Are you a film star?' she asked. 'Should I know you?'

'No,' the Frenchman replied and then, warming to a friendly voice in an alien surrounding, explained, 'but I am the director of a film festival. So I meet a lot of people who make films, stars too.'

'Have you met Bud Booker? "Remove it or I'll remove you." I saw a clip of his new film on the telly last night,' she continued, seeming to have forgotten about Renaud's call. 'There'd be a lot fewer drug addicts lying around the streets of King's Cross if people like him –'

'I think I'm about to,' Renaud interrupted.

'About to what?'

'Meet Bud Booker. If I can get through to Warner Bros.'

'Putting you through now,' she replied, adding with a chuckle: 'Tell him if he wants to come round to my place we could crack open a few tinnies and a lot more besides.'

'Mr Callet, hold on, I'll check if he's here.' Leland's secretary unthinkingly intoned the familiar litany. Of course she knows whether he's there or not, thought Renaud, recalling the old Hollywood chestnut, 'What do you get if you cross a penguin with a William Morris agent? A penguin that doesn't return your phone calls.' However the alacrity with which Walters came on the line indicated he needed a fast answer.

'Renaud. How's Hong Kong? Still Chinese?'

'Still British, to be precise. But not for much longer. Actually I'm in Australia now.'

'Is that still British?'

'Anglo-American. They have the Queen of England's head on the banknotes but they call them dollars.'

'The best of both worlds,' observed Leland, his appetite for small talk now satisfied 'Have you seen the film?'

'Yes, I saw it.'

No studio chief ever asked directly what anybody else thought of a film. If they liked it, people said so unprompted. If they didn't, a plaudit for the lighting was the acceptable reply.

'Listen' – Leland sounded dangerously chummy – 'you know and I know it may not be a classic but there are lot of people out there who go for this sort of thing. It's going to do two fifty million domestic and Bud Booker's as hot as Saturn right now. I think you should consider what the ordinary French people might enjoy.'

Renaud found the advice bordered on the offensive. 'The Cannes Festival is not for the ordinary French people. It exists to set a world standard for the art of film and I do not think that *Black Cops Kill* sets a standard for anyone other than latter-day barbarians.'

There was a pause at the other end. 'So it's no go, uh?'

'I'd like you to come, Leland. I remember Warner Brothers generously celebrated their fiftieth anniversary at our festival. We have a debt to you. I am prepared to place the film on the second Saturday but outside of the competition. It is still a privileged category. It will be shown in the Palais.'

'I see.' Leland paused. 'So that would mean no prizes for Bud. Not even Best Actor?'

'We have a jury that selects the prizes. I am not sure that even if it were in competition they would select him. But I think I understand your problem. We can arrange a small *hommage* to Monsieur Booker at the Cinemathèque in Paris later in the year and, in anticipation of this, perhaps he would accept membership of the *Légion d'Honneur* – which we could bestow upon him at the Palais des Festivals in Cannes before the screening.'

Despite the excellence of the satellite link between Australia and America, Walters bellowed joyfully into the phone: 'Renaud, *mon ami*, you've got a deal.'

As he put the receiver down, Callet lay back on his bed relieved. Despite a relaxing and undisturbed overnight flight he was jet-lagged but too exhilarated to sleep. He undressed and stepped into the shower, anxious to taste the city as an anonymous individual before he resumed the mantle of Festival Director at dinner with Jenny Bates.

A residual, dominantly male image of Australia – peopled by beer-bellied bricklayers and stubbled sheep-shearers – that lay unsubstantiated in the back of his mind was dispelled almost the moment as he stepped out of the hotel. Double Bay appeared to be Australia's answer to Rodeo Drive in Beverly Hills. The shops were a cross between those of his native Paris and California. Only their names hinted at a less established lineage: Yvette's House of Flowers, Franco Di Roma, Mr Leon, Salon de Coiffure, and Adrienne and the Misses Bonney – the last, Renaud reflected, sounded more like a massage parlour than a boutique. Big blonde girls – broader and more muscular than their Parisienne counterparts – in backless tops and topless jeeps, patrolled the carefree streets, occasionally swooping into parking bays which seemed to become available at their whim. Although it was a Monday afternoon in March, the place had a heady holiday air and gave off the confident assertion that no longer did Australia need to keep looking uncertainly to Europe to set the style. It was just possible that Double Bay was the centre of the world.

Invigorated by the atmosphere, Renaud resolved to buy some souvenirs for the girls in the office. Most of the more notable designs in the shops were, however, French and there seemed little point in reimporting such goods as presents, so he settled for some cheaper, more frivolous garments, with gaudy drawings of the Harbour Bridge on them that seemed to catch the spirit of the place. Then on an impulse he decided to go for a swim and he sought out a sports shop to buy some trunks and a towel.

'Would you like a shark-proof cossie?' asked the man in baggy shorts behind the counter, without betraying a scintilla of a smile.

'Do I need one?'

The man glanced at his watch. 'You'll be all right,' he said. 'They'll have had their lunch by now. The beach is just through that little park on the right.'

It was virtually deserted, save for a woman reading a paperback. As Renaud stretched out in the brisk Pacific waters he felt comfortable and at home; it even looked like the Mediterranean with the houses running down to the wooded shore and the bay peppered with polished yachts at anchor. He reflected how simple it was that the brief, friendly conversation of a couple of strangers had managed to make him feel welcome on behalf of a continent.

As he turned to swim for shore he was convinced he saw a figure step rapidly back from the sunlight into the dark shadows of the trees. Ever since he had left the hotel he had had the feeling that he was being watched. But such was his sense of well-being that he did not permit this gentle paranoia to disturb him. In fact, it was a vaguely pleasurable sensation: he had not set out to look for anyone, but that did not mean they might not set out to look for him.

Reaching the small beach he glanced around and, seeing no one, lay down on his towel to catch the fast-weakening rays of the afternoon sun.

It might have been two minutes or maybe twenty before he awoke. The sun had gone down. Or had it? A lean man in brown corduroy trousers and a matching shirt, buttoned right up to the neck, with a blunt, upturned nose and thick glasses too small for his substantial head was standing over him.

'There's something you must see,' he said in a tone just short of desperation.

Renaud sat up and narrowed his eyes at the silhouette.

'I've arranged it for tonight. Don't tell those wankers at the Film Board. I know this projectionist in the Paddington Cinema. He'll run it for us after the last performance. Come at eleven.'

The stranger thrust something into Renaud's hand, then

retreated swiftly into the park before he could answer any questions.

Renaud looked down at the card.

'Tony Birch,' it read, 'Film Critic.' On the back was a crude sketch in pencil of the location of the cinema and the reminder, eleven o'clock, underlined several times.

Back in his hotel suite, he was surprised to discover a crate of Bollinger placed on the window seat. Did the Bellevue spoil all its guests so generously? But when he opened the card on top of the box he found a telexed message from Leland Walters – 'Have notified Booker and he is honoured and delighted. Here's a toast to a memorable Festival in which we will be privileged to participate.'

Well, that's one way to firm up a verbal contract, Renaud thought uncharitably as he started to get changed. He looked at his watch – 6.30. That would be 8.30 a.m. back in Paris. There would probably be no one in the office but he decided to telephone anyway. He rummaged in the bedside drawer for a code-book in order to dial direct and circumvent the friendly delay of the switchboard.

'*Bonjour. Festival du Film.*'

Although he had only been away for eight days, he found it pleasingly reassuring to hear a French voice.

'Hello, who's that?'

'This is Chantal Coutard.' She paused. 'Monsieur Callet, is that you? You're in Australia?'

'Yes, I've been swimming – in the sea. Can you believe that?'

'That's wonderful. It snowed in Paris last night. Still none in the Alps though. *France-Soir* says we should build a ski-slope in the Bois de Boulogne.'

Renaud laughed. 'Chantal, I've come across a film critic in Sydney. His name is Tony Birch. I wondered if we had anything in our files about him?'

'I'll have a look. Can you hold on?'

'Sure.'

Chantal crossed the empty office to a pile of cardboard boxes by the door and soon unearthed a large brown envelope marked 'Australia'. She returned to her desk with it.

'Birch *comme bouleau*?' she asked.

'Yes,' Renaud confirmed.

'I've found him. He's here but Madame Rivette has put a question mark against his name for the Fiftieth. He sometimes does radio, it says, but there are no articles . . . wait, there is something about the new wave in Australian cinema he's written. Their Film Board don't appear to approve of him. There's a note – I can't read the signature – saying he's the sort of person who tends to hang round directors. The journalist as publicist, you know the type.'

'I know the type. That's okay. I just wanted to check he wasn't some kind of weirdo. Anyway, how are you? Why are you in the office so early?'

'I'm preparing a new computer programme,' Chantal was pleased to establish her conscientiousness. 'We'll soon have all the delegates on disc – including your Mr Birch if you approve him.'

'I think I'm about to find out tonight. Goodbye, Chantal. Thank you. My regards to Madame. Only two months to go. Tell her to stay sane.'

'I will. Goodbye.'

Chantal put down the phone. As she watched the whitening street outside the window her imagination warmed itself at the thought of her daily pilgrimage to the Maschou Beach, where she went to sunbathe each lunchtime during the Festival. She was possessed of a desire to see Raoul again. Emotionally they had fallen apart but physically she felt the need for a man, and better a familiar one than an unfamiliar one. Apart from a brief call to see how she was after the robbery in January, she had heard nothing from him. His friend Didier had refused to be drawn on whether he was likely to be reinstated in the Drug Squad – Raoul had been accused of planting heroin on a suspect – but hinted his suspension was likely to become permanent.

On an impulse she dialled Le Mistral bar in Cannes. She knew he would be asleep but she wanted to talk to him. If he sounded accommodating she could fly down for a weekend; the Festival might even pay.

The phone rang for a long time. He was definitely asleep.

Eventually someone answered. 'Hello, hello . . . who is it? Hello.'

It was a woman's voice. Chantal lowered the receiver without speaking.

'Has anyone ever told you that you look like François Truffaut?'

Renaud pushed his hair back from his forehead with both hands and gave a gentle grimace. 'Nobody in Australia has.'

'That's because they've no idea who he is. I'm going to change all that at Christmas,' Jenny Bates pronounced. 'We're going to run a major retrospective of his films. Hurry up, Hal, what's on tonight?'

'A little kookaburra pâté, followed by some grilled koala. They'll throw one on the barbie for you, Renaud.'

Hal Stephenson, the Film Board publicity director, tried to keep a straight face as he read from the only menu at the table. It was not the first time he had employed this gambit with guests from abroad. Renaud looked at him uncertainly.

'If it's possible, I'd like to try some kangaroo.'

'You've come to the wrong state, mate,' laughed Hal. 'Seriously, you can't get it in New South Wales but it's legal food in South Australia – sheepburgers and rooburgers.'

Renaud could see he was telling the truth.

'What does kangaroo taste like?' he said.

'Extremely pissed off, I should imagine.'

Jenny Bates leant forward to intervene before Hal's one-man show took the floor. He was Rigoletto to her Duchess, but like all court jesters he seldom knew when enough was enough.

'If you like fish, I'll order for you,' she said.

Renaud was impressed by her motherly manner – it was direct and very different from that of the women he worked with. 'Go ahead,' he said.

'We'll start with Balmain Bugs – they're like a cousin of a crayfish – and then John Dory, the finest fish to be found in the South Pacific. And as many bottles of Chardonnay as Doyles can keep coming. Hurry them up, Hal, I've got an empty glass.

'So,' she said, turning forthrightly back to Renaud, 'how about *Aboriginal Revenge*?'

'I don't think so,' he replied, angling his head in apology. 'Too exploitative. If only they could have been less obvious. Righteous violence is getting to be a cheap trick.'

She drained her glass and nodded. 'My feeling exactly. But I needed it coming from you. Also it gets Canberra off my tits if you don't put it in the competition. We'll bring the boys over and let them have a romp around the film market. They'll probably make a fortune. And that Boat People thing puts me to sleep, *d'accord*?'

'Agreed.'

'So,' Jenny poured herself a full-to-overflowing refill of Chardonnay and came rapidly to the point, 'that leaves us with *Man of the Media* which has its shitty moments but is not at all bad. You got the cassette?'

'I like it. It's timely. We've had too many films about Australian history. There comes a moment when a nation has to deal with its present.'

'Right on,' she yelled delightedly, holding up her glass for a toast. 'They'll get a bit antsy in Canberra when they hear about it. You see, they don't really know about it yet – the guys had to shoot with a dummy script and a different title because they were afraid of injunctions –'

'From the government?'

'Nah, from Packer or Bennetts or Murdoch or whatever media mogul thought it was about him.'

'Which one is it about?' Callet inquired cautiously.

'None of them,' she reassured him. 'And all of them. You've seen it. Essentially it's about the law of the jungle. Big eats small. But inside this guy there's this primitive urge, he probably wants to demonstrate to his mother that he can outstrip his father. He's like some gladiator who goes round looking for impossible challenges because it's the way of life he has created for himself. And it becomes a hunger no satellite dish can satisfy – that's a line from the poster incidentally.'

'So Ken Turner is entirely fictional?'

'We call him Citizen Ken,' chipped in Hal.

'A promising actor, Ted Barlow,' Renaud observed, 'powerful, yet tender. The jury will be very interested in him.'

'I expect some of them will,' smiled Jenny, spearing a Balmain Bug with her fork.

Tony Birch was pacing nervously outside the darkened

Paddington Cinema, taking rapid puffs on a filter-tipped cigarette. He didn't even bother to greet Renaud.

'I thought you weren't coming. Follow me. We've got to go in by the back,'

They went up an unlit metal staircase at the rear. It reminded Renaud of an old Godard movie where the hero gets so enraged at the way a film is being projected that he leaves his seat, runs round outside the cinema and climbs up some back stairs to the booth where he attacks the projectionist.

An overweight, elderly man in a cardigan was perspiring like a forger as he rewound a roll of film.

'They do this automatically in Hoyts' cinemas,' he muttered to no one in particular.

Birch did not introduce them. Instead, he asked Renaud, 'Do you have twenty dollars?'

The Frenchman pulled a bill out of the wallet in his inside pocket and Birch handed it to the man.

'Come on,' he said, 'we can sit in the balcony.'

As they brushed through the curtain, Renaud thought the time had come for an explanation.

'What is all this? I'm here in a semi-diplomatic capacity. I don't want to get involved in any sort of scandal.'

'There will be an almighty one eventually,' sniggered Birch as he lit another cigarette. 'Just don't worry. I'll explain later. We can't waste time now, Roy has to catch the last bus home.'

Renaud was about to suggest that he would be happy to part with another twenty dollars to get Roy a taxi when the lights dimmed and the old-fashioned velvet curtains parted. A breezy Oriental melody played over a montage of lyrical shots of red poppies, swaying rhythmically in the breeze as if in time to the music.

The lyricism was short-lived. What followed was the most stomach-wrenching scene that Renaud had ever witnessed on film. The setting was Thailand. A Chinese couple, a man and a woman, were seen wandering through an impoverished village, knocking at the doors of huts, clearly in search of someone. A local woman eventually admitted them and, after some bartering, allowed them to take away her baby in exchange for a handful of notes. It appeared, from their assurances to her, that they were only borrowing the child. This was not the case. Once clear of the settlement they undressed the screaming little girl. The man then took out a knife from his bag and plunged it into her belly.

In a wider shot the grotesque couple started to disembowel the infant. The camera moved closer to show them stuffing packets of what appeared to be heroin into her stomach. It was a gruesome, explicit shot. They sewed up the wound, wrapped the baby in grubby clothes, unstained by blood, and set off. The camera cut to their arrival at a border post between Thailand and Malaysia where a sympathetic guard waved through the tired mother and her sleeping infant.

Birch leaned across with an authoritative whisper. 'The baby has to look as if it's asleep so they have to get across the border within a few hours of killing it or its face will be the wrong colour.'

'This is fiction?' asked Renaud.

'Fiction based on fact,' came the sombre reply.

The screen was filled with a close-up of a live chicken clucking desperately, as if aware of its impending fate. A man dressed like a monk seized it and cut off its head with a sword. The body was wrapped in tissue paper and the blood drained off into what seemed to be a bowl of wine. The man looked at the other, much younger, Chinese men in the room.

'After you join the Hung family, you will remain loyal and faithful.' he warned them. 'The wicked and treacherous will die like this cock.'

With the same knife he made a cut in the middle finger of the left hand of each of those present, collecting their dripping blood in the bowl. They were then all obliged to drink from it. After each had sworn a mumbled, liturgical oath, he beckoned them to sit down and listen to him.

'We Triads are not criminals,' he said. 'We are the legitimate rulers of China. Three hundred and fifty years ago we fought to preserve the Ming dynasty from the Manchu terrorists. A cell of Buddhist monks developed the art of Kung Fu to defend themselves but one of their number, Ma Ning Yee, betrayed them. He it is whom we execute in this symbolic slaughter. But it will be you who will die if ever you betray a fellow Triad. Remember your history. We helped Dr Sun Yat

Sen overthrow the Manchus and declare China a republic in 1911. He was a Red Pole – a Kung Fu expert – and so was the noble General Chiang Kai-shek. We fought for them against the Communists and we will do so again.

'But to wage that war we need money. Do not feel guilty if you are asked to trade in goods that you despise. It was the English who taught us. The Chinese emperors tried to ban opium, but the English East India Company forced it on us. That was how they built their empire. Always remember that. Not just the British. It was the French who set up the opium distribution network in the fifties to finance their war in Vietnam. And the American CIA helped the South Vietnamese to grow and export heroin in the seventies. We are not doing anything that these three so-called civilised countries did not show us how to do.'

'The dialogue's a bit starchy,' Birch observed, 'but it puts things in context.'

Renaud said nothing.

The film switched back to the young couple who had murdered the baby. They were now in western clothes, back home in their Hong Kong apartment. Two policemen moved swiftly up the stairs and knocked urgently at their door. At first it looked as though they were going to be arrested. But shortly it became apparent that the man was doing business with the Chinese sergeant who had taken out some money to pay for the heroin. The sergeant was recognisably the monk who had conducted the initiation ceremony.

'There are more millionaires in the Royal Hong Kong police than there are in the Royal Sydney Yacht club,' confided Birch. 'That's what happens when you have a command structure with a lot of *gweilo* officers who don't speak the language of their men.'

'*Gweilos*?' asked Renaud.

'White devils,' came the rejoinder.

The police sergeant was now entering a shabby hotel. A gaunt young man, European, in his late teens or early twenties, opened the door to his room and silently accepted a parcel from him. He went immediately into the bathroom and took something out of his soap-bag. It was a contraceptive. He opened the top and carefully filled it from one of the packages containing the heroin. When he had repeated the process with a dozen more, he joined them together so that they looked like a string of white sausages. Then he tried to swallow them. At first he failed and was violently sick. On the fifth attempt he succeeded.

'It's the most effective way of getting the stuff through customs,' Birch pointed out. 'Sometimes the condoms burst and the carrier is poisoned. Not a pleasant death, but a just one – rather like an assassin being blown apart with his own bomb.'

The police sergeant, as controller, checked onto the same Cathay Pacific flight as the carrier. They did not acknowledge each other. In fact the sergeant, now in plain clothes and looking like a well-heeled Chinese businessman, sat in Marco Polo Class. Their destination was Sydney. The young man, an Australian, passed easily through immigration; the sergeant was more closely questioned but, as a British Commonwealth citizen, he had every right to enter. The film director was playing with the emotions of the audience here. After the earlier scenes there was a natural desire to see these criminals being caught, but set against this was the empathetic challenge of outwitting authority – especially customs.

Both men, still giving each other a wide berth, went through the green, Nothing To Declare, channel. Both were stopped and their luggage was thoroughly searched. The sergeant was allowed to carry on but the Australian was taken away for a strip search. He protested his innocence vigorously. It seemed clear that the officials knew that something was amiss, but nothing was found and he was permitted to proceed. The men were seen checking into different hotels: the sergeant had a corner suite of the Regent overlooking the Harbour Bridge, while the young Australian took a room in a cheap place in Oxford Street.

A day later, he telephoned his controller to tell him that the stuff had safely worked its way through his system. Now it was time for the Chinese White No. 4 – the purest heroin possible – to work its way into the systems of other people, in some instances lethally. The sergeant came to collect the drugs and paid off his courier in a sullen, dismissive manner – almost as if he had contempt for the man's complicity.

The second half of the film began with some travel brochure scenes of sunny Sydney which undoubtedly would have pleased the Minister of Information; surfers on Bondi Beach, sun-blessed children playing tennis in the parks, families with picnics watching a Test Match. At night the city turned into a brightly lit parade: laughing groups of people dining in outdoor restaurants, couples strolling along the brash and blaring streets of King's Cross were interpolated with shots of jazz groups and alternative comedy acts in the late night coffee shops of Darlinghurst.

Then, in a discothèque, electric with lasers fencing to the beat of the band, the camera slowly weaved through the dancers, swaying like carefree poppies, towards an iron-gated lift. It travelled down into the basement where, in a shabby, smoke-filled room, men were gambling frenetically. They were all Chinese. On the wall the symbolic triangle – one side for earth, one for heaven, one for man – confirmed that this was the headquarters of the 14K Triad group, so called because their founding address was at No. 14 Po Wah Road, Canton. The Hong Kong police sergeant, clearly dominant as the Red Pole of the group, was holding an intense meeting round a table.

What they were plotting was tantamount to guerrilla warfare. The main enemy was not the Australian police but other Triads. The action moved onto the mean streets of Sydney where rival Chinese gangs fought for control not only of the heroin trade, but prostitution, illicit gambling and protection racketeering. The last was backed up by vicious retribution. The son of one shop owner who refused to pay had his hand chopped off. There were outbursts of unbridled urban battles between armed youths. After a hectic chase through the streets a Chinese boy, no older than fifteen, wielding an Uzi sub-machine-gun, shot dead three members of a rival group.

One of them was slow in dying. He made it back to his local neighbourhood. His friends, seeing there was nothing more they could do for him, offered him the soothing balm of a heroin injection. The camera panned down from the needle in his arm onto the spreading bloodstain on his shirt, then edged closer until it filled the screen. Gradually the vermilion picture dissolved to the opening shot of swaying red poppies which slowly faded to black. The velvet curtains closed with the finality of those at a crematorium.

'They often use under-age kids to do the killing,' said Birch knowledgeably. 'That way, if they're caught, they usually get off with a lighter sentence. Lovely people. It's not completed yet. What do you think of it?'

Renaud felt distinctly nauseated as he rose on his feet. 'Is it based on verifiable facts?' he enquired unsteadily.

'Totally – only in reality things are much worse than that,' the film critic replied, as if he gleefully relished the idea. 'Want to meet the director?'

'Sure.'

At first Renaud thought that the club they had entered was the one in the film. He looked cautiously around for the iron elevator but it was reassuringly absent. Also, unlike those in the cinema discothèque, the majority of the couples dancing together were men.

'The Kakadu is gay and straight,' explained Birch, as if reading his mind. 'Like so many of us.'

He led Renaud to a table where the noise was less punishing. A pale, thin-featured man, certainly no older than twenty-five, his dark hair gathered back in a small ponytail, was sitting with a bottle of Coca-Cola and an empty glass in front of him. He rose politely to greet them.

Birch introduced him. 'This is Vincent Wall. He made the film. It was his first.' He indicated Renaud. '*Voici le délégué-général du cinquantième Festival du Film de Cannes*. He liked it.'

'Renaud Callet,' said Renaud, offering his hand and sitting down on the padded mock-leather bench beside the youthful director. 'Like is the wrong word. I was shocked, sickened.'

'Pretty hairy stuff, eh?' said Vincent. 'I was too nervous to see it with you. Some of the scenes look a bit amateurish but we hadn't the money for retakes. I thought I might end with a freeze frame of that baby's face.'

Renaud nodded. 'That would work well.' Turning to Birch, he asked, 'can I have a whisky – a big one?'

'Are you going to put it in the Festival?' demanded Birch inquisitorially, as if it were a condition on which depended his getting the drink.

'Yes, I think so,' said Renaud, 'in fact, yes definitely. We need films with that sort of power.'

'You'll get a lot of flak from our government. And the Film Board. They know nothing about it. They'll deny the lot – until they get to Cannes. Then Jenny will support us.'

'I'm used to a lot of flak. Cannes needs its headlines to survive. Now can I have my drink?' He turned to Vincent. 'What inspired you to make it?'

The young man emptied the remains of the Coca-Cola into his glass. His hand trembled as he did so. He stared out at the dancers. 'I had a brother. He was used as a courier. Made the mistake of getting caught in Malaysia. They executed him. Not a pretty end – they've gone back to the old methods. He was tied to a wooden cross in the prison and a gunman shot him from behind. Being a Buddhist, the executioner's not allowed to take life, so he has to pretend he's aiming at the board.'

'Did he know? Did you speak to him?' Was he guilty? Renaud felt a little embarrassed by his own questions.

'He'd never even heard of Triads,' Vincent replied. 'He was a cricketer, on tour with his college team in the Far East. He was going to play for New South Wales one day, maybe even for Australia. They hollowed out the handle of his bat and put the stuff in it before his team left Hong Kong for Malaysia. And then they tipped off the customs there because the authorities already knew a consignment was on board that flight. The big load got through and he was the stool pigeon caught with a smaller amount. It's a tactic the Triads quite often use. Brian was as pure as the driven snow.'

They both sat for a while observing the dancers, not speaking. Renaud broke the silence. 'Has it got a title yet?'

'Yes,' said Vincent quietly, '*Poppy Day*.'

CHAPTER 10

Wednesday 19th March 1997

London and New York

'Never any more,
While I live,
Need I hope to see his face
As before.
Once his love grown chill,
Mine may strive:
Bitterly we re-embrace
Single still.

Was something said,
Something done,
Vexed him? was it touch of hand,
Turn of head?
Strange! that very way
Love begun:
I as little understand
Love's decay.'

After she finished speaking Elizabeth held her gaze, mentally bowed but physically unblinking, towards the half-open door at the back of the chill and cheerless hall. Her sloppy clothes –navy blue sweater two sizes too large, grey track-suit pants, white sneakers and pink leggings – made her look more like a dancer than an actress.

A pencil of light dimly illuminated two people at a desk in the middle of the dark auditorium. 'Thank you, Miss Brown, very good,' muttered a woman in a black checked suit, her iron-grey hair styled severely short. 'Apart from RADA, you haven't done any stage work before?' she enquired without looking up.

'No, I haven't,' Elizabeth replied truthfully. 'But now I feel the need to.'

'This film you play the nurse in, *Jupiter Landing*,' continued the woman, reading from a sheet of paper on the desk, 'when does it open in London?'

'I'm not sure. Some time after the Cannes Festival. June perhaps.'

The woman turned to a crew-cut man with a lean, whippet figure and coiled yellow scarf who was sitting beside her. 'About the time we reach the Phoenix, if it's free,' she remarked. 'I suppose she might get some publicity.'

He scratched his head, clearly absorbed in a different train of thought. Then he looked up at Elizabeth. 'Why did you choose that poem? Most other girls did something directly from *Lear*. Shakespeare wrote some quite good speeches for Cordelia, you know.'

'I do know,' she felt her face flush and looked down at her feet to try and hide the fact. 'I just wanted to express what she might be feeling using other words.'

'Are you implying she had an incestuous relationship with her father?' The woman sounded not a little aggressive.

'Father-daughter, daughter-lover,' Elizabeth grinned deliberately at the man. 'I felt Cordelia's rejection was as strong as that of a jilted lover. I was just . . . I don't know . . . searching for her state of mind. I'm not sure if emotions are things that are already inside us waiting to be released, or whether we acquire them, like new clothes, when we need them. She could have hated her father and just not cared.'

'Is this sort of rejection something you've personally experienced?' The man was showing decided interest.

Elizabeth thought for a moment. 'No,' she said, 'only something I've observed.'

'Thank you, Miss Brown,' the woman intoned conclusively. 'Next. Irene Douradas.'

Elizabeth gathered up her bag, jumped down from the stage and made her way towards the door. As she passed the director he caught her briefly by the wrist and just nodded.

The gesture sent a thrill through her and when she stepped from the gloom of the Notre Dame Hall into the dazzling March light of Leicester Street she shivered with excitement.

'I thought we might eat lunch.'

She knew who it was before her eyes could adjust to see.

'I thought you were at the studio.'

Fyodor had been leaning against his car and came forward to embrace her. He was wearing a tailored blue overcoat and white silk scarf. She kissed him on the cheek.

'It's only a quarter to twelve,' she pointed out.

'I won't tell if you don't tell,' he smiled. 'Just like you didn't about auditioning for Ophelia.'

'Cordelia,' she corrected him. Then, anxious to change the subject, she suggested, 'Chinese?'

'We should be safe,' he remarked. 'There's been drama out here as well. While I was waiting for you a couple of police cars arrived and they took away three Chinese guys from the place next to the See Woo Supermarket. They kicked up a hell of a stink. The police carried away a box of what I suspect was monosodium glutamate.'

As they walked along Lisle Street, he enquired casually, 'How did it go?'

'Not bad – for a beginner.'

'It's good to test a lot. Some actors perfect the art of reading for a part – but when we cast them, they're no use. All they can do is read, not perform. Anyway, you can't do it. It clashes with the Oscars.'

She halted, annoyed. 'How did you know?'

'I asked one of the other girls going in.'

'I only said I'd come if I wasn't working.' She could see the lie float from her mouth, a puff of warm breath in the icy air.

'You promised,' insisted Fyodor.

She caught a refracted glimpse of his imploring expression in a shop window. Once it had enchanted her; now it just vexed her.

Robert looked at himself in the dressing-room mirror, circled with naked light-bulbs, and dabbed some tan powder on his nose and chin to take away the shine. He resisted the temptation to apply any of the variegated sticks of make-up that were ranked like soldiers on the table in front of him. Was it possible to paint away depression, he wondered. As he gazed at his over-groomed appearance he didn't particularly like what he saw. Relationships may be born together, he thought, but they die apart.

And theirs was dead. Ever since Blacklist Thursday, as they both half-jokingly referred to it, the unspoken had insidiously taken over from what was spoken in their life together. Outwardly little had changed. The argument could have been a mere blemish on a harmonious landscape for all that was said. They had made love that night with an exultation fuelled by their division. It was the one time when Tanya exercised sovereign power over him. When their bodies were liberated from their minds there was little contest: she could make him feel dominant or dominated, mistress of the realms of his senses. Following the item on *Hair* in *Arts Action* she teasingly labelled herself his 'chocolate-flavoured treat' – a line from one of the songs in the show.

When they had sex she would repeatedly ask him if he loved her and he would say he did – a cheap reply that now demanded an expensive penance. In a pathetic way he still worried about love, or lack of it. His university affairs had been passing infatuations, although he had often been hurt when they ended, rubbing shoulders with the green devil of jealousy. One night he had stood, shivering and unseen, outside the apartment of the girlfriend who had rejected him, just for the masochistic need to watch her new lover arrive and fail to leave.

But an experience at Princeton had revealed to him that there remained some higher emotional plateau on which he had yet to set foot. One morning he had been walking to lectures across the campus, discussing a football game with his classmate, Hutton. He became aware, as he held forth on the role of the running back, that his discourse was falling on unresponsive ears. Hutton was still with him, stride for stride, but that was all. His attention had travelled ahead to a distant figure in the clearing autumn mist – Lynne, Hutton's girlfriend, on her way to the same lecture hall. Hutton hastened the pace and Robert had tried to keep up with him until his friend could feign it no longer and had broken into a run. When Robert eventually caught up with the couple they were just holding each other, not kissing, not talking, but protected from the world by some mutual aura that no other human could penetrate or disturb.

He realised now that part of his desire to have an affair with Lynne had been to see if that magic would transfer to him. But it hadn't. Indeed he had known, for most of their time together, that he was a temporary custodian of her affections which, eventually, he would have to return to Hutton. One day, he thought, it will happen to me. But it never had. And he had found himself reconciled to that fact, believing that such scales of passion must be the preserve of the very young, or the very pure, or just the very lucky. He had lusted and laughed and lost enough in New York to find wafting pleasures in a continuum of relationships.

With Tanya things were worse. He had acquiesced in her intensity and now everything he might have said or done would be held up to him as innately fraudulent. Many of the things about her that he had initially found exciting had imperceptibly been transmuted into indifferent dross or, worse still, annoying irritants. The perfume that had sufficiently beguiled him to make him sleep clutching her pillow when she left for an early shoot now left a sickly pall in the bathroom. Her outfits, once defiantly original, seemed cheap and childish. Even the way she walked, with a lilting swing in her step – the pimp-roll as Tom Wolfe had called it – now just looked like showing off. Her zappy charm curdled before him. It was as if a Cubist painting he had once admired for its startling originality had broken down into elements that meant nothing.

The more he tried not to signal this change, the more strongly she seemed to promote those aspects of herself that he found increasingly unlovable. He remained a traitor within her camp, anxious to confess his guilt and come clean about the unilateral termination of their affair. But the coward inside him hoped that his unresponsive apathy would cause her to find someone more appreciative elsewhere and relieve him of the dreaded confrontation. Only one of them had committed any moral crime and it was Robert.

'Do you want to shoot him with the mirror behind him, or in front of all those cards and telegrams?'

It was a question that Robert had been asked more than a hundred times during his professional career and it was a question to which there was no correct answer. At this moment, however, he welcomed it as an immediate problem that would temporarily terminate his gloomy rumination on more lasting ones. The star's dressing-room, backstage at the Plymouth Theatre, had been built eighty years ago, when nobody had anticipated the need to accommodate any television crew that might have been sent round to interview the great John Barrymore.

Robert thought for a moment. 'The mirror's a bit of a cliché – let's do it the other way.'

'We'll have to move around some of this clutter on the wall. We can't have a great heart sticking out of his head.' The cameraman preferred mirror shots.

'Wait until he comes offstage. Let him decide. You know how touchy these people are.'

Whether his last remark was overheard by the returning occupant was something which the latter chose not to disclose. Instead dissembled shock was the designed response of the craggy face and noble Roman nose that now came round the door.

'A film crew! What are you doing here? How did you get in?'

Robert stood up. 'Mr Montillion, I'm Robert Barrett, from *Arts Action*.'

'Of course you are, dear boy,' said Edgar Montillion, his expression changing to a professionally beatific smile.

'I thought the publicity agents for the production had told you we were coming. Your dresser let us in. He said you wouldn't mind.'

'My dears, delighted. It must have slipped my mind during the show. So much to carry in so minuscule a vessel. Where is Jeremy?' He called through the door: 'Jeremy, some fine wine and victuals for these doughty mechanicals.'

His dresser, a small, melancholy-looking man in a fawn dust-jacket, had anticipated the command – which sounded like a familiar one – and arrived with a two-litre flask of Californian Chablis and a tube of paper cups.

'How many?' he enquired.

'Enough for all,' insisted the star. 'I expect you would like to film me in front of the mirror. The right profile is probably the less displeasing. Jeremy, make good the lights. Feel free to move my effects, within reason. I have a call of nature to obey.'

He disappeared into the bathroom. Jeremy gave Robert a knowing wink and proceeded to dispense the wine. 'Do him quickly while he's on a high,' he suggested. 'Later he can get a little listless.'

The part of the celebrated English actor on Broadway was an established theatrical role in itself. They came, they were seen, they conquered. For one brief year, on occasions longer, they were the toast, the butter and the marmalade of the town. It began with the import of a sure-fire West End hit which had already received a sufficient rave from the *New York Times* critic, on his annual pilgrimage to London, to underwrite the insurance policy of bringing it to the States. But, however strong the play, the New York public had a limited appetite for writers; they needed stars. So whoever was chosen to take the title role found himself in an automatically elevated position that nothing in his theatrical career would ever match again: a binge of publicity, invitations to parties from people he had only ever read about in gossip columns, by virtue of the fact that they had now read about him in gossip columns, joyously deferential treatment in restaurants (where most of the waiters were, themselves, out-of-work actors), even, if he timed it right by arriving hard on the heels of the coach parties, a burst of applause as he entered Sardi's and, as a memento at the end of that year, to prove to himself and to his grandchildren that it hadn't been a dream, a Tony Award to take back to Britain.

So it was with Edgar Montillion, renowned for his performance – 'machiavellian and magnificent' according to *Time* – in the title role of *Piper*, a musical based on 'The Pied Piper of Hamelin'. The production had broadened its appeal to an increasingly adult audience because, some wrote, it emphasised the perfidy of the town government in failing to honour its bargain but more probably because it sent people home with tears in their eyes and tunes in their ears, humming the rewarding sound of a hit. Secretly the producers looked forward to Montillion going home, too. The part could be improved by a tenor with more voice and less ham.

He returned from the lavatory, looking perceptibly flushed, and sank into his chair with the command, 'Commence!'

'Running,' muttered the cameraman.

'Are you sorry to be leaving the show?' Robert began, knowing that this was intended to be a gentle chat of which no more than forty seconds was likely to be used on air.

'They say it might close without me,' confided Montillion with a penitent look of utter sincerity, 'and that would make me very, very sad.'

The interview went well. In fact, the item was just an excuse to get the hit song from the show – 'Munch on, crunch on, take your nuncheon, breakfast, supper, dinner, luncheon' – with the full cast onto the programme without having to pay Equity and Musicians' Union extract fees. But Montillion was an able and amusing raconteur. When Robert had suggested that nuncheon was a conveniently made-up word – like Edward Lear's runcible spoon – the actor had produced a dictionary with a flourish to prove that it was indeed old English for a light meal.

'New York will miss you,' Robert commented as he concluded the interview.

'Oh, to be in England, now that April's there. But never fear, I shall return,' came the MacArthur-like reply, although both of them knew this was unlikely.

'That was excellent,' Robert leant across and told him when they cut the camera. He habitually said that, but this time he meant it as well.

'You'll stay for a noggin and a nuncheon?' asked Montillion anxiously, as if uneasy about being left on his own.

'I'd better get back,' said Robert, thinking of Tanya, 'I've got to –'

'Yes?'

'Well, a noggin would be nice. I've got a nuncheon waiting for me.'

'I had a feeling you knew what it was, really. Sign of an honest reporter, let the star have the limelight. Goodbye, my dears, well met,' he shouted after the departing camera crew.

After they left he turned to Robert. 'And now, some more substantial nectar. Jeremy keeps the horse piss for those frightful people who come round afterwards. Actors from soap operas with nothing to commend them but their hairlines, overslimmed crones who think that throwing their millions into opera companies and museums somehow gives them a passport into the world of art, stiff-suited senators with wives who used to be hostesses on short-haul airlines and have never managed to rid themselves of the smile, all of them sit here, night after night, hoping for an encore or something. But a glass of warm white Gallo soon spins them out into the street.

> 'All the little boys and girls,
> With rosy cheeks and flaxen curls,
> And sparkling eyes, and teeth like pearls,
> Tripping and skipping, ran merrily after,
> The wonderful music with shouting and laughter.'

He sang spontaneously as he made his way back to his bathroom, returning with a bottle of Polish vodka, barely a quarter full.

'Fine fuel for a musical,' he observed, pouring an over-generous measure into Robert's paper cup. 'Steadies the nerves and speeds up the timing. Just the tonic, which we have none of, in case you were wondering.'

Robert shook his head politely. 'You don't actually drink that stuff during the show?'

'How else do you think I get through it? I've done it a thousand times before. It's not grand opera, you know. Once you've heard these songs for a month or two they're only fit for Muzak in an elevator. But the old potato juice' – he tapped the vodka bottle – 'still manages to give a charge.'

'Have you drunk all that?'

'Most of it. Jeremy will have swiped some. You know, when Richard Burton was doing *Camelot* here he bet a friend of his that he could drink a bottle of vodka during the matinée and another that same night without his Guinevere – darling

Julie Andrews as you will recall – without her noticing. So he did just that, both bottles. And after the evening show the friend asked Miss Andrews for her opinion of Rich's performance and she replied: "A little better than usual, I thought."'

His face creased with laughter at his own story. He took another substantial slug of neat vodka and repeated the last line to himself: 'A little better than usual, I thought,' adding, after a swallow, 'now, cockie, what's the problem?'

Robert looked round to see if somebody else had joined them. They were alone. From that he deduced that he must be 'cockie'.

'Problem?' he repeated.

'Your eyes.' Edgar nodded towards him. 'Dead man's eyes – something very wrong there. Saw it from the moment I came into the room. That's the basis of acting, you know – observation. Have you ever watched a man hobble down the street with a stick and wondered whether he was recovering from a skiing accident or crippled for life? The answer isn't in his limp; it's in his eyes. Did your mother die recently?'

'No,' Robert replied suspiciously, 'about seven years ago.'

'Can't be that, then,' continued the actor, refilling Robert's cup. 'Anyway, I'm not an astrologer, nor a psychiatrist come to that. Going through a divorce?'

For some reason, barely explicable to himself, Robert was seized by the desire, even the need, to let the man into his confidence. Like strangers on a train, he knew they would probably never meet again but an all-pervading revelation came over him at that very moment that he had bottled up his feelings for so long now that Montillion was somehow the genie of their necessary release.

So he told him about Tanya.

The older man listened receptively, only interrupting to return to his bathroom for a fresh bottle of vodka.

'I don't quite know why I'm bothering you with all this,' Robert concluded, 'except you asked.'

Edgar Montillion let loose a theatrical sigh. 'It is the terrible deception of love that it begins by engaging us in play, not with a woman of the external world but with a doll fashioned in our brain – the only woman moreover that we have always at our disposal, the only one we shall ever possess.'

'I'm not quite sure that I follow you,' said Robert, 'and, if I do, I'm not quite sure that's true.'

'It's all right, cockie. Wasn't me that said it. Marcel Proust. *Remembrance of Things Past* – a lot of common sense in there. You seem to be looking for a piece of theatre, not a slice of life. Love as a dramatic device. We all believe in it because it's ground into our formative bones. But it's not real. It's an author's trick, a brilliant agent for tragedy. Take Dr Zhivago – Lara and he find this spiritual oneness for a few fleeting weeks and then she spends the rest of the book searching for him. And when at last she finds him, he dies of a heart attack before they can even speak. Aida – passionate about Radames. So what does she do? Sneaks into the vault where they've walled him up in the belief that the angel of death will take them to eternal happiness in heaven.

'*Di morte l'angelo radiante a noi s'appressa,*' sang Montillion. '*O terra, addio; addio valle di pianti.*'

He paused for a moment in reflection. 'It's evident to all except the irrationally insane that we need that sort of love like we need a firing squad. Look at Ophelia – mad, drowned, gone. Romeo and Juliet, the definitive romance by the master. But he allowed them just one night together.'

He stood up and stared in the mirror. 'Night's candles are burnt out, and jocund day stands tiptoe on the misty mountain tops; I must be gone and live, or stay and die.' He froze for a moment, and turned to Robert with a look of despair. 'Then what?'

'Immortality?'

'It can come cheaper.'

Robert by now was considerably emboldened by the quantities of neat vodka he had consumed. He rose unsteadily and from some cavern in his unconscious brain the words came almost automatically.

'Take him and cut him out in little stars,
And he will make the face of heaven so fine
That all the world will be in love with night,
And pay no worship to the garish sun.'

The ageing thespian applauded him. 'Very good. A show-business reporter who knows his Shakespeare.'

'Not really. It was my father's favourite quotation. They were the words that Robert Kennedy used about his brother. He spoke them at the Democratic convention the year after the assassination. I was named after him.'

'Much better as a totem of brotherly love than in the mouth of the teenage Juliet. I always feel the Bard barked with posterity in mind. His eloquence was too frequently squandered on the picayune. Go now, to your Tanya. Better to endure the squalls of a Manhattan apartment than the eternal silence of Aida's vault.'

'Are you sure?' asked Robert, taking the outstretched hand. 'Wasn't it Shakespeare who wrote "take away love and our earth is a tomb"?'

'No,' mumbled Montillion, shaking his head. 'Wrong there, not Shakespeare.'

The venerable actor closed his eyes, as if deep in thought, but the rhythm of his breathing appeared to indicate he had fallen asleep. Robert put a hand against the wall to steady himself, then quietly let himself out of the door. 'Well, thanks for the interview. And the drinks. And the advice,' he whispered.

But, as he made his fragile way down the steps from the dressing room, he could hear the awakened Montillion continuing their conversation. 'It was Browning, the last great romantic. All poetry is putting the infinite within the finite.' His voice grew louder. 'And it was Oscar Wilde who said: "When you really want love, you will find it waiting for you." Funny how the gays always have the most insight.'

'Nothing will come of nothing, speak again, speak again, speak again.' The words rang in Elizabeth's brain, louder and louder. She woke with a start. At first she thought it was part of her dream. But the ringing didn't stop. It was the phone. She turned on her bedside light – a quarter to five.

She made her way into the hall. It must be her mother; she never could calculate the time zones.

'It's the middle of the night, Mummy,' she croaked grumpily into the receiver.

'I know,' came a familiar voice.

'Fyodor?'

'Yes. Can I come round?'

'No. Why? What will your wife say?'

'She's used to dawn shoots.'

'But we've wrapped.'

'The model unit haven't. I need to talk. I want to see you.'

'America?'

'Yes. I've spoken to some friends. We can stay with them on our way to California. You'll love it.'

'I told you – the play,' she reminded him.

'I rang the director last night – our casting people know him. He thought you were very good, but they need a name so he was only going to ask you to understudy. Listen, I've spoken to Barry Schenck – you know who I mean? – the head of Motivated Management in LA. He's prepared to see you himself. That's unheard of – they say he only talks to God and Bud Booker. Why hang about in draughty church halls when you can have the real thing? I was going to tell you all this when I came round. Can I?'

Elizabeth was by now fully awake and full of fury. She could not believe that Fyodor would take such liberties. An appointment with Motivated Management was no compensation for the intrusive act of talking to the director without her permission. It was as if he had gone through her desk and read her private letters, like some emotional cat burglar. She wanted to scream this at him but measured her restraint.

'No, Fyodor, you can't come round. You've done enough for me for one day.'

The apartment smelt like a flower shop. Tanya had filled it with crocuses and jasmine, daffodils and tiger lilies. And sweet music. She showed no annoyance at Robert being late, nor that he had obviously been drinking, and flung her arms around his neck.

'Name three things that Mozart did in 1791.'

Robert removed his blazer and hung it over a chair. 'Wait a minute, I need a drink before I go on *Wheel of Fortune*.'

'It's here.' She indicated a bottle. 'Pink champagne.' She fetched him a glass from the candlelit table on which was spread a lobster salad, laid out as if for an advertisement in a Sunday magazine.

Robert took a sip. 'First of all, he died.'

'Wasn't that last of all?' she suggested.

'I suppose it was. But just before he died he wrote his Requiem Mass.'

She kissed him. 'Two out of three. Now, for the major prize, the lucky lobster and a night of ecstasy with a partner of your choice, name one more thing.'

He knew the answer but he could not summon up the wish, nor the generosity to provide it. Tanya turned up the volume.

'A clue,' she said.

'No, you've won.'

She indicated the loudspeakers. 'He wrote this – the Clarinet Concerto. Isn't it heavenly?'

'*He* was to be heavenly shortly afterwards,' said Robert.

'It thought you didn't know,' she snapped.

'I didn't,' he lied. 'You just told me. Why the new interest in Mozart? How did you know all this?'

She picked up the box that had contained the compact disc. 'It's all on the cover. Everything you need to know.' Her mood remained combative. 'Are you going to spoil all this?'

'I didn't know we were having a party.'

'It's just for two – maybe just for one, although it's hard to have a party for one with you around.'

He held her to him. 'I'm sorry. Montillion's vodka. He's quite a soak, you know.'

'Did he have anything interesting to say?'

'In a way.' He took another sip from his glass, partly to slacken her grip on him. 'Actors are such strange creatures. You never know what's actually coming from them and what's just going through them. You know what I mean – sometimes they're just conduits for remembered thoughts, as if their minds and their memories were one and the same.'

'So? Is that a bad thing?' She changed the subject. 'Did Hurley get hold of you?'

'No.'

Robert's voice must have carried his anxiety. She quickly reassured him. 'It's okay. You haven't been fired or anything. It's just we've got an assignment together. I fixed it.'

He drew in a substantial mouthful of the heavily scented air. 'The Oscars?'

'No, they wouldn't wear that. Apart from you, it's coming out of the LA office. But I figured that on your way there you could cover the Dyslexia Downhill at Aspen.'

'Spell it,' Robert couldn't stop himself from saying.

She looked at him blankly, as the weak joke sailed past her. 'It's for charity. Some singer who lives there has this dyslexic child and he gets a lot of celebrities who come over and race. I suggested it to Jim and he okayed it. Fast action and famous faces, that's what we're about. It'll be great.'

'I wonder – trapped in a ski lift with a box of soap stars adjusting their make-up? I'm never sure about giving publicity to these charity things. They tend to be career advancement exercises: people turn up so that they can be seen in the right peer groups. It usually turns out to be the charity that's benefiting the stars.'

Tanya sat down at the table, close to tears. 'You're too fucking heavy. It's not a sociological investigation into human motivation, Robert. It's a goddam ski race for kids who can't speak straight.'

'Spell,' he interrupted.

'Whatever. And you want to dump on it, like you want to dump on everything nowadays starting and ending with me. I thought it would be a chance for us to get away, have a change of scene, cheer you up. You like to ski. We could ski together.'

'You can't ski.'

'I'm prepared to learn, Robert. I'm prepared to learn how to ski and how to spell to try to hold on to something that once was good. But you don't seem prepared to do anything except put me down. You're a shit.'

'I am,' he agreed. 'I'm sorry.'

He raised his glass of pink champagne. 'Sure. We'll go. Here's to Aspen.'

CHAPTER 11

Friday 28th – Sunday 30th March 1997

Aspen, Colorado

Tanya was right. From the moment they sank into the back of the aptly named Mellow Yellow taxi at Pitkin County Airport an invisible burden seemed surreptitiously to lift from their shoulders. The young driver, untutored in the shrug and snarl of his combative Manhattan counterparts, engaged them in cheerful conversation as if they had been friends for years. The streets of Aspen appeared to offer a simpler, more considerate way of life, long forgotten by blinkered city-dwellers. By the time they reached the Jerome Hotel, Robert had even managed to lodge a few layers of objectivity between himself and his recent unsettling introspection.

The snow lay late on the Rockies that year, champagne powder sent from further on high – a rich, deep, luxuriant carpet for the most perfect skiing in the world. The smell of wood-smoke cut into the pure, thin air inducing a curious nostalgia for a time that neither of them had ever known, when people were much more dependent on the elements and thus reminded every day of their puny place in the universe. As they lay in the steaming outdoor jacuzzi after dinner, dwarfed by the silent sentinels of Pyramid Peak and Maroon Bells, Tanya tipsily proclaimed that there were more stars in the heavens here than she had ever seen before and started to count them, until sleep came to rescue her from the impossible task.

Aspen seemed to cloak them in its own personality, as if there were some unwritten local by-law that prohibited friction and erased bitter memories. The following morning they ambled along the snow-dusted streets arm-in-arm, spotting the shop signs that signalled the laid-back humour of the place: My Mane Man Hairstyling Saloon, Footloose and Fancy Things Jewellers, Downhill Donuts and the Chip Chip Hooray Cookie Company. What European ski resort could boast a true New York deli, Schlomo's, serving matzoh ball soup on the very edge of the slopes? Tanya, sensing that their relationship was regaining a surer footing, announced that she intended to open a video store and stay there for ever. She let loose a yelp of delight and hugged Robert protectively to her.

The jovial atmosphere informed the Dyslexia Downhill as well. The social orders of Beverly Hills were temporarily set aside as film and television personalities came down to earth with a succession of crashes, humbly spread-eagling their way to the foot of the slalom slope in front of an admiring crowd. That night the uninformed stranger could be forgiven for thinking he was at an amateur talent contest in the Ute City Banque restaurant. Stars, of less permanent tenure than those that decorated the Colorado sky, sang round the piano and reminisced. As the evening wore on their stories grew longer and taller, most harking back to the commonly repeated point of departure that, in show business, everybody started as nobody. It also provided amusing television, just the sort of casual spectacle which made *Arts Action* as undemandingly addictive as a glossy gossip column.

The following morning Tanya suggested that Robert should go and ski himself. She insisted on taking the video-tapes to the airport, saying that she then intended to embark on her own downhill career by joining a beginners' class of Powder Pandas at Buttermilk on her way back. Robert offered to accompany her, promising he would teach her to ski, but she was adamant that she would be better off on her own and that he was likely to find more excitement on the steeper mountain.

He felt exhilarated and uniquely alive as he stepped out of the Silver Queen Gondola at Sundeck, the uppermost station, eleven thousand feet above the worries of the world. The day looked good; only a few niggling clouds occasionally blotted out the strong March sun. He went to the outside bar for a coffee, half-hoping that he might come across somebody with whom he could ski. Although he had a map of the mountain, the routes were unfamiliar to him. With slow deliberation he applied a coating of oil to his face and white zinc to his lips, but there seemed to be no one else on their own.

He set off by himself. It had been three years since he had last skied but as he gathered speed over the glistening snow, his body, as if by some internal memory, relaxed into a practised position, lowering his centre of gravity, dropping his arms forward in front of him and passing his weight from ski to ski as he carved precise turns through the tonsured mogul-field. His confidence grew. He took off from the tops of bumps with soaring pleasure, landing with pneumatic ease, eager to seek out others. The physical release seemed to trigger a chemical reaction in his brain making him feel not only unchained but newly purged and powerful, dominant somehow over his own destiny. Purposely he sought out the toughest runs – Bear Paw, North Star, Glade 3, Jackpot, rounding Kleenex Corner and plunging down the forbiddingly named Niagara to traverse across Schuss Gulley until he reached a distant lift that would take him back up the mountain.

He had been so absorbed in his reawakened skills that he failed to notice, until he had lowered himself onto the moving chair, a dramatic change in the weather. It had started to snow heavily. He looked down at his navy-blue salopettes and to his surprise saw that they were thickly coated. As he cleaned his sunglasses and looked ahead up the mountain, the slope and the sky had seamlessly merged into a white-out.

'Shame about the weather. I hope it'll clear soon.' The person sitting next to him was a woman – he could tell from her voice and neatly padded figure – but not one he was ever likely to recognize again. A white balaclava and fogged goggles disguised her completely, like some mountain terrorist.

'I hope so, too,' he replied. 'I don't know these runs and I doubt if even a white stick will help me find my way down.'

'We get to a bar called Ruthie's at the top of this cable,' she informed him. 'You'd do better to nurse a hot rum there till the storm passes. It can't last all day.'

As she spoke, the lift came to a juddering halt. The snow was descending in solid curtains ahead of them, making it impossible to see the couple on the chair in front. Robert looked round behind and could just make out the following chair which was empty.

'It looks as if you're going to have to wait a little longer for your rum,' his companion remarked.

She pushed her goggles up onto the woollen turban on her head. Her eyes, wide and other-worldly, seemed to reflect the missing sky of that morning. Her lips were pale in the cold and only came to life when they parted.

'Were you one of the crowd at the Ute City Banque last night?' she enquired.

'Yes – no,' he corrected himself. 'I was present. Not really part of it, though.'

'Present and not part of it?'

'I was covering it. I'm a television reporter. For *Arts Action*.'

'I've never seen that programme. Is it about parties?'

Robert smiled, a broad engaging deliberate smile. 'Pretty well. Anything, except matters of consequence.'

'That seems a good idea. I shall watch out for it.'

'I wouldn't bother.'

She appeared to ignore his reply. 'Would you think it terribly rude of me if I sat a little closer to you?' she asked. 'Two bodies can be warmer than one. Scott of the Antarctic and all that.'

Without waiting for his assent she snuggled up to him, the curves of her body neatly jigsawing into his. He caught the light aroma of her scent – a musky fragrance that was new to him. For some reason he felt too shy to look at her again.

'Scott of the Antarctic,' he repeated. 'You British really love to turn your losers into heroes. You *are* English, aren't you?'

'Yes, I am. But no – he wasn't a loser.'

'I thought Amundsen beat him to the Pole. That's how we were taught it. Do they give you the result the other way round in British schools?' he teased.

She pulled her body away from his. 'That's so American. The race didn't matter. What mattered was the way it was run. What mattered was that Captain Oates walked out into the night because he was lame with frostbite and was holding the others up. And Scott kept writing his scientific journal until the moment he could no longer move his hand.

Can you believe that? What mattered was that he and his men died with dignity.'

'Better to live with dignity,' Robert suggested.

'Oh no,' she contradicted him, with a shake of her head. 'It's something some of us are prepared for from childhood. Haven't you read *Peter Pan*? When Captain Hook is about to make the Lost Boys walk the plank, Wendy tells them that she feels she has a message from their mothers, that they hope their sons will die like English gentlemen.'

'To die,' Robert replied, 'would be an awfully big adventure.'

She leant her body back against his, smiled and squeezed his arm. 'There's a story they tell in the Alps of a ski instructor who went missing on a glacier and his body was never found. Thirty years passed and one hot summer, the hottest of the century, the man's son was skiing on the same glacier which had melted as never before and it yielded up the dead body. Only the father now looked younger than his own son.'

'Is it true?' he asked.

'I don't think it matters. It's just the notion of defying time, defying God really. We'd all like the power to do that. To preserve somebody at their most perfect. "Porphyria's Lover" – remember? The moment he knows she really loves him, he strangles her with her own long yellow hair. "And all night long we have not stirred, and yet God has not said a word!" Can you think of anything more romantic?'

Robert had not heard a woman refer to a poem since he was at Princeton, and possibly not even then. The essence of her beauty, he thought as he glanced at her, was in itself poetic. Set against this wild, swirling background she seemed slightly surreal and entirely desirable.

'It's hardly romantic,' he argued. 'She's dead. He hasn't preserved anything.'

'Yes, he has,' she insisted.

'What?'

'A memory.' She stared out into the snow, her gaze unfocused by her own thoughts.

'Is a memory something we have, or something we've lost?' he asked.

She turned slowly to him and fixed him with a stare, as if she were trying to find the solution in his eyes. 'That's an intriguing question.'

'Not mine,' he acknowledged. 'I think it comes from a Woody Allen film.'

'And what's the answer?'

He shrugged his shoulders. 'There is no answer. It's a pure conundrum.'

'You're wrong,' she corrected him with assertive certainty. 'A memory is something we have. It can never be taken from us, it can be more precious than the present.'

'Do you really believe that?'

'More precious than my present –' she began, but as she spoke the chair jerked forward and the lift started to move again.

It was as if the spell of those few stationary moments had been abruptly broken and Robert sensed that their shared intimacy was over.

'Do you know these mountains?' he asked her.

She nodded. 'My father used to bring me here when I was quite small. When we lived in Washington. What's your name, by the way?'

'Robert.'

'Same as Scott. Robert Falcon Scott. I knew I'd found the right person for warmth. He died eighty-five years ago today – did you know that?'

'How come you know so much about him?'

'Dad. He named me after Captain Oates.'

The snow was thinning now and the wooden outline of Ruthie's became visible as their chair swooped down to the dismounting area. Together they raised the bar and then slid off to separate sides of the lift.

'After a man?' Robert shouted, perplexed.

'Grace,' she grinned, pulling down her goggles. 'Lawrence Edward Grace Oates. But I think he preferred to be known as Lawrence.'

She turned away from him and made to point her skis down the hill.

'Stay.' The word fell involuntarily from his lips.

'I can't. The weather's lifting. You'll be okay.'

'Couldn't we have lunch?'

'I have to go.'

'Can't we meet?' he implored.

'We just have,' she laughed.

'Again?'

'Who knows?' she called back over her shoulder, weaving speedily and stylishly down the mountain as the snow enveloped her diminishing figure. 'I'm going outside. I may be some time.'

Robert stood watching her slip away, feeling futile and frustrated. Would he have been prepared to wind her yellow hair around her neck to preserve that moment? For the first time in his life he had some inkling of the sort of emotion that might drive a man to do that. He didn't want her to be just a memory, for he suspected that a memory was something that was lost.

CHAPTER 12

Tuesday 8th April 1997

Los Angeles

The Yoshikata Yoda was microwave hot. Fully automatic with voice-activated controls and a respectful Japanese voice attempting to control the driver if he failed to fasten his seat-belt or release the handbrake, its air-conditioning had nevertheless sighed and resigned the moment the outside temperature had reached the eighties. The further Robert travelled down Wilshire Boulevard away from the verdant, sprinkled lawns of Westwood and Beverly Hills, the hotter it became. As he turned through MacArthur Park and under the Harbor Freeway the downtown streets of Los Angeles appeared to be sweltering under a transparent grey dome which filtered the sun and trapped the heat. He had opened the Yoda's windows – a voice-activated method of obtaining Mexican air-conditioning – but it made little difference. His evening shirt was limp and damp, and he didn't have a spare.

Sandra Lewis did. Robert left the microwave to cool in its allotted space in the University of Southern California car-park. As he crossed the road – already stagnant with traffic – towards the Shrine auditorium, she was waving it at him.

'I thought you might need a replacement,' she called. 'Fifteen-and-a-half-inch collar, thirty-three sleeve. Right?'

He responded with a look of mock disappointment. 'No good. Thirty-four-inch sleeve, I'm afraid. I like to show a bit of cuff.'

'Oh dear. I knew I'd fuck up. You'll just have to appear in that sweat-flavoured one. We'll tell the viewers you have a glandular problem.'

'You think of everything. You have the computer mind of a

Yoda, only yours works,' he exclaimed, putting a thankful arm around her shoulder.

'I told you not to hire Japanese,' she reminded him, 'the Oriental mind can't cope with the Southern Cal climate.'

She had been assigned as his producer. For the past week they had worked together in the head office of *Arts Action*, a bright orange building situated at the junction of Cahuenga and Hollywood Boulevards. It was just around the corner from the Tussaud Hollywood Wax Museum – 'the place actors go to perfect their Christopher Walken stare,' Sandra had solemnly informed him on his arrival.

He had warmed to her immediately. She was passionate about show business and, from the start, had briefed and bullied him on the Oscars like a trainer preparing an athlete for a crucial race.

She had already put together a twenty-five-minute retrospective, *Seventy Years of the Academy Awards*. In 1927 the newly formed Academy pronounced that it would 'encourage the improvement and advancement of the arts and sciences of the profession by the interchange of constructive ideas and by awards of merit for distinctive achievement'. In fact Louis B. Mayer and his fellow studio bosses were just trying to buy off the labour unions. Movies made that year were eligible for the initial ceremony in 1929 and one of them, *Wings* with Buddy Rogers and Clara Bow, was the first Best Picture. The Warner brothers were upset that the thirty-six members of the Academy did not give it to *The Jazz Singer*, but their film was considered to have an unfair advantage on the grounds that it had sound.

'That's some neat footage Tanya Neris found on the first television coverage,' Sandra remarked. 'Is she your girlfriend?'

'Sort of.' Robert was taken aback. 'What made you think so?'

'That's what she said on the phone.'

Sandra had juxtaposed footage of the memorable moments when the Best Actor Oscars were awarded to two notable non-attendees – Sacheen Littlefeather's tedious and extensive monologue on behalf of the absent Godfather, Marlon

Brando, and Goldie Hawn's screech of surprise when she opened the envelope to see the boycotting George C. Scott's name as winner for *Patton* – with a linking soundtrack of Woody Allen playing his clarinet, something he had chosen to spend the evening doing in Michael's Pub in New York instead of collecting the statuette for *Annie Hall*. In 1973 David Niven made an instinctively witty ad-lib to one of the world's largest television audiences when a naked man streaked across the stage behind him: 'Isn't it fascinating that probably the only laugh this man will ever get in his life is by stripping off his clothes and showing his shortcomings.' The next time the streaker made it into the papers was when he was found dead in a San Francisco sex shop.

Sandra's video ended with close-ups of a tearful Elizabeth Taylor accepting a posthumous career Oscar for Richard Burton, who had been nominated seven times but never won the award.

'Very moving for a night of glitzy schmalz,' Robert observed when the tape finished.

'You mustn't think of it like that,' Sandra admonished him, switching off the machine. 'People need these things, they're an antidote to all the crime and poverty and inhumanity on the news. Adult fairy tales.'

She devised a game called 'Oscar Trivia' which they played on car journeys and in restaurants. The idea was to gear him up with information so that if there were any lulls in his live half-hour telecast from outside the Shrine he would be able to fill in the time.

'Who was the youngest person ever to win an Oscar?'

'Tatum O'Neal – Mrs McEnroe – aged ten.'

'And the oldest?'

'I know . . . er . . . Henry Fonda. When he was seventy-six. He was too frail to come to the ceremony – there were shots of him in his hospital bed and he went home to die a few months later. How about that?'

'Wrong. George Burns – for Best Supporting Actor in *The Sunshine Boys*. Aged eighty. Who was nominated for both Best Actor and Best Supporting Actor for the same movie?'

Robert held up his hand for time to think. 'Don't tell me.'

'I won't.'

He noticed the way she chewed the ends of her lank blonde hair whenever she was excited. She was a genuine California girl – perfect teeth, total tan and long legs that managed to be athletic and sexy at the same time. In truth, in her late thirties, Sandra Lewis was more of a career-girl than a girl but by applying the methodical planning that she brought to her career, she intended to have a husband and a family by the time she was forty, whether or not the right man came along.

'Larry Fitzgerald,' said Robert.

'Barry,' she corrected him.

'Hey, I was ninety per cent right.'

'Ninety per cent right is wrong.'

Robert strove for the extra ten per cent. 'It was 1944. It was *Going My Way*. He only actually won Supporting and Bing Crosby got Best.'

Sandra was not yet satisfied. 'And why hasn't it happened since?'

'They changed the rules. The actors' section now determines the category – quite arbitrarily, like Timothy Hutton got Best Supporting Actor for *Ordinary People* even though he had the leading role in the film.'

'In which year was *Citizen Kane* voted Best Film?'

'1941, of course. Make them harder. Next.'

She punched him, none too lightly, in the stomach. 'That hard enough? *Citizen Kane* didn't win Best Picture. It was beaten by *How Green Was My* fucking *Valley*. And Orson had to make do with the screenplay Oscar. Now I don't know what you're doing with yourself nights but I suggest you get back to the reference books.'

He had felt like a student again.

In the beach houses of Malibu and the mansions of Bel Air and the designer ranches nestling in the canyons the movie community was on the move. The hills were alive with the hiss of hair-spray as heads and smiles were fixed for the evening ahead. It was barely four o'clock but since the ceremony started at six, in order to accommodate the East Coast viewers for whom it would be nine in the evening, there were already ever-lengthening traffic jams of lilac limousines

– this year's colour – snaking down Appian Way and Lookout Mountain and Benedict Canyon. These latter-day quinqui-remes of Nineveh bore precious cargoes of emeralds and tiaras, exotic perfumes from Saint Laurent and Dior and Rochas, and Palm Springs sun-tans displayed in frocks from Christian Lacroix and Donna Karan and Gianni Versace. The label was infinitely more important than the look.

More precious still than these spices and silks and satins (indeed, the financial springs from which they gushed) were the composed and, for the most part, silent men in dinner-jackets, satisfactorily burdened with the knowledge that they were the highest-paid people in the world. Ten million a year minimum to run an agency, twenty million to head a studio, fifteen to fifty million to play the lead in a picture – agents, executives and stars alike had long since been able to put aside their initial fears that one day someone would pull away the carpet from underneath Hollywood and force them out into the chill, real world.

Leland Walters took a pragmatic approach to this particular occasion. The days had long gone when the major studios like Warners could control the Oscars by relying on the loyalty of their staff. With no such manipulation of block votes it had become a fairer fight. Very often it proved to be the passionate dream of an independent producer rather than the committee product of a studio hierarchy that carried off Best Picture. But the studios could still benefit; there was an art in spotting a likely winner ahead of time – big themes were always the favourites for big Oscars – and then picking up the North American rights before the ceremony. Warner Bros had initiated the trend when they bought the cheaply made British winner, *Chariots of Fire*, in 1981.

Win or lose, the Oscar ceremony was more than three hours of free publicity for the industry on prime-time television and countless weeks of world-wide column inches during the build-up. Besides, it was a very special night out for Leland's teenage daughter, Samantha, who sat excitedly beside him in her long pink dress, like a kid going to the movies.

'How was Aspen?' Leland addressed the question politely to the man opposite him, only half trying to conceal his irritation at the smell of Gitanes that was filling the car. Surely even Europeans knew by now that Beverly Hills was a non-smoking zone.

'It snowed,' replied Fyodor.

'I'm told it does,' Leland observed. 'Evidently it helps with the skiing. Although if it doesn't, they can always make the stuff. No sense in being too reliant on nature to provide one's pleasures.'

'Well, skiing is no pleasure of mine.' The Hungarian patted the knee of the young woman sitting next to him. 'I nearly lost this little penguin in a storm. I had to wait for ages at the bottom of the slopes until at last she came out of the snows – like Omar Sharif in *Lawrence of Arabia*.'

'Wasn't he on a camel?' asked Samantha innocently.

'So young and so perceptive,' acknowledged Fyodor. 'I meant that she emerged like a mirage.'

As if she had not noticed that she was being discussed, Elizabeth continued to gaze out of the limousine window at the never-ending river of domestic opulence. Nearly every mansion seemed to come complete with neo-classical colonnades, a loud convertible Mercedes and a gleaming dark Jaguar.

'I see,' Samantha stared at the couple opposite. 'How romantic.'

Leland, anxious to soften his daughter's bluntness, attempted to bring Elizabeth into the conversation. 'The appointment with Barry Schenck, it went okay?'

There was no response; her thoughts were elsewhere.

'Elizabeth,' Fyodor tapped her more firmly on the knee, 'Leland wants to hear about your meeting at Motivated Management.'

She turned from the window and offered the studio boss an apologetic smile. 'I'm so sorry. I was miles away. Motivated Management . . . yes . . . er . . . crikey, what a zoo. Have you been there? They had these young people at reception, barely out of school, pretending they're air traffic controllers or something. They've got these mini head-sets and microphones and all the time they're saying to everyone "Motivated Management, can you hold? Motivated Management, can you hold?" I don't think anyone ever gets through. All of Hollywood is on hold to Motivated Management.'

'In thrall to it, certainly,' Leland chuckled. 'They deal the cards and we play them.'

'Anyway,' Elizabeth continued, 'these infant receptionists seem to manage to ignore you *and* let you know that they've noticed that you're there. Then eventually you're led past a long row of sheep-pens containing impeccable young men in striped shirts and expensive haircuts, all of whom look as if they should be playing doctors in daytime soap operas, to the den of the almighty Schenck – who seemed to think I'd come to provide a one-woman audience for his phone-calls.'

Leland poured himself a lime-flavoured mineral water from the mini-bar in the back of the limousine. 'He's the top man, you know. Difficult to see. Maybe he had a busy day. A lot of people are leaving for out of town around now. Especially those who haven't been invited to the right parties.'

'I know. I'm grateful to you for fixing it. He just seemed to me a man who made lunch appointments and got upset because he hadn't the right season ticket for the Lakers. And on the phone he kept asking a million, two million dollars or more for actors I'd never heard of, then winking at me and covering the receiver so that he could proudly let on he hadn't read the script they were talking about.'

'He's not paid to read scripts,' Fyodor interrupted. 'He's paid to make his clients richer.'

'He thinks he's creative,' Elizabeth retorted, becoming distinctly more aggressive. 'I know because he told me so. He actually managed to read the first line of my press handout – "Elizabeth Grace Brown" – and suggested that it would be "beneficial" – his word – if I called myself Grace because it would remind people of Grace Kelly.'

Fyodor lit another Gitane. 'If he agrees to represent you, you're made. Just wait till he sees you in *Jupiter Landing*.'

'Oh, he watches movies, does he? Well, that's an improvement.'

Leland laughed. 'Everybody does. They screened the version with the new ending for me last night, Fyodor. Much better without all that Foreign Office medal stuff – it doesn't mean diddly over here. Also my guys want you to re-voice the ship's captain: he comes across too faggy.'

'You mean re-dub Howard with somebody else's voice?'
Elizabeth was shocked by the suggestion.

Fyodor gently took her reluctant hand. 'No problem,
Leland, as long as you pick up the tab for it. It's in the contract.
Section 22d, I think.'

Various attempts had been made to glamorise the usually
scruffy surrounds of The Shrine, but only in an incomplete
way that would suffice to make it look good on television. The
opposing tiers of ascending wooden benches were supported
by flaking green scaffolding and the red carpet that ran
between them was unevenly worn. When Robert and Sandra
arrived an old man in grubby cord trousers and a grey T-shirt
with the words 'Termite Control' written on the back was
vacuuming it. The crowd was actually quite small, hundreds
rather than thousands, but enough to fill the screen. At least a
third of the area had been assigned to reporters and television
crews. But those members of the public who had secured
places in the bleachers reacted with the well-trained response
of a television studio audience, standing up and trying to gain
the attention of anyone they half-recognised. The familiar
urban odour of junk food filled the air. Many of the spectators
were extremely overweight. As the limousines deposited
their occupants at the end of the crimson corridor it seemed,
Robert thought, an instance of the poor and fat looking down
on the rich and lean.

Not that he said so on the air. There was a necessary
conspiracy to preserve the mystique of the event – fans had
been queuing all night to get seats, stars had flown in from
every corner of the globe for this glittering ceremony. An
Oscar was a passport to roles and riches. This last observation
was intriguingly disputed by one of the lesser-known women
up for Best Supporting Actress who stopped to be interviewed by Robert on her way in. She, too, had been doing her
research. Half of her, she said, was afraid of winning because
of the Oscar jinx. She mentioned Kim Stanley who disappeared from films for nearly twenty years after being nominated for *Seance on a Wet Afternoon*, until she turned up again in
France in 1982. And, sadder still, Luise Rainer, the ex-wife of
the playwright Clifford Odets, who shared with Katherine

Hepburn the distinction of being voted Best Actress for two years in succession but whose career then took a violent downhill slide, so she went off to Lake Lugano to paint.

'Well, good luck,' Robert said at the end of the interview. 'Or, if you prefer it, bad luck.'

'There's no such thing as luck, darling – just karma,' advised the actress, blowing his viewers a kiss and trotting off on the arm of her much younger escort.

Although the crush of arrivals was now at its worst as, indeed, were people's tempers – 'relax, man, you'll win,' a publicist audibly advised his client; who screamed back, 'don't you tell me to fuckin' relax!' – the number of stars had noticeably diminished. The reason was quite simple. Many of the major stars who had been nominated had also been engaged as presenters. They didn't know who the winners were but they did know that four-fifths of their number would otherwise remain dejectedly in their seats throughout the evening, not always an appealing position for those accustomed to the limelight. So they were accorded the certainty of a brief, shining moment on stage and had been inside rehearsing it since earlier in the afternoon.

'Not to worry,' Sandra whispered to Robert, during a commercial break. 'The director's releasing them as soon as they're finished. They'll come out of the back of the hall, get in a limo and be driven round the front. But pretend they've just arrived.'

'What if I don't?'

'If you don't, you won't be standing here next year. Neither will anybody from *Arts Action*. Ten seconds.'

'Welcome back, welcome back.' Robert smiled at his invisible audience. 'It's less than fifteen minutes to go now until the first envelope will be torn open at the 1997 Academy Awards and I can see coming towards me the person likely to be the most worried man in the building, conductor Herbie Larner who has precisely half a second in which to decide which of five prepared themes the orchestra will play. You know ahead of time, don't you, Herbie?'

The grey-haired man looked astounded at the suggestion. 'I do not.'

'So what happens? Do you just wait for the presenter to read out the names?'

'Too dangerous. We can't always hear. What we do, Bob, is to rehearse all five themes but we try and make the first bar of each as similar as possible so if anyone begins to play the wrong one – and it happens – nobody notices. We've got a colour code and numbers on the sheet music and we've all got ear-pieces. The moment the winner is announced, somebody screams the number in our ears, and that colour and the winning name is flashed up on our television monitors. It's what we call a fail-safe situation.'

By now a steady flow of leading names had been chauffeured the two hundred yards from the back of the theatre to the front. The atmosphere was suffocating with the sound of superlatives as Robert and the competing crews dutifully recorded everyone's delight at being there. The fallow period came in the final five minutes, after nearly everybody had gone in but before the networked telecast began.

'Don't worry,' Sandra had reassured him earlier. 'We'll be taking a clean feed from another remote. The boys in editing will have a three-minute montage ready to roll at any time from five-fifty onwards.'

But Robert had noticed a frail, elderly lady, dressed as if for afternoon tea at an elegant hotel in another age, sitting at the very front of the bleachers. She had not been applauding, using one hand to hold up a small, lace parasol to shield herself from the sun, but she had been observing everything with an intelligent curiosity. On a hunch he signalled to the cameraman to follow him across to her.

'Madam,' he enquired respectfully. 'Is this your first Oscar ceremony?'

'No, young man,' she replied, 'it is not. My father took me to the *first* Oscar ceremony. We saw Charlie Chaplin and Douglas Fairbanks – senior, not junior. I was only twelve. 16th May, 1929. Outside the Roosevelt Hotel. A night just as hot as this but without the – what do you call it? – smog.'

'Jesus Christ,' Terry, the director, yelled into his earpiece. 'Hold the highlights tape and let's go with her. This looks like vintage stuff.'

It was. But as Robert continued to dig deeper into this

accidental treasury of oral history, he failed to notice Leland Walters and Samantha, followed by Fyodor and Elizabeth, moving hurriedly along the carpet behind him. They were late.

'You set her up, didn't you? She's from central casting. I've seen her on a yoghurt ad.'

'Honestly, I'd never met her in my life before.'

'She's a great-aunt. You gave her a pile of film history books and rehearsed her till she was word perfect.'

'She just caught my eye. I could see she was taking everything in so I supposed she might have something to say. She might have been goddam Lithuanian!'

'Luck,' chided Sandra. 'Beginner's luck.'

'You know what Pasteur said: "Luck favours the prepared mind."'

'Lucky and pompous. When can we get out of this place and get a proper drink? At least there's liquor when it's at the Dorothy Chandler Pavilion.'

They were in the vast tent at the back of the Shrine where the press were corralled. All were in dinner jackets or evening gowns and most were chatting casually between sips of coffee, casting an occasional eye at the giant television screens staring from each corner. Several were typing fervidly on portable computers, copy that would go immediately by modem into newspapers in their home states. Possibly a local citizen had won an Oscar for set design or best sound. One or two older journalists stood calling the results into phones, as if they were reporting a sports match, fearing perhaps that a grid failure would prevent the copytakers on their newspapers obtaining exactly the same information from the television.

People crowded to the front when the first recipients came into the tent, clutching their Oscars as tightly as hand-grenades. In 1979 Meryl Streep had been so overcome after winning hers that she made straight for the lavatory. As she was leaving she heard one woman shriek to another, 'somebody's left an Oscar in the bathroom!'

At this stage the winners of the technical awards stood smiling silently before the press, untroubled by any questions; instead the journalists asked the more famous presenters whom they were dating and what their next film was going to be, the two most pressingly repeated topics of the evening.

The *Arts Action* crew had now moved inside but they did not bother to cover any of this for the highlights programme later that night. 'Let's wait,' Sandra insisted. 'If *Luria* gets Supporting Actor and Special Effects, the domino theory comes into play. It'll sweep six, maybe seven, including Best Picture. It smells like a winner. Russian-American co-production, we provided the stars, they provided the story and the roubles.'

It was a remarkable film. *Luria* was a Russian neuro-psychologist whose most celebrated patient, S. V. Shere-shevskii, was cursed with the ability to remember everything. He had been a reporter on a Moscow newspaper where his editor noticed that he could memorize long and complicated messages. There was no limit to the amount of material he could commit to memory: Luria would give him extensive lists of hundred of words and digits and, twenty years later, the man could reproduce them exactly. Luria's research on Shereshevskii demonstrated that memory is a visual skill. The reporter would close his eyes and take an imaginary walk from Pushkin Square down Gorky Street and read the lists of words off the walls he had mentally written them on. His rare errors occurred when he couldn't decipher one because the corner was too dimly lit by a street lamp. For him sound was turned into colour and taste. If he ate in a restaurant with sweet music his food tasted good; if there was a hammering on the roof, the same food would taste vile. Strangely, he couldn't remember a human face if it had been smiling the first time he saw it and scowling the next. His talent became his tragedy. Later in life he became a music-hall performer and was afraid to cross even an empty street because he could still visualise the traffic he had seen on it a few moments earlier.

Robert had been absorbed by the movie when he first saw it but as he watched the extracts now on the monitors they assumed a different significance. 'A memory is something that can never be taken from us . . . more precious than the present.' The English girl on the ski lift had integrated herself in his thoughts. However much he concentrated on his preparation for the show, the desire to see her again remained dominant. He had no idea where to begin. Should he return to Aspen and comb the hotel registers in search of a Grace? He had never mentioned her – there was no one to mention her to – and sometimes he even wondered if she actually existed. Was she perhaps just the product of some white-out that had temporarily fused his brain during the snowstorm?

Sandra was right. From the moment *Luria* won the special-effects Oscar – the visions of the hero's mind had been realised with brilliantly surrealist skill by the American technicians – it began to sweep the board, as Robert had none too confidently suggested on camera before the ceremony.

He left before the final awards to get to his next location. The air-conditioning in the Yoda was working again now that the temperature had dropped down into the low seventies and so, Robert discovered, was the car phone. He was on a high. He knew the introductory programme had crackled along; there had been messages of congratulation from both the LA and New York offices afterwards. 'Everybody's watching us – that's what matters,' an exultant Jim Hurley had shouted. 'The overnights are going to look very nice.'

So he called Tanya in New York. She lifted the phone but, before he had time to speak, snapped: 'Who's crazy enough to ring in the middle of the Oscars? Call back tomorrow.'

'It's Robert.' He managed to get the words in before she cut him off.

Her tone changed. 'Where are you?'

'I'm just leaving The Shrine and I'm heading west towards Le Moulin de l'Abbaye. How are you?'

'I'm fine.'

'Did you see our show?'

'Sure.'

'And?'

'That was fine, too.'

'So what's wrong?'

'Nothing,' she said, in the clipped, lowered voice that people use when they mean 'everything'.

'Nothing?' he echoed.

'Jesus, *Luria* just got cinematography. Who wants to see that shit?'

'Are you all right?' he asked.

'Well, you sure are.'

'What do you mean?'

'From what I hear, you're fucking Sandra Lewis.'

He was damned if he was going to flatter her with a denial. 'Who says?'

'Everyone who's seen you together. Didn't take you long to forget Aspen.'

'I haven't forgotten Aspen,' he protested, adding, with some measure of truth, 'I don't think I'll forget Aspen as long as I live.' But his transmitted memories were not received. She had already put the phone down.

'May Mu Wang and his eight steeds come and spirit me out of here.' Elizabeth looked at her watch for the twentieth time that evening. For no immediately identifiable reason she was overwhelmed by a surge of homesickness. She looked around her at all the alien, sun-tanned faces and she felt a ravenous craving to be somewhere else, anywhere else.

'I have to go to the loo,' she whispered to Fyodor in desperation. She waited for the next commercial break and left her place. Almost immediately a young woman in an evening dress sat down in it – the Academy hired fillers-in for the audience to make sure the viewers always saw a full house.

Fyodor followed her. 'What's wrong?' he asked anxiously when they reached the corridor.

'Nothing.'

'You seem ill or upset or something. I can't see why. Everybody's here. It's an incredible night.'

'Not for me,' she replied, close to tears. 'I know it's stupid but I'd rather be at home watching it on TV. I just don't want to be a part of it, it doesn't feel right. Can we go home? Or can I, at least? I'll take the bus.'

'You're crazy,' Fyodor was becoming irritated. 'Nobody here takes the bus.'

'Maybe that explains why I shouldn't be here,' she pointed out defiantly. 'I love buses, especially upstairs. I do my thinking on them.'

'You're being silly. Come back in We'll miss best director.'

'We won't miss anything. It'll be *Luria* again. Once they've decided, they give everything to the same film. There's no discrimination in this town.'

Fyodor placed his hands on her shoulders. 'Please.'

She relaxed her body and put her head against his chest.' 'I'm sorry,' she said. 'The heat, I expect.' And followed him meekly back to the auditorium.

She was right about best director.

It was not hard to find 'Le Moulin', as it was known. The restaurant nestled in the stretch of Melrose Avenue that aspired to be European – bistros, boutiques, curiosity shops and, most bizarre of all for that four-wheeled city, an area where people actually walked. The entrance was crowded with disaffected TV crews and paparazzi who had failed to gain admission and there was an outer ring of bystanders who managed to find sufficient entertainment in watching them.

Robert handed the car keys to 'varlet parking', as Sandra persisted in calling it, and the temporary downswing that Tanya had brought about in his spirits was immediately corrected by the young man with gold epaulettes who took them. 'Hey, how about that old lady? Do you know, someone came out and gave her a ticket for inside after they saw her on your show?'

He didn't and the news gave him a philanthropic buzz. Le Moulin was certainly the place to be on Oscar night. It had a sense of the bygone Hollywood, dominated by the *ancien régime* of stars who had once reigned supreme but had now slipped into the twilight movie roles of passengers on ships or airliners that were about to be smitten by disaster, and brief cameos on current television soap operas, plus the endless coating of magazine-cover stars – actors and actresses who didn't have the talent to carry a film but were content to coast along in secondary roles, enjoying a much greater notoriety than some of the serious leading players because they were happy to offer the theatre of their private lives – marriages, affairs, babies, divorces – to papers and magazines and the new breed of television programmes that had grown up to feed off precisely this. *Arts Action* considered itself just a cut above such reporting but as Jim Hurley, once picture editor on a national magazine, used to remind his directors when they were going out on location, the most popular photograph with the public is that of a famous person with their house behind them.

Homer Mangold was easy to find. He was at a table with two other agents, not the sleek modern Schenck version, but the older, more crinkled variety, the sort of men who might still puff a forbidden cigar or actually read a script. They seemed almost oblivious to the Oscar ceremony which was coming to its predictable conclusion on television sets dotted around the room, but were engaged in a combative discussion about the old days, a time which clearly held more fascination for them than the present.

'They imported the locusts from China. In sealed containers.'

'That's crap. It was a rumour dreamt up by some flack.'

'It's true. George Hill – not George *Roy* Hill, *George* Hill – went to China and filmed the whole place, millions of fucking feet. It kept cropping up in other MGM pictures – he came back not just with the film but clothes, houses, villages, temples, animals and locusts. And then he killed himself.'

Robert sat down, intrigued. Homer greeted him with a confident aside. 'It's all okay. Bud's primed. Your exclusive.' He turned to his friends. 'This is the guy who did the interview with that girl, the one with the karma who didn't want to win and had her wish fulfilled.'

The others laughed. The bald man with a cigar that stretched halfway across the table waved it at Robert. 'But she was talking about Luise Rainer in *The Good Earth*. That movie gave everyone connected with it the kiss of death. Even Irving Thalberg was in his grave before the picture was released.'

'That cannot be true,' said the man next to him, who had enjoyed sufficient wine to challenge every assertion.

'It's true. Run the movie. It says at the front "To the memory of Irving Grant Thalberg we dedicate this picture – his last achievement." Aged thirty-seven, pneumonia. One of the few visionaries this town ever had. Now they give a memorial prize in his name' – he pointed the cigar towards the television set where endless final credits were now rolling –

'to some asshole producer who has only ever made a bunch of spy thrillers, never risked a dollar on an original idea. Thalberg rebuilt China in California for that picture. Four hundred acres of countryside, terraces, villages, you would have thought you were there. And it was a great story. From the moment Paul Muni leaves Luise Rainer he loses touch with the earth, his roots. You see he hasn't just betrayed her. When you betray another person you betray yourself. And it takes this plague of locusts –'

His narrative was drowned by the rising decibels of a commotion at the door. People were shouting and jostling each other and the hand-basher lights of the television crews flooded blindingly into the restaurant. All heads turned. It was Bud Booker, acknowledging the attention with a practisedly modest wave, as if he had just won an Oscar rather than having only presented one. Leland Walters was with him, attentively followed by Fyodor.

Homer Mangold was by his side the moment he came through the door. He pumped Bud's hand with excessive relish, the better to reassure himself and remind those present, of their close relationship. 'How are you? How you doing?'

'How did I do?' asked Bud, sitting down, without thinking, in Homer's place at the table. 'Can I get a vodka tonic?' he called out to no one in particular.

'You were great, the rest was a bit of a drag,' said Homer, hovering uncertainly behind him. 'Three hours of people congratulating themselves, who needs that?'

'Yeah, but how was I?' Bud became more emphatic. 'That line about us calling Oscar night Passover at our house because the awards always pass over me seemed to go down all right.'

'It certainly did,' agreed Robert, thinking it had also gone down quite well the first time Bob Hope had used it.

'Did you meet Robert Barrett, from *Arts Action*?' Homer's persona had changed. Gone was the confident, all-knowing operator; in the presence of his major star he became a concerned and willing flunkey. And round the table the atmosphere changed, too. No time for anecdotes now, the only permissible subject was the man with the golden aura.

Film stars were there to be listened to and never to be contradicted, a state of affairs that frequently had the effect of merely compounding their ignorance. This was especially so in the case of Bud, whose main educational achievement had been his ability to kick-start a motor-cycle.

He shook Robert's hand with a minimum of interest and muttered, merely, 'Hi.'

'Can you tell these goons that we've got permission to come in?' Sandra's voice shrilled authoritatively across the renewed chatter. She and the crew were standing at the entrance, their way barred by two solid men with short-cropped hair and thin moustaches, purpose-built to repel the unwanted.

Robert rose and dashed across to her. 'Where did you get to?' he asked.

The bouncers, noticing he had just come from the side of Bud Booker, let her through without further hesitation. Sandra beckoned to her crew to follow her. 'Set up in front of all those pastries and desserts,' she instructed the cameraman, 'nobody's going to eat them – they're all on diets in here.'

She turned to Robert. 'Hi. I went back to production control. They've got a window when they'll take Booker live at ten-forty. Isn't that Leland Walters from Warner Bros over there talking to him? I followed him up the steps. He was with his daughter and that stubby man next to him was with a girl that I assumed was *his* daughter, until they had such a stinking row in the street. She just turned on him and ordered the car to take her back to the hotel. I wish I'd had that nerve at her age.'

Robert indicated to Homer that they were nearly ready to go. The agent guided Bud and Leland across to the interview position but the studio president stood sufficiently apart from the star to indicate that he had no wish to be included.

Robert was now linked up to the control room again on his ear-piece. Terry's voice came over, tired and terse. 'You have only four minutes maximum and no overrun. So keep it snappy. We just crash out of you at the end. No handover. Counting five, four, three, two, one and take it.'

'Bud Booker. One of the luminous stars of tonight, or any night.'

Robert felt self-consciously obsequious, but Bud merely blinked both eyes in acknowledgement.

'And *Black Cops Kill* is, well, killing them, I hear.'

The star put on his meaningful expression. 'I think this film has caught the public imagination. People no longer want to see an America where crime goes unpunished, where there are sub-communities outside the reach of the law. We've got to show the world that if we find any imperfections in our system of justice, right-thinking people will blast them out, root and branch.'

Elizabeth poured herself a neat vodka from the complimentary bar in the corner of the suite and drank it straight down. The air-conditioning in the room did little to cool the heat of her emotion. She had acted impetuously and maybe foolishly. But she could no longer endure the man she respected as a film-maker and a thinker toadying to people like a stall-holder in a souk. Even with Leland, for whom she had some respect, Fyodor agreed to every change in *Jupiter Landing* and to what she thought was a meretricious marketing campaign without a whimper. When the car had reached the restaurant she could take it no longer. She had pleaded to go home on the grounds that she was exhausted and Fyodor had called her a stuck-up little bitch.

The remark stung, the more so because she acknowledged to herself there was a hint of truth in it. She paced the room, too tense to sit down. The vodka had no calming effect whatever. Punching the button on the television set by the bar she caught sight of the familiar features of Bud Booker. But Elizabeth had had enough of Oscars for one night and didn't bother to turn up the sound. The picture cut to a long shot and she could see Leland Walters in the background. The programme must be coming from the restaurant Fyodor was at. Suddenly the screen was filled with a smile that had lingered pleasantly in her memory for the past ten days. That's God's way of punishing you for your tantrums, Elizabeth, she heard her nanny saying.

Robert attempted a little more edge. 'And when is the rest of the world going to see your perfect system, Mr Booker?'

'That's a great honour. We've been invited to participate in this year's Cannes Film Festival. As you may know, it's their fiftieth anniversary and could well be the most celebrated event in the history of cinema – with the possible exception of tonight.'

'So in addition to the millions of dollars, you could find your brow wreathed in laurels with the Palme d'Or.'

'Keep him short, you have less than ten seconds,' came the command in Robert's ear.

'After due discussions,' continued Bud, with the formality of a man reading a press communiqué, 'we have decided it would be unfair to compete against films from Third World countries, but I am happy to tell you that I will, on that occasion, be invested by their Secretary of State with membership of the French Foreign Legion.'

CHAPTER 13

Friday 9th May 1834

Cannes

Lord Brougham was feeling overweight, undervalued and out of sorts. Throughout the dismal, dank winter he had suffered from this nagging illness – possibly just a cold, maybe something worse. It had been an arduous parliamentary session. The initial, self-satisfied pleasure that the office of Lord High Chancellor had conferred – second only in rank to members of the Royal Family and the Archbishop of Canterbury – was tempered by tedious hours on the Woolsack listening to his fellow peers endlessly arguing about their own privileges in the House of Lords. At home his situation was little better; his family seemed, if anything, more irritating. His son and heir, derisive of London society, had offhandedly rejected the advantageous match his parents had arranged for him and had run away with a French actress.

So Henry Peter Brougham decided to shut up house and head off to the Mediterranean for a rest. He travelled overland with a minimum of staff, intent on a peaceful sojourn in Nice. But, about twenty miles from the town, his party was halted by a platoon of soldiers who had erected what appeared to be a temporary customs post across the road. Brougham, a short and short-tempered man, informed the sergeant who had stopped them exactly who he was and demanded to see the officer in charge. A French lieutenant was duly summoned but confirmed, respectfully, that his lordship could go no further. Nor was there any prospect of his being able to do so for the next few weeks or, indeed, months. There had been an outbreak of cholera in Nice and a *cordon sanitaire* surrounded the town.

'What the devil do you expect me to do, then?' demanded Brougham, as if the hapless lieutenant were himself responsible for the disease.

The officer took a map out of his military document case and pondered over it. 'If you strike downhill from here, sir,' he suggested, 'south towards the sea, you'll find a small fishing village. I'm sure they can arrange some temporary accommodation.'

Tired and irritated, the Lord High Chancellor followed his instructions, reaching the village after darkness had fallen. His mood was marginally improved by the warm Provençal reception he received in the modest home of the local butcher.

The next day dawned excellent and fair. From his bedroom window Brougham could see a perfect, unspoilt bay that curved alluringly to the east. The sight lightened his burden and lifted his spirits. Since there seemed little chance that summer of reaching Nice, a few miles away beyond a distant promontory, he decided to remain where he was and build a house there.

The only blot on the iridescent Mediterranean horizon remained his son, who was persisting in his relationship with the Frenchwoman.

'If you do not quit her, I will stop your allowance,' Brougham wrote to him.

The reply came back: 'If you do not double it, I will marry her.'

Brougham reluctantly agreed to do so. This was the first recorded deal struck at Cannes. It was 1834, the year the British finally abolished slavery – a cause to which Brougham had nobly devoted himself. Four years later, just before the outbreak of Britain's First Opium War with the Chinese, he devised the one-horse closed carriage that bears his name to this day. But it was to be more than a century before anyone devised the Cannes Film Festival.

The port itself had existed for two thousand years. Ships would set sail with olive oil and fine wines, leather and sweet-scente soap produced locally in Grasse, returning with cargoes of coffee and cocoa, tallow and soda from Spain, sailcloth and cedarwood from Sicily. The tower that still dominates the town was built in the twelfth century so that the local people could watch out for Saracen counter-attacks during the Crusades. Five hundred years later a church was built beside it: Notre-Dame de l'Espérance – Our Lady of Hope. In 1687 the mysterious Man in the Iron Mask – thought by many to be the twin brother of Louis XIV, the Sun King who ascended the throne of France at the age of five – was brought to the Ile Sainte-Marguerite, just off the coast, and imprisoned near the Roches Plates. This area later became celebrated as a place where people could sunbathe naked without fearing imprisonment themselves under section 330 of the French Penal Code of 1863. The nudists were kept well out of sight of the oldest monastery in western Europe on the nearby Ile Saint-Honorat.

Others of similar fortune were not slow to follow Lord Brougham's example and build holiday homes in Cannes. Work started on a harbour in 1838 and it fast became a popular resort, soon fashionable enough to challenge its neighbour, Nice. The change of century celebrated the age of the grand hotel, and the Carlton – a deliberately imperial structure, promising absolute privilege and luxury to those who could afford to walk through its haughty portals while delivering an unspoken warning to those who could not – assumed the commanding position on the Boulevard de la Croisette, to be followed by the Majestic, the Martinez, the Gonnet, the Grand, the Gray d'Albion and, inevitably, the Hilton. Each of the original sea-front hotels had a wooden jetty to receive any travellers who might choose to arrive by boat – fewer in 1997 than there would have been at the beginning of the century – and owned a private beach, although not an entirely natural one. Every year, a week before the Film Festival, a crocodile of trucks arrived importing fresh, clean African sand and a fleet of bulldozers, like so many cooks icing a cake, spread it across the shore from the Croisette to the Mediterranean.

The weather in mid-May was always variable, uncertain enough to keep away the tourists, so what better way to start the season two weeks early than by filling the hotels with movie buffs who were not hostages to the vagaries of the climate, since they had ostensibly come to spend their days in the cinema? Thus, a Festival was born.

But nothing can have prepared the local Cannois for the invasion that was to take place. What had been planned as an intellectual riposte to Mussolini's gaudy Venice Film Festival – a reminder to Il Duce that the art of film had, if anything, a more rightful home in France than Italy – was unfortunately delayed by the ambitions of another country with an equal claim to the same art. The first Cannes Film Festival began on 1st September 1939 – the same day as Hitler invaded Poland – and closed the following morning. So it was not until after the Second World War that Cannes got under way properly. And what had started out comparatively modestly was thrown into the world spotlight by a widely reported act of immodesty. In 1954 a French actress, Simone Silva (who wanted to be France's answer to Marilyn Monroe but managed to match her only in her subsequent suicide), threw off the top of her bikini and embraced Robert Mitchum. The Festival authorities ordered Silva out of Cannes but the hordes of cameramen present had already struck gold. The resulting photographs travelled round the globe and, from that moment, the notion that the true glamour of the movies was to be found in Lord Brougham's sedate resort was imprinted on the international consciousness. As with all such myths, reality itself was soon happy enough to live up to it.

On Friday 9th May 1997, however, Renaud Callet was far from happy. The Director had left the Festival headquarters in St Honoré in Paris deliberately early to try and avoid some of the last-minute hysteria that rose in an uncontrollable crescendo at the end of April. As he sat in his Cannes office in the Palais des Festivals looking out at the cheerless, grey Mediterranean, he knew that the telegram in front of him was not a problem that could be solved with the traditional French response: '*non*'.

The wording looked cannily like a request but the content was undoubtedly a command. 'The Principal Private Secretary to Monsieur Henri Chaillot, Minister of Foreign Affairs for La République Française, presents his compliments and offers the Director and his staff sincere good wishes and congratulations on their fiftieth anniversary. As a measure of goodwill Monsieur Chaillot would be happy to come down to

Cannes for this historic occasion and, if pressed, would consider clearing his diary to serve as a member of the Festival jury.'

'If pressed,' muttered Renaud as he crumpled the telegram for the fourth time that morning. He already had a jury. He and the board of directors had spent the past six months putting together the nine French and foreign personalities as laid down by Article 7 of the Rules of the Festival International du Film. The arguments and permutations had been never-ending until they had come up with a collation as artfully prepared as a menu at a five-star restaurant: an Italian director whose name was revered but who was readily available since his last three films had been flops, making him virtually unbankable; a German producer who had earned a fortune out of electronics but was now one of the most powerful forces in the European cinema; an attractive Australian actress who had actually been born in Egypt and now worked mainly in America, thus adding most usefully to the compulsory mix of nationalities; a British film critic, since the nation of proliferating newspapers seemed to have many more film critics than directors; an American independent producer who always let Cannes have first shot at his films and reliably delivered the stars for gala evenings; a Russian director whose name had been put forward by Moscow as a true talent, which meant he would be true to the current controlling interests in the Russian cinema; and three Frenchmen, an actor, a director and an historian – the last the current holder of the Prix Goncourt for biography, an appropriate president of the jury in this anniversary year.

So where did that leave the French Foreign Minister? Did *he* want to be president of the jury? And would any of the other members – especially the Russian – resign when they heard of the appointment?

Renaud despondently lifted the phone to Paris. The matter would have to be tackled head-on. He was put through to the Principal Private Secretary, who was evidently relieved to hear from him.

'Monsieur Callet, at last. You are difficult to track down. We feared you had returned to Australia.'

Renaud brushed aside this attempt at a joke. 'Thank you for

your kind wishes. I have passed them on to my staff. And for the Minister's offer to serve on the jury. It is gratefully received but it would be a wholly unfair burden for him to involve himself in such an onerous duty.'

'He is involved already,' came the quiet reply.

'How?' Renaud queried, slightly too abruptly.

'Your Festival, you possibly forget, is presented under the auspices of *Le Ministère de la Culture et de la Communication* and *Le Ministère des Affaires Étrangères*. Monsieur Chaillot is looking forward to contributing more personally this year.'

'What if some great affair of state were to blow up?' Renaud was determined to put up at least some token resistance.

'Let us be the judge of that, *Monsieur le Directeur*. It is a matter of which we have considerable experience.'

'But does he have any experience of films? Does he have the time to see any?'

'He has time to see the twenty films in competition. Does he need to see any others?'

Renaud knew he was beaten. 'I don't think I can make him president of the jury.'

'That will not be necessary. *Monsieur le Ministre* will be happy to serve as an ordinary member. Perhaps you would be good enough to reserve him a suite at the Majestic. We will look after the additional security but I understand that the jury's accommodation is paid out of the Festival budget.'

One problem down and a thousand more to go, Renaud thought as he replaced the receiver. Every year some nation singled itself out to be more irksome than the rest and in 1997 this prize had already gone to Australia. Their government had considered itself gravely offended by the inclusion of *Man of the Media* which, according to their ambassador's telegram, 'portrayed Australians as cultureless worshippers of Mammon'. But this was nothing compared to the furore that was unleashed when they learnt of the selection of *Poppy Day*. 'It makes Sydney look like a sewer,' Dick Lockwood had screamed over the phone. Nevertheless Renaud had stuck by his decisions. 'It's only a film festival where people come to enjoy themselves,' he told the ambassador, 'not a state of siege.'

*

'But I booked the goddam room when I checked out last year. You, of all people, should remember that.'

Hetty Berman glared at the back of the retreating receptionist. He *should* remember it, she thought, since he'd been happy enough to pocket the three hundred dollars. Perhaps she hadn't given him enough? With considerable ceremony he had unscrewed the cap of his fountain pen to write down her reservation in ink on a list of names most of which were written in pencil. They might as well have been written in water, she had reflected at the time, for all the chance they had of finding themselves with reservations next year.

Now next year had arrived and on this uncomfortable morning her luggage, a contrasting pyramid of smart Lacroix suitcases and shabby cardboard boxes containing press releases – a monument that closely matched Hetty in height and girth – remained uncertainly on the porter's trolley behind her. A squat, determined New Yorker, her head a turbulent sea of grey curls, she had not built up her public relations company by losing battles like this one. Besides, she had occupied the same room in this hotel every Festival for the past twelve years.

But as jet lag involuntarily lowered her eyelids and she could see a general shaking of heads in the back office, she feared today might be the day. The Boisse Hotel had been taken over during the winter by another chain and, although they had retained many of the same staff, all bets – and bribes – were off. It had happened to a friend of hers. But it was not going to happen to her. Careers could come to an end in her business if you were not seen to have the right room in the right hotel for the Festival. She had given the address to everyone and she knew that if people thought that she, a revered New York press agent, could be seen off by a Cannes hotel receptionist, then it was probably time to hang up her gloves.

The man made his way back, the expression behind his rimless glasses saying more than his halting English would be able to explain.

'I am sorry, Madame Berman' – at least he remembered her name – 'but we have a problem with the security. We have an important government minister in Cannes for the Festival and he has many staff and bodyguards and we have very few rooms.' Although the receptionist knew who the Minister was, he was unaware that the Foreign Ministry had laid plans for Chaillot's arrival well in advance of their cable to the Festival Director.

'But why my room?' she moaned. 'My room, the one you wrote down in ink, remember? *Avec l'encre*. What about the pencil rooms?'

The man took out a Bic and began to draw a small diagram on the blotter in front of him. 'You see your room – what was your room, last year – with the balcony and the pleasing view, on a sunny day. From there it is possible to see clearly l'Hotel Majestic.'

'Thank you. I know that. So?'

'Well, for the security, it is the best position to keep an eye on who comes and goes to that hotel. And so they take your room,' he added, finishing his explanation with a degree of pride.

'But don't you have another room?'

The man shrugged. 'You said you specially wanted that one.'

Hetty stood on tiptoes and leant across the desk towards him, three hundred pounds of unbudgeable New York prime rib. 'So you *do* remember.'

Although trapped, he was still in a dominant position. It was unlikely that he would find himself up before the magistrates for obtaining money by false pretences. The system of bribes for procuring rooms in Cannes during the Festival was almost institutionalised, like the *mordida* in Mexico.

'And the hotel is full,' she said slowly.

'*Complet.*'

'Completely full.'

Wearily she put her Louis Feraud handbag on the desk top and took out her passport.

'Then perhaps you would be kind enough to get me a reservation in another hotel, this side of Nice if possible.'

The receptionist took the passport and bowed. '*À votre service.*'

As he returned to the office, Hetty made a mental note of the things she had to do: ring the Majestic to make sure they had a booking for Fyodor and that new girl of his, look after the projectionist for the *Jupiter Landing* screening in the Rue D'Antibes (she'd have to find out how much projectionists were getting bribed this year to show the reels in the right order), get her local French runner to note down the relevant press-box numbers for invitations to the party on the beach, book the fly-past planes, confirm the dinner reservations at the Moulin de –

Her list was interrupted by the return of the receptionist. Once again, his expression told the story before he spoke.

'I am happy to inform you, Madame Berman, that we have had a last-minute cancellation. A smaller room – no balcony, I'm afraid, but much quieter. There is no need for us to keep your passport; you are a trusted guest.'

He gave it back to her minus, naturally, the five hundred dollars she had sandwiched in its pages when she had handed it to him.

Chantal Coutard was having problems getting in, too. She hammered at the door of Le Mistral but there was no reply. It seemed madness for a bar to be closed just when thousands of people were arriving in town for the Festival.

'Looks like it's shut.'

She turned to find a friendly face, César, a young fisherman whom she knew slightly from previous Festivals. He and his partner Jean would offer her fresh prawns if she passed the harbour while they were unloading their catch. She returned the gesture by giving them spare passes for screenings. They liked American police films.

'Have you seen the owner? Has he gone away?'

'Who knows? I think he drinks a little too much.' César downed an imaginary glass with his hand. 'Ah, Chantal,' he called back as he continued on his way down to La Pantiero. 'You get me Bud Booker tickets and I bring you something nice. A big fish for a big fish.'

She felt guilty, knowing that she should really be at her desk in the Palais in case there were any early arrivals among the English language press. But everyone was entitled to a lunch hour and she was desperate to see Raoul.

Chantal had lived the life of a nun since the robbery in January. The sordid experience had haunted her as insidiously as if she had actually been raped. Although she had gone on dates with other men, she could not bear them to touch her. But returning to Cannes had triggered a turbulent sexual frustration that had never been very far from the surface. Although her romance with Raoul was over, she was upset and offended by the way in which he had so mysteriously excluded her from his life. Also, in an admission to herself of unsuppressible candour, she needed to make love.

She sat, waif-like, on the steps and glanced at her watch. One-fifteen. She would wait until half-past and then leave him a note. It was still overcast, threatening to rain, and the boats in the Old Port, crammed together like library books, rose and fell individually as an imperceptible swell crept into the harbour. Chantal had considered quitting the press office altogether after the raid but her relationship with Madame Rivette had temporarily improved and, in truth, she had nowhere else to go. Now Madame was back to her neurotic worst and the next two weeks would be the usual running river of complaints.

Without any warning the door opened. It was Raoul.

She stood up. 'I knocked. You didn't answer.'

He did not appear very pleased to see her. 'How could I know it was you? I thought it was someone –' He stopped abruptly. 'It doesn't matter.'

'Were you going out?' she asked.

'I was.'

'I'm sorry. I didn't know when I could get away.' Chantal stared at him. His ragged blond fringe, hulking frame and battered rugby forward's nose still held an undeniable sexual temptation for her. But something was wrong. There was a defensiveness in his manner quite alien to the old Raoul Bazin.

'Are you all right?' she asked.

His eyes refused to meet hers. He looked out at the harbour and then up the street as if he were expecting someone. 'Come in,' he said.

The bar was dark and empty. He led her to a small back room, barely furnished with a sofa and a television set.

'Cognac?' he enquired.

She nodded. As he went to the bar to get a bottle, she called after him, 'Why are you closed?'

'My partner's ill. I can't be here myself all the time. There are no barmen on the Côte d'Azur, they've all got jobs in the hotel for your fucking Festival.'

She ignored the insult. 'What about your suspension? Have they given you a date for a proper hearing?'

He handed her a glass. '*Santé*. There won't be a hearing. I've resigned. I'd never be taken back into the drug squad whatever the outcome and I don't want to spend my days handing out parking tickets.'

Chantal was amazed. 'So what are you going to do?'

'Why all these questions? Live life. I don't need to be accountable to anyone.' He was stoking the fire of his own irritation. 'Why did you come here? We parted friends. We agreed we had no future.'

'But we had a past.'

He poured himself another brandy and sat down beside her. 'So don't spoil it.'

'Are you seeing anyone?'

Raoul put his head back against the wall and stretched his legs out in front of him. 'From time to time. Nothing permanent, not for me, you know that.'

The soft burn of the cognac settled in her stomach. Almost instinctively she leant across and touched him. He stirred responsively. With one hand she started to undo his belt and with the other unzipped his jeans. He made no attempt to prevent her. His member was hardening. She flicked her tongue around its rim and, when it had grown to its full strength, slipped it deep into her mouth.

He bent across and pulled her shirt and jumper over her head in one movement. She wasn't wearing a brassière. He guided her head up to his lips, easily lifting her light body, running his hands down from her naked shoulders to the bottom of her back, and started to unbutton her skirt. She helped him and eagerly kicked off the rest of her clothes. Then he lowered her gently onto him. She was ready. She had been ready for him for the past three months. He moved her up and down on top of him, slowly at first and then with quickening pace.

It was not quick enough for her. She clung limpet-like to his neck and turned her soft, brown body into a human piston, accelerating faster and faster and screaming with relief into his ear.

She could feel him come inside her, warmer than the cognac, and desperately used the remaining moments of his rigid tumescence to bring herself to orgasm. She had lost all control by now and shivered unrestrainedly when she came as if she had been plunged into a frozen lake.

Their bodies fell silent and remained motionless. After several minutes, Chantal twisted her arm to look at her watch. Five to two.

'I've got to get back,' she said. 'Madame – as usual. Listen, my darling, I know it's over between us. But just for the Festival, couldn't we pretend? I don't know what you're doing but I know what you do to me.'

He looked at her nervously, as if she were accusing him of something. 'It's not possible. Not now, not any more. There are things I can't go into at the moment, things that are difficult to explain. You mustn't come back here, Chantal. You mustn't even talk to me if you see me in the street. And you mustn't ask why. My life is not easy at the moment.' He kissed her with a chill finality. 'There's no one like you. I've never loved anyone so much. But don't come back.'

She got up to dress, humiliated and close to tears.

CHAPTER 14

Saturday 10th May 1997

Cannes

Few of the large and angry crowd, growing larger and angrier outside the glass doors of the Palais des Festivals, took much notice of the rain which had stealthily increased from a soft Mediterranean drizzle to a persistent Provençal downpour. Nor did they give much thought to the crude, granite edifice they were so anxious to enter. From its inception until a dozen years previously the Festival had been accommodated in a noble building that had proudly rubbed shoulders with the grand hotels along the Croisette. People would come out of a film to be greeted by a vista frequently more impressive than anything they had just seen on the screen. From the top of the steps they could gaze over the immaculately raked beach with its red umbrellas moving gently like poppies in a cornfield to the Baie de Cannes, peppered with yachts of ascending degrees of opulence, suspended in a cyclorama of infinite blue, with no perceptible dividing line between the end of the Mediterranean and the beginning of the sky.

The old Palais had gone now, swatted out of existence by the giant metal yo-yo of a construction company to make way for yet another hotel. The *cinéastes'* loss was the hall porters' gain. Instead there had arisen, on the site of the old Casino, one of the eyesores of modern Europe. Biscuit factories looked more beautiful. When it first appeared, several delegates took quite seriously the *canard* that the new Palais had been based on the designs of an underground car park which, through some terrible misunderstanding, had been built above ground. Even the local French acknowledged that this was a vast and irremovable stain but were quick to point out, in mitigation, that the architect had been British.

The main reason for a monstrosity of this proportion was to house the growing market-place – *Le Marché du Film* – a windowless basement. Stall-holders from many nations would stand in front of what they termed 'product', flickering from television screens, and beckon passers-by as they might do in an Arab bazaar. An effort had been made to give the connecting passages a pedigree by endowing them with the names of distinguished directors – it was possible to go up Lindsay Anderson's alley, pass along Franco Zeffirelli's and emerge from Pasolini's – but most of the real business of the Festival was conducted elsewhere, in hotel suites and on terraces. The market today was infiltrated by brazen entre-preneurs trying to sell semi-pornographic films to territories such as South Korea. In truth it had been designed with the other satellite festivals in mind that clustered round the premier film event. People now awarded each other Golden Palms for twelve-second advertisements. Television, music, washing-machine and lawn-mower festivals had adopted Cannes in the hope of finding some left-over glamour in the closet.

But the journalists huddled in the rain, like the litigants in *Bleak House* clamouring to get into the Chancery Division, were anxious to register for the real thing. However, they had fallen foul of a particular piece of Madame Rivette's bureaucracy: in order to get in to collect your accreditation, you had to have an accreditation to collect your accreditation. This usually arrived at their newspapers and television stations at the eleventh hour – Madame had found that journalists were more appreciative of the honour of being accredited if they did not take it as a *fait accompli*. But none of this frustrated band – further frustrated as they watched their colleagues from other countries sail past and obtain admission with ease – had received the vital blue *laissez-passer* in the post. A group of writers and critics from such luckless territories as Spain, Switzerland, South Africa, Saudi Arabia and Sri Lanka remonstrated with the security guards to let them in. They had no idea of what it was that united them in their adversity; neither had anyone in the press office. It would take another forty-eight hours to unravel the situation. In the interim the problem was solved by the officials at the door with *le mot juste*: '*non*'.

Tony Birch skipped through clutching his blue accreditation-to-obtain-accreditation in one hand and a bunch of red carnations in the other. Sometimes it paid to be Australian. Young Vincent Wall, who had failed to notice the bow of respect he had been accorded when the guard had seen from his credentials that he was the director of a film in competition, followed, slightly awe-struck, in his wake.

'Looks like an aviary without any birds.' Birch indicated the glass-roofed atrium as they ascended the escalator, past the massive blow-ups of famous actors and actresses who had visited Cannes in previous years, exhibited with the reverence accorded to Davids in the Louvre, proof – if proof were needed – that the Festival paid as much respect to the stars of Hollywood as it did to the art of film.

Birch was inwardly congratulating himself: he had done it again. He did not work for any newspaper, contributing only spasmodic outbursts of vitriol about the decline of the Australian cinema to an underground magazine. But by sending in a shrewd manipulation of cuttings and by putting 'ABC radio' on his application form – he had, two years ago, been briefly interviewed on an arts programme – his credentials had once again come through. Many applicants sent in articles about Cannes from journals which had no bylines, such as *The Economist* in England, although this was a tactic that was beginning to be rumbled.

Vincent Wall watched impressed as Birch bounced up to the array of tanned hostesses, waiting like car rental girls in their fuchsia-pink Izet Curi suits to greet the arriving journalists. He presented his card to one of them and within minutes she was back with the precious brown envelope which meant, for him at least, that Cannes had begun. Noticing the carnations she enquired, 'You would like to see Madame?' and ushered them both behind the counter to a complex of partitioned offices.

Madame Rivette's door was ajar. She was talking agitatedly on the phone – with a second waiting receiver cradled to her breast – and attempting to carry on a conversation with two

Yugoslav journalists in front of her at the same time. It was a position she was likely to find herself in for most of the Festival.

Birch waved the carnations to obtain her attention and, when he did, pointed to Vincent with them, mouthing the words '*Poppy Day*'.

'Beautiful poppies,' replied Madame, whose command of English was not good.

Tony decided against attempting any further explanation and laid the flowers on a desk by the door, backing out of the office which was already bedecked with so many bunches of late-spring blooms that it looked like the ante-room of a crematorium.

The private jet was an extravagance, even Fyodor acknowledged that. But Hetty Berman had insisted it was essential for his image. Just one foreign distributor, she pointed out, who spotted them arriving at Nice airport in such luxury, might up his offer on *Jupiter Landing* sufficiently to cover the cost of the plane a hundred times over.

The producer knew that one must never be seen to be short of cash in the film world. Even if you were bankrupt, you still stayed at the Ritz in Paris and travelled by Concorde; it was the only way to show you were credit-worthy and thus be able to raise film finance. Especially at Cannes, with international movie moguls watching each other like buzzards, it was vital to overspend. In the early seventies the Salkinds had flown fleets of planes over the beaches at lunchtime to proclaim that *Superman* was coming. What had initially appeared merely to be a speculative fantasy later became a profitable one. In the early eighties the Israeli cousins, Menahem Golan and Yoram Globus, had covered the town and fattened the trade magazines with advertisements for films not even financed, let alone made, and yet had found no shortage of willing buyers. In the early nineties the Stella sisters from Luxemburg had attracted millions of dollars into their widely advertised European Cinema Coalition. Neither they nor the money were ever seen again.

So a Lear jet, with leather armchairs, an unwanted buffet of smoked salmon and strawberries, and two hostesses to dispense champagne, took the place of a row of Club Class seats on the Air France airbus for the short ride from London to Nice. Tim Lawrence was happy enough to sit analysing his directional talents for the benefit of the sole show business reporter on the plane. Give one guy an exclusive, Hetty had advised, that way you can control the story more and make the opposition papers hungrier.

Elizabeth had disliked the journalist on sight. She had read several of his articles – he had been writing variations of the same one since before she was born – and they had all seemed to be self-congratulatory essays on his purported friendships with the stars. He had greedily helped himself to a plate of smoked salmon even before the plane took off, and had presumed an unreciprocated, matey friendship with her from the moment they were introduced. She sensed that the only subject which really interested the weasel was her relationship with Fyodor – 'such a shame Mrs Lasky couldn't make it this year,' he had observed, 'we've had marvellous meals at the Colombe d'Or in the past' – so she hid behind a paperback in a corner seat.

Fyodor was in the opposite corner, ostentatiously on the phone, although his calls seemed solely to confirm arrangements already made and reconfirmed a dozen times by his secretaries. Howard and Douglas, having found a pack of playing cards, were noisily trying to remember the rules of gin rummy – which neither of them actually knew in the first place.

If a heat-seeking missile were to blast them out of the skies, Elizabeth thought, she wouldn't be too disappointed. She was miserable. Fyodor had forced her to come, insisting it was her duty to the film while silently implying that it was her duty to him.

When does an obligation come to an end, she wondered. Her remorse was compounded by the fact that it was she who had given their affair the green light. It had been an impetuous act but she had feared that if she had not seized that moment, then she would have been forced to relive it with nagging doubts in years to come. When you are old, her grandmother had told her, you rarely regret the things you have done as much as you regret the things you wished you had done. At this moment, Elizabeth wished she had left the wrap party that night alone.

America had been a disaster. She steadily lost respect for Fyodor as she watched him defer to the power of the studio. It wasn't just the cuts in the film and the brash advertising campaign that upset her. The producer hadn't even had the guts to tell Howard that his part was being revoiced; he had asked his agent to do so. But the worst crime was the music. That first night on their way home from Pinewood Fyodor had slipped a digital cassette into her car player. It was a combination of soaring martial and soft melodic music, unlike any she had heard before. The 'Jupiter' Symphony, Fyodor had informed her knowingly, the last one Mozart ever wrote. 'He never even heard an orchestra play it. So, in dedication, we will give it the largest and finest performance there has ever been for my film.' Fyodor had always intended to use it as the main theme. But, in America, he had readily agreed that his orchestral score should be replaced by music from an Atlanta rock group who were currently in vogue. The Fyodor whom she had often heard wax philosophical on the metaphorical strength of the story had turned into a small, greedy man out for every dollar he could get.

She resented the way he had drawn her into his life, almost by the same exploitative methods, without any consultation. He seemed to think that just because they slept together he had rights over her whole personality. And she sensed, especially at the Oscars, that she was being used as a marketing stratagem for Fyodor himself. Their relationship had never recovered from their row that night.

He still exercised some perplexing dominion over her, otherwise she would not be there. But as she looked up from her book and watched his stubby fingers light another Gitane, awkwardly holding onto the phone at the same time, she acknowledged to herself the summation of her thoughts: she never wanted to sleep with him again.

A fat German passenger jet landed just ahead of them at Nice airport and, since there was no one from protocol to usher them to the front of the queue, they had a frustrating twenty-minute wait behind the tourists.

Fyodor unleashed his irritation on a uniformed official. 'I thought we had dismantled customs barriers. Why is there this delay?'

'Drugs,' the man replied. 'And security.'

Hetty Berman, her ample form displayed to the world in a lime-green jogging suit, was waiting agitatedly on the other side of the barrier.

'They promised me you would get priority. It was all fixed, they assured me it had been taken care of. And then I rang today and they told me the man had gone on vacation. Can you imagine that? Vacation during the Film Festival? So I asked them "what are you going to do about it?" and they said there would be no problem. I got here two hours early, two hours ago and, would you believe, nobody could help me. It has been the most agonising two hours of my life, do you realise, standing here powerless. And the camera crew from *World of Cinema* that promised to cover your arrival isn't here. When I see that reporter again, I'm just going to remind him of the meals I bought –'

Fyodor managed to stop her. Hetty was beginning to hyperventilate. Her outburst actually had the effect of calming him down. 'Have you got someone to collect the luggage?' he asked.

'No, I thought you would have organised – here, porter! . . . I'll go, I'll do it myself.'

Fyodor put a steadying hand on her shoulder. 'We need to talk. Howard, would you be so kind as to look after the bags? Elizabeth and I will go with Hetty in the first car and perhaps you would follow in the second. You did hire some cars, didn't you, Hetty?'

'Lilac stretch limos,' she smiled, regaining her composure, 'the only two on the whole Riviera.'

In Los Angeles Elizabeth had felt increasingly isolated and trapped but, as she looked out at the passing villas nestling among the pine-clad hills of Provence, she fantasised that, like some prisoner in the Second World War, she could at least escape from here and make her way home across Europe.

Fyodor followed her gaze. 'John Robie retired to one of those houses. After he gave up his career as a cat burglar, remember?'

She was mystified. Hetty was not.

'*To Catch a Thief*. Cary Grant. She's too young, Fyodor.'

'They said Grace Kelly was, as well. She was only twenty-four and Grant was fifty. He came out of semi-retirement for that picture.' The Hungarian seemed to be making a personal point, but the return to Europe had in some measure reinvigorated his sense of romance. 'Do you remember their picnic, it was in these hills? She asks him: "Do you want a leg or a breast?" and he replies: "You make the choice." And then she says: "Tell me, how long has it been?" She's teasing him. "Since what?" he asks, and she answers . . .'

'"Since you were last in America,"' Hetty completed the dialogue; movies were in her bloodstream, too. 'They filmed a love scene on the Moyenne Corniche,' she recalled dreamily. 'And Grace asked who lived in the great palace that was down beneath them and they told her it was Prince Rainier. The following year she came back for the Film Festival. *Paris Match* set up a publicity stills session with her and the prince and –'

'Life followed art – or, at least, photography,' said Fyodor.

Elizabeth was intrigued but felt excluded and changed the subject. 'What do we have to do when we get there, Hetty?'

'We've taken out a double-page spread in *Screen International* to say we're showing the film today, Sunday and Monday afternoons at the Star in the Rue d'Antibes. That way we drum up press interest. It's not easy here if you're not part of the official selection. There are ten thousand movies being screened in this town during the next ten days so you have to spend to draw attention to yourself.' Hetty addressed the information pointedly at Fyodor. 'Then next Tuesday we have the party on the Majestic Beach. All the major international journalists and television crews have been invited and that's when we finalise the schedule for interviews and further publicity.'

Fyodor fiddled worriedly with an unlit cigarette. 'Are you sure about this *son et lumière* stunt of yours? I don't want people to get the wrong idea about the film.'

'You're not going to get any television coverage unless you have a stunt,' Hetty insisted. 'There are two hundred television crews roaming about Cannes pissed off with taking pictures of people sipping champagne in fancy clothes. They're all waiting for something to happen.'

*

The Majestic Hotel had, for most of its life, been a haven of comparative calm amid the frenzy of the Festival. But when the new Palais was built on its doorstep, even the Majestic bowed to the commercial pressures of the market-place. Its once peaceful pool and garden were now surrounded by thirty-foot-high advertisements for films. An enormous Elvis Ho, with a raging sea battle behind him and the words *The Yellow Pirate* slashed across his chest, gazed down at the crush of people and traffic on the Croisette, as congested as his native Hong Kong.

The lilac limousine edged slowly towards the hotel. 'I can remember when the Majestic was like a club,' Fyodor observed ruefully. 'Everybody knew each other and the staff remembered you. Now, look at it, Hetty. It's like Las Vegas.'

The publicist sat unusually silent beside him. A vast poster with an ocean liner on a collision course with what appeared to be a spaceship hove into view, dominating the corner of the hoarding. On top of it the words *Jupiter Landing* spelt out in blue neon flashed on and off with the urgency of a police siren.

The poster was not visible from Chantal's windowless office in the Palais. But the lack of a view didn't detract from the pleasure she felt at finally getting into action after the months of preparation. She was glad she had stayed. As she glanced at the computer screen in front of her, she smiled in satisfaction as she noted that the record of her alleged affair with the man from the London *Observer* had mysteriously disappeared from her file. It intrigued her to put faces to names she only knew through their written work. Critics who fulminated with loquacious indignation, shredding the attempts of the German cinema to address itself to modernism, cutting renowned Italian directors down to lifeless stumps, attacking the Festival authorities in past years for their muddle-headed selection of films and woefully mistaken choice of prizes, more often then not turned out to be mild, nervous men, maladroitly dressed in corduroy clothes, frequently flecked with dandruff.

'Don't worry about the British,' Madame had instructed her. 'Give the old brigade full board for a fortnight and a few of the promising ones six days but no meals and I doubt if you'll have much trouble. They're happy with a pass to the ordinary press screenings; they never complain about the starting times.'

The hierarchy of accreditation at Cannes was thought by some to have been based on a blueprint from the court of Louis XIV. The humble press pass merely admitted the bearer to two screenings at the most inconvenient times of day: eight-thirty in the morning when most people would normally be eating breakfast, and nine o'clock at night, when they would normally be having dinner. An intrepid London critic had once pointed out to Madame that if one had been enjoying the Lucullan delights of the local restaurants the previous evening, eight-thirty was a little early for a morning movie – with the popular ones people had to get to the screening by eight to be sure of entry. But Madame, with watertight rationality, had pointed out that if one had, instead, taken an early dinner, attended the nine o'clock screening the night before and gone sensibly to bed, the system worked perfectly.

The American press were less eager to fall in with this logic and were accorded more comfortable credentials, some given a gold dot that admitted them to a wider choice of screenings and some even made *Soiristes*, which meant they could even get into the nightly premieres at which evening dress, or *le smoking*, as the French called it, was *de rigueur* – although smoking itself was rigorously prohibited.

It was two such passes that Chantal pressed into the grateful palms of the clean-cut couple who were sitting in erect chairs opposite her as if they were in a registry office. The man wore a dark navy blazer with the obligatory, Oxford-style button-down blue shirt. The woman had straight blonde hair, her white linen skirt revealing an enviable pair of legs, the well-turned product of many miles of Californian jogging.

'Where are you staying?' Chantal enquired.

'The Carlton,' the woman replied.

Chantal wrote it down. She need hardly have asked; they were the sort of Americans who would opt for little less.

'Can you tell me your room numbers?'

The couple looked at each other uncertainly.

'I'm in 309 and Robert is in –' Sandra glanced across at him. 'What room are you in?'

He smiled. '710. Right up in the attic. Away from the noise.'

Chantal had not asked the question by accident. There was in fact no need to know their room numbers but she was curious to find out how much of a couple they really were. Robert Barrett, she thought, was agreeably free of the usual switch-on charm of television reporters. He was slightly hesitant, introspective. She liked that. And he seemed interested in her. Not in an overtly flirtatious way, but with a genuine sincerity that was not a customary calling card at the Festival.

'We do not get *Arts Action* in France but I have read about you. The *New York Times* is the paper that closes plays and you are the man who keeps them open.'

Robert was flattered. 'Only one. I can't make a living out of it.'

'We are happy to have you here. I hope you will give a good impression of us. How many programmes will you make?'

Sandra took the initiative. 'We're going to do two live specials on Sunday and Friday. We'll shoot material during the day for packaging and then Robert will anchor the show from the roof of the Palais around midnight. There'll be a delayed transmission to a lot of stations in the west but quite a few in the east will take us live with a repeat that night. We could be getting audiences of up to twenty million, maybe more.'

Chantal had little time to be impressed. A harassed Madame Rivette burst into the office, the rictus of panic on her face more dangerously pronounced then usual.

'Excuse me,' she apologised to the two Americans, then turned to Chantal. 'We have a tragedy. The Festival is one day old and we have a tragedy. I have on the line in my office the Ambassador from Sierra Leone. It is the first time that they have a film in the Festival, and yet their leading critics' – she looked down at the piece of paper she was carrying – 'from the *Freetown Times* and the *West African Gazette*, I think it is, say they have no accreditation. They telephoned him to report that they have been turned away.'

'Not possible,' Chantal assured her, 'I processed both applications myself.'

She moved back to the computer on the desk beside hers and, with the panache of a church organist, punched in the code to open the press programme. This year Chantal had proudly filed the nations in English. Moving swiftly through the alphabetical list, she confidently stopped the cursor at Sierra Leone and called it up. For several seconds she just gazed at the screen. Then she tapped some more keys and suddenly her shoulders stiffened. There was nothing at all appearing under 'S' in the accreditation list. 'Oh my God,' she said.

By the time Robert and Sandra emerged from the Palais the weather had cleared but the disaffected crowd had not. They made their way through it and past a little playground, lively with chirping children, to the seaward side of the Croisette. The pavement was dense with people, both local and foreign. It took no gift for languages to distinguish them: the former moved at the stately trundle of the promenade, the pace of people with no particular place to go, a speed further reduced in the case of the innumerable elderly ladies with miniature dogs on leads.

'They're taking them home for lunch,' Sandra observed, slipping her arm through Robert's, almost without thinking. She felt good: they were on the Riviera, the rain had stopped and she was glad to be with him.

He laughed. 'Apparently they taste much better if you can put them in mortal fear immediately before death. It produces an adrenalin that tenderises the meat. It's a tip the Koreans picked up from cannibals who'd cooked missionaries.'

'Can dogs have mortal fear?' she asked, adding, 'How come you know so much about it?'

'I'm a mine of incidental information. I sometimes think there's a microchip in my brain with a random access memory for anything except things that truly matter.'

Sandra stopped and, swinging him round to face her, looked earnestly into his eyes. 'And what really matters to you, Robert?'

He stared at her for a moment, temporarily taken aback by this apparent lurch into seriousness. He looked up and searched the sky, opening his mouth and running his tongue along the back of his teeth to indicate he was pondering the question. Then he returned her gaze.

'Lunch,' he said.

They ate at an outside table where they could observe the continuing parade. Cannes was prepared to lift up her skirts and shake a saucy leg in deference to this event that had put the town on the map. The rows of palm trees, graceful reminders that the deserts of Africa lay but a hop and a skip across the sea, temporarily sacrificed their dignity to bear the aberrant fruit of advertising posters: *Revenge of the Nuclear Ninjas*, *Nazi Sadists on Skis*, *Stir Crazy Nymphs* and *Who Sucks Wins*. Ninjas, Nazis and Nymphs, preferably sexually voracious women prisoners, had long been cultural favourites in the Cannes market-place.

Pavement artists jostled for position, potential Leonardos and Van Goghs vying for space to lay down their chalked Mona Lisas and Sunflowers, and a cap to collect the centimes. Young female students, dressed in black, plucked guitars and paid questionable respect to the memory of Edith Piaf by the toneless incantation of her saddest songs. Tall black Ethiopians in long white djellabas, some with monkeys on their shoulders, wandered among the tables offering neck-laces and bracelets made of jaguar teeth. Men in laterally striped sailors' shirts and tight black trousers, their rubbery faces painted white, attempted to attract a few francs by silent, jerky slow-motion routines, frequently featuring invis-ible panes of glass.

Robert regarded them abstractedly. 'I remember an uncle taking me to the circus when I was about four. As we sat down, he whispered to me, "There's something you should know – clowns are not actually funny," I've never forgotten that and I've always wondered whether the reason I don't find them funny is because he told me so, or because they really *aren't* funny.'

Sandra broke a piece of bread off her roll and popped it in her mouth. 'Mmm. Do we see anything as it really is, or just as we want to see it, or as we've been conditioned to see it? I'm not sure I ever found clowns very funny but I liked to be among people laughing at them. It made me feel warm. I was often sad for the clowns.'

'The maternal instinct stirs early on.' He picked up the menu. 'Anyway, what are you going to have? They say the Border Terrier is delicious on Saturdays.'

She cupped her chin in her hands. 'What were you like at four? I bet you parted your hair just the way you do now.'

'I had it parted for me by my mother. My problems began when I had to do it myself. I've been looking for someone else to do it ever since.'

They drank too much wine. That and the strong sun and their jet lag and the festive atmosphere of the town made them both feel light-headed and somnolent.

'What do you want to do now?' Sandra asked as Robert paid the bill.

'Same as you want to do,' he answered cryptically.

'I'm not sure. I think we should see a movie. After all, we're in Cannes. It says in this little magazine that there are preview screenings all along the Rue d'Antibes. We should be able to get in with our passes.'

She thought she spotted a flicker of disappointment on his face as he warned, 'I'll probably fall asleep.'

'Yes,' she replied teasingly. 'That's why I'd rather see a movie.'

It was a relief to escape from the crowds and the afternoon heat into the cool and shabby Star cinema. The film was already underway when they crept into two vacant seats at the very front.

'If I snore, wake me,' warned Robert.

He dropped off almost immediately but Sandra ignored his instruction. She kept a benevolent eye on the sleeping face beside her, feeling briefly maternal – men seemed to revert to childhood expressions when they fell asleep. She had to fight hard to stay awake herself but the task was made easier by the extraordinary things that were happening on the screen. It appeared to be a documentary about fishing. A large net was being lowered from the side of a ship to bring in the catch but when the blue fish-like creatures were eventually lifted on board they began to stagger in a semi-human fashion along the deck. A young woman, primly dressed in a white uniform, helped one of the struggling creatures into the ship's surgery where she started to dress its wounds.

Robert moved in his sleep, then half-opened his eyes and leant across to Sandra. 'I dreamt we were trying to make a programme but there weren't any cameras and this girl kept calling out – my God!'

'She said what?'

He was transfixed by the screen in a state of total bewilderment.

Sandra was amused by his reaction. 'Don't worry, they're from Jupiter.'

'But the girl –'

'Not her. I think she's English. Kinda cute, too.'

He was by now fully alert and wholly agitated. 'What's her name? Did they say her name?'

'Sister Florence, I think.' She patted his arm to reassure him. 'She's just an actress, Robert. Go back to sleep. It's only a movie.'

CHAPTER 15

Sunday 11th May 1997

Cannes

Elvis Ho wished he hadn't come. The expectant crowd in front of him seemed infinitely more intimidating than any stunt he had ever set himself. Journalists from all over the world, carnivorous for copy, were waiting to write down whatever he might have to say or record it in their tiny cassette machines. Behind them more than twenty television cameras made the inquisition even hotter with their searching lights. Elvis was a man of action, not words. He just made his films and people seemed to enjoy them; there was nothing in them that could be improved by analysis or discussion. And the one fact that might be of conceivable interest to the press – that he would never again return to Hong Kong – was certainly not something that he intended to reveal at this stage.

'Since he's called the *Yellow* Pirate, are you trying to imply that he's something of a coward?' The speaker was a broad-beamed American woman, her green-rimmed glasses bearing little chains that attached them to her neck.

Ho shaded his eyes from the lights to see who was speaking. 'Does he look like a coward?'

'No, I thought his actions were on the surface very brave, not to say foolhardy. But I wondered if you were somehow implying that within himself he's compensating for a deep-seated cowardice, maybe he failed to help his sister out of trouble when he was a child. Something like that.'

'He had no sister. No childhood. He went to sea as soon as he became a boy. He is the yellow pirate because his skin is yellow. Like me. No make-up.'

The appreciative laughter indicated that the room was on his side. A pallid young man in a patterned sleeveless sweater held up his pencil. He had a nasal, reedy English accent and a pedantic manner to match.

'Quite clearly you've paid homage to *Alexander Nevsky* in the way you've edited your battle scenes, especially the deep focus shooting and the contrapuntal use of the score. It seems to me that you've achieved, to some extent, the filmic fourth dimension by your synthesis of metric, rhythmic and tonal montage which does not, of course, appear at the level of the individual frame but only through the continuum of the projected film. Could you elaborate on the influence of Eisenstein in your work?'

Ho was genuinely confused. 'Eisenwho? Eisenhower? I think when he command a sea battle he stay on the shore. Cheung Po Sai always in the thick of it. No running away. Very brave. Not yellow.'

The approving applause added to the embarrassment of his intellectual inquisitor. A voice ran out from the back of the room, its owner unidentifiable in the darkness behind the television lights, 'Mr Ho, are *you* going to run away?'

Ho looked alarmed. 'What do you mean?'

'I think you know. When the communists take control of Hong Kong next month, will you still be there? Or, like so many of your fellow countrymen, will you be elsewhere?'

'Hong Kong is home for Ho. These are my people. We have been promised . . .'

Sandra turned to the cameraman beside her. 'You might as well turn off, Vik. This is yawn city.'

Robert looked at her questioningly. 'Are you sure? It's a big issue.'

'Not in California it isn't,' she replied dismissively. For reasons she failed to comprehend, his previously flirtatious attitude towards her seemed to have terminated abruptly from the moment they left the cinema the previous day. Maybe he was upset that they hadn't gone to bed that afternoon. Anyway, whatever it was, an undoubted *froideur* had descended on their relationship.

'We need something a bit controversial,' Robert insisted. 'I'm going to interview him afterwards.'

Sandra got up from her seat. 'Tape is cheap, but my time isn't. I'll see you back at the hotel later.'

Robert was accustomed to handling interviews with feature-film directors who demanded to position the camera and take over the whole shoot themselves. Elvis Ho was no exception. He was adamant that they conduct it by the unsightly television trucks at the back of the Palais. It was not the location that Robert would have chosen and he imagined how derisive Sandra's reaction would be when she watched the recording.

'You just ask me one question,' Ho demanded.

Robert was taken aback. 'I rather hoped we might take up the issue that was raised inside about your future in Hong Kong.'

'No Hong Kong. No future.' Elvis was not budging. 'But I give you good answer. You ask me if I do all my own stunts and you, Vik and Erik,' – he indicated the Belgian camera crew, whose names he had made a point of learning – 'you stay on me.'

There seemed to be no option but to comply with him. Robert felt more like a stooge than ever as he fed Ho his own question. The actor-director flared his nostrils, firing his reply at the camera.

'In Hollywood everything is fake – all models and special effects and stunt men. In Hong Kong everything is real – otherwise nobody believe us.'

With that he turned and sprang onto the bonnet of the truck behind him, scrambling up the windscreen and onto the roof. He ran along it, jumping across the ten-foot gap to the top of the truck beside it, and then on to the next from which he made an impossible leap onto the lowest balcony of the Palais. Finding a foothold in the corner wall he climbed up to the one above and, using the same process, shinned up and up, clambering from balcony to balcony until he had reached the roof of the building.

When he got there – more than a hundred feet above the ground – he turned and shouted down triumphantly, 'You get that, Vik?'

The Belgian, too experienced to make a sound while his

camera was still running, raised a thumb in acknowledgement.

Fyodor Lasky sipped his coffee in the cheerful morning sunlight, morbid in a cloud of gloom. Elizabeth and he had slept in separate beds last night. This was not a situation that he intended should continue. But he was unsure what to do about it.

This personal setback seemed to be robbing his professional life of much of its savour. Usually there was nothing he liked more during the festival than to sit in the glamorous surrounds of the Majestic pool and do deals.

Jupiter Landing was already in profit thanks to pre-sales and the contract with Warners who had bought the North American rights. Fyodor had well-established connections in the boardrooms of Burbank and Century City. Although the studio executives changed places with the regularity of a children's game of musical chairs, the significant difference in Hollywood was that nobody ever took a chair away. So it was not uncommon for someone who had been fired for being a calamitous head of production at Twentieth Century Fox to surface as the great white hope of MGM two months later.

Fyodor also knew how to pitch ideas. Most studio chiefs liked to have at least one picture shooting in Britain; it gave them the opportunity for more frequent trips to Europe. Even before the project was outlined, it was worth going into details of the Royal Charity Première, an unfair bargaining factor that British-based producers had over the Americans. The usual speech about British technicians and craftsmen being the best in the world was a traditional prelude to pointing out how much cheaper they were as well, thanks to the rate of exchange.

Studios were more likely to back films that shadowed recent hits and the notion that the rest of the universe might be inhabited by aliens who were not necessarily bellicose had found fresh favour in Hollywood with the 1996 money-maker, *People of the Pleiades*. Also, the novel on which *Jupiter Landing* was based had enjoyed huge paperback sales and Fyodor had diverted part of the budget of his last movie to option the book while it was still in proof stage.

But the ultimate weapon to close a contract with an outwardly confident executive who had little more idea of what would be next year's hit movie than the average Detroit cinema-goer was to hint that other studios were hungry for it. The man at Universal who turned down *Star Wars* or the one at Fox who rejected *Crocodile Dundee* or the executive at Paramount who passed on *Reagan: The Movie* remained demons of Hollywood mythology.

Leland Walters had been nagged by the worrying thought that *Jupiter Landing* just might be that runaway success. Since it had no stars, it was relatively cheap to make and all Lasky was asking was a North American distribution guarantee and the promise that the studio would spend fifteen million minimum on prints and advertising. Leland had forced Fyodor to go fifty-fifty on the North American video and broadcast rights which would return more than the box-office. The Hungarian was happy. He had expected to have to surrender all video rights plus South America. But the big studios had lost interest south of the border. Although Brazilians and Argentinians were among the most inveterate cinema-goers in the world, the returns from these territories were minimal, thanks to the low price of admission and the relative worthlessness of their currencies.

Once it was established that Warners would take the film, it had been an easy matter for Fyodor to go to even the staidest banks and raise the capital for it. And it was these sixty million dollars – seventy-five million as far as the press or any potential buyers were concerned – that now comfortably looked after his every domestic need: housekeeper, chauffeur, first-class travel, suites at the Pierre in New York and the George V in Paris, office expenses, an allowance to his wife, meals in restaurants, refurbishment of their house and even school fees (these last appeared in the weekly budget print-out as petty disbursements). All this before he paid himself three million dollars as a producer's fee which, annoyingly, attracted tax. This was, in some measure, compensated for by the fact that nobody in the Inland Revenue could pin down which expenses were or were not attributable to making a vast, special-effects movie. For the most part, money could be spread with tax-free abandon.

So, as he sat by the pool under the awning of the outside bar of the Majestic – he hated the sun as his thick wool jacket and heavy shoes indicated – he was already healthily in profit well in advance of the film's release. The nervous Dutch distributor sitting opposite him, sipping a mineral water which had cost the price of a glass of champagne in Amsterdam, was well aware of this and knew he was negotiating from a supplicant position. Hundreds of millions of dollars were won and lost in these crowded bars during the ten days of the Festival – many more than were spent in the Port Canto casino.

Fyodor usually enjoyed this daily game of Movie Monopoly, happy to trade territories which he had already in fact sold, in the knowledge that he could ask for impossible guarantees, confident that they would never be met but strengthening his bargaining position in those territories that remained. The Dutchman had made the cardinal error of actually having seen *Jupiter Landing* and had made the further mistake of admitting he liked it. Here his inexperience was palpable. The preferred stratagem of any buyer was to glimpse a showreel of highlights and to take the position 'we both know it's pretty average rubbish, but drop the price enough and I can dump it on a local circuit for you'.

Thus was the future cinema entertainment of the world visited on an innocent public by contracts concluded in this exclusive open-air film bazaar – a meeting place which, like the Savoy Hotel, was open to all.

'I can go to one and a half million for Brazil,' offered the Dutchman.

'Cruzeiros or dollars?' asked Fyodor.

The other man smiled – movie deals were always done in dollars.

'That's a possibility,' the producer continued. 'Make it a round two million and I'll throw in the television and video rights as well.'

The man's face fell. 'My offer was to include television and video, you know that. There is no market without them. And satellite.'

'There I cannot help you,' Fyodor acknowledged, quite truthfully. 'Satellite rights go before all others nowadays.

Men with cheque books arrive the moment you say you're going to make a movie, anxious to invest in anything to fill up the skies.'

His gaze travelled upwards to emphasise his words and, as it did so, it settled on Elizabeth who was standing on their balcony. Still wearing her white hotel bathrobe she held herself erect, merely touching the rail with one hand, looking across at the Palais. Fyodor knew he had lost her – although he refused to admit the fact either to her or to himself. Affairs with actresses had come and gone before – they, too, were part of the tax-free advantages of producing a movie – but more painful than her rejection of him as a lover had been her implicit rejection of him as a man and what he stood for.

Nobody had ever challenged him in the insidious and unwitting way that Elizabeth had managed to do. It was commonplace in the film industry to wax lyrical about Flaubert at a dinner party and then go and work on a film about Flash Gordon the next day. There was nothing incongruous in that: if you were a financial success, who questioned whether your money was made from marketing Schubert or schlock? Only Elizabeth, it seemed.

Neither Fyodor's wife nor his previous mistresses had paid much attention to his business methods. He was a mogul, he spoke like a mogul, he behaved like a mogul. Bankers courted him, journalists quoted him and flashlights popped at him at premières. Only Elizabeth had begun to divine the thin web of niggling compromises which had made him what he had become. The price he had paid for enjoying the directness of her youth was to face the abandoned aspirations of his own. In part, and in England, she had inspired him to do something about them, but in Hollywood he had instinctively reverted to type. Movies there were about money, not about lofty motives.

He was only too aware of what had caused the cooling of their relationship and he knew his life would be infinitely more harmonious if it cooled completely. But he could not readily accept being deprived of someone with whom he had, unexpectedly, become so passionately entangled.

'Okay, a million five,' he said casually, his eyes and emotions still targeted on the unmoving figure above them.

The Dutchman was sure that he had not heard correctly. 'A million and a half? Television and video included?'

'The lot. And you can have Peru as well. They never pay and they're nothing but trouble.'

Somehow the thrust and parry of a well-fought deal had temporarily lost its edge. Fyodor rose abruptly from his chair and stretched out his hand. 'I have to go. One of my stars . . . a little temperamental . . . you understand.'

She was still on the balcony when he got to the room. He quietly closed the door and moved across to her, putting his arms around her waist from behind.

'What a glorious day. I've already offloaded Brazil for three times what it's worth. Glad you came?'

She stiffened. 'I'm not sure.'

'Of what?'

'Of anything at the moment.'

He put his head next to hers, nuzzling her neck with his chin. It felt unshaven. The smell of Gitanes made her slightly nauseated.

'Let's make love,' he said, slipping his hand inside her robe and cupping her breast.

She shook her head. 'Not now, not just now.'

'What's wrong?'

'I'm just not very sure of myself at the moment, Fyodor. Nor of us, either.'

'How can you say that? Why do you say that now?'

'I told you the night of the Oscars what I thought.'

'That was a fit of temperament. What about the good times, the nights, we've spent together? Don't they mean anything to you?'

She turned to him and he could see that she had been crying. 'They did, of course they did, at the time. But at the moment I feel very confused. I wish I hadn't agreed to come. I need time to myself, to clear my mind. I'll do what I can for the picture. I know what it means to you. I'm sorry.'

'You're a cunt,' he said.

'When you say reasonable laundry expenses, what do you intend by reasonable? I mean, socks and underwear, yes –'

Later on that Sunday in the darkened conference room of the same hotel, its curtains drawn against the penetrating afternoon sun, the Festival jury were concluding their first meeting. The British critic was holding sway.

'– but I would have thought that a maximum of ten shirts was too low. What if you spilt some red wine on your dinner shirt, for instance? Are you suggesting that I should have brought a spare one from London and that I should take them both home dirty? I mean, I had to hire a dinner jacket and I thought that would be allowable but evidently it's not. And then there's the question of lunches. I know we get a free dinner each day but lunch at the hotel comes to two hundred francs against an allowance of only one hundred francs. I mean, are we expected only to have lunch every other day? And I don't have time to go anywhere else because I have to get this book on Molly Ringwald finished by the end of June and the publishers are ringing me up all the time. Telephone calls, there's another problem. It seems to me the allowance is all right for French jurors but with international calls –'

Renaud Callet could bear it no longer. 'The precise allowances for jurors were made clear to you when you gracefully accepted your appointment. They have been arrived at as a result of similar submissions made in previous years – very often from our dear colleagues at the other end of the Tunnel. If you care to put in writing your suggestions for future amendments, they will be considered by my Board in September. But, for the moment, the answer is –'

'*Non*?' suggested the British critic.

'*Oui*,' Renaud replied. 'I think that concludes our discussions – your discussions, I'm so sorry – for the moment. The next meeting will be here at six o'clock on Thursday. I'm sure it would help the debate if our friend from Italy had stayed to the end of at least one of the competition films by then.'

The named juror grimaced as they filed out past Renaud. 'A Chinaman who thinks he's Errol Flynn, an Australian who thinks he's Mussolini and another Englishman lamenting his lost empire. Where is the true cinema of today?'

He was through the door before Renaud could muster a reply. One member of the jury remained behind, the only one who was wearing a formal suit and tie and who had made his contribution from a sheet of neatly typed notes. Henri Chaillot, the Foreign Minister, ran his hand through his thick silver-grey hair, as a positive gesture of relief, and refilled his glass with Badoit water.

'What was so wrong with Mussolini?' he asked. 'He founded the Venice Film Festival, didn't he? Do you always ask such bizarre types to be jurors? If the French system of justice were run by people like them we would bring back the guillotine. Why do they all hate films so much? They're only toys for the adult mind after all.'

'They probably see too many of them. Excess makes the heart grow harder.' The Director walked to the window and pulled back a curtain to look down at the people in evening dress sipping their twenty-dollar Kir Royales on the terrace before they went across to the Palais for the evening film. A young man was swimming in the pool, the curve of his bronzed back bringing a Hockney to life in the limpid blue water.

'This dinner I'm giving on Friday,' Chaillot muttered irritably, 'do we have to invite them all?'

'Only those with clean evening shirts.' Renaud's attempt at humour met with little response. 'It would be the correct thing to do. We have on our computer the list of approved guests in each category and the highest would include the jury. There are ways round it in some cases. We have a tradition at the Festival that we do not send invitations to people at their hotels until one or two days before, or in some chosen cases, one or two days after a party or reception.'

Chaillot nodded approvingly. 'My office had a call from the Swiss Embassy mentioning some problem with invitations or accreditations. Was that sorted out satisfactorily?'

'Of course. No problem. You know the Swiss. Always complaining. Everything must go like clockwork. The dinner is for the Australians, though. They were a little over-excited by our choice of films. It will repair matters diplomatically.'

The Foreign Minister glanced through his file. 'Yes. They've submitted an enormous list of names. Don Bates, Minister of Information, Dick Lockwood, Ambassador to France – nobody of any distinction.' He uncapped his pen. 'Why don't we ask Ken Turner, the Man of the Media? That's just the sort of person who might interest my wife; she can't stand diplomats.'

Renaud eyed him with suspicion. He presumed he meant the Australian actor, Ted Barlow, who had played Ken Turner. It's only a movie, minister, he managed to refrain from saying.

By seven twenty-five the first première of the evening was well under way. The steps leading to the Grand Auditorium Lumière had been covered in a lush vermilion carpet. Spreading crowds on either side craned their necks to see who was arriving. Like the rats and children of Hamelin, they had been summoned from their houses and streets and cafés by the amplified strains of a military band bellowing forth familiar themes – most frequently Strauss's *Also sprach Zarathustra* – to add an imperial dignity to what, after all, was a show-business event.

The French, having finally got rid of their monarchy more than a hundred years previously, seemed paradoxically to love the trappings of royalty more than any other nation. The biggest crowds in the history of the Festival had turned out in 1987 to see the Prince and Princess of Wales come to the movies. And tonight, although there were no monarchs or princes present, as on twenty-two other occasions throughout the Festival the triumphal entry into the evening screening was accorded a mock-regal status. Dress rules were enforced with draconian inflexibility. In years gone by men, especially Americans who had not realised they needed to bring a tuxedo, would be admitted in a lounge suit, provided they also had a white shirt and bow tie. People wearing sneakers were always turned away in disgrace. But today it was either *le smoking* or no admittance; indeed there were those on the Board who lobbied that a white tuxedo should become essential dress. Cannes maintained its pre-eminence in the world league of film festivals because, however low the standard of the movies might fall, the standards of glamour were steadfastly maintained.

Not that most of those arriving were in need of rules to dictate their apparel. They had been preparing for this moment all day; some had been preparing all year. A ticket to a Cannes première was as precious as one to the Wimbledon final or the Super Bowl. Women wore full flowing gowns, diamond tiaras and deep tans. Their escorts frequently sported white bow ties and velvet cloaks with golden clasps. They could have been arriving at a banquet thrown by the Sun King at Versailles; in fact what they were going to do was to sit in the dark in closely packed seats and watch a film with French subtitles set in a bauxite mine in Sierra Leone.

Bringing up the traditional end to this cavalcade were the stars and directors and producers – tonight not faces immediately recognisable, but generously welcomed at the top of the thirty-five steps, nonetheless, and bathed in a downpour of camera flashlights. There, escorted by a guard of honour, provided on alternate years by the Gendarmerie or the more vaunted Compagnies Republicaines de Sécurité, they turned to acknowledge the crowd. It was Renaud Callet's duty, as Director, to greet them at this moment, not a task which he always approached with the relish of his predecessors.

After they had gone in, the screening could start. The more knowing members of the crowd lingered, aware that real, larger-than-life stars needed to reassure themselves of their status by arriving late. The record for this was held by Elizabeth Taylor at the fortieth Festival who turned up at an important film shortly before the screening ended. Tonight there was a rumour that Bud Booker might be coming, but only an ageing French pop singer trotted in the wake of the cast, delight enough for many in the crowd.

Jenny Bates gazed down on the glittering scene from the Australian Film Board balcony on the fifth floor of the Gray d'Albion apartments, directly across the Rue des Serbes from the Majestic. She was not planning to attend the première as was clear from her apparel: striped surfers' shorts and a yellow T-shirt with a blood-red poppy emblazoned on the front of it. She had been piqued to learn about Vincent Wall's film second-hand and further piqued that the information should have come from the abhorrent Tony Birch. But when she saw it she left the cinema in an awed daze, stunned by the sheer power of the piece. Without hesitation she had committed herself and her staff to promoting it.

A Swedish journalist with an open notebook was earnestly trying to get a story out of her.

'Is it now the case that you no longer have the government backing to make the good movies?' he enquired.

Do they all speak like that because they've seen too many Bergman movies, she wondered uncharitably.

'Not true at all,' she bellowed. 'Governments don't make movies, inspiration makes them. In Sydney we have the Hollywood of the future: we have the talent, the expertise, the resources, the sun and the stars.'

He wrote all this down. 'Is it stars like up there?' he queried, pointing at the evening sky.

'No, mate,' she laughed, indicating the Palais with her lighted cigarette, 'stars like down there.'

'I hope you don't mind my questions, yes?' he asked. 'My newspaper needs a story and we have the problem with the credentials.'

'Carry on,' she assured him. She didn't mind. They had a table booked at La Mère Besson at nine and it had been a whole year since Jenny's taste buds had been quickened by the thought of La Mère's *feuilleté* of asparagus.

'For a young industry you have made many strides, no?'

'We wear many strides,' she replied to the amusement of Hal Stephenson, her press officer, who was uncorking another bottle of Coonawarra Sauvignon. 'No, you've got it wrong. We're the oldest bloody film industry in the world. We were making movies more than a hundred years ago. *The Early Christian Martyrs*, sponsored by the Salvation Army, no less, began shooting in 1887. We had the first two-reeler, *The Story of the Kelly Gang* – Ned Kelly, you know, was much more of a buckaroo than Jesse James or Butch Cassidy. *And* we invented sound.'

'How do you spell buckaroo?' asked the Swede.

'Any way you want to.'

'The Marsupial Marauder,' the reporter enquired, indicating a poster on the inside wall, 'is that a man or an animal?'

Jenny picked up her glass of Sauvignon. 'Well, he's a man. But there you touch on the heart of the picture. He's born months prematurely without a placenta. You understand? So his mother brings him up like a marsupial, in a pouch on her stomach, until he can fend for himself. But because he's like a marsupial he has a very small brain and he goes berserk. It's a beaut film.'

'And this Man of the Media, is he marsupial, too?'

'More like a mammal really. He's this whale who devours newspapers and television stations like so much plankton.'

Before the journalist could ask her to spell plankton, and to extricate herself from further questioning, Jenny called across to her assistant. 'Hal, will you get Ted Barlow out of the dunny, this man should really talk to him.'

Hal obediently went and rapped on the lavatory door. 'Ted, Jenny needs you.'

The voice of the actor who had portrayed the upright media baron, Ken Turner, came from within, drunk and desperate. 'Hal, you got any crack, mate?'

'No, you'd better get out here.'

The door cautiously opened and a stoned and staring man, his flies undone and the tail of his shirt outside his trousers, made his unsteady way to the balcony. He seemed hypnotised by the flashing *Jupiter Landing* sign across the street.

'Those fucking pigs,' he shouted at it, 'watching me day and night. I can't wait to get out of this shit heap. What do they expect you to do, sniff the sand?'

He threw the crumpled lager can he was holding in his hand in the direction of the sign, then slumped over the balcony. A trickle of yellow vomit fell from the corner of his mouth onto the striped awning beneath.

'Have you met Ted Barlow?' Jenny cheerfully asked the amazed journalist, 'a rising star of the new Australian cinema.'

Had he but known it, the apartment that Barlow was inadvertently decorating contained sufficient white powder to keep him sniffing until kingdom come. Not that any of the men assembled around the dining room table availed themselves of it. Several were smoking cigarettes but the only refreshments on display were bottles of mineral water and Coca-Cola.

The table was covered with various sets of plans and a chunky Frenchman indicated details on them with his stubby forefinger.

'This is the Plaza President Georges Pompidou. The only cars that can get in here are the official Festival Renaults, police vehicles, of course, ambulances, if necessary, radio and television hook-up trucks, which are stationed here all the time, and repair and delivery lorries. But every one of them has to have an official stopping or parking sticker.'

The man at the head of the table turned to a colleague on his right.

'We have those, yes? From Paris?'

The man nodded. Behind the tortoiseshell reading glasses he looked not unlike the young Alain Delon.

'But you can get into the Palais des Festivals from the underground car park,' the Frenchman continued. 'There you just have to pay to get in or, rather, to get out. Nine hundred cars on two levels. They're covered by cameras, of course, and inside the Palais there are a further sixty-five video cameras, not all of them obvious. They're monitored by screens and every ten seconds each of them records a picture on tape. Now here' – he pointed with a ruler – 'there's a cordon known as the sacred perimeter that's protected outside the Palais. Both there and inside there are regular patrols by the CRS – they're the hot-shot brigade, more powerful than the gendarmes, you can see them walking in twos and threes with portable radios and sub-machine-guns.'

He stood back from the map, twitchily pushing a matted strand of flaxen hair out of his eyes. 'Now every morning of the Festival at nine o'clock there's a security committee chaired by the Under-Prefect for the Alpes-Maritimes. They constantly update the arrangements –'

His flow of information was interrupted by the man in charge of the meeting.

'It is not relevant. We will take action when the time is right.'

'When might that be?' enquired the Frenchman timorously.

'When we can get maximum publicity.'

CHAPTER 16

Monday 12th May 1997

Cannes

'They thought the show sucked.'

'That's not so. Nobody said so. Hurley seemed quite happy last night.'

'Believe me, Robert, that was the general opinion.'

'Whose opinion?'

'Raymond Rainier. He said if he'd had to review it, it would have been a big thumbs-down.'

'I don't give a toss what he thinks, he's a venomous fag.'

'Oh, calling people names, are we? Lucky he isn't black as well.'

'That's not fair.'

'You're not fair.' Tanya's voice tapered off.

'I can't hear you,' Robert shouted into the receiver.

'I'd stopped speaking.'

'Well, thanks for calling to tell me how much you hated it. Just the encouragement we needed.'

Her voice became distinctly audible and her tone not a little sarcastic. 'How are *we*?'

Robert exploded. 'Jesus Christ, Tanya, grow up. Men and women work together in this world and it may not be your experience, but some of them actually manage to do so without fucking each other.'

'That's not fair,' she echoed.

'Why don't you lay off Sandra?'

'You, too.'

'I'm going to put the phone down,' he warned.

'No, don't do that. I won't be able to go to sleep. It's late. I needed to talk to you.'

Needed to check up on me, Robert thought, glancing at his watch. It was five to eight. He had better move fast to make the morning screening – they were going to interview the director immediately after it.

'I meant to be positive,' Tanya apologised. 'Only it didn't come out that way. They didn't actually hate the programme but I heard Hurley talking to LA afterwards. They seemed to be happy with all that colour shit – they liked the loony who thought he was the reincarnation of Charlie Chaplin and that crazy Chinese waiter clambering over the multi-storey car park – but everyone's seen those bimbos on the beach and people pimping up the steps before. Hurley said it was all flab and no muscle. He wants news.'

'There isn't any.'

'Then I suggest you make some. But not with Sandra. I love you and I only meant to help but now I'm going to sleep. Goodnight.'

'I love you, too,' said Robert but fortunately she had put the phone down before his distant deceit reached her.

Outside, Cannes was already rising and shining. Water vans sprayed the early morning streets, maids aggressively polished hotel plaques, waiters washed already pellucid restaurant windows, stooped gardeners were carefully replacing any flowers that had begun to fade in the neatly groomed beds which ran along the middle of the Croisette and, down on the beaches, young men in white shorts and striped T-shirts were sweeping the sand and arranging the sun-beds in military rows at right angles to the sea wall, as if a brutish sergeant-major were about to come and inspect them. The whole town, Robert reflected, was being cleaned like a dance hall after the night before, its ashtrays emptied and the left-over liquor poured away. The Almighty, too, was playing his part in scrubbing the morning – the unblemished aqua-marine sky and the purity of the Mediterranean air defied everybody to feel other than good.

Not that it did a lot to uplift Robert's spirits as he half-walked, half-jogged along the sea front towards the Palais. Tanya was right. Last night's programme had been a stinker. The visuals had been clichés that could have come out of a film

library, the live interviewees had lapsed into stale superlatives, the critics had all tediously agreed with each other and
the promised star of the show, Ted Barlow, Man of the Media,
had arrived so coked up that he had to be carried down from
the roof of the Palais before the show began and laid out,
comatose, on the beach below.

He blamed himself, not just for the sloppy programme, but
the schism that had opened between him and Sandra which
undoubtedly had contributed to it. He had been unable to
explain to her what had happened in the cinema that
Saturday afternoon; he had hardly been able to explain it to
himself. Sandra had wanted to leave but he had persuaded
her to stay, doggedly waiting for the final credits.

Elizabeth Brown – probably a stage name, he thought. But
he was certain, as certain as anybody could be in the
hallucinatory atmosphere of Cannes which daily became
more fictional than factual, that she was Grace, the girl from
Aspen. No other human being, he told himself, could possess
such eyes, sapphire blue in pools of umber, nor a look so
wistful and other-worldly and beguiling. In the intervals
between working on the Sunday programme he had made
desperate efforts to find out how he might contact her. A
temporary receptionist at the Warner Bros press office had
offered the grudging information that the film's producer,
Fyodor Lasky, might be in town for the Festival but she had
no idea where he was staying and, besides, Warners were not
handling the movie outside the States.

The flashing blue sign of *Jupiter Landing*, anaemic in the
morning sun, winked reprimandingly at him as he reached
the Palais des Festivals. Jay Gatsby failed, he thought. But it
was not a failure he could continue to accept. Whatever it
might cost in pride or his present relationship, he was
determined to devote himself to tracking this woman down.
He anxiously scanned the faces of every female he passed in
the street, convinced that there was a reasonable chance that
she might be here in Cannes. Grace – he had looked up her
name – the undeserved mercy of God. Well, if God's mercy
didn't deliver her, he would find her for himself whether he
deserved her or not.

Madame Rivette was at the entrance barrier watching the

journalists and critics arrive. A few of the older hands stopped to have a word with her. They knew she always welcomed some opinions on the previous night's competition entry. Like most of those who worked in the administration, she rarely had time to watch a film during the Festival, but was obliged to talk knowledgeably about them at official receptions and dinner parties. Mischievous newcomers, cognisant of this, had been known to add car chases to period melodramas or deviant love scenes to peasant tales of Indian village life for her benefit. It did not take a computer error for such journalists to find their credentials missing the following year.

'How did it go last night?'

Robert was jolted out of his daydream; the question appeared to be addressed to him. He had put away his press card and was about to sprint up the steps, but he turned and saw Chantal, fresh and smiling like the morning, her urchin red hair vibrant in the sun. He walked the few steps back down to her.

'It went.'

'Not good?'

'Not good, not bad. It was technically okay. The harbour lights looked pretty. We'd intended it as a scene-setter but back in the States they wanted something more, or different, or both. They're getting a bit blasé, if you know what I mean.'

'I do. It's a French word. Perhaps I can help.'

Robert was grateful. 'Sure. I'd welcome it.'

Chantal responded to his open smile. She was desperate to talk to somebody and yet was afraid to contact Raoul again. He had become withdrawn and strange. Whereas Robert, she thought, looked a bit like one of those clean-cut heroes in American movies who manage to effect a rescue without ever putting a hair out of place. 'Do you want to have lunch? We have only a brief break. But normally I go to the Maschou Beach at one, for a *salade niçoise* and a little sun.'

'I'll meet you. Thanks. I'd better get inside.'

'Your friend has already gone in. Maybe she's saved you a seat,' she called after him, adding puckishly, 'or maybe she hasn't.'

*

'We have reservations. I made them myself, confirmed them myself and reconfirmed them myself. These are stars of a very important movie and not accustomed to being treated like this.'

It cut no ice with the head waiter at the Plage Victorine. Everybody insisted they were stars of a very important movie.

'Let me handle this,' Hetty Berman continued, a superfluous remark since neither Tim nor Douglas nor Elizabeth showed any inclination to do so. 'Couldn't we just squeeze into that space over there?'

'I bet that comes out of the budget of the bloody film,' observed Douglas, who had been soothing himself on Ricard since that morning, as he watched Hetty pass a wad of notes to the unsmiling head waiter. 'No wonder you never get any money from your percentage points.'

An uncomfortable table was hurriedly made up for them, well away from the beach and on people's route to the lavatories.

'You've got to know how to work the system,' Hetty announced, proud of her triumph. 'I've been coming here for nearly twenty years and it's only now that I'm beginning to beat it. The *pommes frites* at the Victorine are heaven.'

'Do you think we could have a bottle of wine?' asked Douglas.

'Red, white or rosé?' Hetty enquired, anxious to be of service.

'I should imagine one of each to begin with.'

None of the passing waiters appeared to notice Hetty's windmill gestures or the accompanying squeaks employed to gain their attention. In frustration she got up to go to the bar herself. A waiter arrived immediately she had disappeared.

'A bottle each of red, white and rosé,' Douglas demanded, 'and *le menu*.'

Elizabeth could see that Tim was appraising the other tables, bubbling and alive and cacophonous with chatter.

'Europeans seem to be at home in restaurants,' she remarked, 'they've been going to them since childhood. You can spot the Brits because they're so much more starchy. It's the legacy of nannies who won't let you speak during meals and maiden aunts who take you to punitive afternoon teas where the ring of bone china is louder than the hush of conversation.'

Tim leant back in his chair authoritatively. 'The advertising festival's much better. There are no foreigners at all – well, just some Americans to make it seem international. My agency hired a villa once up by the Colombe d'Or in Vence – the hotel with the doves and the Picassos. Cocaine Castle our place was known as, not without justification, although why you have to go through all that tommy-rot when a good whisky will do the trick and cheaper beats me. There's something in human nature that draws people to pleasures simply because they're illicit. I bet booze was never more fun than when you had to go to a speakeasy in Chicago.'

'I think it's pretty good fun now,' Douglas interjected, waking up like the dormouse as Hetty returned with a cargo of red, white and rosé at the same time as the waiter placed three further bottles on the table.

She appeared not to notice, so anxious was she to unburden her good news. 'I bumped into Myron Spada of Spadapix and got us all invited to his party out at La Napoule. It's a really historic château – Napoleon landed there – and it's going to be a very, very exclusive occasion.'

Douglas filled up his glass from the nearest bottle. 'Not that bloody exclusive.'

Hetty turned on him. 'What do you mean?'

'Well, they're advertising for people to go. I saw it in that dreadful little magazine you can't stop them pushing under your door at some unearthly hour every morning. You know the one, full of frightful fat Americans all smiling foolishly at each other at parties given by laboratories. You could tear the invitation out of the magazine and provided you had a dinner-jacket and you were prepared to sit through some ghastly film – *The Ponce and the Pendulum* I'm sure it was called – a bus would take you to La Napoule afterwards.'

He swallowed his white wine and, with a passing observation of 'filth', switched to the rosé. Hetty ignored the insult to her size and her nationality – but she was not prepared to accept any criticism of her professional abilities.

'*Those* people will stand around in the courtyard at the pay bar. We will be inside at one of Myron's select tables. I see you've ordered.'

A waiter had begun to spoon *bouillabaisse* into the brown bowls placed before them.

'I only asked for *le menu*.' Douglas started to sound contrite.

'*La carte* is the French for menu' – Hetty's revenge was swift and satisfactory – '*le menu* is a five-course meal here, starting with the soup.'

'Look,' Elizabeth pointed with delight, 'mine's got a fish's head in it. It looks just like you did in the film, Douglas. You laid this on specially, didn't you, Hetty?'

The American was about to deny it but then caught the sparkle in Elizabeth's eye. It was the first time, since they had arrived in Cannes, that the girl had evinced any outward cheerfulness. Hetty could see her evident relief at being away from the shadow of Fyodor and in the more carefree company of her fellow actors.

'Doesn't look like me at all,' said Douglas, 'I was blue.'

'Blue-blooded. An aristocrat from outer space,' Elizabeth teased. 'I'm sure all the science-fiction magazines will want to talk to you. Has any one seen the film yet, Hetty?'

'There were screenings at the weekend and there's another tomorrow. The response has been very good, but you've no idea how hard it is to promote a movie with no stars in it. It's like selling perfume without a sample. You can't *describe* Chanel.'

Douglas refilled his glass with rosé. He was the only one who was drinking. 'I thought we *were* stars. That's how you got the table.'

'You'll all be big, big stars once the movie's released in the States,' the American assured him. 'At Cannes we've got to use different tactics. They're slow but they're working. People are queuing at my room from dawn for their free *Jupiter Landing* cotton bomber jackets and we're clean out of those ship's log leather diaries.'

'I never got one,' Tim was visibly put out.

'Don't worry, I'll make sure you do.' Hetty fumbled in her bag for a Gucci note-pad. 'What colour would you like?'

'I think I'll try a little red,' Douglas replied, seizing the bottle with both hands.

'Blue,' Tim stated affirmatively, 'like Douglas's blood used to be before it turned to wine.'

'I've got a full schedule for you on Thursday, Elizabeth,' Hetty went on, 'two American movie magazines anxious to hear about the British brat pack, a modelling session with a French teenage monthly and some English Sunday newspaper wants to do a day in your life.'

'A night in her life, more like,' Douglas suggested, none too softly.

Elizabeth decided to ignore the remark; she enjoyed a bit of bitchiness in the English theatrical tradition. 'I don't know how to model,' she confessed to Hetty. 'And I'm not sure that I want to know.'

The publicist was half-way through her third giant Mediterranean prawn. 'It's a euphemism, darling. They just want to take your picture in a bikini.'

Biting her lower lip, Elizabeth enquired with trepidation, 'And what's the British brat pack? There was an American brat pack ten years ago, but they grew out of it. I've never heard of a British one.'

'Journalists need a line. I gave them that one. Some of them have to be led, you know, they can't think for themselves. Just name three or four young actors and actresses and you've got a brat pack. Simple.'

Before Elizabeth could say that she couldn't think of any, Tim broke in, querulously, 'What about me?'

Hetty waited until her mouth was free of prawns. 'The only director anybody's interested in Cannes is the director as star. Polanski, Fellini, Godard. Doesn't matter if you're churning out garbage as long as you've got a name. But you, Tim, have got to wait for the critics – especially the ones who think you made the movie on your own. We just need a couple of notices talking about Tim Lawrence's *Jupiter Landing* and we can start marketing the *auteur* angle.'

'But the posters already say Fyodor Lasky's *Jupiter Landing*,' Tim pointed out.

As if summoned by an assistant director, the producer appeared at the foot of the steps and made his entry into the restaurant. He surveyed the table with an ironic eye. 'I hope you're all getting enough to eat and drink. Deaths from malnutrition in Cannes are comparatively rare, I'm told, and you'll be happy to hear Howard's recovering from his food-poisoning. Oysters, I think. Always better to have an "R" in the month, whatever the French say.'

Hetty was on her feet, still savouring her first taste of *gigot d'agneau*. 'Here, Fyodor; take my place. I'll get another chair. Waiter!'

Fyodor remained standing. 'Thank you, no. I have to take another meeting. Hetty has given you all the details for tomorrow. We would like you to wear your nurse's costume, if you would, Elizabeth my dear.'

Both the information and the offhand way in which it was delivered made Elizabeth prickly with discomfort. She stared nervously at Hetty who appeared to be starting another anxiety attack. 'Everything's under control,' the publicist assured Fyodor. 'I was going to tell them over dessert. Profiteroles – you'd die for them.'

'We will pay in cash. There is to be no record of this hire agreement anywhere in your books nor are you to mention it to anyone, understood?' Raoul Bazin spoke softly into the phone. His back was to the bar which was busy with lunchtime customers.

'Understood,' said the voice at the other end.

'I cannot emphasise this enough. If any word of this gets out, the repercussions for you will not bear thinking about.'

'I said I understood. Don't threaten me. Just turn up on time.'

How can the French eat so much and still keep anorexic figures? Robert thought, hoping that his sunglasses prevented anyone from noticing that as he walked he was conducting a survey of the topless brown bodies lying torpidly on the shore. He did not feel particularly aroused by the sight. There was little mystery in encountering a girl who was almost entirely naked; it was like being bearded by a stranger at a party who insisted on telling you their entire life story in five minutes. After that, what?

Behind, the symmetrical succession of beach restaurants, each parading its individual canopy like battle colours, was thronged with Festival delegates, not burdened by the need to attend movies in the afternoon nor spend their days in the unappetising dungeon of the Film Market. People sat in the sun in shorts and swimming costumes and set about their *loup de mer* and *steack tartare* as casually as if it were the divine right of every human being to enjoy such privileges. The South of France, he reflected, looked like an advertisement for itself.

When finally he reached the Maschou Beach, Chantal had already finished her salad. Her shirt hung over the back of her chair and she sat in a pink bikini top and neat khaki skirt, sipping a small cup of coffee.

'I'm sorry I'm late,' he apologised. 'Never do an interview with a new-wave director, they have a beginning, a middle but no end.'

She laughed. 'I was early. Would you like a coffee?'

'A big one – double, treble. In the States they give you a large cup and they fill it up as many times as you want for no extra charge. Here they offer you a thimble and it costs the same again for another thimble.'

'It's the quality,' she smiled. 'Less is more – like our movies.'

He dropped down into the chair opposite her. 'Would you like a proper drink?'

She shook her head. 'I have to get back. I've thought of two things that might help. You should go to Mougins – it's only twenty minutes away up behind the town – to the restaurants there. Pretend you're doing interviews with the chefs – they're always keen on the publicity – but try and get a look at their reservation books. A lot of the big stars come to the Riviera at this time but they stay away from Cannes itself. They're dotted around on yachts and in villas and they eat out every night. Their friends tend to flaunt their names to get the bookings and the best tables.'

Robert made a note in the diary given to him by the Andalusian film industry.

'At the other end of the scale,' she went on, 'you should go to Le Petit Carlton, on the Rue d'Antibes, just behind your hotel. Young film-makers and producers hang out there. They talk and drink and drink and talk. The patron will keep it open until six or seven in the morning if need be. That's where you hear the true stories of Cannes, the ones which are not in the trade magazines or handed out to everyone at press conferences. That should give you some leads.'

'That's great. We'll go tonight. Thank you.'

'Where is Miss Lewis, by the way? I thought she might come with you.'

'She's with the crew, taking some shots of the Old Port.'

'Is everything all right?'

'It's fine.' Robert tried to sound as casual as he could, but to prevent their conversation going in a direction he did not wish, he started to ask Chantal some questions.

'How long have you been doing this job?'

'This is my third year in the press office, but I've been with the Festival for five years now, starting as a secretary.'

'And do you like it? How long do you think you'll stay?'

'I like it well enough but – ' she began but was interrupted by a waiter with a large espresso and the bill. Chantal had money in her hand ready to pay, but Robert would not let her.

'You're very kind,' she said.

'You're a mine of information. Why the but?'

'I'm sorry, I don't understand.'

'You said you liked it "but". But what?'

'Oh, nothing. This may be my last year. We'll see.'

'You have another job lined up? Another way of life. A man, perhaps?'

'No, nothing like that.' The timbre of her voice changed as if he had trespassed on forbidden territory.

Robert tried to remedy his false step. 'Just a change then?'

'Maybe. I don't know.'

Chantal took her shirt from the back of the chair and unthinkingly began to put it on, as if it were natural for her to dress in front of him. Robert found her action strangely suggestive – a paradox with so much naked flesh around them. She stood up and tucked it in, and a formality returned to her demeanour.

'I must go. Thank you again for lunch.'

As she stepped past him, some inexplicable instinct made him reach out and grab her elbow. It startled her.

'What is it?' she demanded defensively.

'Could you sit down? Just for a minute.'

She did as she was told. He took a slow sip of coffee to give himself time to prepare his words.

'Forgive me for saying this, but French girls don't usually ask strangers to lunch.'

She pursed her lips. 'Why not? You are our guests.'

'When you suggested it this morning, there was something you wanted to say, wasn't there?'

'I have told you. Mougins and Le Petit Carlton.'

'No, there was something more. Something that mattered more.'

'You're wrong.'

Robert's voice grew softer and more confident at the same time. Her words might not confirm his suspicions, but her manner did. 'I am not wrong. But there is nothing I can do. You have two alternatives. You can either leave now, as you were about to, or you can tell me.'

'Look,' Chantal exclaimed, pointing upwards. 'The planes are coming, bringing messages from the skies. "You cannot afford to miss Man of the Media. Tomorrow he may be your boss." They're always so difficult to understand, like crossword puzzles.'

Robert remained deliberately silent. Her eyes followed the planes for a while and then she looked down at the table, avoiding his gaze.

'It's nothing really. In the winter there was a robbery at our office in Paris. The men were masked – they were never caught. They didn't take any money but I'm sure they were looking for something else. Everyone seemed to forget about it. But not me. They said I only kept worrying because I'd been tied up. I was the only one there. But I knew there was something more. And ever since I have come to Cannes I have had a feeling that something is wrong here. I told myself to forget it and not to be silly. But last night I heard a voice, just someone in the crowd after the film. I didn't really recognise it but my senses reacted before my mind. I'm certain it was the man who threatened me. He's here in Cannes.'

'The baby you used in your film. Was it a real one?'

'Well, I should have thought it was fairly obvious. In some

shots it was, but not when it was dead. We used a lot of prosthetics – make-up sort of thing.'

The balcony of the Australian Film Board suite was beginning to fill up with journalists and other visitors as it tended to at happy hour every evening. The provision of free lager by a sponsoring brewery was just as strong an attraction as the films. Possibly more so.

Vincent Wall, nursing nothing stronger than a cup of tea, sat at a table opposite three Greek critics. One of them was getting fairly hostile.

'So when you say at the end that *Poppy Day* is true, that is not so.'

'We don't say that. We say that it is based on things that have really happened.'

'But I understand there's been a great controversy in your native Australia about your movie coming to Cannes.' The speaker appeared to be foaming at the mouth, not out of anger but due to the substantial topping of frothy beer spread across his walrus moustache. 'I didn't get here in time to see the cassette but the whole world will know about this film when it's shown at the weekend. Now, Melbourne has the largest Greek community outside of Greece. Isn't this sort of sensationalism unfair to them?'

'The only people who are likely to be upset by *Poppy Day* are criminals and I'm not too worried about them,' Vincent replied. 'Besides, it's set in Sydney.'

A woman in a scarlet shift with lipstick to match came to his rescue. She held a small microphone in front of her ample frame.

'Mr Wall, what is your personal attitude to drugs?'

'I'm against them. Unequivocally. I think that even the smallest amount obtained for personal use is still feeding major crime syndicates. We discovered that – '

'Vince, Vince, can I have a word in your ear?' Ted Barlow was standing uneasily beside him. 'Can you let me have fifty bucks? I've got a guy downstairs and he's going to start cutting up rough if I don't square things with him.'

'Mr Barlow, the Man of the Media,' the lady in red was delighted. 'Can I have you on my radio programme?'

'Any time, darling,' Ted replied, drawing up a chair and

seeming instantly to forget about his problem. 'Your place or mine?'

'Vincent, can you come here for a moment?' The urgent face of Tony Birch was at the French window.

'Excuse me,' Vincent said to the trio of journalists who now appeared to be otherwise engaged.

He got up and went across to Tony who dramatically whipped off his glasses and ran the back of his hand across his brow. 'The Festival's been on the phone. The print of *Poppy Day* which they sent away for sub-titling has gone missing. Where's our back-up copy?'

Vincent was mystified. 'You know where. It's at the apartment, in the packing case in the kitchen.'

'Not any more,' said Birch, 'we've had a break-in.'

'Oh shit. But hang on – we've still got the video here that we show the journos before the interviews – '

'That's just terrific. You can't win the Palme d'Or with a fucking video.'

Despite a substantial gratuity to the concierge at the Carlton, Robert had been unable to get a reservation at Le Moulin de Mougins. But the man had found them a table at Manon's, a restaurant that was just as good, he had informed Robert. Good enough, anyway, for the concierge to retain the gratuity.

Sandra started to warm up a little as she took the first icy sip of her champagne. She was aware that they could not continue to work in the chilly atmosphere that now obtained between them, but she felt it was up to Robert to explain his distant and frequently distracted behaviour. He managed to forestall the issue by dwelling on the menu. The waiter seemed only too happy to help him, as if trying to explain the workings of the combustion engine to a man about to buy a Bentley Mulsanne.

'The *quenelles de brochette* is made from pike, pounded with a mortar into a purée with just enough body to hold its shape when it is poached. We add truffles and nutmeg and a little whipped cream – not enough for *madame* to worry about – then it is cooked for fifteen minutes before we pour it over a *pâte à choux* – a cream puff pastry. With it, may I recommend half a bottle of white Burgundy?'

Robert motioned with his head as if he had taken it all in. 'And the *pigeon en soupière*?'

'We take the young pigeon, we poach it for seven minutes, then we add the French beans, artichoke hearts, raw ceps, celery, miniature carrots, lettuce hearts and we cook them all together. It is *formidable*. Or perhaps *monsieur* would prefer *le baron de lapereau à la vapeur d'hysope*. We take the saddle and hind legs of a young rabbit – '

Sandra closed her menu abruptly. 'I'm just going to have a steak. *Bien cuit*.'

'Me too,' Robert agreed. 'And *frites*.'

The waiter bowed and left, not in the slightest disappointed. He had had American customers before.

Robert topped up her glass. 'I'm sorry about the programme. My fault. It was all there, thanks to you. With some better timing and a bit of luck and some truffles and nutmeg and raw ceps I daresay it would have worked.'

Sandra looked at him forgivingly. 'It was okay. Next time we do okay plus. Are you okay?'

'Not really.'

'Tanya?'

'In part.'

'I guess I came along too late.'

'Just a day or two.'

'A day or two can change a lifetime.'

'A minute or two can do that.' He tasted his own drink and, anxious to change tack, simply asked her, 'What makes you so nice?'

Instead of shrugging this off as a flippant compliment, she picked up her fork and started to play a game of invisible noughts and crosses on the table-cloth with it.

'When I was a little girl in Canada I was always looking for approval. I suppose all kids do but I was aware of it more. Yet I never did anything to boast of at school, you know, at sports or in the end-of-term play. Nothing that was a concrete achievement, anyway. My father used to take me swimming on Saturday mornings and we'd dodge in and out of the fountains and go down the slide and horse around with a rubber ball. Then one day, without saying anything, he started to take me up to the deep end – I can only have been about six or seven – and he would teach me how to do racing dives. He turned it into a game of sorts, but I knew what he was trying to do. And on the day of the school swimming sports the girl who was the best swimmer in our class was sick and I came second. I got a green badge. I always remember it was green. And I sat in the kitchen wearing it, waiting for my dad to come back and see it. But he never did.'

'He died?'

'No, nothing so dramatic. My mother and he had been planning on splitting up. They never said so but I knew. And of course I saw him again in a month or so when he came to take me out. But I never showed him the badge. I never showed it to him ever. After my mother and I moved to California I saw him less and less. And I sometimes think that I'm still looking for people's approval and if I'm working with a man and he's the right man and I want to be with him, where's the harm? So you wouldn't have been the first guy I slept with on location, and I doubt if you would have been the last.'

Her hand slipped into Robert's while she was telling him this and he squeezed it as tightly as he could without hurting her. But he knew he already had.

Despite the fact that it was a quarter to two in the morning the crowd at le Petit Carlton fanned out from the café into the road. Robert felt self-conscious as he guided Sandra to the bar. They were overdressed. Most people were in leather jackets and T-shirts and jeans, as if they had just parked their motorcycles outside, although there were none to be seen.

Tanya's style, he thought. The barman raised an eyebrow to acknowledge his presence, so he yelled, *'Deux pressions.'*

'What's that?' asked Sandra.

'No idea. It's what the guy ahead of me ordered.'

It had been a good dinner. She had recounted stories of her various relationships with men with the wry perception of a third party. Robert had thought of telling her about Grace, but then thought better of it. Compared with the dispassionate maturity of her affairs, his feelings would seem fanciful and adolescent.

The barman brought them two substantial beers. Sandra seized hers and took a gulp. She felt tipsy and reckless.

'Right. Where's the action? Where are the stories? We're gonna sock it to 'em.'

Robert tried to quieten her down. 'Let's go outside.'

They stood among the throng in the Rue d'Antibes watching stout men in dinner jackets lurch down towards the more expensive hotels and the odd pair of new-found lovers strolling slowly uphill home to bed, taking their time in the knowledge that their time now belonged to each other.

'Do you have a light?' A tall man with heavy dark-rimmed spectacles too small for his face brandished a cigarette in front of Robert.

'I'm afraid I don't – ' he began, but then, feeling in his pocket, remembered he had taken some from the restaurant. He held them out.

The man glanced at them disdainfully. 'Manon's. Are you Americans?'

Sandra went on the offensive. 'We're journalists. We're covering the Festival for *Arts Action*, the top-rated entertainment news show in America.'

'Ah,' said the stranger. 'I want to introduce you to a friend of mine. He's called Vincent Wall.'

The Nice docks were still and silent at this hour. There was nobody to observe the twelve men discreetly loading luggage from the back of an anonymous van onto an ageing fishing vessel on the Quai de Marseille.

Three other men stood apart from the main group, shadowed by the van from the distant neon lights.

'You must pay him now. That was our agreement.' The burly Frenchman in his shirt-sleeves turned to his slender colleague who, despite the warm weather, was wearing an immaculate blue Burberry. The boat's owner, his unshaven face beery as a retired bosun's, waited in anticipation.

'*Your* agreement,' the lean man replied. He glanced about him, then drew a compact Colt.45 with a silencer from his raincoat pocket. There was no need for a second shot. The fisherman slumped lifelessly to the ground moments after the bullet penetrated his heart.

'Now,' he ordered the Frenchman, 'carry him on board.'

CHAPTER 17

Tuesday 13th May 1997

Cannes

'Chantal, could you step into my office for a moment?'

Madame Rivette had the deliberately cultivated knack of reducing all such requests to the level of the schoolroom.

A florid, middle-aged man with an insanitary beard and a matted tangle of greying hair vainly trying to cover his bald head was seated opposite Madame's desk. His dilapidated suitcases were deposited on either side of him. He made no effort to get up when Chantal came in. She wondered whether this lapse in manners was due to any embarrassment he might have caused himself by wearing long grey woollen socks and a loud tartan kilt, predominantly red but with a jarring clash of yellow, as the temperature outside was now well into the nineties. But no; she could tell from the dour expression on his face that such gestures were not part of his usual mode of behaviour.

'Mr MacCormick is a late arrival,' Madame stated on his behalf, 'but this does not mean that he should be a non-arrival.'

'I filled in all the wee forms,' the man declared in a voice not unaccustomed to complaining, 'and I made it absolutely clear that I would not be coming till the second week of the Festival. I cannae afford just to be hanging around all the time. In, get the story, and out again.'

'Really? What story?' Chantal was genuinely baffled.

'Bud Booker, of course. What else? We're not interested in a lot of artsy-fartsy stuff about foreign films. My editor wants a two-page spread on Booker next Sunday morning. With photographs.'

'The story is immaterial,' Madame was emphatic. 'Mr MacCormick is without accreditation.'

The name did ring a bell in the back of Chantal's mind. 'Gillian MacCormick?' she enquired.

'Gillan,' he corrected her. It was a mistake that he had long been obliged to allow people, even Frenchwomen. 'Gillian is a lassie's name.'

A flickering image of Elizabeth Taylor with a long-haired dog passed through Chantal's imagination but, collecting her thoughts, she persisted. 'I'm sure we did receive your application. And if Madame Rivette agreed to it, I don't see why you're not on our computer.'

'Chantal is our computer expert and looks after the English-language press,' Madame explained. 'In fact she is such an Anglophile that she keeps all the accreditation records in English – sometimes I think it's to confuse the rest of us.'

'Well, I'm not,' muttered MacCormick.

'Not what?' Chantal was puzzled.

'Not English and certainly not an Anglophile, either. How can you be after what those lordly bastards did to us? Have you forgotten James IV? He died for you French on the field of Flodden. What about the Auld Alliance?'

Chantal was not anxious to get into an historical argument. 'On your form, you put United Kingdom as your country of residence?'

The man rose to his feet, immediately revealing that his kilt would benefit from a trip to the dry cleaners.

'I did not. I put Scotland. Scotland wi' a capital S.'

'Chantal.' Hearing the sound of her name she turned to the door, temporarily relieved of the need for an explanation. It was Renaud Callet.

'I'm sorry, Madame Rivette. I didn't realise you had company.' He indicated the standing Scotsman. 'May I borrow Chantal for a moment?'

'Of course, Monsieur le Directeur. But Chantal, you will solve Mr MacCormick's problem, I hope.'

'I think I've solved it already,' Chantal assured her, following Renaud out of the room. 'It's a case of confused nationality. If he comes to my office tomorrow morning, his credentials will be in order.'

'Do I get a free room?' MacCormick shouted after her.

'We will see,' she called back sweetly.

Renaud led her round to her own office. 'The Australian party tonight, the one on the beach,' he said. 'I need to look at our list.'

She trembled slightly as she called it up on the computer.

'Are you all right?' he asked.

'Yes, I think so. Just a little tired.'

'We are all tired. But in seven days it will be over and everyone will be telling each other that the Fiftieth Festival was an event to remember. At least I hope they will. Nothing else is worrying you?'

What was worrying her most immediately was the prospect of the Director seeing her name inserted on the Australian party list. For a moment she considered opening up to him about her greater concern but she hadn't worked out how to express her fears without sounding silly and, besides, she felt that now was hardly the time.

Renaud sat ruminatively on the edge of her desk rubbing his eyes with the back of his hands, then brushing back his hair. 'No Festival ever runs perfectly smoothly. There are always problems. But we have a staff to solve them. The laboratories in Paris, would you believe, have lost the print of one of the Australian films, *Poppy Day*. So it goes.' He shrugged his shoulders. 'It will probably turn up. And if it does not we'll show their other copy with a translation and no subtitles. I will explain to the jury. They will find it sensational either way.'

He looked across at the Festival poster, a Phoenix, like an eagle with red and golden plumage, rising from the ashes. Every Festival dips a little in the middle. Forty thousand people sit in the bars and the restaurants and on the beaches waiting for something to happen. And yet nothing happens. It's just a lull. And then the feeling disappears, they look forward to the second weekend, to the big stars arriving, maybe to the awards and then to going home. It is the same every year. Things always pick up again. Yet during this temporary tranquillity this feeling of expectation is contagious. It affects us all. I'll be relieved when it passes.'

Renaud leaned across to the screen and took a pencil from

the desk. 'There. We need some more people for the Foreign Minister's dinner.'

He copied several names down into his diary. 'You don't want to come to that, as well?' he asked Chantal, good-naturedly.

She felt herself blush.

'I want to go home.'

'You can't go. Not today. You must wait for tonight, at least.'

'Oh Fyodor, you don't understand. Tonight's the reason I want to go.'

'I thought I was the reason you wanted to go.'

Elizabeth caught sight of him in the mirror. His reflection made him look shorter than he was. Somehow his neck seemed to disappear when he was angry.

'I can't keep apologising,' she said. 'But I'm sorry.'

'If you're sorry, you'll stay.'

Fyodor never lost sight of his business strategy, whatever the tempests of his private life.

'It seems so stupid,' Elizabeth exclaimed. 'If you'd told me about this stunt earlier I never would have come.'

'I know.' He sat on the bed, half-smiling. 'That's why I didn't tell you. But now you're here and you owe me this final favour.'

'Why not just let me go, Fyodor? Let me drift out of your life like I drifted in. Maybe we could salvage some decent memories. You seem determined to leave us with an everlasting taste of bitterness.'

'Me?'

'I know. I'm the guilty one. Put it down to inexperience. Maybe I can't cope with you. Besides . . . your wife, your daughter . . .'

'They didn't seem to worry you when we were sleeping together – if you can remember that far back.'

Elizabeth had grown to hate these arguments; his application of cold logic to something that was illogically emotional was an unfair ploy. She decided to terminate this one in the only way she could – by agreeing.

'I'll stay. For tonight only.'

Fyodor had won his battle. He got up. 'Good. I've got to take a meeting. Hetty will confirm the arrangements.'

He left the room without attempting any form of embrace or farewell. Elizabeth felt used and dishonourable. She flung herself on the bed and began to pray. 'Kuan Yin, Goddess of Mercy, come and take me away from all this.'

'It seems to me that although the Canadians have cracked the commercial market-place with *Mountie Mac*, they have a fair way to go in making, shall we say, slightly more mature films that address relevant topics. From the little I've seen in Cannes, the Australians are certainly making progress in that field.'

Although the voice sounded familiar she was unable to place it immediately. But when she looked up at the television set which Fyodor kept permanently tuned to the closed-circuit Festival channel, she had no difficulty in placing the smile. She had seen him on television before, interviewing Bud Booker the night of the Oscars: Robert, her Aspen hot-water bottle as she liked to think of him. Indeed, there was something warm and reassuring and just attractively normal about his demeanour. In her recent despair her thoughts had frequently travelled back to those peculiar moments, frozen in time and space. She regretted skiing away without even telling him her real name, but she comforted herself with the thought that he was probably married, had plaid golf trousers, a wife called Holly and an estate car full of children and pets.

And if he wasn't, well, maybe Kuan Yin, Goddess of Mercy, would deliver him to her. She had certainly brought him as far as Cannes.

'*Monsieur Barrett, du programme américain*, Arse Action, *bienvenu à Cannes et merci. Et maintenant, Jo-Jo.*'

A swirling disco singer bounced Robert's image from the screen.

The heat was getting to Hetty Berman. So was Roger *le traiteur*.

'You've let me down,' she screamed into the phone. 'I distinctly requested six marzipan *bateaux*, each three feet long. There are people in this room who will testify that I said that.' She waved her arm in the direction of Monique, the thin – anorexic by Hetty's standards – French student who was acting as her secretary.

'*Gâteaux*,' Roger insisted, not for the first time.

'*Gâteaux*, yes. But *gâteaux* that look like *bateaux*. That's the whole point. You must have seen the poster outside the Majestic. The boat is the image of the film.'

'But outside the Majestic, that is a pirate ship. Like the one Roman Polanski left in Cannes.'

'Not that poster. The one beside it, with the flashing blue light.'

'With the men from the moon?'

'Exactly.'

'That is a spaceship, not a *bateau*.'

'But the earth people, what were they standing on?' Hetty was getting somewhere.

'You mean the people at sea?' Roger asked.

'Yes.'

'You want a boat like theirs?'

'Six of them.'

'But there is only one in the poster.'

'We have to feed three hundred guests. Can you do it?'

'Turn the *gâteaux* into *bateaux*?'

'Yes.'

'I can try.'

'Will a hundred dollars make you try any harder?'

'Rely on me, Madame Berman.' Roger sounded willing. 'You are a good customer.'

Hetty replaced the receiver with relief and put another tick on her check list.

'I do not think you need to give him more money,' Monique observed, 'already for the Festival his prices are times two.'

'Are you suggesting he was two-timing me?' Hetty smiled appreciatively at her own remark. 'Is that what *traiteur* means?'

'*Un traiteur* means a caterer,' the student solemnly assured her. 'A traitor in French is *un traître*.'

'I see,' said Hetty, although she didn't really. 'The hotel is looking after the rest of the food and that should be fine. We've invited two hundred journalists, none of whom have replied because they never reply to anything in Cannes except anything they haven't been invited to. And you have two hundred press packs to hand out to them when they arrive. My God!'

Hetty had caught sight of the empty box by the door and emitted a stricken wail. 'They've been stolen. Someone's stolen the press packs. What pervert would want to do a thing like that? Ring hotel security. No, get me the printers. It's too late. All this trouble. Fyodor will never forgive me.'

Monique did nothing. 'I sent out the press packs with the invitations, madame. It was Monsieur Lasky's idea.'

Hetty stared at her, half-angry, half-relieved. 'Why didn't you tell me, for goodness' sake?'

'I thought *he* did.'

'He's always too busy, too preoccupied with that girl. Now: have we got additional security for the French Foreign Minister or did he say he was bringing his own?'

Monique looked surprised. 'Neither, madame.'

'What does neither mean?'

'As far as I know he is not coming.'

'Why not?'

'He was not on the list you gave me.'

'The jury, Monique, he's on the goddam jury. What have you done?'

'But you told me that you thought Monsieur Lasky should personally sign the invitations for the jury and the Festival administration. You put them specially – '

' – in the drawer,' sighed Hetty simultaneously, jerking it open with both hands to reveal the neat pile of large cream envelopes inside. 'Oh fuck!'

The speedboat cut through the rising swell with a succession of triggered thuds. The air had become more humid as the sun began to go down and the growing turbulence in the ocean indicated that a storm might be on its way from Africa.

Tuesday night was traditionally party night in Cannes. Although parties were given every day and all day from before the opening gala until after the closing ceremony, for no precise reason – or perhaps because it fell precisely in the middle – this was by far the most popular day for parties.

Those not invited to one on the Tuesday of the second week had every right to consider themselves social lepers.

Sandra had decided they would start with the flashiest gathering, given by a previously unknown Kuwaiti oil billionaire on a yacht the size of a nine-hole golf course, that dominated the bay. In case anyone should have failed to notice it, three helicopters had been ferrying guests to and from the reception on board since early evening. Sandra suggested that they should arrive under their own steam by boat – 'I just hate having to wait for a helicopter home.'

Their host was dressed distinctively in Arab clothes and headgear, which was just as well since the one thing all of his guests appeared to have in common was that none of them had met him before. An American public relations woman – a blonde, much sleeker and statelier than Hetty Barman – led him amongst them. As he sipped his orange juice, he graciously thanked each guest individually for coming to swallow his vintage champagne and consume his caviar.

He had seemed surprised when Sandra requested that they should video a short interview with him, but his unflagging politeness ensured that he could not turn them down.

'Why are you here?' Robert asked when the camera rolled.

The Arab gave an uneasy smile. 'Why are we all here? This is the greatest film festival in the world.'

'But why are you giving this party?'

He fiddled nervously with his robes, throwing a questioning glance in the direction of his PR lady in the hope that she might furnish him with a reply. 'It is for my friends, my new friends in the film industry.'

'And what films are you involved with?'

'You ask me these questions and they are too soon. I have met one or two very influential people in the British cinema and they have invited me to Cannes. It is wonderful. Now I meet their friends.'

'Have you invested in any of their films yet?'

'No, not yet. We are having talks. I think there is a great future in the European cinema. The American, too. And now I must return to my guests.'

'That was about as stimulating as a treasury spokesman giving details of the budget deficit,' Robert complained as he helped to load the equipment back onto their launch.

Sandra was defensive about her idea. 'Listen, it's not a bad story and it's a good one visually – Arab robes, luxury yacht, bathsful of champagne. Okay, no crime's been committed but I think that guy's being set up. Someone has got their hands on his wallet, prised it open enough to give a party like that and now the eager bees are swarming all over his boat to see if he's good for a few million bucks to finance their films. It's all part of the picture down here, a relevant part. Emphasise it at the end of your lead in and we'll cut to the helicopter landing on board.'

A soft evening sun, the colour of Provençal rosé, was spilling across Cannes from behind the twelfth-century tower that presided over the Old Port. It had the effect of backlighting the town, giving it a shadowy and mysterious profile when viewed from the sea, like the set for the final act of a tragic opera.

Robert was in a separate boat from Sandra and the crew. She wanted to shoot him crossing the bay at what was known in film terms as 'the magic hour', a time that was neither day nor night when the light could play tricks on the eye and the imagination.

'Can't you go any faster?' she shouted through her loud-hailer, like a cox at a regatta.

'It's too choppy. This thing will break up. You want me to die on camera, don't you?'

'It would sure make good television. Imagine the ratings "Tonight on *Arts Action* watch Robert Barrett die, live from the French Riviera."'

'It's not live,' he hollered back.

'Neither will you be. Okay, let's give it a twirl. Ready, Vik? Erik? Plenty of zip and authority and make sure you don't fall over.'

This last piece of advice was the most pertinent. The sea was turning from choppy to heavy. Waves that ended as attractive two-footers when they hit the shore originated in a ten-to-twelve foot swell out in the bay where they were filming.

'Okay, I'm ready.'

When the boats were nearly parallel Sandra yelled, 'Action!'

'They take their movies seriously here in Cannes at festival time' – Robert clung tenaciously to the wheel of his boat like a Grand Prix driver entering a chicane – 'Already there's been the mysterious disappearance of one of the favourites for the Golden Palm, *Poppy Day* – an Australian film about drug-smuggling, which, some say, has been smuggled out of town by rivals who consider it a bit too hot to compete with. And did you ever hear the story of the producer who put his own money into a movie? No, neither did I. But they rarely have the slightest hesitation in extracting it from other, less informed people. The secret is to blind them with the glamour of the game. This yacht ahead of us now was bought with millions drilling black gold and now its Kuwaiti owner has, himself, become a drilling field for not always honourable – Christ *Almighty* – what the hell – what in *fuck's* name – '

The overpowering noise made Robert loosen his grip on the wheel and he fell back into the boat which swerved ungovernably out of control, crashing around on the crest of the waves. For a moment the din abated slightly and then it came again, if anything more thunderous than before. Robert had sufficiently recovered his composure to count the four single-engined planes roaring overhead, flying so low that they caught the spray of the sea on the underside of their wings as they headed for shore.

He scrambled forward and grabbed hold of the throttle, managing to curb the craft's restless circling. As he raised himself by the wheel another wave of fighters was upon him, and then another, each group of four arriving in tight military formation.

His gaze followed the last one – he counted twenty-four planes – as it flew towards the town. He couldn't believe his eyes – or ears. They were dropping depth charges which threw up plumes of white spray amidst the already choppy surf. Their attack seemed to be centred on the Majestic beach which had now become alive with explosions and lights and screaming people running backwards and forwards in panic.

The planes soared up over the hotel and banked round to the left to the back of the Old Port ready for another run.

'Let's get out of here,' he shouted to Sandra, but she and the crew had disappeared. Instead the waters around him were now filled with small boats that had emerged from the twilight and were heading for the beach. The craft were crewed by men dressed like bob-sleigh teams in shiny blue body suits with matching metallic helmets. At first they seemed to be holding torches, but as they came nearer Robert could see that they had state-of-the-art automatic weapons in their hands, and powerful rays were sweeping the shore to seek out targets.

He had never been closer to combat before than the set of a war film and, now that he was in the thick of it, he realised the full horror of being nakedly exposed with no place to hide. The whole experience had the properties of one of his nightmares about the Crusades, the worst kind in which he knew he was dreaming but wakefulness refused to come and rescue him. The second phase of the airborne attack was coming in again, more furious than the first, and the noise and confusion on the beach rose in an alarming crescendo. The leading group of boats had now landed, and the noise of light arms fire crackled menacingly in the night air as they made their way up the beach.

As if drawn by the pyrotechnics of the spectacle, he opened up the throttle and followed the last group of boats in. It seemed odd that none of the invading force had taken any notice of him, as if he were irrelevant to their committed mission. Perversely this made his situation even more unnerving. He felt he was a trespasser in a private war, equally vulnerable to both sides.

A brilliant spotlight on the shore picked out a stooped, white-haired man who appeared to be the leader of the invaders. He looked less than human as he dragged his blue scaly body up the beach towards a small outnumbered force of sailors, lined up in their white officers' uniforms.

The man straightened himself out and, holding his weapon high above him like someone playing Henry V at Stratford, pronounced in a deep voice, as English as old oak: 'We come in peace.'

The besieged officers immediately burst into applause. A large blue neon sign behind them came to life with the flashing words 'Jupiter Landing' and the theme from the film quadraphonically boomed out from the corners of the beach.

Robert was thankful for the cover of comparative darkness as he pulled his own boat onto the shore. He felt extraordinarily foolish. Everybody else except him must have known that this was just an elaborate stunt advertising the film. Through the clearing smoke he could see Sandra and the crew filming the remaining action on the beach.

Bruised and aggrieved at being the victim of such a subterfuge he decided not to join them straight away. He should have been expecting it. As a director Sandra liked to model herself on Sam Fuller, who was known to play tricks on actors to get more realistic performances from them. Fuller would rehearse a scene with an actor coming into a room and pouring himself a whisky from a bottle on the mantelpiece. But then, for the take, he would hide the bottle in a cupboard and let the camera run on the man's frustration as he looked for it. Doubtless Robert's reaction to the first wave of planes, once the expletives had been dubbed out, would be another of Sandra's 'spontaneous moments'.

The invading forces, primarily off-duty French policemen, had pulled off their helmets and were helping themselves to bottles of beer and wine. An extensive array of cold cuts and quiches and salads was laid out on three trestle tables. Each was bordered by large marzipan ships, like book-ends, which were quickly being dismantled by hungry guests.

Suddenly it hit Robert like a newsflash: Elizabeth Brown must be here. The very thought had a numbing effect on his mind. He had no idea what to do. Moving up the beach, slowly at first, not daring to call her name, he anxiously scanned the clusters of people nearest the shore. Then he broke into a trot, despondent, confused, perspiring with the onset of panic. He ran agitatedly from group to group, like a father who has lost his child in a crowd.

'Got a problem, old chap?' His way was blocked by an elegant man in naval uniform casually puffing a cigarette in a holder, as if he was a refugee from a Noël Coward comedy.

'No, nothing.'

'The drinks are over there if you're looking for them,' the

officer indicated, adding patronisingly, 'no hurry though, there are plenty left.'

'Thank you,' said Robert. And then, as the man turned to go, he shouted. 'Wait!'

The officer froze, then slowly swivelled back to face him.

'Yes?' he coolly enquired.

'You were in the film,' Robert blurted out. 'The captain, very British, most inspiring. Congratulations.'

Howard's expression melted quickly. 'Did you think so? How very kind.'

'At first I didn't recognise you from your voice.'

Howard stiffened.

'But now I know,' Robert continued. 'And you must know – Elizabeth, Elizabeth Brown.'

'Only too well. Not that she's going to be the most popular passenger on the plane tomorrow. Left after the photocall, said she couldn't stand the bangs.'

'Tomorrow? You're going home?'

'I think I had enough of this town yesterday and she seems to have had enough of our producer – or vice versa. Don't touch the oysters, by the way.'

Before Robert could squeeze Howard for any further information, Sandra and Vik arrived.

'That should put some life into the next show,' she grinned. 'Give the Vets a buzz anyhow. Come on, we've got to cover the Australians. Their party's only five beaches along.'

'Who organised this?' Robert demanded.

'That little woman over there. The one munching the ship's funnel. You might know her, she's from New York.'

Robert ran across to Hetty and breathlessly extended his hand. 'Robert Barrett, *Arts Action*.'

'Pleased to meet you. I think we spoke on the phone once. Did you enjoy our show?'

'Incredible. Most life-like. It'll look great on the air. We just need an interview with that nurse actress – I forget her name . . .'

'Elizabeth Brown?'

'Brown, yes. Just to round off our report.'

'I'm not sure that will be possible. She's not feeling too well and I think she's going back. I tell you what, there's a good slug with her in the electronic press pack. I'll have it sent round to your producer.'

'You're *sure* she's ill?'

Hetty nodded.

'If you see her, you couldn't give her a message . . . just say' – he had to think quickly – 'just say you saw a falcon on the beach.'

'A falcon?' Hetty was puzzled. 'Is that some kind of code?'

'Sort of,' said Robert.

The only solution, as he could see it, was to get astronomically bombed. There was no shortage of medicaments on the Australian beach, nor did he find himself alone in his quest. Here was a nation, he thought, that knew how to pull out a cork and swallow its worries. That's why they kept assuring people they had none. Drinking seemed positively healthy in this environment, not the furtive act of getting stoned in a New York bar but a religious affirmation of the sheer joys of booze. Most modern societies used it to shake off inhibition; in Australia there were few inhibitions in the first place – drink was an end to be celebrated in itself.

This was of little benefit, however, several hours later when he attempted once more to interview Ted Barlow aka Ken Turner, the Man of the Media, who was five days more drugged and drunk than he was.

'I presume you used aspects of all the Australian media moguls to build up the portfolio of the part?' Liquor released a loquaciousness in the reporter not best suited to the terse interview.

'Portfolio? Are we talking about the same film, mate?'

'To create a larger than life character you must have borrowed from – well, from life.'

'I would never borrow. I'm an actor. It's all in here.' Barlow rapped his stomach with his fist. 'It's all inside.' A look of horror came over his face. 'And I think it's coming up to join us.'

Vik kept the camera running as Ted decorated his Nikes.

Cautioned by Barlow's example, Robert decided to find some food to help sober himself up. There was plenty left, extensive tables laden with meats and sweetmeats like the remains of a banquet given by a medieval monarch. He helped himself to an entire baby chicken and took a bread roll to go with it. There was nowhere to sit; this was evidently one of those parties where you either stood or fell.

Making his way unsteadily down the beach, he reached a low wooden breakwater and snuggled in behind it. He contemplated the chicken with a glazed expression. The sea was less restless now and the waves broke more contentedly on the shore. The night sky had cleared and a crescent moon dangled like a decoration over the Arab yacht.

'Which do you prefer, leg or breast?'

As though someone had given him a shot with a hypodermic needle his whole system quickened and became alert. If he had needed confirmation of the owner of the voice, which he didn't, the tang of a never-to-be-forgotten fragrance sweetened the night air. Even in his befuddled state he endeavoured to retain some composure.

'What is the name of that perfume? I looked everywhere for it, but without a name you're lost. You just go around sniffing stupidly.'

'Like a dog,' Elizabeth agreed. 'It's called "Betrayal". At the moment you can only get it at one store in London, but if it catches on everybody will want some.'

She was wearing a simple white T-shirt and blue jeans. Climbing over the breakwater she sat down beside him. 'Aren't you going to ask me to share your dinner? I hoped the invitation might still be open.'

'That was for lunch. You remembered?'

'I read about you in the *Hollywood Reporter*, with that little old lady at the Oscars. Was she a plant?'

'No,' said Robert. 'Are you?'

'Yes. Belladonna – do you know what that is?'

'A beautiful gift?'

'Wrong. Deadly nightshade. Tell me, how long has it been?'

She had wrongfooted him. 'Since when?'

'Since you were last in America?'

Was he drunk or dreaming? 'Have we had this conversation before?' he asked.

'*We* haven't,' she smiled and stretched her hand across to

his plate. 'I'll have the leg. Breasts are greatly overrated, don't you agree?'

They sat silently for a while as she ate it.

'I couldn't sleep,' Elizabeth said, 'so I went down to reception to see if they had a newspaper. But the only paper they had was your message. Falcon – a bird of prey.'

'So you answered my prayers.'

She gave him an affectionate push. 'I thought Americans didn't deal in puns – it's an English disease.'

'They teach a course at Princeton. it's either that or Scott Fitzgerald.'

'Do you have a cigarette?' she asked.

'I don't smoke. Wait a sec – I think I have a sample pack from that yacht. Would you like one?'

'No, you have it. I'd just like to watch you smoke and see how it smells. It's always different, you know.'

He lit one up and put an arm around her. 'Would you mind if we sat slightly closer together? It's beginning to get a little chilly.'

She relaxed her head against his shoulder, watching the smoke drift into the darkness.

'I'd like us to stay sitting here,' said Robert. 'Just till dawn. It can't be long now.'

He stole a surreptitious glance to gauge her reaction. Her eyes seemed to acquiesce but he noticed they had lost a little of their lustre since Aspen, as if she had lost something else as well.

'Why stop at dawn?' she asked.

CHAPTER 18

Wednesday 14th May 1997

Cannes

In the morning they made love.

The beach cleaners and the dawn had arrived simultaneously to interrupt their sitting slumber. Saying nothing, Robert gently helped her to her feet. The Carlton Hotel was just across the Croisette. Clinging supportively together they walked under the giant cardboard horse with Mountie Mac astride it and into the vacant lobby, where the concierge offered Robert his key and a trade magazine bearing the headline 'Lasky's Raiders Wake Up Dull Festival'.

'Do you want any breakfast?' he asked when they got to his room. 'There's chilled brandy and sickly chocolate in the mini-bar.'

'I'd prefer brunch,' she replied, pulling off her jeans and T-shirt which she threw onto a chair and sliding into bed.

He undressed and followed her.

'Would you rather sleep or make love?'

'You decide,' she said, turning to him and putting her hand against his cheek. She drew him to her and kissed him softly and unceasingly.

Every part of her excited him: he could feel her breasts harden against his chest, her stomach warm and soothing against his stomach and her legs securing a safe mooring as she wrapped them around his.

'I guess you want to go to sleep,' she said.

'Guess again.'

'Oh.' She tightened the grip of her whole body around him. 'Did I remember to take my knickers off? I think I forgot in all the excitement.'

274

He slid his hands slowly down her back and, hooking the garment with his thumbs, removed it in one unbroken movement.

'You've done that before,' whispered Elizabeth.

'Not with you.'

She giggled. 'Wasn't there some little man who wanted to make love to Dorothy Parker and she said, "If you do and I find out, I shall be most annoyed."'

'Will you be most annoyed?'

'I will be if you don't hurry up.'

He entered her with ease. She stiffened for a moment and gasped, then relaxed back onto the pillow, murmuring his name as he moved on top of her with as much control as he could manage in his fatigued state. Her eyes were firmly closed but her mouth carried all the contentment of someone who was happy and at home.

He came abruptly and unexpectedly, long before she had any chance of orgasm.

'I'm sorry,' he breathed, dropping his head onto the pillow beside hers.

'Oh Robert,' she said sleepily. 'Robert.'

The Warner Bros jet lowered its ailerons and commenced its final approach to Nice airport. Bud Booker picked up his winnings with glee – fifty-five dollars from Leland Walters, the President of the studio, and sixty from Homer Mangold, his press agent. The star counted out the notes as eagerly as someone who had just collected his social security. Twenty million dollars for a picture was not, somehow, an assimilable sum but these hundred and fifteen bucks won at seven-card stud were real. Moreover he had had the added pleasure of watching people open their wallets and pay it over.

His agent, Barry Schenck, had declined to play, preferring instead to make endless free telephone calls throughout the journey. Did he now collect ten per cent of Booker's winnings, Leland wondered. He had been amazed at the actor's restraint in refusing all food and sipping only iced water on the eleven-hour flight. Male stars, he often thought, tended to take care of their looks far more solicitously than female ones, who quite often turned forty and to the bottle at about the same time.

The chaos at Nice Airport was quite like the old days, a successful piece of manipulation by the publicity firm of Pascall and Swern, who had been informing journalists for the past week that there would be no chance of Bud speaking to the press when he arrived at exactly 10.17 a.m. on Wednesday. Since early that morning French fans had been crowding the roof of the airport building and the railings were covered in large hand-written banners: 'Bonjour Bud' and, less accurately, 'Bub Booker – Welcome in France'. The only dissent in this sea of approbation was a small group of well-dressed young men and women parading a placard which read 'Unfair to the Unification Church', but the police had manoeuvred them into a shaded corner, pretty well out of sight. There was little doubt where the gendarmes' loyalty lay.

The piercing and prolonged screams that greeted him as he walked down the aircraft's steps – his blond hair perfectly lacquered into controlled disarray – managed to drown out the dying whine of the jet's engines. Bud stopped, looked surprised – even though he had been inspecting the crowd for the past five minutes as the plane taxied in – then pointed his forefinger up at the throng and fired. They loved it, and him, even more.

It seemed that the entire Nice police force had been prepared to sacrifice their day off for a glimpse of a man who stood for a form of policing which many of them secretly believed in and which, indeed, had been influential in causing some of the younger officers to join up. He moved through their ranks, nodding appreciatively and stopping occasionally, like the Duchess of Kent passing through the corridor of ballboys at Wimbledon, to talk to anyone who was especially short or black.

There was no suggestion of any customs or immigration. The only people who wanted to question him were the four hundred reporters and television crews who had immobilised the arrivals hall, hungry for just one quote that would enhance their story. There was nothing television news hated more than an airport arrival without a brief sound-bite.

Bud knew that. He stood there, lean, loose and unblinking. Then he held up his hand for quiet. Even Moses could not have had such rapid results – the expectant hush was such that the journalists might well have been waiting for a message from a prophet.

'It's good to be in France and I'm glad you liked the movie,' was all he said, well aware that few of them had actually seen it but that the remark would be bounced twenty-three and a half thousand miles up into the sky where a cluster of geodesically stationary satellites would bounce it back to millions of sitting rooms in the four corners of the globe.

Renaud was relieved to see the arrival on his office television. With hindsight he realised he had been mistaken in his initial reluctance to accommodate the American star. The Fiftieth Festival had made a solid impact in France but, as yet, no other territories had given it more than cursory coverage as an afterthought on the arts page. Now Cannes had a chance to hit the headlines.

His phone rang. It was Henri Chaillot. 'All that business with the planes last night, was that in order?'

'Not uncommon. A little more exaggerated than usual perhaps.'

'*Jupiter Blinding*'s not one of the films in the competition, is it?'

'*Landing*, no, too commercial.'

'So they could have asked the jury to their reception on the beach?'

'I expect you'll get an invitation in a day or two.'

'Not me, you understand. My son and his friend were in town. They might have enjoyed it. I hope arrangements with Bud Booker will be a little more efficient. We will have the opportunity of a private meeting with him, will we not?'

'Minister,' said Renaud, 'I shall see to it myself.'

Robert was awoken by a hammering at the door. He knew immediately who it was. How was he going to explain this to her? He felt caught, like an errant schoolboy. Then he noticed, to his surprise and relief, that Elizabeth had gone. No clothes on the chair, not a trace of her save a faint musky aroma in the air.

'Wake up,' yelled Sandra. 'All hot-shit reporters should be up by lunchtime. That's the way they get their scoops.'

'It's open,' he called out to her.

She entered the darkened room and went across to draw the curtains. The dazzling morning came pouring in.

'Welcome to another wonderful day at the Cannes Film Festival. The place where you can lie on the sand and look at the stars, or vice versa.'

Robert eyed her anxiously. Was she making a personal point, or just an old joke?

'What time is it?' he asked.

'Past eleven. What time did you get in?'

'I'm not sure. Late. Shit! Did you say eleven? What about Bud Booker? We've missed him.'

'Relax,' Sandra assured him. 'Vik and Erik went to pick him up. They called in just now. Usual airport scramble. Warners were on the phone offering a ten-minute photocall at his hotel early this evening. I told them to forget it. We need something better than that.'

Robert eased himself gingerly out of bed. 'I'll contact Homer Mangold after lunch. He should be able to square a decent interview.'

Draped in a sheet he steadied himself against the wardrobe. 'Boy! What do Australians put in their drink, do you suppose?'

Sandra laughed. 'You should know – you had enough of it. You'll be telling me next you saw little blue men crawling up the beach.'

'The Festival had you booked into the Majestic,' Leland confided to Bud as they sank into the back of the Rolls. 'Madness. You'd have been mobbed from morning till night. Much better at the du Cap. I've been going there for years – they're always booked twice over but they made a suite available the moment my secretary told them who it was for. Wanted to know if you preferred Russian or Polish vodka in your room. It's that sort of place.'

Indeed it was. Lying fifteen miles to the east of Cannes, on the far side of Antibes – a town best known during the Festival for its eternally constipated traffic system – the Hôtel du Cap, exclusive and resplendent on the brow of a hill, was the Versailles of the Côte d'Azur. To stay there was to have arrived. It was not just a question of wealth, although if the prospect of a thousand dollars a night for a room or ten dollars a leaf for a salad was intimidating, then it was the wrong hotel in the first place. It was a confidence in the belief that other delegates would be prepared to break off from their crowded schedules on the Croisette and spend at least an hour on the journey each way in order to do a deal with you there.

For American studio heads it was a traditional home from home. The moment that anyone became the temporary custodian of the cash and clout that went with such a post, the rules of the Hollywood Hills that aspiring movie Mohammeds must come to the mountains transferred effortlessly to the Hôtel du Cap. So it was with some of the major agents in a custom pioneered by the veteran deal-maker Swifty Lazar, who knew that a sun-bed at the pool next to the right person could end up with a contract worth ten per cent of ten million dollars – or at least enough to cover the tab. At that very hotel, three years previously, Leland had been invited to make up a tennis four and met the man who subsequently offered him the job at Warners.

Inevitably the spivs and shamans of the industry, indistinguishable in their Gucci loafers and Cerruti tennis-wear from anyone else in the business, were prepared to risk a few thousand dollars on a long weekend at the hotel – it was a better bet than they would find on the roulette wheels of Monte Carlo – to press their unwelcome presence on the regular residents. Nature has provided no creature with a thicker skin than an independent producer touting a script in need of finance.

Some guests miscalculated badly and found themselves isolated in this priceless purdah, sentenced, like prisoners in an exercise yard, to walk endlessly up and down the spacious drive that ran from the Grand Trianon of the hotel to the Petit Trianon of the Eden Roc restaurant by the water's edge. If they were lucky, a passing studio boss such as Leland might remark 'nice day' to alleviate their lonely misery. He remembered the occasions when – as a show-business lawyer with a lean client list – he was in a similar position. Once the perfunctory game of tennis had been played, there was little else to do in the hotel except contemplate expensive food and deals.

The staff at the du Cap were trained like courtiers, attentive to every need – from a thimble to a thesaurus – and mightily unimpressed by famous names. They had seen monarchs come and monarchs go and the only general rule of thumb was the bigger the reputation, the smaller the tip. Nevertheless an unusual *frisson* of anticipation ran through the stately lobby that Wednesday morning in May. Although none of the staff had seen Bud Booker's latest film, *Black Cops Kill*, they were conversant with its content from newspaper articles and non-stop pre-publicity on television. Even those with a limited command of English could manage the famous line: 'Remove it, or I'll remove you.'

'Is that it for today?' Bud asked Mangold as the Rolls snaked up the winding coastal road to the hotel.

Homer shrugged. He was just along for the ride and the meals – and to bask in the reflected glory.

Leland Walters took out an itinerary from his attaché case. 'I spoke to our publicity people at the airport. They feel we should capitalise on the arrival footage with something more.'

Barry Schenck leant back from the front seat to defend his client. 'Bud said he was glad they liked the film. That was very quick thinking.'

Bud held up a finger to still him. 'Hold on a little bit. What do you reckon, Leland, a photo-call in front of a poster?'

'Something like that. Pascall and Swern suggested that we allow twenty television crews, the ones that will give us the biggest international exposure, say a ten-minute question and answer session – enough so each one can make it seem exclusive to them.'

'Five minutes,' said Schenck.

'Whatever.' Bud was in an amenable mood. He didn't get the sort of welcome he had just received at the golf club every morning.

'Fine,' Leland was delighted. 'At six tonight.'

'Seven,' replied Bud, for no other reason than the professional instinct of every star that if you proved too cooperative, people might start taking you for granted.

The police had managed to head off all the cars that were tailing them by the simple expedient of closing the road, a cause of more than a little annoyance to other guests trying to get to the hotel.

Bud beamed obligingly at the welcoming party in the foyer, lifted up the manager's six-year-old daughter who had presented him with a bouquet and planted a kiss on her cheek for the benefit of the sole house photographer.

'Now everybody's going to start talking about you and me,' he remarked, getting a laugh from those in earshot.

'I've got to get some shuteye,' he announced to the lobby. 'Playing all that poker makes a man tired.'

Leland was met in his suite by an attentive delegation of his European staff. 'I've considered your suggestion and I've told him he should do a brief press call this evening,' he informed them. 'But I've decided to make it seven o'clock and five minutes maximum.'

As he was leaving, his Paris manager turned to him. 'By the way, there are two English guys outside. They said you'd agreed to see them and your secretary confirmed it. I thought you'd like to get it over and done with.'

It was true. They had been pestering him for weeks in Los Angeles. One of them was related to someone on the Warners' board so Leland had reluctantly offered to spare them a few minutes if they happened to be in Cannes.

They were both in their late twenties and not an attractive pair. The shorter, wearing a blue shirt covered in bananas and cherries and oranges, buttoned up to the neck, and a lank pony-tail, appeared to be a man who took his showers by the week rather than the day. The taller, more respectable in a charcoal suit and a moustache to match, looked as if he had come to peddle Watch Tower Bibles.

Ever since it had passed into movie folklore that Richard Attenborough had launched himself on a successful career as a director by acting out the script of *Oh What a Lovely War* in the office of the President of Paramount, other British producers had frequently tried to follow suit. It was a tedious process.

'Just imagine,' began the pony-tail, after introductions had been briefly effected, 'a young English girl arrives in Calcutta today. As she takes the bus from the airport she is catatonic with culture shock. The streets are alive with hundreds of thousands of people carrying out every sort of human activity imaginable and some unimaginable: cobblers, carpet sellers, food stalls with fruit and fish crawling with flies, children in rags playing in the gutters, mothers with babies – drugged to make them look ill – begging for baksheesh, everywhere beggars, crippled, one-legged, twisted people stretching out thin imploring arms, people living in huts made of cardboard boxes along the side of main roads, others sleeping on the pavements, cattle walking amongst them and, most distressing of all, dead bodies being carried through the streets in open coffins, some of them little children – '

Leland stood up, the only way he could interrupt the flow. 'What's this film about?'

'I'm coming to that,' the Englishman snapped back impatiently, forgetting for the moment that his own arm was metaphorically outstretched, begging for finance. 'The girl is called Emily Eden and she is the direct descendant of the author of this diary' – he waved a green leather-bound book in the air – 'Emily Eden, the sister of the Viceroy, Lord Curzon, who made that same trip to India a hundred years previously. What she did was to record the British summer move – when everybody left the suffocating streets of Calcutta, where the heat made life impossible, for the cool fresh air of the hill station at Simla.'

'Did they take the entire population with them?' Leland tried to look as innocent as his distaste for the man would permit.

The homunculus fixed him with a condescending look, the irony of the remark passing him by. 'No. Just the British, of course. And so Emily, our Emily, sets out on a fantastic voyage in the steps of her ancestor. But here's the twist that's really going to get to people. When she arrives at the holy city of Benares where people bathe at dawn to purge themselves of their sins, she immerses herself totally in the Ganges and when she surfaces she has become the old Emily. The clock has gone back a century and she starts to live the life of the British Raj. Incredible.'

'It's certainly that,' acknowledged Leland. 'It sounds a bit too dreamy for me. Is there any action in it?'

The charcoal moustache could barely contain himself. 'Fantastic action,' he proclaimed, leaping to his feet. 'She finds herself right in the middle of the Indian Mutiny – we're taking a bit of poetic licence with the dates but the morons who go to the cinema today will hardly notice. She actually finds herself in the siege of Cawnpore, binding the wounds of the bloodied and decimated British troops as they wait in vain for Sir Colin Campbell to come and relieve them. It's the story of quite astounding bravery in the face of terrible savagery.'

Leland had by now taken a substantial dislike to both men. Not only had they forced themselves on him but they were patronising him as if he were one of the morons who made up the audience they so despised.

'Wait a minute,' he said. 'What caused your Indian Mutiny? Wasn't it the sepoys whose religion stopped them from greasing their guns with fat because it came from slaughtered cows? So when you talk of savagery, who exactly are the savages? Those Indians trying to uphold their religion? Or the British officers who were ordering them to ignore it?'

Both men were taken aback. Apart from balance sheets, Hollywood studio chiefs were supposed to be ignorant of everything – especially the Indian Mutiny. The pony-tail tried to cover his surprise with indignation. 'They massacred us at Meerut. And the siege of Lucknow was unforgivably brutal, British soldiers were starving.'

'But hold on,' Leland was almost beginning to enjoy the argument. 'What were the British doing there in the first place? Didn't the East India Company just march in, start trading and then declare itself the government of India? And didn't the British just as irresponsibly march out again two hundred years later, leaving the Hindus and Muslims to slaughter each other in their millions?'

'That's putting it a bit strongly,' complained the pony-tail.

'Sorry, gentlemen, India films went out with the eighties,' Leland announced, clapping his hands together to terminate the audience.

'So what's hot now?' asked the Bible salesman. 'We've had Russia, after the Oscars.'

'The Far East,' Leland replied, unthinkingly.

'I've got it,' the fruit shirt was not leaving with his pony-tail between his legs. 'What if the diary belonged to a woman who was on the Long March . . .?'

By six o'clock all the chosen television units and press reporters – with the exception of the *Arts Action* crew – had gathered at the curved swimming pool by the Eden Roc restaurant in order to secure the best position to record the thoughts of Bud Booker. In fact there was no best position since it had not been established where Booker would actually stand. Nevertheless people jostled and jockeyed for places as if they were acting out a pre-ordained ritual which, in their way, they were. Sound recordists, by nature the most passive of characters but men driven to the edge of eccentricity because they spent their working lives listening to people's words half a second after their lip movements, were sympathetic to each other's problems, offering to patch feeds together and work out a communal way of obtaining the best results. Cameramen, on the other hand, always more combative and wiry than their frequently overweight partners, displayed no such generous spirit of co-operation. Their tripods were their castles, protected by experienced and instinctively aimed elbows, and anyone who dared to interrupt the view from their lenses was the target of immediate vilification.

Matters were exacerbated by a posse of uninvited guests, few of them aware that they were named after a character in the film that had won the Palme d'Or at Cannes thirty-seven years previously: *La Dolce Vita* – Fellini's dream-like satire on Rome at the height of Italy's economic miracle. Marcello Mastroianni played a journalist caught up in a slick, sick society accompanied by Walter Santesso as his sensation- hungry photographer – Paparazzo.

Cannes now hosted the world's annual convention of the paparazzi, not a gathering which required any invitations since they were, by definition, the uninvited. They roamed the streets like a guerrilla force that had occupied the citadel of the city, lone buccaneers, most of them garbed in semi-military vests with batteries of motor-driven cameras hanging from their necks and pouches of celluloid ammunition at their waists. Thousands of near-identical photographs would land on the picture desks of newspapers and magazines and television stations throughout the world each day of the Festival. It was the remorseless aim of every vigilante paparazzo to catch that treasured, unplanned moment that was different.

More than three dozen, thanks to tip-offs and radio eavesdrops and fast motor-cycles, had made it to the photo-call, and all the imprecations of the young publicist with the upward shock of dyed yellow hair who had arrived to try and control the assembled crowd, that they should leave or Bud would cancel the appointment, had about as much effect as asking starving wolfhounds to abandon their bones.

Leland was awoken by an arpeggio of anxious cries from outside his window. He was initially thankful to be shaken out of a dream in which he was working as a chef in an Indian restaurant. He had refused to grease his frying pan and so the poppadoms had stuck to it.

'Leland, *Le*-land.'

He pulled aside the lace curtains and opened the French windows onto his ground-floor balcony. Homer Mangold, paunchy in matching lemon tennis shorts and shirt, bearing an outsize racquet and capped absurdly in a pink peaked hat, was standing on the other side of the flower boxes in a state of advanced agitation.

Leland tried to stifle his amusement at the image before him. 'What's the matter, Homer? A heart attack or tennis elbow?'

'Much worse than that,' Homer appeared not to notice the flippancy. 'It's Bud. He's still asleep.'

'I would be, too, if it weren't for you.'

'It's past seven o'clock' – Homer indicated his watch with his racquet – 'and there's a real wild crowd of press and TV people down at the pool. They're likely to get ugly if he doesn't show.'

'So wake him up.'

'I don't want to. It's not my job. There's a nasty side to him, you know that.'

'So get Schenck to do it.'

'He's disappeared. Gone off to see some Arab on a yacht.'

'He moves fast.'

'We've got to move fast.' Homer hammered with his racquet on the stone edge of the balcony. 'We can't afford negative publicity.'

'You'd better come in,' said Leland.

Homer made it over the balcony on his third attempt and headed straight for the drinks table by the door.

'Help yourself at the bar,' urged his host. 'The Dutch courage is in the brown bottle on the right.'

Homer gulped down a substantial scotch. Picking up a green book as he refilled his glass he asked, 'What's this?'

'It's a Bible belonging to two guys who were lecturing me on how to colour the world map red.'

'Communists?'

'No, Brits. They had the colour first.'

'What are you going to do?'

'I told them to forget it.'

'No, about Bud.'

'Ring his suite,' Leland suggested.

'I tried to. He's taken the phone off the hook.'

'Well, go round there. You're good at shouting outside windows.'

'I'm afraid.'

'Of what?'

'I'm afraid he's in there with some chick.'

'So what else is new?'

Homer grew embarrassed. 'His wife's my sister. You didn't know that, did you? We agreed to keep it quiet. Bad for business.'

'Good for your business, I would have thought.' Leland had always wondered why Bud had tolerated this social gadfly who was out to lunch in more ways than one.

'You go, Leland, please. I'll owe you one. I can fix a Friar's Club roast in your honour. Anything.'

The studio boss seemed to be left with little alternative but, even as he prepared to get dressed, the door of the suite was flung open and there was Bud Booker, dressed in a three-piece hand-made Vercotti suit with an open-necked primrose shirt and even the closed yellow rose – plastic in fact – that he habitually wore as a screen detective.

'Homer, you asshole, why didn't you wake me? I haven't even had time to do my hair.'

However the flaxen tangles had contrived, perhaps instinctively, to arrange themselves in the controlled disarray that usually took half an hour and half a can of hairspray to achieve.

Bud managed to disarm the waiting press with his opening remark. 'I'm sorry I'm late but I thought I'd give you a chance to enjoy the view before I came and spoiled it for you. Did everybody get a drink?'

Nobody had been offered one – there would not have been much change out of a thousand dollars if they had. But now the anxious publicist shot off towards the restaurant with a promise to Bud that drinks were on their way.

Booker stood imposingly on the weathered Mediterranean rocks, looking like a Western hero at the end of a classic film. It was not by accident that the setting sun enhanced his rugged features with a diffused, rose-tinted key light. He had carefully chosen where best to stand and had earlier calculated from his bedroom window the exact moment when the sun would be at its most effective – the real reason he was forty minutes late. Leland, watching him from the far side of the pool, ruminated, not for the first time, that although the studios might claim that they created stars, they were always reliant on a more powerful, even divine force doing the groundwork for them.

The publicist came running back, assuring the assembly that drinks would be served afterwards. He tried to stop the clicking of cameras so that the television reporters could have their turn but his pleas had no effect.

'Okay, boys, let's hold it,' growled Bud quietly. Almost immediately the shutters were silenced. 'I gather you want to ask me a couple of questions.'

'What do you think of Cannes?' It was a Dutch reporter who led off.

'I haven't seen it yet. I've only seen the inside of my suite and the inside of my eyelids. I hear there are one or two good restaurants, though, might stake those out.'

'Are you disappointed that *Black Cops Kill* is not in competition?'

'Not in the competition? I didn't know that. Hey, Leland – that's Leland Walters, the President of Warner Bros and the man who flew me here in his nice plane – how come we're not in the competition?'

The star was, of course, entirely conversant with the fact that they had been turned down, but Leland secretly admired the way he passed the buck so adroitly. He had been ready for the question. 'Unfortunately we had to open in some territories outside of the United States before the Festival so that rendered us ineligible. It contravenes Article three Section two of the rules, I'm afraid.'

It was a section that was more honoured in the breach than the observance but nobody thought to challenge it.

'I'm not sure that I believe in competitions,' affirmed Bud. 'Except the one that says you have to fill up cinema seats and we're doing quite well in that one.'

There was an appreciative response from the press who had been effectively won over by his apparent frank charm. This cheerful atmosphere was punctured by a middle-aged Englishman in a white safari suit. 'Mr Booker, Sidney Saxon from *World of Cinema*. It seems to me that in *Black Cops Kill* you have a severe case of muddled morality. For nearly two-thirds of your film you appear to be championing these vigilante thugs who are persecuting the Chinese, the clear message being that they have no right to their own enclave within San Francisco. And then your violent retribution is, if anything, more prejudiced. What's happened to truth, justice and the American way?'

Booker looked as if he had just taken a left to the stomach, which indeed he had. 'Well, your wonderful unarmed police force in England isn't the most effective in the world – you just have to see movies like *Hungertown* with that crazy picking off people as if he was shooting rabbits. And you have the Irish Republicans who seem to be able to blow up a British army barracks whenever they feel like it – '

Leland sighed inwardly as he mentally knocked five million dollars off the UK box-office. It was too late to stop him now. But, miraculously, his silent wishes were granted when two hooded men in black, both armed with rifles, suddenly appeared opposite him on the other side of the pool.

The press were startled at first, then greeted this pre-arranged stunt with laughter and applause. One bold paparazzo yelled, 'Bud, can you go and stand between them for a picture?'

Booker was disconcerted. Homer had failed to tell him about this – another reason he should get rid of him. But he was relieved to be interrupted, realising he had stepped into dangerously controversial waters with his mention of the IRA, so he complied.

The photographers and television cameramen crowded round to get a better shot – at last an image that was an improvement on a talking head. But the two men permitted him to pose only briefly, then grabbed him roughly by the arms and led him the short distance down the steps to the sea.

Bud was now visibly disturbed. 'Homer, what is this?' – he yelled over his shoulder.

Homer had no idea. He was as surprised as everyone else. He looked at Leland and Leland looked back at him.

The man beside Bud poked a gun in his ribs, indicating that he meant business. A speedboat with two more men, also hooded and clad like executioners in black, was waiting at the jetty and the star was unceremoniously tumbled into its back seat.

Every moment of what happened was minutely recorded on film and tape as the boat shot off along the burnished amber path of the lowering sun. Far out to sea it veered sharply to the left, setting a course round the point of Cap d'Antibes, heading for Nice or Monte Carlo or maybe Italy beyond.

'Nice idea, Mr Walters,' said Sidney Saxon, his camera panning back to focus on Leland. 'Now does your studio stand by Mr Booker's, if I may say, controversial views?'

'What the fuck are you talking about?' Leland yelled at him. 'Why didn't some of you guys do something? What's the sense in taking pictures when a man's life is at stake?'

'I presume it was a stunt,' Saxon went quickly on the defensive. 'You've just arrived. These things happen all the time in Cannes.'

Leland's eyes moved from the young PR man whose dyed hair seemed in a greater state of a shock than before, to the publicity partners, Pascall and Swern, standing sheepishly at the back of the crowd, to Homer Mangold, still absurd in his lemon tennis-wear, gripping his racquet so tightly with both hands that his knuckles were as white as his face.

'Tell me it was a stunt,' said the studio head.

Nobody spoke. For the first time that evening, by the swimming pool of the Hôtel du Cap, there was complete and utter silence.

CHAPTER 19

Thursday 15th May 1997

Cannes

'Where the fuck were *you*?'

'I've told you. There was nothing new in it for us. The movie's old hat in the States. We had the airport footage. All they were offering was a photo-call and a couple of questions. He was only likely to get interesting when he arrived in town with all the hoop-la here.'

'Only likely to get interesting when he arrived in town.' Jim Hurley repeated Robert's words with cutting irony, his anger swelling higher than the turbulent Atlantic that fortunately separated them. 'You do realise that it led the network news on all three channels? CBS ran it at six minutes. And the photographs are on the front page of every single first edition. It is probably the biggest show-business news story of the decade. One of the most famous film stars in the world is brazenly kidnapped in front of a battery of international television cameras. But not ours. My chairman is asking me for an explanation. I have no explanation. My job is probably going to go quicker than yours.'

Robert held the receiver a little further away from his ear as Hurley's rage reached its climax.

'There's no need to fire me, Jim. I resign. And I take full responsibility. Sandra was out of town doing a recce when it happened. It was my decision.' Sandra, who was listening on another line, made as if to interrupt with the true story but Robert succeeded in stopping her.

'There'll be plenty of time for resignations when you get back here.' Hurley's voice came over more vehement than before. 'What we need is a fucking brilliant programme from you guys tomorrow or you won't be alive to resign. What have you got lined up?'

It was only seven in the morning in Cannes, one a.m. in New York. Hurley was being deliberately provocative. Robert and Sandra had spent most of a sleepless night following various leads that led nowhere. It seemed as if the whole town had stayed awake after they heard the news. People lingered in bars and cafés and hotel lobbies until dawn, energised and excited by the incident, as if it somehow made them more important simply by being there. The mid-Festival lull had come to an abrupt end.

'We're putting together a package on security,' Robert began. 'What went wrong.'

'What in hell *did* go wrong? How do two masked gunmen march into a hotel, gatecrash a press conference and walk away with a movie star as if they were taking their grandmother out of a sunshine home for an afternoon stroll?'

'They didn't march into the hotel. That's the whole point. Everybody's credentials were checked at the gate and there was staggered perimeter security, not much but enough to spot interlopers. But they didn't anticipate the possibility of anybody coming by boat.'

'Well, why did nobody try to do anything about it when they led him away?'

'They genuinely thought it was some kind of stunt. Even Booker thought so. He went and posed with the guys. You saw that on TV.'

'Not on our programme,' snarled Hurley, rubbing in the point.

'These things are happening all the time in Cannes. People are fighting for media attention. There was a full-time beach landing two nights ago, just to push some space movie. We've sent back the material. It had me fooled to begin with.'

'But it wasn't real.'

'Movies aren't real but they're the reason we're all here.' Robert was managing to regain his stride. 'This place isn't real. For fifty weeks a year these people spend their lives creating fantasies. And then for two weeks they take a break and invent a living fantasy which they can inhabit themselves. They go down the rabbit hole into their own wonderland – Disneyland with asparagus.'

'Save the poetics till you're on camera. What's the latest? Have they asked for a ransom yet? And who the fuck are they?'

'Nobody knows. There's been absolute silence. Some people think it could be the ETA – the Basque separatists. It has the hallmark of one of their operations. It could even be the IRA – the timing was certainly appropriate considering what he was saying. Seems unlikely though if they're looking for money – they're hardly likely to alienate the American public where most of it comes from. There's even a possibility that it's a French underground group – *Action Directe*.'

'What do they stand for?' asked Jim.

'Nobody really knows. They've never published any aims. They're just generally angry and carry off the occasional kidnapping or killing to let people know they're still around. They're a sort of middle-class hangover from the Baader-Meinhof gang in Germany. It could be the Mafia, but that's very doubtful. The most intelligent speculation is that it's probably professional criminals looking for a ransom.'

'Well, whatever it is, find out. Or better still, find Bud. Get him on the show for a live interview and all is forgiven.'

'Believe me, Jim,' said Robert, 'we're trying our best. Can I speak to Tanya? Is she there?'

'Sure.' The programme editor's tone softened a little. 'And good luck.'

'Thanks. It's time some came our way.'

Tanya's voice took over the line, very quiet and distant. 'Hi Robert, how are you?'

'You can imagine how I am. How are you?'

'Oh I'm fine,' she replied in a deliberately flat and emotionless tone.

He affected to ignore it; this was hardly the time to deal with their personal problems. 'Could you do me a favour? You remember Hutton Craig, my friend at the *New York Times*.'

'Sort of.' She sounded even more defensive.

'Well, he's in Paris now. Can you ring him there and ask him if he could find out whatever he can about a break-in at the Film Festival offices in the Faubourg St Honoré at the end of January. I'm not sure that it was even reported in the press but he must have some contacts in the police by now. Would you do that, Tanya, and ask him to fax any information to the Carlton here?'

'Why don't you do it? You're in France.'

'I've tried but I can't get hold of him and we're going to be out running all day. It's not necessarily that important. It's only a vague lead.'

'Why bother then?'

'It just might help, that's all.'

'I don't know that I can. I have to go to Atlantic City. There's a casino story.'

'Fine. Don't worry then.'

He could hear the catch in her throat. 'Robert, there's something you should know. I'm seeing somebody. I'd be lying to you if I didn't tell you. It's nothing serious, at the moment. But you should know.'

'It's okay. I understand. I've got to go. We're under a lot of pressure.'

'I'll ring you,' she said.

'Do that.'

After he heard the click at the other end, he lowered the receiver and juggled it from hand to hand. He looked across at Sandra who had continued listening on the other phone, and smiled weakly. 'As they say in this business, you're as good as your last show.'

'I insist that we close down the Festival. It is not possible to carry out any controlled investigation with forty thousand people milling around this town. Besides, what is there to be festive about? This is a stain on our country. Whatever the outcome, the Americans will probably never return here. It makes a mockery of all our security procedures.'

The *Sous-Préfet* for the Alpes-Maritimes had summoned the daily security meeting an hour early at eight o'clock. Although he was the chairman, his eyes anxiously flickered from face to face as he spoke, hoping to read the concurrence of the other participants in what he was suggesting. He sensed the majority were against him, led by the formidable presence of the French Foreign Minister, Henri Chaillot, who sat beside him, tersely drawing on a thin cigar.

'The Americans will come back,' Chaillot pronounced with confidence. 'Remember 1986. They moved the Sixth Fleet into the Mediterranean and bombed Libya. Colonel Gaddafi swore that he would take his revenge. On American television news, night after night, they carried scare stories about what might happen at Cannes. That is why the Excelsior Plan was evolved and this very committee was set up. So they stayed away that year – led by their hero, Rambo. But the security worked. There was no bomb, no shooting, no terrorists. And the next year all the Americans returned, more than before. If we close the Festival we make it a bigger scandal than it is already. Is that not so, Renaud?'

The Director had been pencilling notes on his daily schedule. He had not expected to become involved in the discussion so soon, but he knew what he thought.

'I agree – we should continue. I spoke to the President of Warner Bros this morning. Walters was with Booker at the Hôtel du Cap – well, you saw him on the television news. He has heard nothing. Obviously we will not now go ahead with the showing of *Black Cops Kill* – it was not, I must confess, a film that would have enhanced this event in any case. Instead of putting in a replacement I will keep that evening free as a mark of respect. But I hope, by then, this matter will be over. Apart from that things must go on as normal. I doubt very much if the people responsible for this deed are coming to screenings every day, so what good would it do to cancel them?'

Chaillot looked across the table at the five uniformed men, their faces funereal as they listened to Renaud's suggestions. Behind the scattered row of empty coffee cups sat the Lieutenant–Colonel in charge of the Municipal Security Services, the Cannes Police Commissioner, the Head of the Fire Brigade – the proudly named *Corps des Sapeurs-Pompiers* – and the Commandant of the élite CRS who ranked above the regular police force in their powers of investigation and arrest. It was to this last man that Chaillot addressed his question.

'Commandant, when are we going to hear something?'

'We have our contacts, but it's early yet.' The bearded officer, even when facing a senior member of the government, was experienced enough to hint that secret activity was furiously taking place behind the scenes, while not fully revealing his hand. In truth, his organisation's contacts in the notorious Nice underworld had come up with nothing, making it seem doubtful that this was a local gangland kidnap to extract a few million dollars from the purse of Warner Bros. Nor had his opposite numbers in Italy been able to get any leads from those members of the Mafia who cleverly doubled their income, and ensured their immunity from arrest, by acting as police informers.

Chaillot appeared to read his mind. 'Do you think it's a Mafia job?'

'Not their style,' replied the Commandant. 'Evidently they have a good relationship with Hollywood.'

Chaillot turned to Callet. 'Is that true?'

Renaud permitted himself a slight smile. 'It was said that there was an unspoken agreement on the early Godfather films that if they were not portrayed as drug dealers they wouldn't cause any problems and that seems to have held true since. As long as the Mafia is seen to be glamorous and only really a threat to rival families, that's the movie image they appreciate. I daresay if they were shown to be as heavily into heroin as apparently they are, they might get a little upset.'

'So not the Mafia,' Chaillot put a small cross on the list of options in front of him.

'There is one vague possibility that we shouldn't rule out altogether.' The members of the meeting turned more intently towards Renaud. 'It could actually have been a stunt. Not orchestrated by the studio, of course, but by students possibly – maybe even some maverick publicist.'

'Are you serious?' asked Chaillot.

'Half-serious,' Renaud replied. 'And half-hopeful. You know . . . Cannes . . . Festival time.'

'If it were a prank we would have heard by now.' The Divisional Police Commissioner had no doubts.

'Could it be personal?' Chaillot was reverting to his pre-government role as a *juge d'instruction* where his pertinent questioning from the bench had brought him to the notice of the elders of his party.

'First reports indicate not.' There was a hesitation in the Commandant's voice. 'But these police films that Monsieur Booker makes are evidently not to everybody's taste. I gather the Moonies were not too pleased about this last one, nor was the National Association for the Advancement of Coloured People, although these institutions sometimes pretend to get upset about high-profile movies in order to obtain some publicity on the back of them. We have an officer with Leland Walters at the moment pursuing this line.'

'What results from your men?' Chaillot fixed the Lieutenant-Colonel in charge of Municipal Security with a searchlight glare that made the man feel, for a moment, that he was being accused of masterminding the kidnap himself.

'We're fairly certain he's not in Cannes.' The Colonel tried to make this negative supposition seem as positive as possible. 'He would be recognised instantly. Anyway, put yourself in the minds of the men who did it. It would be the last place they would go. We've carried out spot checks on the more remote farms and villas in a line from Vence to Grasse but nothing so far. Nobody has even seen the boat since it rounded the Cap. We had a full-scale speedboat and helicopter search under way in less than half an hour but by then, as you know, it was dark.'

'Is it possible that he's still on the Cap?' Chaillot seemed enamoured of his own suggestion.

'It is possible. We just don't have the men to comb it.'

The Minister became even more convinced. 'You shall. Let me set an example by allocating my personal guards to your force, and I suggest we commit every available person to this search.' He threw a pointed glance at the Commandant of the CRS. 'I think your men would be better employed out there looking for Booker, rather than back here waiting for him to come to them.'

The Commandant agreed with reluctance, but thankful to have had the decision taken for him.

'I am sure it is essential,' continued Chaillot, 'that everything should go on as normal. We must give the appearance that we are waiting to hear from them before we act. A communiqué should be drawn up to that effect. That way we buy an element of surprise in our measures. Apart from an expression of condolence for Madame Booker, I intend to host my dinner for the Australians at the Majestic tomorrow night as if nothing had happened.'

'Who gives a toss about some fascist film star? If they hijacked the whole of Hollywood and dumped them in the Pacific we'd be better off. They've polluted the cinema. The glamour's gone – all that remains is the greed.'

Tony Birch did not appear to be too upset about Booker's disappearance. He was more upset about the prospect of the Festival closing down – rumours to that effect had been coursing up and down the Croisette all morning – and by the fact that both prints of *Poppy Day* were still missing.

'When did you say this guy was coming?'

Vincent Wall looked down from their apartment window at the clock above the jeweller's shop on the other side of the Rue de La Tour Maubourg. 'He should have been here an hour ago. I'm sure he said one o'clock. I don't think he's going to turn up.'

Birch lit up his umpteenth cigarette of the day. 'Are you sure he said here? I mean, if he was from the Festival wouldn't he have wanted you to go there?'

'I told you I'm not certain. He just came up to me in the Petit Carlton. Maybe he was from the laboratory. His English wasn't that good.'

'But he understood the address?'

'Sure, he wrote it down.'

'And he said our print was safe.'

'I told you.'

'Fucking French,' Birch flicked his ash contemptuously on the carpet. 'Can't trust them to look after the films or the stars.'

The buzzer from the downstairs door stuttered out its broken message. Without bothering to ask who was there, Birch lifted the wall phone and shouted 'Third floor', pressing the button to let the arrival in.

Neither of them recognised the burly figure of Raoul Bazin. They hadn't even been as far as the Old Port, let alone entered Le Mistral bar during their time in Cannes. But they could see he didn't much look like a Festival official, clad in blue jeans and sneakers with both his hands firmly in the pockets of a shabby leather jacket.

'Where's the print?' Birch demanded. 'What's happened? I need to see it before the screening to check the sub-titles – not that there's anything we can do at this stage if they're all to cock.'

Bazin remained standing in the doorway. Since before the Booker kidnap, his services appeared to have been dispensed with and he had still not been paid. Here was a chance to make a little freelance money.

'I know where your film is,' he told the two Australians in halting English. 'You may have it back at any time you like but first you must pay one hundred thousand francs in cash. It is the reward.'

Birch rounded on him in anger. 'Reward? There is no reward. What are you on about? Are you trying to blackmail us? C'mon, Vince, let's go to the police.'

Bazin barred their way. He drew an expired drug-squad ID from his pocket. 'No point in that,' he informed them, adding, as he took a pistol out of the other one. 'Bring the money to the Square de Verdun at three tomorrow afternoon. Come alone.'

'I am going to hit this man if he asks me once more if Bud had any enemies.' Leland Walters clenched and unclenched his fists in silent desperation.

The patient police inspector had already filled one standard-issue notebook as Walters, Mangold and Schenck retraced the last twenty-four hours in their lives. Methodically, he had brought another one.

'The pilots on your private plane, was there anything suspicious about them? Where did they go when you landed?'

'They work for me,' said Leland. 'I've met their wives and children. They went off to Monte Carlo to lose some money. We didn't need them again till the weekend.'

'Talking of children, why did Monsieur Booker never have any?'

'I don't know. It's not a thing I ever discussed with him. Maybe he and Mary couldn't, maybe they didn't want any. What's it got to do with this?'

'In this situation the family is very often involved. Frequently they will make secret deals without informing us, hand over large sums against our advice. Sometimes the kidnappers get the money and the family get back a corpse.'

'Have they asked for any money yet?' demanded Barry Schenck.

'You tell me, Mr Schenck. I think you will be the first to know.'

'We'll pay,' insisted Leland. 'Whatever it is the studio will pay. Unless it's absurd.'

'I hope you will be guided by us on that.' The young inspector looked reprimandingly at the tycoon.

The Frenchman turned his attention to Schenck. 'The other three gentlemen went to their rooms to rest after their arrival. But they informed me at reception that you made eight telephone calls and then ordered a car. Is that so?'

'How is it relevant?' Schenck eyed him derisively.

'Everything is relevant when a man's life is at stake. I believe the car took you to the Port Canto. And there you boarded the tender of the yacht *Princess Sophie*, that is still at anchor in Cannes Bay.'

'If you know all this, why are you asking me?'

The inspector ignored his question. 'What were you doing on the yacht?'

'I was doing a deal. Why else do you think I came to Cannes? To show my tits off on the beach?'

'These negotiations were with an Arab gentleman, were they not? And did they involve Mr Booker?'

Schenck's face flushed. 'That's confidential. I'm not going to talk about that.'

But Leland could see the logic in the line of questioning. 'He has a point, Barry. Who else is on board that boat?'

'Apart from the entire Popular Front for the Liberation of Palestine, nobody who matters.' Schenck was both annoyed and embarrassed that it had come to light that he had used the trip, funded by Warners, to conduct his own private business. 'The guy lives in London. His crew are Goans or something, I think. I had an entirely separate fiscal negotiation with him. Nothing to do with Mr Booker.'

'But you did tell him you were here with Bud?' Leland had taken over the questioning.

'Sure, his daughter wanted to know what he was like.'

'And you did tell him he was staying in this hotel?'

'Where's the harm in that? Your publicity department told the whole fucking press corps he was here!'

The impending friction between them was broken by the telephone. Leland answered it. 'Yes, put her through.'

'Is it them?' Homer was anxiously on edge.

'No, it's Mary.' Leland saw this as an opportunity to get rid of the policeman, at least for the moment. 'Inspector, could you excuse us? This is very personal.'

The Frenchman rose slowly and made his reluctant way across to the door. 'You must tell me the moment you hear from them. Two or more of my men are permanently in the lobby. And can you cast your minds back, all three of you? There is one central question and the answer may unravel everything. Did Bud Booker have any enemies?'

Leland shook his head disbelievingly at the other two as the inspector left the room. Mary Booker came on the line. 'Mary, are you all right? Did they get in touch with you before the television news? Where were you?'

'I'm fine. I was out playing golf. I'm in Palm Springs. The studio have been very good, thank you, Leland. They've kept the press out of my hair. I made a simple statement saying how distressed I was, that's all. They don't seem to know that Bud and I – '

Leland interrupted her. 'Mary, I'm fairly certain this line's got a tap on it. We're still waiting for some contact from the kidnappers and they may well ring me.'

All three men in the room knew that Booker's marriage was presented as hale and harmonious to enhance his public image but, for the past eight years, he and Mary had ceased to live together as man and wife. They merely shared the same home occasionally.

'Is he going to be okay?' she asked. 'Who did it? I hope they release him in time to see all the publicity. He'll love it.'

'We don't know who did it. Some nuts looking for money probably. We'll square them.'

'There was a report on the television last night that you plan to re-release a few of his old films, evidently as some kind of tribute. He's not dead yet, you know.'

'Just some kid in the publicity department going a bit too far.' Leland tried to sound as dismissive as possible. In truth he had harboured considerable doubts about setting this plan in motion. But, he reassured himself, he still had his shareholders' interests to think of, as well as those of his leading star.

The floor of Fyodor and Elizabeth's suite at the Majestic was covered with photocopies of newspaper articles.

'Look at that,' said Hetty Berman, letting another sheet float from her hand. 'Burma. Who would have thought that they'd be interested? Page seven of their second largest circulation newspaper – with a photograph. The stuff has been jamming the fax machine for twenty-four hours non-stop. I've had to get another girl in to help me sort it out.'

Fyodor, looking almost biblical in his white dressing-gown and sandals, stubbed out his Gitane and picked up the piece of paper nearest to him.

'This one's from the *Daily News* in Mexico City.' He cast an eye over the article. 'It's in English – just. "France last night witnessed the biggest seaborne landing since D-Day . . ."'

'I gave them that line,' exclaimed Hetty proudly. 'Lots of them have used it.'

'"Thousands of Aliens from Ursa Minor . . ." did you give them that line, as well?'

Hetty eyed him circumspectly. 'Isn't Jupiter part of Ursa Minor?'

'Not when I last looked up. It might have joined since, of course.'

'Who cares? We're talking column inches, not planets. When you think of the tens of thousands of movies being shown here, this sort of free publicity is quite incredible.'

'It wasn't free,' Fyodor observed quietly. 'I had to sacrifice a day's shooting to budget for it.'

'So that's why Tim had to cover the blast-off scene in two days instead of three.' Elizabeth was sitting on the edge of the bed leafing through the daily Festival magazine.

'If he had had twenty-two days he would still have made a

botch of it. It was all sparks and smoke. The emotional heart of that scene wasn't a firework display. It was the distraught face at the window. Yours. And he nearly missed that.' In normal circumstances Elizabeth would not have let this pass, but the delicacy of their present position made her hold back.

'Let's hear some more of that Mexico stuff.' Hetty was equally anxious to avoid any tension.

'They obviously picked this up from a wire-service or a syndication agency. It's amazing how you can rely on some journalists to do your exaggeration for you – they always want things to be the biggest ever, the most spectacular, to break all records.' Fyodor's respect for show-business reporters was no higher than that for his director. 'D-Day? We only hired eighteen boats and two of those broke down. Anyway, Muriel Lowry was under the illusion that she was there, or she wants her readers to have that illusion. "I felt like an old fashioned war correspondent as I dug into my foxhole on the beach seeking cover from the bombardment by smoke bombs." Foxhole? Bit of artistic licence there. "This is a crazy town full of crazy people," Muriel informs us, omitting to mention that, crazy or sane, she is not one of them. "You don't have to go to the movies at Cannes. They come to you. In all its fifty glorious years this star-studded, sun-kissed movie-fest has rarely seen a stunt of more stunning audacity to promote yet another multi-million dollar space extravaganza."'

He dropped the article on the floor. 'She doesn't even mention the name of the film. And it isn't set in space.'

Hetty was not in the mood to accept criticism. 'Just count your lucky dollars that we didn't coincide with the Booker kidnapping. We wouldn't have got a paragraph. Talk about audacity.'

'You didn't arrange that one, did you, Hetty?'

'No, I did not and I think it's very tasteless – ' Hetty realised that Fyodor was sending her up. 'What news, anyway?'

'I finally got through to Leland after lunch. Things are bad. This damned business has interrupted everything. He's cancelled all meetings, including our lunch to confirm the

302

sequel. He says he has to stay by the phone – surely someone else could take care of it. The man is probably dead by now. That's why I don't want to stay here with those crazy people around. The place doesn't feel safe.'

Elizabeth closed her magazine and got up off the bed. 'That's what Muriel of Mexico said – lots of crazy people.'

'You're booked on the seven-thirty out of Nice. Economy, I'm afraid, they had no seats left in Club.' Hetty made it sound like a national catastrophe. 'They've had to lay on two extra Jumbos. People are leaving this town like lemmings. Even if Booker isn't dead, the Festival is. If the French had any repsect they'd cancel it now.'

'Are you going?' Elizabeth unexpectedly addressed the question to Hetty.

'No, not yet. I need to follow up on this. Besides, there's a couple of other possible clients I have to see. This is the best place in the world to pick up new business. There are millionaires owning publicity agencies today who started out getting black-market tickets for producers in Cannes.'

'I don't want to go, either,' Elizabeth announced. 'We've got this suite till the end of the week. I'll fly back then.'

'You've got an open ticket,' Hetty informed her. 'I'll buy you lunch at the Colombe d'Or if you're serious. The way things are going we may be able to get a table.'

'Don't be stupid.' Fyodor's clipped words curtailed their arrangements. 'Of course you're leaving. Hetty, will you excuse us?'

'I'm sorry.' The corpulent publicist looked doubly uncomfortable as she bent down to pick the papers up off the floor.

'Leave those.' Fyodor's temper was barely under control. 'And leave us.'

Hastily gathering her bags and belongings, Hetty made a swift and undignified exit.

'Why do you have to talk to people like that?' Elizabeth asked.

'Why do you have to make such silly statements in public?'

'It's not a silly statement. This place is beginning to get interesting now it's been infected with some reality. I genuinely want to stay.'

'I don't understand you any more.' Fyodor lowered himself into a chair and lit up another cigarette. 'Could it be that you're staying because I'm going?'

Elizabeth sat on the floor beside him, cross-legged like a schoolgirl. She had rarely felt so ill at ease with a man as she had with him during the past three days. He had respected her wishes and kept his distance but at times she felt it might have been better if he hadn't, if he had forced himself on her in retribution for her cold treachery. When she had come home the previous morning she had found him, fully clothed, asleep in the same chair he was sitting in now.

She had said nothing and he had asked her nothing. Instead he picked up the open book at his feet and pointed out a passage to her. 'It says here the Romans in Britain used to make sacrifices to Jupiter, the king of the gods. They would kill cattle, feast off the best bits and offer him the parts they didn't want, the feet and the offal. A very practical religion. Apparently, paganism was suppressed late in the fourth century and now as we enter the twenty-first it's back again.'

His generosity seemed a way of torturing her further. She wanted to provoke him. She needed their relationship to become combustible so that it would explode and shatter. Yet Fyodor, however crassly and insensitively he behaved to those working for him, was prepared to treat her as the prodigal daughter.

She watched him sitting there in his towelling robe, puffing twitchily at his Gitane. He looked pudgy and badly out of condition, a film of sweat on the flesh around his neck.

'You become like a bull when you're angry,' she remarked. 'I can see you scratch your cloven hoof in the dirt. I wouldn't like to be a toreador in your sights.'

'I'm not angry. I just don't understand you any longer.'

She said nothing. There was little she could say. She had checked repeatedly at reception to see if Robert had left a message but there had been none. Logically she realised that he must be off somewhere covering the Bud Booker story but emotionally she feared that, for the first time in her life, it had been a one-night stand. She knew so little about him.

Maybe there *was* a station wagon and a wife called Holly and, despite her desperation to see him again, it was not her intention to flee from one married man to another.

She felt Fyodor's hand on her shoulder and looked up. His eyes were red and rheumy.

'I don't want to lose you, Lizzie,' he said.

She turned away and contemplated the pile of papers on the floor.

'There's no one else, is there?'

'No,' she lied.

It was him, standing beside her at the kiosk. Chantal was certain. That smell, like bitter-sweet saffron, she would never forget it. She glanced at his face. She had seen those eyes before, piercing and passionless. His skin seemed too dark for Chinese. Maybe he was Japanese or Malaysian. She wasn't knowledgeable enough to be sure. Speaking imperfect French with an English accent, he asked for two packets of spearmint chewing gum. Would he remember her? She turned away quickly. He hadn't betrayed a flicker of recognition. Thank goodness there were other people behind them.

He paid for the gum and walked off in the direction of the Old Port. Chantal remained frozen to the spot, trance-like.

'Yes, what is it?' The old lady behind the counter was getting impatient.

Chantal had no idea what she had come for. 'A bar of chocolate,' she spluttered, 'and an apple.'

She was determined not to let him out of her sight. He hadn't gone far. Down on Le Pantiero, the section of the wharf reserved for the fishing boats, he was occupied in an intense conversation with two of the sailors.

She had no idea what to do. There were no police to be seen – most of them had been drafted for the search. Even if there were, what could she tell them? Demand to have him arrested? She needed to get to a phone. As she made her way back towards the Palais the solution dawned on her. Raoul.

The man was still talking to the fishermen. Chantal crossed to the other side of the street and, when she was sure there was no chance he could see her, broke into a run, accelerating past the pavement restaurants, all of them much emptier than usual in the early evening.

Le Mistral was closed. She banged on the door but there was no response. There must be a way in, she thought. At the back of the building she found a low wooden hatch, like an animal entrance, where deliveries could be made. The hinge was loose and, using her nail file, she managed to work it off with surprising ease. She crouched down and crawled through it into a store-room full of crates. It was cold and slightly damp. A door led into the dark, silent bar.

'Raoul,' she called nervously. 'Raoul.'

He wasn't there. At least she could leave him a note. She felt her way apprehensively along the counter and ducked under it. Up on her left she reached for the light-switch by the door of the back room.

He was there, after all. His body lay contorted on the sofa. Fresh blood oozed from his stomach where somebody appeared to have attempted a Caesarean section with a meat cleaver. The rictus of terror on his face indicated it had been a painful and unpleasant death. His tongue had been partially torn out and hung from his puffed lips in a glistening stream of blood.

Chantal retreated slowly from the sight, dizzy with nausea. She turned round to vomit in the basin behind the bar but her way was blocked by a stubby arm, fat to the point of deformity, stretched out across the doorway.

CHAPTER 20

Friday 16th May 1997

Cannes

The weather changed on the morning of Friday 16th May and so did the character of the town. A solid sheet of grey cloud canopied the Mediterranean and a chill, unfriendly breeze swept off the sea into the streets. Those vestiges of summer that had attempted to arrive earlier in the week were banished as if they had never been. The waiters, glancing at the sky, made an automatic decision not to lay the outdoor tables, let alone set out the miniature tubes of sun cream. People wrapped themselves in sweaters and raincoats, moving quickly through the streets at a pace normally associated with big cities as opposed to the leisurely promenade of Cannes.

Renaud Callet's office had now become an operational headquarters. The Commandant of the CRS and the Colonel in charge of municipal security had both established rights there, although neither was present at that moment. Henri Chaillot was. He had had an uncomfortable morning. His opposite number from Washington had been on the line, communicating little of the bonhomie that he had radiated at the recent Foreign Ministers' conference in Rome. He had proposed moving a destroyer from the United States Sixth Fleet into the Bay of Cannes – it was less than two days' sailing·away – with the suggestion that the sailors might help in the land search as an operational exercise. Chaillot had rejected the offer; this was a problem that France must solve on her own. When the Secretary of State had pressed him for details of their intelligence operation, pointing out that American spy satellites could provide minute coverage of the area, he had dismissed that proposal as well. It was unthinkable that the United States should spy on the charmed hexagon.

The Elysée had been just as irritating. The President wanted a full report on what was happening. What good was a full report at this stage? It only occupied valuable man-hours that could more profitably be devoted to the search. Chaillot had the uneasy feeling that his own political future might depend on the success of this. The Fiftieth Cannes Film Festival seemed to have turned into a horror movie providing the watching world with a ghoulish entertainment. Why had he been so stupid as to get involved himself? He had been right in thinking that the event would give his name a wider global prominence – but he had had no precognition of the circumstances that would attend this notoriety. It should have been an underling down here facing the music. Then he could still be comfortably in his office in Paris, demanding full reports himself.

The jury had been unofficially discharged – although neither the press nor the competing film-makers had been informed – a decision made easier by the fact that two of its members had expressed their intention of returning home anyway. The Minister quite clearly could no longer be seen to serve on it while the crisis continued, and he was secretly relieved at this.

'Do you really sit through all those films right to the end?' he asked Renaud, who was reworking the screening schedule on the wall opposite.

'Not always. As you know, sometimes when the *sommelier* gives you a taste of the wine, you can tell it's no good without having to finish the bottle.'

'Then why did we have to?'

'Film-makers would get upset if you were not to see the complete film you are judging. There's always the chance of a revelation in the very last scene that would put the whole work in a different context.'

'That it was all a dream, for instance?'

'Something like that.'

'This is a nightmare,' said Chaillot, twisting the cap of his pen restlessly in his fingers. 'Thirty-six hours, more. What do they want? Why don't they ring? Who are they? What happens at this stage in the plot in all those movies that you see?'

Renaud thought for a moment. 'Something has to happen. He can't just disappear and never be heard of again. The audience needs an ending, preferably a happy one. If not, at least an heroic one. What usually happens at this stage is that a lone detective, ignoring the bureaucratic rules that are bogging down all his colleagues, makes a dramatic breakthrough, rather like . . .' He hesitated.

'Rather like what?' demanded the Minister peevishly.

'Rather like the parts Bud Booker usually plays.'

'I still don't like the look of that Arab yacht.' Leland gazed across the immaculately groomed gardens of the Hôtel du Cap to the distant vessel that did indeed seem more sinister under the lowering sky. 'Did you get a good sniff round it, Barry?'

Schenck stopped dialling the call he was making. 'I told you a thousand times. The guy's straight up. He went to Oxford University, there's a plaque on the wall says so.'

'What does that prove? How can you be sure he's not fronting for one of those Palestinian or Libyan outfits?'

'How can I be sure you're not fronting for them? Nobody knows anything. What I am sure of is that if I were to kidnap somebody I wouldn't take him to some fucking great liner that's there for everybody to see. The French cops have been through it twice, backwards and forwards.'

Leland left the balcony and returned to the room. 'That doesn't mean diddly. I'd like to see how long he hangs around when our boys get here. I doubt if he wants to rub shoulders with a United States warship. Will you get off the phone, it's meant to be kept free.'

'Just one more call,' pleaded Schenck. 'It's a beautiful package. The icing's set and I only have to put the cherry on the top. If I can get Molly Ringwald, everybody doubles their money before we shoot a frame.'

'How can you concentrate on something like that when your prize client may be lying out there dead?'

'It helps to take my mind off it,' said the agent, trying the number again. 'Besides, who can survive on ten per cent of a dead man?'

Before he could finish dialling, the hotel operator broke in. 'I'm sorry, sir, there is a call for Mr Walters.'

'Tell them to hold,' shouted Schenck. 'I've an important contract that needs to be finalised in the next half hour.'

Leland strode across the room and snatched the telephone out of his hand. 'This is Leland Walters. Who is that?'

'Putting you through now, sir,' said the operator.

'Hello, hello,' Leland found his voice rising stridently, fuelled by impatience and tension.

'Mr Walters, I am speaking on behalf of your friend Mr Booker.' To Leland the man sounded French, or maybe Spanish or Italian. 'He is well and in good hands. I am authorised to inform you of the steps you must take to ensure he remains this way and may be safely returned to you.'

'How do I know this isn't a hoax?'

'It will be your loss if you think it is. But we shall give you some reassurance in a moment. Would you be so kind as to write down our requirements? Do you have a pen?'

By the phone there was a pad with the hotel's crest on it and a pencil to match. It slipped through Leland's fingers as he tried to pick it up and clattered on the parquet floor.

'Are you still there?' The voice on the phone became agitated, betraying the nervousness behind its earlier precise calm.

'Yes,' Leland affirmed, retrieving the pencil. 'Go ahead.'

'There will be a press conference at nine o'clock tonight in the ballroom of the Hilton Hotel in Nice. If you are asked by the police or the security forces why this reservation has been made, you must say it is your intention to appeal to Mr Booker's captors for clemency. In fact, our organisation will use this occasion to make public our demands. The Hilton in Nice, you understand?'

Leland found himself perspiring, as if gripped by an unexpected fever, and placed a steadying hand on the table. 'I understand.'

'At the same time,' continued the voice, 'you are to make arrangements for twenty million dollars in non-consecutive lira notes to be collected from the Chase Manhattan Bank in Rome before it closes this evening. The manager of the Warner Bros Italian office is to pick up the money and take it in a taxi to the western entrance to the Baths of Caracalla. He must inform no one where he is going, nor must he be followed.'

'I'm sure they don't carry that sort of money,' Leland pointed out desperately.

'It is there. A request was made on your behalf yesterday. All that is needed is your personal authorisation. I must emphasise, Mr Walters, that all these instructions are to be carried out to the letter and in the strictest secrecy if Mr Booker is to remain alive.'

'How do I know if he's alive now?'

'You don't. You must trust me. But I will play you a recording he made this morning.' There was a pause, and then the click of a tape recorder being switched on. 'Say your line,' instructed a voice, more high-pitched than the one that had been speaking previously. The familiar low whisper of Bud Booker came faintly over the phone. 'This bullet doesn't know if it's aimed at a black man, a yellow man or a white man. It just knows it's going where I tell it. Okay?'

Seven minutes later the Commandant of the CRS triumphantly brought a tape of the conversation into Renaud's office.

Chaillot had already been briefed on its contents. 'At last,' he said. 'Why did they wait so long?'

Armed with the evidence, the Commandant felt more secure in expanding the Minister's previous initiative. 'May I suggest, sir, that we now concentrate all our resources on Nice. Even if we only pick one of them up, it's a lead. The only lead we've got.'

'Of course.'

'May I further suggest that you personally come to Nice, ostensibly to give moral support to Mr Walters, but in case we are faced with any delicate political decisions.'

The Minister pursed his lips and formed his fingers into a pyramid, a position he habitually assumed when he wanted to be seen to be seriously considering a proposal. In fact he had already made up his mind.

'That would be playing into their hands. Just because the press have blown this up into an issue of international magnitude, that doesn't mean the government of France is giving it the same importance. It is only the question of one man's life, after all. No, I shall stay here and host our dinner

311

for the Australians at the Majestic. It will stop people panicking. Of course, you will keep my chief of staff informed by phone.'

Renaud's secretary looked timidly round the door. 'It's Leland Walters for you, sir.'

The Minister lifted the phone.

'Monsieur Chaillot, you've heard?'

'I have, Mr Walters. I am hopeful we are about to see the beginning of the end.'

'It's my intention to carry out their instructions. The caller must have expected my phone to be bugged so I guess they'll be anticipating a strong police presence round the Nice Hilton. But I don't want any gun-happy cop trying to make a reputation and putting Bud's life in danger. That guy's worth several hundred million to my shareholders.'

The paradox of life possibly imitating art in this fashion was lost on both men, but not on Renaud who was listening on an extension.

'They will be ordered to exercise restraint,' Chaillot reassured him. 'But I am not sure we shall see Mr Booker until the money has been collected and counted, and I'm afraid I must inform you that such an act is illegal.'

'I know damn well it's illegal,' growled Leland. 'Blackmail's illegal in any country.'

'You misunderstand me.' The Minister was carefully taking every step possible to cover himself. This conversation would go on the record and he did not want to be complicit in a breach of international relations. 'It is illegal under Italian law to pay a ransom.'

Leland was incredulous. 'So what's that supposed to mean?'

'The initial opinion among the experts here is that this is a straightforward Italian kidnapping for money. Not Red Brigade, not Mafia, just criminal. The most effective way of calling their bluff is to reject their financial demand. There is a well-documented case in Italy of a man whose daughter was similarly kidnapped. When they asked him for the ranson he told them: "You may keep her. I have six other healthy daughters at home who are just as much a pain in the ass, so one less will make no difference." She was released unharmed the same day.'

'Are you advising me to tell them to fuck off? I'm not prepared to play games with a man's life. Twenty million dollars is not that much money by Hollywood standards, you know.'

'As you will.'

'Is it your intention to inform the Italian authorities?'

'Of what? You have done nothing illegal yet.'

Chaillot knew perfectly well that Warners would pay but he was not now seen to be a party to it.

'By the way,' he added, 'there is another law in Italy. It says you may always break the law if your intention is to save a human life.'

Rumours had been going round town all day, like seagulls circling a rubbish dump. Some said Bud was dead, others that he had been sighted in Paris, others that Leland Walters had found his severed finger on his breakfast tray that morning.

But they came to an abrupt halt with the dramatic announcement that at seven o'clock Madame Rivette would be issuing some kind of new credentials and giving details of a formal communiqué on Bud Booker. The post-film press-conference room was too small to hold the several hundred journalists and reporters who turned up, so the meeting was transferred to Les Ambassadeurs on the fourth floor. There was an unseemly scramble up the escalators to get to the best positions.

Madame was dressed severely in black, as if in mourning. 'There will be a statement tonight on the unfortunate incident concerning Mr Bud Booker.' She could not bring herself to say the word kidnap. 'It will be given by Mr Leland Walters, President of Warner Bros, in the ballroom of the Hilton Hotel in Nice. You will require these special passes' – she held one up – 'to gain admission. We shall be laying on coaches for any members of the press who do not have their own transportation.'

'Wonderful,' Robert remarked drily to Sandra. Their live transmission was due to take place at eleven-thirty that evening. 'Two days without sleep to put together the most comprehensive report on what's been happening here and it's scuppered by some statement that every goddam station's going to carry. What about the Chaillot exclusive – he's not talked to anyone else – and the other guys we've scheduled for the Palais roof tonight?'

'Scrap them,' she said unhesitatingly.

Questions started to fly.

'Have they heard from the kidnappers?'

'Have they found Bud?'

'Why do we have to go to Nice?'

Madame had a prepared answer for the last one. 'It is more convenient for Mr Walters to get there and it is possible that he will be going on to the airport immediately afterwards.'

'Doesn't he realise it's more convenient for us here?'

'Where's he flying to?'

'Will he be taking Bud with him?'

She waved her hands in front of her to stop them. 'I have no further information. If you wish to attend, please collect your passes. The buses will depart in forty minutes exactly.'

The television crews began to wrap their equipment in haste. They had covered Madame Rivette's statement – every word of this affair was news, even the departure time of the buses – and now fought to get out of the room with as much urgency as they had fought to get in. At the same time word went out like a fast-spreading stain among the journalists and reporters that it was, in fact, the kidnappers who had dictated the terms of this announcement, and Walters was merely the helpless victim of their demands. The more people discussed this, the more logical it seemed.

Robert wanted to find Chantal to try and uncover the real story. There was something about the arrangement that seemed suspiciously organised, manipulative even. He rushed down to her office but found it closed. The receptionists at the counter said that they had seen her earlier but nobody knew where she was. He made his way back to Sandra who was waiting impatiently in the crew van behind the building.

'Hurry up,' she yelled when she saw him. 'If we miss this one, we're dog meat.'

'I just need ten minutes,' he replied. 'Five. What I need most of all is a break. Wait for me. I'll be back.'

He disappeared among the television trucks, jumping over their cables, and ran in and out of the rows of dark Renaults, their pennants fluttering officiously in the breeze. He sprinted past the little café on the Croisette – usually thronged with people but now deserted – and through the children's playground. A tinkling music was playing and empty horses bobbed up and down on the turning merry-go-round, but without any children it had a morbid, faintly sinister air about it. He dashed down the steps onto the shore cutting an absurd figure, had there been anyone around to watch him, as he raced along in his double-breasted blue blazer, sharply creased grey flannels and black leather shoes.

On long-distance training runs at school Robert used to count the landmarks as he made for home and he did the same now as he ticked off the furled beach umbrellas, restless in the quickening wind: *Goeland* – pink and white; *Gray d'Albion* – yellow; *Plage Royale* – blue and white; *Cannes Beach* – green; *Sportive* – blue; *Grand Hotel* – white; *Club des Sport* – yellow.

At last, the red of the Maschou Beach, Chantal's lunch-time retreat. It was deserted, as all the others had been. But he could see a dim light in the glass-fronted restaurant that nestled under the sea wall. Exhausted, he summoned up the energy to make his way across the sand to the door. It was locked. He rapped urgently on the window. There was no response. He rapped again, louder and longer. A reluctant waiter eventually arrived.

'I'm sorry, sir, we are closed. There is no custom tonight.'

'I'm here,' shouted Robert. 'I'm custom.'

'We are still closed. A decision has been made.'

Over the man's shoulder he could see a lone figure sitting at a table. He brushed past the waiter. 'I'm sorry,' he apologised. 'there's someone I have to see. A friend.'

Chantal was less than sober. She sat slouched over a glass of wine as if all the bones had been filleted from her body and her eyes were wounds of tears. She wasn't pleased to see him.

'What's wrong?'

'Nothing.'

'Don't be silly.'

'My boy-friend. We have split up.'

'Can I buy you a drink?' Robert sat down opposite her.

She shook her head. 'Please,' she said, 'please go.'

'Maybe I can help.'

'Nobody can help.'

'Listen, Chantal. This is the biggest news break in the history of the Festival and you're sitting at a bar getting drunk. Something's wrong.'

'I can't tell you,' she stammered.

He seized her arm. 'You *must* tell me.'

'They will kill me,' she insisted. 'They will kill you, too.'

'They? Who?'

Chantal shook her head tearfully from side to side. 'No. No!'

'You can trust me, Chantal. You helped me once before.'

'I can say nothing. They only let me return to the office today because it would raise suspicions if I were absent. Robert, these are terrible men. They know where my sister lives in Moûtiers. They will murder her if I speak to anyone. Please go.'

'What men?'

'I don't know. Men. Foreigners. Please, Robert, you must say nothing.'

'I promise. But you must know something more.'

She took a sip from the glass in front of her. 'Truly I don't. There are only rumours.'

'Like what?'

'You know the Ile Sainte-Marguerite?'

'Where the monks are?'

'Just along from there. There is a cave where they kept the Man in the Iron Mask.'

'Yes?'

'I met a friend, César . . . the fishermen think they are holding Bud Booker there.'

'Have they done anything about it? Have they told the police?'

'They don't talk to the police. There is bad feeling between them. They won't let them spread their catch on the quay in the summer, because of the tourists.'

'Has anyone been to look?'

'They're too scared. They say there are many men on the island.'

'How can I get there? Do you know anyone with a boat?'

'Nobody will take you,' said Chantal. 'I have never seen them like this. They're all terrified.'

He caught Sandra and the crew just as their van was turning out of the car-park onto the Croisette.

'You idiot!' she screamed at him through the open window. 'You suicidal idiot! We're going to miss this thing. It could start early. It's all that matters today and you keep us waiting till it's too late.'

Robert stood panting in front of the van, his hands resting on the bonnet to stop it moving any further. 'I don't think we should go. Something else is happening. There's something going on on those islands. I think we should try and get out there.'

Sandra opened her door and jumped onto the pavement. 'You're crazy. Just because you're almost certainly fired already there's no need to die a double death, you know. Word gets round. Ever thought how difficult it might be to get a job if you have a reputation as a man who runs away from stories?'

He held her by the shoulders. 'I'm not running away. Everybody's running to Nice because somebody's clicked their fingers and said that's where the action is. But I don't think it's dead in Cannes yet. I've checked this out, Sandra. You have to trust me. Just this once. You need never listen to me again after this.'

'I can't, Robert. We have to go. Whether you come with us or not we need to be at that hotel.'

'I'm not going. I've got to follow this lead somewhere. And I need Vik and Erik. Listen, go yourself. Take a taxi. You can do a deal with a French Sygma crew for their footage. Pay whatever they ask. I can voice-over any questions when you get back – live if necessary. But just this time, please, Sandra, go with what I say. Let me hang myself. I have that right, don't I?'

She froze for a moment, holding herself motionless as if in shock, then kissed him on the lips with unexpected passion.

'Die then,' she called over her shoulder as she sprinted across the road to the taxi rank.

Without any warning the ominous opening chords of *Also sprach Zarathustra* crashed into the night air. It was hardly an appropriate time for a hymn to Nietzsche but the overture for the evening screening was part of the policy that things should continue as usual. Only a few spectators clustered round the carpeted steps up to the Palais and the polished ranks of the CRS were reduced to two men at the top. An Armenian film about Turkish atrocities was not likely to cull a full house at the best of times. Tonight a reduced trickle of ticket holders made their way past the unmanned barriers and up to the Grand Auditorium.

The lights still illuminated the stairway to the stars but there were no television cameras. Only a couple of photographers were on hand to record the sparse crop of expensive gowns. The skies had darkened prematurely as a growl of thunder made itself distantly audible, somewhere far out across the sea towards Africa.

'What do you want us to do, then?' demanded Vik, clearly upset at missing out on the events in Nice. 'Shoot Armenian film stars? I have no idea what they look like.'

Robert climbed into the front seat vacated by Sandra. 'No, it's not like that at all. Let me explain. There's a chance that Booker is here in Cannes. Not here exactly but on an island, the one you can see out there. We've got to check it out.'

The cameraman looked at him as if he had taken leave of his senses. 'I can't see any island.'

'It's too dark now. But just because you can't see it doesn't mean it isn't there. It's where the monks make that liqueur and people go to sunbathe nude.'

'Not right now, they don't.' Vik replied, glancing accusingly at his watch.

Robert was accustomed to a degree of rebellion from film crews, although the relationship with the two Belgians during the Festival had been harmonious, thanks primarily to their respect for Sandra's decisiveness. Now that she had departed he felt more vulnerable.

'We've got to get out to that island,' he insisted. 'If Booker's there we've got the story of a lifetime.'

'And if he isn't?' asked Vik.

'Then I've fucked up but you haven't. It's not your fault. All you have to do is what I ask you to and I want you to come with me out there.'

'How?' Vik seemed more stubborn than ever. 'The Service

des Iles has stopped running and the Gare Maritime is closed.'

'Let's drive round to the Old Port. We'll find a boat.'

In the waterside restaurants by the wharf small groups of early diners were attacking substantial plates of Claires No 1. Nobody would dream of ordering six oysters in the South of France; they seemed only to come in multiples of a dozen. Opposite the crescent of cafés on the Quai Saint Pierre, their awnings and boundaries of potted plants stealthily annexing extra space for more tables on the kerbside, lay luxury yachts with the names of their home ports – Barcelona, Piraeus, Rio – romantically inscribed on their hulls. Few of them had lights on to give any indication of life. And the fishermen, who retained a special landing stage by La Pantiero at the northern-most end of the port, had clearly gone home for the night, their ropes coiled neatly by their swaying boats.

'Stop the van! Stop. Wait.' Robert spotted somebody on board a scruffy, rusting vessel, wedged between two sleek white ocean-going cruisers.

He jumped out, ducked under the railing and leapt onto the stern of the boat. It had known better days. Several of the wooden planks on the deck were broken and the wheelhouse was lopsided with cracked windows, as if it had seen service in battle. A man in a grubby yellow vest and black shorts was sluicing out the forward end with a bucket of water.

'Do you speak English?' Robert realised he had bellowed the question in the way people do when anticipating the answer no, somehow hoping that the sheer force of decibels will translate it for them.

At least the man heard him. He put down the bucket and turned deliberately round.

'English, can you understand? I need a boat.' Robert spoke more softly but gestured clamorously with his hands.

'You've left it rather late. You can't see much at this time of night.'

Robert was taken aback. 'You *do* speak English.'

'Just about.' The man came towards him, drying his hands on a dirty strip of towel. 'They tried to knock most of it out of us at Charterhouse but luckily one or two traces remain.'

'Hey, I'm sorry. I didn't realise. My name's Robert Barrett. I'm with American TV.'

The Englishman eyed him suspiciously. 'Shouldn't you be over in Nice? I gather they're having a spot of bother with one of your countrymen.'

'That's why I'm here. Or, at least, that's why I'm not there.'

The man settled himself on top of an oxygen tank, appearing to relish the company of a stranger. 'That seems rather perverse to me.'

'It probably is. I just had a hunch, well a sort of tip-off and a hunch, that it was all a red herring.'

'Don't get many of those in the Med. Mainly off Aberdeen when the socialists are in power.'

It was Robert's turn to look askance.

'Just a joke. How can I help you? We set off at eight tomorrow morning. Got a full house but I dare say we could fit you in.'

'I need to go tonight. I'm not interested in underwater fishing, I want to get out to the Ile Sainte-Marguérite.'

'Whatever for? Bit dark for sunbathing.'

'The fishermen . . .' Robert began. 'Listen, a friend of mine heard from the fishermen that there's something suspicious going on out there. I know this sounds crazy but I thought there was one per cent of a chance that that's where they're holding Bud Booker. Look, I've got a film crew in that van you can see. I hope this doesn't insult you, but I'll pay you anything if you take us out to the island.'

The Englishman picked up the mask of an aqualung and started to clean it with his towel. 'Doesn't insult me at all. I could do with the cash. We've got off to a rotten start this year – the weather. Look at it now. There's a storm coming up the Mediterranean. You'd have to be mad to go out in that, especially in this old tub. I'm sorry, I can't help you. Nobody can.'

Robert could tell the man was being genuine. 'Thanks anyway. Not my lucky day, I guess.'

As he began to clamber back over the hull of the boat, the man got up and followed him. 'You're right about one thing,' he whispered in a deliberately low voice. 'There is something going on out there. Something to do with NATO, I suspect.

We've all been warned off till tomorrow. There was a serious incident last night. Some young guy drowned. They found him and his boat this morning. I think they're trying to hush things up until the Festival is over. Bad for tourism. You know the French.'

'Many people think the *entente cordiale* is a French phrase. In fact, it was invented by the British. And for two nations who have been at war with each other for most of the past thousand years, it is perhaps not the most felicitous expression. But tonight I want to propose a toast to the *entente australienne*. To two countries who have never been at war – except in the mud of Le Parc des Princes. Indeed we have been staunch allies throughout this century.'

'Hear fucking hear.'

Henri Chaillot glanced over his pince-nez at the cluster of tables in the centre of the Majestic dining room, ingeniously arranged beneath the ponderous chandeliers so that it would not be too obvious that a place which could hold a thousand guests was occupied by only about a hundred and fifty.

'Hear fucking hear.'

Chaillot could see that the member of his audience so assiduously agreeing with him was none other than Ted Barlow, alias Ken Turner, Man of the Media. It had, perhaps, not been the best decision in the world to invite him. Admittedly he was wearing a dinner suit, but his pair of splattered sneakers was not the expected footwear for the occasion. The fact that speeches were taking place before the meal had, the Minister thought, lessened the likelihood of drunken interventions. But Barlow was currently completing day seven of what he termed 'a beaut of a binge'.

The actor rose vertiginously to his feet, ignoring the attempts of Jenny Bates to restrain him, and held up his empty glass. 'We fought together in Gallipoli, we fought side by side in Vietnam – and where were the bloody Pommies there, I might ask? – and we'll fight together again against the imperialist yoke.'

Jenny managed to pull him back onto his seat and the search for another glass of wine temporarily diverted him from his peroration.

Chaillot cleared his throat. 'I thank Monsieur Turner for his expression of solidarity. Of course we did not fight shoulder to shoulder in Vietnam but Australia nobly joined the United States in the cause for which so many French lives were needlessly sacrificed. But now your nation is leading the world in another great battle. Your entrepreneurs – like Citizen Ken – have grasped the fact that the future lies in the skies. No longer will we have to wait for the latest movie to be shipped to us from Sydney. It will fall, like pure snow from the heavens, into our cinemas the moment it is completed in its home studio. So I propose a toast. To a great continent and a great future.'

People slowly rose from their seats and sipped their Sancerre. Ted Barlow did not. He sat almost erect in his chair, his eyes closed and a benign look of childlike contentment on his face. Nobody had the heart, nor the desire, to wake him.

There was considerably more animation in the ballroom of the Nice Hilton, which had taken on the air of an American political convention. The room was raw with excitement. All semblance of security appeared to have broken down. The throng on the floor consisted not only of reporters and photographers but hotel staff and guests and their friends who had somehow managed to get in, and innumerable plain-clothes police. At the far end of the hall lay the stage, glaringly empty in the lights save for a podium and a table bearing a forest of microphones. On a raised horseshoe platform opposite, the television crews were packed elbow to elbow. The cameramen restlessly panned left and right and focused and refocused as if they were doing invisible target practice. The only elements that were missing were the balloons, the straw hats and the bands.

It was nine-fifteen and still no one had appeared. Madame Rivette stood anxiously by the door, fending off persistent enquiries with the honest excuse that she had no idea herself what was happening. Some of the television crews had already been transmitting live back to the States, their reporters interviewing other journalists for want of anyone better. Sandra had joined forces with a crew from a British satellite station, Moonbeam, who had been covering many of the same events as *Arts Action* earlier in the Festival. On the premise that the main activity would undoubtedly be shown on the networks, she worked with their director on behind-the-scenes coverage, managing to get a live trail back to New York. She thought it perverse and insane of Robert not to be there but was secretly pleased to have a personal moment of glory, appearing in front of camera herself to report on the all-enveloping tension.

Suddenly, without any signal, an infectious silence spread stealthily through the room. Seconds later the fragile hush was broken by a firework display of flash bulbs as Leland Walters walked to the rostrum. He started to speak but his words were drowned by the yells of the sound engineers directing him to the lower table where their microphones had been positioned.

He moved slowly, as if burdened by grief, and put on his reading glasses as he sat down. 'My name is Leland Walters,' he began unnecessarily – his name and photograph had been on television and the front pages of most newspapers for the past two days. 'I am President of Warner Bros. A short while ago I received this letter.'

He reached inside his pocket and opened it in the manner of someone revealing the winning nominee at the Academy Awards. 'It says: "Leland, thank you for sticking by me. I'm safe and I should be with you by midnight."' He looked up. 'That's all.'

Some people cheered, others groaned, most remained silent. Leland removed his glasses. 'It's his writing. I've no reason to believe it's a hoax. The best we can all do is sit it out.'

Robert was beside himself with rage, frustration and despair. Vik and Erik thought he must have gone partly insane. He had charged onto a Yugoslav yacht – about the only one with several people visible in the main cabin – and gate-crashed a dinner party, demanding that they take him out to sea. After he had been escorted off, the film crew prevented him from boarding any other boats. They had managed to persuade him to calm down and have a drink at the Clemenceau bar, but he had almost got into a fight with two fishermen who refused to admit that anything was amiss and would not entertain the idea of ferrying him to the islands.

Defeated and dishevelled he had returned to the roof of the Palais, now dampened by a light drizzle, to set up ready for their live transmission back to the States. Even there things had begun to go wrong. There was a note from Chaillot's assistant saying that, in the circumstances, the Minister would be unable to appear on the programme. Robert sent a message to Renaud Callet, to see if he would come instead.

But the request was to prove irrelevant. Sandra was shortly on the line from Nice. Vik passed him the portable phone. Bud Booker, she said, was due at the Hilton some time before midnight. New York had decided that *Arts Action* would carry that live and put the Cannes link merely on stand-by.

'Our nation is just a little bit older than your republic. Who knows what would have happened if, instead of decapitating your royals, you had deported them to Australia.'

Don Lugg, the Minister of Information, his red wave frozen and effulgent with hairspray and neatly matching the ribbon bearing the Order of Australia which hung decoratively from his neck, was concluding his reply to Chaillot's speech.

'What if our fair continent had been settled by a fleet of French nobles instead of boatloads of British shirtlifters' – the squall of laughter from Jenny and Hal's table caused him hurriedly to check his notes – 'I'm sorry, shoplifters, then our wine industry could have started a hundred years sooner and we wouldn't have to be humiliated by the West Indies on the cricket field every four years.'

The general incomprehension that greeted this made even Lugg realise it was time to close the innings.

'So God bless you and your Festival. And join me in a toast. *Vive le Bud Booker libre* and *Vive le Cannes libre.*'

Two floors directly above him Elizabeth Brown was lying on her bed with one eye on the television. It was a quiz game about numbers and letters which she had sometimes watched in London. The British played it light-heartedly but the French approach was much more intense. In her hand was a note on Carlton Hotel stationery which at last had been left for

324

her at reception. It simply read: 'You forgot to say goodbye. You mustn't leave till you do that. R.'

The memory of him warmed her with pleasure. Fyodor had gone home. She was on her own and she at last felt free.

Four further floors above her, at the very top of the hotel, Elvis Ho strode out onto his balcony to make one final survey of the town by night. Grasping the iron railing he involuntarily went into a light work-out routine, dropping down onto his haunches and running a check on his muscles like an airline pilot warming up his engines. In less than twenty hours Ho would be taking off himself. He could see distant daggers of lightning far out on the horizon of the Mediterranean. Nearer to the shore there were small intermittent bursts of light. At first he thought they were buoys but they now seemed to be flashes of torchlight coming from approaching craft. The fishermen were probably returning early to seek shelter from the storm. Tomorrow night at Pornic Studios, he thought, he would see the fleet setting out from Vancouver Harbour. And he would be free.

Nice was crammed to the gills with thousands of undercover police and soldiers. Every hotel, bar, restaurant, club, kitchen, shop, office block, apartment building and even garage in town had its complement of unfamiliar visitors, vigilantly observing and waiting.

'What was that?'

Down on the Quai des Anglais a young officer, posing as a fisherman, nudged his colleague.

'I don't see anything.'

'Listen.'

The man did as he was told. He could hear it now, the sound of a motor-boat steadily approaching. There was no sign of any lights. Levelling their rifles they moved to the water's edge. The noise of the engine grew closer, as if the vessel were targeting itself on them.

'Can you put those things down? Somebody might get hurt.'

The voice was familiar. And, soon, so was the face. Bud Booker was standing at the wheel cautiously guiding the boat to the shore. He was wearing the same suit he had last been seen in. It and his hair were both more dishevelled than usual.

The officer, who looked as if he had seen a ghost, lowered his rifle with shaking hands.

Within minutes Bud was in the back seat of an official police Citroën.

'They kept their word,' said the colonel accompanying him. 'Were they French?'

Bud blinked at him, wondering if the two statements were connected. 'I don't think so.'

'Are you all right?' the officer enquired.

'I am now,' he replied tersely.

'There is a press conference at the Hilton but the feeling of the *Sous-Préfét* is that you should not attend. Why give them more publicity when you are safe?'

'I've got to go,' the star insisted. 'It's part of the bargain. Besides, I want to tell my folks I'm okay.'

He looked pityingly at the Frenchman. This guy was trying to prevent him from playing to the biggest single audience of his career.

'There's a phone call for you.'

Robert was standing in front of the camera on the roof of the Palais des Festivals as Erik handed him the receiver.

'Who?' he mouthed.

'Your wife.'

'I don't have one.'

The Belgian shrugged. 'She sounded like a wife.'

She did. It was Tanya, ringing from New York. 'For Christ's sake, what are you doing? We've been getting that bitch Sandra Lewis simpering away at the Bud Booker thing. Hurley's blowing his top. He wants to know why you're not there.'

'I'm still in Cannes. We've divided the story. It's not dead here yet.'

'Well, *you* are. You'd better get your ass across to the Hilton.'

'You don't understand. It's in Nice. At least an hour away at this time of night. Don't come on so heavy – how are you?'

'Pretty pissed at you. Something seems to have gone seriously wrong since we split, Robert.'

So they had split. Tanya could always be relied upon for precision timing. Wearily he supposed a token protest was in order. 'Listen, when I get back to New – '

'It's not Tanya, Bob, it's me.' Even at three thousand miles' distance Jim Hurley had no need to introduce himself. 'Can you just tell me what's happening? We've got a hundred and seventy stations standing by to take a syndicated report at any time. And you seem to be the one journalist on the French Riviera who's in the wrong place.'

'I can explain.' Robert felt frustrated and foolish. 'The fishermen are worried about something – '

'What the fuck has it got to do with fishermen?' Hurley was getting angry.

'There's no guarantee, just because the kidnappers dictate that the action's going to be in Nice – hold on a minute.'

Robert could hear ill-tempered shouts far below him to his right. From his vantage point on the top of the Palais des Festivals he could see what looked like a scuffle at the entry to the Majestic Hotel. The first people to leave the Armenian première had made their way there – the bar of the Majestic was a traditional watering-hole after evening screenings – but it appeared they were being turned away at the gate.

'Jim,' he yelled into the telephone, 'there's some action here. It may be something or it may be nothing. We'll come to you early if it's any good.'

'You're not making this up?' The voice at the other end sounded disbelieving.

'I would if I could,' cried Robert, cutting him off. 'Vik, Erik, let's get a camera on this.'

They moved a camera to the edge of the roof. It was now apparent that the gates to the Majestic had been closed and no one was being allowed in. Outside, men and women in evening dress were remonstrating loudly, with angry gestures.

'Robert, come here. Take a look through the camera.' Vik was unusually animated.

'On the other side of the gate. Men with rifles. Not gendarmes, not CRS. They are wearing, how you say, *passe-montagnes noirs*.'

'Ski hats. Black ones,' explained Erik.

'Balaclavas,' nodded Robert as he looked through the powerful zoom lens.

Erik was perplexed. 'Where are the police? Why are they doing nothing?'

Vik grabbed the camera again and urgently flicked it into action. 'They haven't the strength. Most of them are in Nice. I think that was precisely what someone intended, eh, Robert?'

'Precisely,' said Robert. A comforting glow of vindication began to settle in his abdomen; at the same time the palms of his hands became clammy. 'Better keep your camera steady, Vik, we may be sitting on something hot. I'm getting back to New York. My bet is we'll be reporting live in about ten minutes.'

The soft mist that was in the air had by now very definitely turned to rain.

An impromptu honour guard of secret service men, identifiable by their dark glasses and ear pieces, escorted Bud through the mass of soldiers and police who crammed the lobby of the Nice Hilton. The assembled troops cheered as the movie star progressed past them and he acknowledged their approbation with a casual wave.

As he entered the ballroom he could not have been greeted with a louder or more sustained ovation, nor been carried live by television to so many countries if he had just received the Republican nomination.

Bud sprinted up the steps to where Leland was standing by the table. The two men clutched each other as if they had just clinched a two-hundred-million-dollar contract. The camera flashes were so incessant that they joined seamlessly together into a continuing explosion of light.

Leland eventually broke away from their embrace and leant over the microphones. 'Bud,' he said, 'we missed you.'

Renewed applause broke out. Booker remained very still, permitting just a soupçon of a smile to play on his lips. As long as they were prepared to clap him, he was prepared to stand there. He waited until the noise began to subside before he moved across to the microphones. Leland, knowing his place, stepped aside to let him assume the limelight on his own.

Bud looked innocently at the phalanx of television cameras trained on him. 'Can someone tell my wife that I'm okay?'

'Who did it?' yelled an eager reporter from the floor.

'I don't really know. I was kept blindfold most of the time.'

'Were you tortured?' The questioner's voice carried the faint hope that he had been.

'Not apart from the blindfold,' said Bud, pausing for a beat, 'and the food.'

An appreciative round of laughter went up from the hall. Then the questions ricocheted off the walls in overlapping waves – 'Who did it?' 'What did they want?' 'Where did they keep you?' 'How did you get away?'

Bud held his peace and waited for the journalists to silence each other.

Sandra noticed that although the floor was now attentive to Booker, feverish whispered discussions were taking place among the police and Festival officials at the entrance to the room. She tapped the Moonbeam producer on his shoulder and pointed this out to him.

'I was in a small boat,' Bud began, oblivious to the behind-the-scenes activity. 'Then in a bigger boat. Then in some room. Then another boat and another room. They kept moving me on until I found myself in a motor-boat pointed at – where are we, by the way?'

'Nice,' came the chorus from the floor.

Sandra was getting more and more worried. Something pretty terrible must have happened – she could tell by the faces at the door. She tried to get down from the horseshoe camera platform to find out, but her way was completely blocked.

'Always wanted to visit Nice,' Bud remarked, tugging an earlobe, 'in my own time, though. I guess these guys were after a few dollars. Forgot to ask my agent unfortunately.'

'Who were they?' came the repeated cry.

Sandra tried again to edge her way towards the door but she could see that her journey was now unnecessary. Madame Rivette was preparing to come onto the stage.

Bud scratched his temple and gave a slight grin. 'I got a sight of a few of them at one stage. You're never going to believe this but there was a black man, a yellow man and – '

His sentence went unfinished, the flow interrupted by the busy figure of Madame Rivette. She apologised nervously to him and then bent over the microphones.

'Monsieur Booker, excuse me. We have a further emergency. It seems that all is not yet over. We have just been told that the Majestic Hotel in Cannes has been occupied by terrorists with – ' she paused, emotionally, to catch her breath ' – with the French Foreign Minister inside.'

'The most worrying aspect for the French is the presence of their Foreign Minister, Henri Chaillot, among the hostages. In the past France has been accused by her European partners of giving in to terrorism a little too easily and there's a definite fear in Cannes tonight, among the Americans and the British especially, that whoever is holding the Majestic will have their demands accommodated by the French.'

It's amazing how quickly you could learn to sound like an expert on international affairs, Robert reflected. A researcher in the New York office had faxed the relevant press clippings across to him in a matter of minutes.

'As yet, nobody knows what those demands might be. What does seem certain is that the kidnapping of the American actor, Bud Booker, who was released unharmed in Nice almost exactly at the time of the takeover, was a subterfuge – a smokescreen which effectively weakened the security here in Cannes. It seems some of the terrorists were already in the hotel, and reinforcements came by truck and some by boat into the Old Port. So while people were watching a film about Armenian terrorists in the auditorium beneath me, a real life drama was taking place just a few yards away. At the moment there are no reports of any casualties. Armed and masked men cleared the bar and the main lobby of the hotel at gunpoint, forcing people out of the back door into the Rue St Honoré. They've now isolated the east wing. About two hundred people were attending a French-Australian banquet in the dining-room on the ground floor and they, including Donald Lugg, a senior Australian minister, are understood to be held captive.'

Erik made a circular motion with his finger to indicate that New York had told him it was time to wind up.

Robert gave him an imperceptible nod to indicate he had got the message. 'The initiative at the moment is with the hijackers. You can see them behind me, masked, heavily armed, on every floor right up to the roof. They have issued just one warning: any attempt to storm the building will result in the execution – they call it execution, I call it murder – of everyone in there. We will bring you further reports the moment there's any change in the situation. This is Robert Barrett, *Arts Action*, in Cannes, France.'

'Coupe,' whispered Vik. 'Very good – I go in on those two men who are lit up blue by the flashing sign from *Jupiter Landing* – very powerful.'

Jupiter Landing. The warm rain that had been falling on Robert's face turned to ice as it dawned on him. She was in there.

CHAPTER 21

Saturday 17th May 1997

Cannes

A *cordon sanitaire*, just like the one that prevented Lord Brougham from reaching Nice a hundred and fifty-three years previously, now surrounded the Majestic Hotel. It was under siege from within and without. Rolls of barbed wire formed lines of demarcation in the adjoining streets and a quartet of AMX–30 tanks stood sentinel, one at each corner of the blighted building. During the night the country's leading anti-terrorist paratroop force, under its commander, General Le Prince, had flown down from their stand-by position at Paris's Charles de Gaulle Airport. Two French naval frigates had been dispatched from their base in Toulon and were anchored ominously in the Bay of Cannes, directly in alignment with the hotel.

The Esplanade Georges Pompidou at the foot of the Palais steps facing the Majestic was barely recognisable under the spread of sandbags, machine-gun emplacements and more barbed wire. The nature of military engagement seemed to have changed little in the eighty years since Ypres and Passchendaele. Robert and the crew had lost their commanding position on the roof of the Palais. That was now topped with troops and artillery who also decorated, like fortified hanging gardens, the roof and upper storeys of the Gray d'Albion which was situated on the opposite side of the Rue des Serbes from the occupied wing of the Majestic.

A prematurely funereal air permeated the town, eradicating the *joie de vivre* of the Festival, as if in anticipation of a tragedy that was about to happen. Certainly, there seemed very little chance of any terrorist getting out of the Majestic alive unless he provided the waiting paras with an extremely persuasive reason to hold their fire.

A reason was exactly what General Le Prince was waiting for as he sat in his command position in Renaud's office. Two sketch artists were drawing up a plan of the hotel, indicating which areas the terrorists were known to be holding.

'You miscalculated,' said Le Prince. Even without the trappings of his rank and reputation he still looked a formidable man. Short grey hair bristled back from his heavy brow, his jaw was solid and certain and his broad body was clearly in peak condition.

No one in the room had slept much the previous night but the *Sous-Préfet des Alpes Maritimes* looked as if he hadn't slept for a week. 'How were we to know?' he replied lamely. 'Think of our relationship with the United States. My first priority was to secure the safety of Bud Booker. The publicity was extremely adverse.'

'You will know the meaning of bad publicity,' the General observed, 'if we have to storm the hotel. There are going to be a lot of innocent corpses around. The name of Cannes will become synonymous with catastrophe. Remember Fréjus, along the coast, after the Malpasset dam disaster? The first rule of any operation is to cover your rear. With the security you left here, a kindergarten class could have taken over the Palais – or anywhere.'

'Who do you think it is, in the Majestic?' The Commandant of the CRS seized the chance to change the subject.

'Professionals,' Le Prince pronounced confidently. 'A well-planned operation, an effective diversion and nobody killed or wounded as far as we know. So public opinion will hardly wear us charging in there with guns blazing, for the moment anyway. And they've got a prize scalp, Henri Chaillot. The President's been on to me twice this morning already. On no account must Chaillot be exposed to any harm. He's insisting on a negotiated settlement even before we know who we're negotiating with. They'll have anticipated all that. That's why they're making us wait. And that's why they're professionals.'

Renaud Callet was conscious-stricken at what had happened, as if it were somehow his fault. He feared he would go down in history as the man who presided over the Fiftieth Cannes Film Festival – and the last one. He sensed that the room expected him to speak but he had little to say. 'Which professionals?' he asked dispiritedly.

Le Prince set about enumerating them, as if he had a tacit respect for the opposition he was trained to combat. 'Not the IRA – not their style, too well organised for one thing. Not the ETA either – they're a spent force, most of them can't even speak the Basque language any longer. *Action Directe* – too cowardly. Same goes for the Italian Red Brigade – very good at murdering elderly politicians but shit scared of the Mafia.'

"What about the German Red Brigade?" The head of the *Corps des Sapeurs-Pompiers* was keen to air his outdated knowledge of international affairs.

The General laughed. 'Middle-class maniacs. After the Baader-Meinhof gang did away with themselves, the next bunch came mainly from the Heidelberg psychiatric patients collective. The Japanese Red Army are the ones to watch out for. They nearly pulled it off at the Atlanta Olympics. Remember Shigenobu Fasko? The Women are always the most ruthless. They buried half their group alive because they claimed they had anti-revolutionary failings. If I thought it was the Japs I'd be in there, President or no President. They'd be cooking Chaillot for breakfast right now.'

He could see he had the attention of the gathering. 'No, it's either Middle Eastern or South American. The Interior Ministry is checking to see what foreigners we've got in jail at present. Some of them are going to be very happy boys with a fistful of free air tickets by this evening. I can't quite put my finger on it but it smacks of South America.' He turned to Renaud. 'If we could get rid of all those television cameras on the Croisette, we'd be in much stronger bargaining position.'

It was Callet's turn to feel uncomfortable. 'I think it's too late now. If we started asking the press to leave Cannes – especially the Americans –'

He was saved by the bell. The phone in front of the Director rang out like an amplified alarm clock, jerking the assembled men into a state of jittery apprehension. The secretaries had been instructed that the only call permitted to disturb the meeting was one from the Majestic. Renaud looked at Le Prince. 'Should I answer it?'

The General nodded. It had been agreed that any negotiations would initially be conducted by the Festival Director so that the terrorists would be less aware of the chain of command with which they were dealing.

An electric silence fell on the room as Renaud cupped the receiver to his ear. He began to take notes with his left hand. 'Yes . . . yes . . . yes . . . I see . . . yes. At five . . . seventeen hundred hours . . . five this afternoon,' he repeated as he put the phone down.

'Who the hell are they?' demanded the Commandant, impatiently. 'You didn't even bother to find out.'

'We'll know soon enough,' Renaud replied. 'They've asked for the American reporter who covered the events of last night to take his crew into the hotel by the Rue Saint Honoré door. Evidently they want to put their demands on television.'

'Why should we agree?' The Cannes Police Commissioner was keen to curry favour with the General. 'Starve them of publicity. They've had enough already.'

Le Prince studied the completed plan of the hotel to see which entrance they meant. 'At this stage they are in the driving seat. We've got to know their demands. It would be a shame to slaughter the lot of them and never find out why they did it.'

'You're going to be late.'

'I'm hurrying.'

'Have you found your costume?'

'What do you think I'm looking for?'

Ellen Lasky returned from the bottom of the stairs to the kitchen. It was a bright room overlooking an extensive Kensington garden, the unvarnished wooden surfaces and cheerful jasmine walls bearing the unmistakable stamp of a professional interior designer.

'We need a new au pair,' she said. 'The child is beginning to be cheeky.'

Her husband sounded a grunt of acknowledgement, without removing his eyes from the weekend edition of the *International Herald Tribune*.

'If you were at home a little more, we might see an improvement in her behaviour.'

Another grunt, less affable than before. Ellen sat beside him at the table. Without any make-up and her hair drawn back in a severe bun, she made no attempt to shed any of her forty-four years. She lifted the percolator and tried a different avenue of contact.

'More coffee?'

'No, no thanks. I'll take her to swimming.'

'Why?'

He looked up from his paper. 'Why not? I feel like it.'

Having obtained his attention she was eager not to let it go.

'They're not going to die, are they?'

'Of course not. It's just a game – of sorts.'

'It could have been you.'

'But it wasn't.' He bit off a piece of toast.

'Is everybody from *Jupiter Landing* back? Are you sure?'

'Everybody.' He poured himself a refill of coffee. 'Those madmen are very thoughtfully giving us free international publicity as long as they keep showing our hoarding on television. The commercial half of me hopes that they spin it out for a few more days.'

'Nobody's still there?'

He became irritated. 'I told you.'

'But that girl – Elizabeth – her picture was on the television news this morning. She's there, isn't she?'

'They got it wrong.'

'But she didn't come back with you.'

'Hetty's looking after her. She says she met a boy called Falcon. They've probably flown off together. She's young – and romantic.'

Ellen eyed him challengingly but he refused to meet her stare.

'Are you sure you shouldn't do something?' she asked.

'I'm sure.' His face lightened as he threw down his paper and stretched out his arms. 'Pola, my little princess, pigtails for daddy.'

His daughter ran across to him. 'I'm so glad you're home,' she said, 'you make us safe.'

As he squeezed her tightly to him, the nauseous sensation of self-disgust in his stomach became overpowering.

'You don't have to go.'

Sandra had been jogging. She sat at the end of Robert's bed in her kumquat singlet and satin shorts, the sweat still glistening on her shoulders.

'Where have you been?' he asked, propping up a pillow behind him.

'Oh, along the beach. I thought I might get a little closer to the hotel that way. But two goons with machine-guns had other ideas.'

'Terrorists?'

She playfully threw her towel at him. 'No, you idiot, although they looked pretty terrifying. The French are getting heavy about this thing. It looks as if their entire army's in town. I hope they've left some troops on the Russian front – this could be another diversion.'

'France doesn't have a frontier with Russia.'

'I know, Robert. I'm joking. Lighten up.'

'I'm sorry. Do you want some coffee or something? I'm starving.'

She got up and studied herself in the mirror. 'I rang room service already. Club sandwiches and Valium for two. Did you manage to sleep?'

'At first I didn't think I would and then I didn't think I'd wake.'

Sandra patted her stomach. 'Remind me to sue my callisthenics instructor when we get back to California. His programme is quite hopeless in the face of French food.'

She removed a Diet-Coke from the mini-bar and came and sat at his end of the bed. 'I don't want you to go, you know. They're sending someone round to explain. Tell him the deal's off. There are professional people trained for situations like this. You're not one of them.'

Robert shifted against his pillow. 'It may be the only chance I ever have to be truly professional.'

'The equation's all wrong. This is life and death stuff and if they don't let you walk out of that hotel again, the odds are on death. Whether by the guerrillas or the French army that's

lined up outside I don't suppose will concern you too much.'
She paused to let the thought sink in. 'It's not your problem.
Stay out of it. I've spoken to Jim in New York. He's ordered
you not to go. Tanya rang, by the way.'

'What did she want?'

'She's thinking of coming over. Guess you've made it back
into favour. Can't think how.'

'Jesus.'

'You're okay for forty-eight hours. She can't get away. The
flights into Nice are full, anyway.'

'What happened to Bud Booker? Did you manage to film
anything?'

'Just a goodbye wave. He made it out of town very
snappy. The Warner jet just swept them away like a mother
hen. The whole thing's a bit too real for the boys from
Tinseltown.'

'All the more reason for us to put on a good show.'

She moved up beside him on the bed. 'You sound like an
astronaut.'

He kissed her lightly on the cheek. 'An astronaut and a
swimmer.'

'Terms of endearment. Very rare coming from you.'
Sandra lay back with her head on his chest. 'A condemned
man's allowed one last treat. I think I could probably make it
memorable.'

She was interrupted by a commanding knock on the door.

'Come in,' she called, not bothering to move.

The door was pushed open and a clanking trolley wheeled
into the room by a stooped waiter in a maroon jacket. He
was followed by a man in a dark blue suit, his tie slack
around his neck and his thick dark hair, flecked with grey,
tousled as if he had just come off a rugby field.

Sandra sat up abruptly and put down her Coke can, as if
she'd been caught drinking illegally.

'I do apologise,' said Renaud Callet. 'I didn't know you
had company. I am –'

'We know who you are.' Sandra took the initiative in a
flash. She bounced off the bed and held out her hand.
'Sandra Lewis, *Arts Action*. Listen, I think this whole idea's
mad. Worse than that, it's suicidal –'

'Sandra,' Robert stopped her. 'Mr Callet, it's good of you to come yourself. I'm Robert Barrett. I apologise for being in bed.'

'Where else would anyone want to be on an inclement afternoon like this? Especially with no films to look at.' Renaud threw a wry glance in Sandra's direction.

'Please sit down,' said Robert. 'I didn't expect to see you. I thought you must have been in the hotel. Did you escape?'

'Nobody has escaped. We appear to be up against a tough team. I should have been at the dinner but it was agreed that I would come later when I had news from Nice. By then it was too late.' Lowering himself into a chair by the window, he could just see the two frigates on the right-hand side of the bay. 'Part of me wants to be in the hotel. A form of expiation, I suppose. It's hard to interpret the way fate ordains these things. Maybe she has some worse ordeals in store.'

'Well, fate hasn't ordained that Robert go in there. Nor can you order it.' Sandra poured out a cup of coffee and brought it solicitously to her reporter, as if he were convalescing.

'Neither fate nor the state has ordered it. But I must admit I have come to talk about it.'

'It's a French problem, send in French television,' Sandra remained on the offensive.

'We would. But the hijackers know we would send in a trained army crew, that's probably why they asked for you. They also know what you look like from the television last night. You will be accompanied, however – if you decide to go – by two intelligence officers who can operate the camera equipment.'

Robert took a long sip of his coffee. It tasted hot and strong and ambrosial. Ambrosia – he could hear his classics master saying it now – the drink of the Greek gods which conferred everlasting youth and beauty. He closed his eyes and thought of Elizabeth. In that moment it suddenly hit him how scared he was of dying. And how desperately he wanted to see her again.

'If I go,' he said, 'I'd feel safer with Vik and Erik. They're the Belgian crew we've been shooting with. A few of these guys may have been in Cannes for some time and seen us working together.'

Renaud nodded in agreement. 'The final decision rests with you.'

Robert looked across at Sandra. 'Can you get in touch with them?'

She remained seated. 'Unlike you, they have wives and families, you know.'

'So do many of those inside,' Renaud pointed out.

'I'll use the extension in the bathroom.' She managed to indicate her continuing distaste for the venture by the off-hand manner in which she crossed the room.

'Who do you think they are?' asked Robert.

Renaud pursed his lips and drew in a breath. 'Some form of nationalist movement, probably. The army think they're Libyan-trained.'

'And what do they want?'

'Publicity to start with. They've certainly won that battle. And prisoners released, most likely. Not just France. They've got Australians, Americans and British in there, as well. They could go for all four countries. In fact they could ask for anything they damn well please. But the sooner we know, the sooner we can plan our next move.'

Robert looked at him in some amazement. 'Are you in charge?'

Renaud shook his head. 'Very far from it. The President of France will ultimately decide. And he's got Le Prince, the commander of the paras, just chomping at the bit to put all their training exercises into action.'

The bathroom door swung open and Sandra fixed Renaud with an accusing glare. 'Vik and Erik had already been asked. They agreed. They're preparing their equipment.';

Renaud shrugged, half-apologetically, and glanced at his watch. 'In just over an hour someone will come and get you. There's a briefing first from internal security – what to look for in the hotel, numbers of men, types of guns, condition of hostages – all that sort of thing.'

He got up and came to the bed to shake Robert's hand. 'You'll be okay. Thank you. Sorry to have interrupted your afternoon nap. There's still time to finish it, I think.'

'By the way,' he added, as he reached the door, 'I'm sure your gesture will not go unnoticed by the *Légion d'Honneur*.'

'Is it awarded posthumously?' Sandra inquired acidly.

'*Non.*'

'But I *have* to get in. All my mates are there.'

'Nobody is there.'

Vincent Wall pointed frustratedly up to the balcony of the Gray d'Albion apartments. 'Yes, they are. I can see people – and guns.'

The officer patted his own revolver. 'Exactly. The whole of the Gray d'Albion is currently under military occupation. All civilians have been evacuated.'

'But I've got mates in the Majestic, as well.'

'Then I'm sorry for you. The Festival business has now been moved to the Martinez Hotel. I suggest you go there for any information.'

At least the streets were less clogged than usual, Vincent reflected as he made his way back along the Croisette. Tony Birch had been panic-stricken and retired to bed after Bazin's visit, fearing for his life if they went to the police. Vincent had immediately taken the initiative, ringing the laboratories in Sydney to ask them to make an urgent new print of *Poppy Day*. Without Tony knowing, he had gone to the Square de Verdun at the appointed time but there had been no sign of the man in the leather jacket. Probably some nutter, he thought.

Birch had recovered sufficiently to attend the fateful dinner the night before, but Vincent had decided against it, waiting in the apartment for a call from Sydney to say the new print was ready. Besides, he didn't have much time for official dinners or government ministers, Australian or French.

'Monsieur Wall, Monsieur Wall.' He was surprised to hear his name being called as he entered the Martinez lobby.

A pretty girl he vaguely recognised with striking red hair came up to him bearing a bunch of envelopes. 'You are greatly in demand. I think you are the only Australian who escaped. They all want to interview you.'

'Forget it,' said Vincent. 'This is a circus. I don't want to be interviewed. I've got enough problems.'

'I understand,' she replied. 'I'm Chantal, from the press office. Perhaps you would like to come out to the swimming-pool and we can talk in peace.'

He thankfully followed her out of the hotel to a table on the far side of the pool.

'Who are those bastards?' he asked as they sat down.

'We'll know soon enough. They intend to broadcast their demands this evening.'

'This town is insane. Is it always like this during the Festival?'

Chantal managed her first smile in forty-eight hours. 'No,' she assured him, 'this is a bad year.'

Vincent bit his finger-nail in frustration. 'All those Aussies in there. And that guy Booker. And some crazy starts threatening me about my film.'

Chantal was intrigued. 'What crazy? Not an Arab?'

'Nah, French – great hulk of a blond fella, looked like an All Black.'

She didn't follow him but it began to confirm her suspicions. 'With a blond fringe, as if he cut it himself!'

'Yes, you could say that. Do you know him?'

'I did,' she replied sombrely as she watched a light wind drive a broken twig across the empty pool.

'Who is he?'

She found it hard to formulate the words. 'He was working for them – those men in the Majestic. And then, I am sure, when he showed his face to you and they no longer needed him, they killed him. I was threatened, too. They said they would kill me, and my sister, if I told anyone. But now the soldiers say there is no longer any danger.'

'I guess not,' said Vincent, as three police cars, their sirens howling hungrily, raced past the other side of the hedge along the Croisette. 'Only to the poor buggers in the hotel.'

CHAPTER 22

Saturday Evening
17th May 1997

Cannes

For the past fifty years the Régence Hotel on the Rue St Honoré had been home to the more impoverished class of Festival delegate. A tolerance of cockroaches and a sunny disposition when joining the queue for the bathroom were the minimum requirements for the guests. But generous room rates, proximity to the Palais and the affability of the Fouquet family who ran the place brought the same people back year after year. The clientele were, in the main, intense young and not-so-young *cinéastes* who tended to write articles for monthly magazines that frequently seemed longer than the films they were analysing.

Now La Régence was to take on a significance that had been denied it in the past. It was the closest hotel to the rear doors of the Majestic, which were ten metres away on the far side of the street. In the years before the Gaddafi scare they slid obediently open when anyone set foot on the thick, welcoming mat. Bolder residents of La Régence would skip in after breakfast to collect an armful of daily trade magazines from the Majestic foyer and even take an early dip in the luxury hotel's swimming pool. At a Festival as status-conscious as Cannes, it was not unknown for people to give the Majestic as their address in the Who's-Staying-Where register, but in fact take a room at La Régence. They would pick up their mail every day from reception at the neighbouring hotel that was at least a dozen times more expensive. A better class of invitation was usually procured that way.

There were no *cinéastes* in La Régence today, just soldiers. The front windows and door had been sandbagged and heavily fortified. A masked man with a sub-machine-gun could be dimly seen through the glass doors of the Majestic, moving deliberately in and out of the shadows. Outside, the closed street separating the two hotels took on the forlorn air of a Cold War customs post.

'They had people in there already, that's for sure. Didn't even have to break the glass. Beautiful operation. Clean as a whistle.'

Colonel Bresson from French military intelligence, who had been deputed to give Robert his final briefing, had a more than grudging admiration for the enemy. Not so his colleague, Madame Melville, a dark-suited woman from the Ministry of the Interior who chain-smoked obtrusively.

'They are the worst kind. Total efficiency – total ruthlessness. It is the Japanese Red Brigade, I am certain. The ones that got away in Athens. Not interested in their own lives, or anyone else's. There are two sorts of fanatics: fanatics and Japanese fanatics.'

These were not words guaranteed to reassure the three men who were about to enter the fortress. Erik tried to catch Vik's eye, hoping perhaps for an indication of a change of heart, but the cameraman had dodged a few bullets in Southeast Asia in his time and had no intention of running away from this crisis.

'The British have a children's party game,' began the Colonel, 'Kim's game. It is quite simple. A number of small objects are placed on a tray which is then covered. The tray is brought into a room and the cover is taken off for thirty seconds. The trick is to see which child can remember most objects.'

'And the secret,' added Madame Melville, 'is to relate the position of the objects to one another. The memory is a visual tool.'

'Shereshevskii,' murmured Robert.

'Who?' she demanded, stubbing out a barely started cigarette.

'He was a Russian who could remember everything.' Robert was pleased to have put her off-guard. He had taken an immediate dislike to her clinical approach to the crisis, treating it as if it, too, were a game without any real people involved. 'There was no limit to the amount that his brain could take in, but he sometimes had difficulty with people's faces. If a man was smiling when he first met him, he wouldn't remember his face if he was frowning when he saw him again.'

'Are you sure?' queried the woman, trying simultaneously to take notes and light another cigarette. 'He is not taught on our course.'

'He was a freak,' Robert replied. Obviously *Luria* had not yet opened in France, or maybe Madame Melville was just not a cinema-goer. 'His imagination was too vivid to be of help to ordinary individuals.'

'We can't help much either,' confessed the Colonel. 'What we need most of all is an estimate of how many of them are in there. Try and keep a count. I doubt if you'll have the chance to remember many faces, smiling or not. But I should imagine that whoever's going to deliver the statement will show his. If he doesn't seem to want to, point out to him that it's futile to try to persuade people of the justice of your cause from behind a mask. We believe there are not enough of them to occupy any of the hotel west of the lobby. Take a look upstairs, if you can.'

Madame Melville nodded her agreement. 'It's less important to find out who the hostages are. We think we know and they may be spread over several rooms by now. Just make a quick count of the number still in the dining-room. It will help to minimise casualties when we go in.'

'You're going in?' Erik exclaimed nervously.

'Not for a while yet,' the Colonel assured him. 'Every hour that passes they get a little weaker. Vigilance is a diminishing resource, especially when it's allied to a lack of sleep.'

'Look at these photographs,' Madame Melville opened her ministry brief-case and passed them around. 'This is Henri Chaillot, the Foreign Minister. Acknowledge him and watch his face for any message.'

Robert studied the confident features and polished silver hair. 'Should I ask to speak to him?'

The Colonel shook his head. 'No, stay passive. However friendly or normal they may seem, remember you're dealing with fanatics. They're like animals – any sudden movement, anything out of the ordinary disturbs them. Do exactly as they say.'

A sergeant in full battle-gear put his head round the door and offered a casual salute. 'Seventeen hundred hours, sir.'

'Well,' – Colonel Bresson squeezed Robert lightly on the shoulder – '*bonne chance*. You'll be fine. Don't forget to tell them there's a plane waiting and a safe passage out of the country any time they care to march out with their hands up.'

'Is there?' Robert asked.

The Colonel smiled back enigmatically. Madame Melville released a coil of smoke disdainfully towards the ceiling.

'Yes, and a bunch of grapes and a garland of lilies each.' General Le Prince and the senior members of the Excelsior committee had been listening to the radio receiver in Renaud's office. A live transmitter had been attached to Erik's recording equipment without his knowledge.

'Plus burial at sea with the cause of your choice.' The Commandant of the CRS joined in with an uncertain laugh.

Renaud had been uneasy at the idea of bugging Robert's crew – if discovered, it could give the terrorists a justifiable reason for holding onto them – and was further disturbed by the bellicose attitude that the military and the police were starting to exhibit. It was as if they had already begun to discount the lives of the hostages.

'You seem to have rejected their demands before they've been made.' He surprised even himself with his provocative approach. 'I doubt if Monsieur Chaillot would approve of that.'

The General gave him a patronising glance. 'Unfortunately, Monsieur Chaillot is likely to be the first to go.'

'Raise your arms.' The voice came unexpectedly from behind Robert as he stepped out into the empty street.

Involuntarily he did so. Erik followed suit, the video-recorder hanging from his beefy neck, and Vik held out his camera in front of him like a peace offering. A second camera covered their progress from a third-floor window of the hotel they were leaving.

Robert became disturbingly aware of the cocktail of emotions that was inside him: surface excitement, deep-seated fear and a charge of ecstasy at the prospect of seeing Elizabeth again. It was an all-time high that not even the purest cocaine could reproduce. To his amazement, when he stepped on the large mat bearing the Majestic insignia, the glass doors parted electronically. He found his legs were becoming reluctant to take orders from his brain and he had to make a deliberately conscious effort to place one foot in front of the other.

The doors closed with silent precision behind them, like a see-through drawbridge cutting them off from the real world. A short man, his features masked by an Arab head-dress, emerged from behind the lifts. He appeared to be unarmed but the two terrorists in balaclavas who materialised at the top of the stairs had their Kalashnikov AK-94s trained on the three arrivals. Robert could see a sheen of sweat above the eyes and mouth of the man nearer to him and inwardly wished he would keep his finger a little further from the trigger.

The Arab stopped in front of them but did not proffer a hand. 'Now you are here we can conclude this matter quickly and without unnecessary bloodshed.'

He spoke with a guttural American accent, acquired perhaps from living there or maybe just from watching their television programmes. Robert noticed his arms. They were unnaturally ballooned, as if pumped up by a permanent thrombosis. The man motioned to the two guards who came rapidly down the stairs. The perspiring one kept his rifle about a foot away from from Robert's face while the other carried out a rough but practised body-search. Vik and Erik were subjected to the same, but the terrorist fortunately appeared to be inexperienced when it came to camera equipment and gave it a cursory going-over.

'Hurry. We must not waste time.' The Arab was becoming impatient. 'Follow me.'

He walked in front of them towards the main lobby of the hotel. Through the glass door Robert could see another AMX-30 tank newly stationed at the bottom of the drive. It was turning its gun turret from right to left in an unhurried way that seemed to make it all the more menacing. The dismaying thought occurred to him that possibly the diversion game was being played again, only this time by the other side. Had he and the crew been sent in as decoys to distract the terrorists while the paras stormed the building?

Such thoughts compounded his sense of unease as they were led down the wide corridor, past empty armchairs and tables still littered with copies of *Nice Matin* and Festival magazines and stacks of publicity brochures, the garbage of blithe days that now seemed light years away. The banks of television monitors, usually chattering out interviews with the stars, film clips and relentless analysis of the movies, stood forebodingly silent.

From the moment they entered the dining-room Robert could feel the fear; it was all around him, like undetectable white noise. People were huddled in groups in the corners of the room, some sitting on the floor with their backs to the walls, others lying in front of them and one or two trying unsuccessfully to find a comfortable position on the upright dining-chairs. Everyone was in some form of dinner dress; several of the women were now wearing men's jackets.

All the indications were that they had spent an uncomfortable night on the floor. It was unlikely that anybody had slept very much. They had the air of passengers who had emerged from a prolonged trans-continental flight, their faces sallow and worn, the men unshaven, and their eyes stonily devoid of sparkle. They seemed to Robert like revenants from another age who had come back to haunt the room, an image reinforced by the remains of the previous night's banquet that lay before them. Rumpled napkins and unfinished bottles of red wine and ashtrays with half-smoked cigars littered the tables. The intruders appeared to have descended on them before the end of the feast.

Their arrival seemed to breathe new life into the dinner guests. People stirred but nobody spoke. Several looked anxiously at the four masked guards who were in charge of them, two at the main door and two by the French windows that led out to the Jacuzzi garden. Three of the prisoners, including Don Lugg, his expression as lifeless as his flopping red hair, had abrasions on their faces. There must have been some form of resistance or disobedience. The Arab pointed at them individually.

'You, and you, and you, come here.'

The three men rose wearily to their feet and approached him, clearly apprehensive that there was further punishment in store.

'Stand by the door,' the Arab snapped. He turned to Robert. 'Now, film the rest of them. We want to show the world that we are treating our hostages humanely.'

Robert gestured his permission to Vik and Erik. As the two men prepared their gear, he had time to study the faces more thoroughly. His eyes travelled from woman to woman desperately in search of Elizabeth. They seemed to have held up better than the men. Some managed a wan smile in response and Jenny Bates of the Australian Film Board gave him a defiant wink. The guard by the garden window gestured with his rifle to intimate that he had noticed this. Robert went round them once again to double check but the conclusion remained the same: she wasn't there. Perhaps she had escaped; perhaps she had gone home.

'Is this everyone?' he asked.

'Shut up,' replied the Arab. 'No questions. Just do what you're told.'

People stared passively and resentfully at Vik's camera as he tracked across their faces. Two of the women and one man were crying. Only Ted Barlow showed any real spirit, making a double thumbs-up sign from his supine position, like a soldier in a wartime newsreel. But in the eyes of many of them lay the resigned expression of people who instinctively knew there was a genuine probability of death, either at the hands of their captors or their liberators. A few men stood up and tried to retain some dignity but the degradation of their position militated against it. They had ceased to be individuals; they were just hostages, whose lives and destinies were no longer theirs to control. They had become mere bargaining factors in a contest which they were not themselves permitted to join.

'Call Kwang.' The Arab's command was barked abruptly. The guard nearest the door stiffened in a military fashion and left the room. Whoever these people were, Robert thought, it was evident that they were a thoroughly trained unit.

Vik looked up from his camera. 'Can I speak?'

'What is it?' The Arab's intolerant tone betrayed his continuing nervousness.

'The light level. It's too low. We're not getting much.'

'Let me see. Play it back through the camera.'

Vik signalled to Erik who stopped recording and pressed the rewind button. The Arab marched across and seized the camera. 'Run it now. No tricks. We expected professionals.'

He looked at the pictures through the viewfinder. In the furthest corner of the room the man who had been crying began to weep loudly, attempting to stifle the noise with his handkerchief. Robert braced himself as he waited for the verdict. All eyes turned apprehensively to the stocky emperor of the Majestic dining-room.

The Arab gave a murmur which could have indicated either satisfaction or lack of it. Finally he took his eye from the camera. 'It's good enough. We're not making an MGM musical. Continue.'

At the very moment he handed the camera back to Vik, the unmistakable and pitiable figure of Henri Chaillot came into the room. His bloodshot eyes suggested an excess of brandy and an absence of sleep. Although he had obviously made some attempt to smarten himself up, his silver hair had lost its sheen, his shirt collar was scuffed and stained and his confident expression severely dented.

In contrast, the Chinese man who followed him in was beamingly alert. He was considerably leaner and slightly taller than the Foreign Minister, with tight-fitting black trousers and a freshly laundered white shirt, open at the neck. His glistening black hair indicated that he had recently showered and his springing walk was that of someone anxious to exude an impression of physical fitness. He had a mild, almost academic demeanour very far from the wide-eyed expression expected of a dangerous fanatic. Nevertheless, Robert surmised, this must be Kwang.

Without introducing himself he pointed peremptorily at Vik. 'Put your camera there,' he ordered, indicating a position by the French windows. 'I shall speak first and then Monsieur Chaillot.'

Vik loyally looked at Robert before carrying out this instruction but a brief nod of acquiescence was enough to spur him into action. Robert tried to catch Chaillot's attention but the Minister refused to meet his eyes. It seemed the order of events had already been worked out and the Frenchman was ruefully resigned to his role.

While the camera was being repositioned, Kwang went across to his captives.

'I hope you are all as comfortable as can be expected.' The friendly tone of his voice was somewhat undercut by the manner in which three of the masked guards trained their guns on the dinner guests as he spoke. 'The end is in sight. Now the television is here I do not expect we shall have to detain you very much longer. Two days at the most.'

An audible groan echoed around the room, more animal, Robert thought, than human. Some people began to speak to each other only to be silenced with a barked 'shut up' from the Arab.

Kwang now addressed Robert. 'You will see to it that everything that I and Monsieur Chaillot say is shown uncut. We will be brief. The tape will be made available to every broadcasting organisation that wants it.' He let loose a dissonant and disconcerting sound, half-laugh, half-giggle. 'I have a feeling that most will.'

Robert signified his compliance while managing, with ease, not to return the smile. He could see now, behind the studious exterior, the unbalanced drive of somebody obsessed with the naked pleasure of power.

'Well, are we ready?' Kwang strode over to the camera. 'There is not time for a wasted moment in these circumstances. Do I look all right?'

Vik boldly ignored the question. 'Can you move a little to your left so that the daylight is directly on your face. Stop. That's fine. Fine by me.'

'Sound?' Kwang demanded, eyeing Erik with a cold stare. The large Belgian edged the microphone closer to him.

Robert took up his position behind Vik. 'Okay, let's roll.'

'Speed,' said Erik.

'In your own time,' Robert murmured.

Kwang's surface calm had the effect of making him seem intimidatingly unearthly. When he began to speak, the words appeared to be coming not from him but as though he were receiving them from elsewhere.

'What you have witnessed during the past twenty hours,' he began, 'is not an act of terrorism but an act of humanity. We are attempting to redress a gross injustice and, having explored all peaceful negotiating channels, we have reluctantly had to resort to this final military solution.'

His captive audience stirred with intrigue. They were about to be told the bargain in which they were the human factor.

'In six weeks' time the United Kingdom is prepared to hand over the Crown Colony of Hong Kong to the People's Republic of China. This is an act of perfidy on a scale the world has seldom seen. It is both contrary to international law and, more faithlessly, against the wishes of ninety-five per cent of the indigenous population of the territory. The people have a right to self-determination. We, in the Hong Kong Liberation Front, have fought this despicable act but have failed to prevent the British treating us with the treachery that they have shown to every one of their former colonies.'

No editing, thought Robert – he'll be lucky.

'On the eve of this final betrayal we are demanding one right. It is not a matter on which we will take no for an answer.' He looked round the room, his expression now bitter and glacial. 'The Government of the United Kingdom must amend the British Nationality Act of 1981 and the subsequent agreements of 1984 and 1994 to give every citizen of Hong Kong, not just the favoured few, a full British passport, permitting them to settle in the UK, or Canada or Australia if they so choose. The British Government has until seven o'clock French time tomorrow night to give its solemn pledge to this effect before the United Nations – or nobody in this hotel will remain alive. That would be a heavy price to pay for rejecting a simple and honourable request.'

He beckoned Henri Chaillot over. The Foreign Minister walked towards him, his legs moving leadenly as if restrained by invisible chains. He took up the indicated position beside Kwang and removed a piece of paper from his inside pocket.

'I have had long discussions last night with Mr Kwang.' He glanced anxiously at the man beside him, almost seeking approval to use his name. 'I have no doubts about the veracity of his case nor . . . nor any . . .' He stumbled and appeared to lose his place. 'Nor any . . . nor do I doubt that his threat is equally genuine. He is prepared to kill us all. I implore the British government to accede to his demands. At the end of the day humanity will be the winner and in strict international law his request has a legitimate foundation which –'

His speech was cut short. Kwang moved him to one side and stepped in front of the camera. 'There are to be no tricks. We have an independent communications system which will monitor the UN. The lives of the people you have seen in this room have just over twenty-four hours to run. Their fate is now in the hands of the British Government.'

In Renaud's office General Le Prince tipped back his chair and shook his head pensively. 'Not much the Elysée can do now. It's all up to the British. And if I know them they won't give an inch. We should have taken them out this morning before they were expecting us. Now we're going to have civilian blood all over the floor.'

'Fifty per cent fatalities?' suggested the Commandant of the CRS.

The General perused the map of the hotel. 'Seventy per cent if they're any good,' he replied. And then, after a pause for further consideration he added: 'maybe worse.'

'Was I all right?'

Robert could hardly believe his ears. Here was a man as lethal as a nuclear burn-out asking the same modest question that every interviewee did.

'Yes, you were fine. They'll get the message.'

'If they get it, they'll act on it.'

'I hope so,' said Robert, unnecessarily.

'You go now,' Kwang ordered. They had left the dining-room and were standing outside in the corridor which was empty apart from the inevitable guard with a gun. Chaillot had been granted no special privileges for his placatory efforts and had been left inside with the rest of the guests. Vik and Erik were also in there, packing up their equipment.

'What about my crew?' Robert asked defiantly.

'They will stay. We may need some more pictures from inside if the French try anything silly.'

Without thinking, Robert waved the video cassette in his face. 'No, that's not our deal. If they stay, I stay.'

Kwang bristled at the unexpected resistance. 'It makes little difference to me. The message is recorded. We can deliver it ourselves.'

'Yes, you can. But if you do, it will be apparent to everybody that you are not capable of keeping your word. You're asking for a bargain from the British, but they'll see right from the start that they are dealing with a man who has no honour.'

Kwang snatched the tape away from him. 'They are not dealing with honour. They are dealing with the deaths of two hundred people. That is a bargain that they understand only too well.'

'There aren't two hundred in that room.' Robert's instinct for self-preservation impelled him to prolong the dialogue.

'We have hostages in rooms throughout the hotel. You tell them that. If they attack us, they have no idea where our prisoners are. There is no chance that anybody will escape alive.'

'I can't tell them that if I'm here.'

'You will go, you and your crew. We have enough people here.'

Robert felt relieved and emboldened by this victory. Clearly his argument had had some force. 'I have a favour to ask of you. There is possibly a girl in here. She is staying in one of the rooms. I would like to talk to her.'

'Why?'

'She is a friend.'

'Who?'

'An actress. An English woman, blonde and young. Too young to –'

'Too young to die.' Kwang completed his sentence for him. 'Exactly. I know the one. The girl from the film. She is here.'

The information caused Robert's spirits to soar and to crash at the same time.

'If you let me see her, I'll – I'll –' – his mind failed to contrive a plausible bargaining factor – 'I'll make sure *Arts Action* transmits your speech in its entirety.' As he said the words he knew they formed an insignificant, pathetic offer.

'We don't need your help. The world is waiting. Is she your girl-friend?'

'No, not really. We just –' His thought-processes fused and went completely numb but, like a secondary power supply, his emotions came to their rescue. 'I'm going to marry her.'

Kwang smiled. 'So you would like the British and French governments to act sensibly in this matter.'

'I don't know much about Hong Kong. I'm an American. But I do believe in people's right to self determination.'

Kwang spread his arms and opened the palms of his hands. 'That is all we are asking. Nothing more. It could have been done without this unpleasantness. But now the world will understand our desperation and there will be justice for all. Including the residents of this hotel.'

Robert's confidence grew. 'If you believe in justice, let me see her. Five minutes. Then I'll do everything in my power to make sure your message is heard and acted upon.'

Kwang tapped the video cassette on his chin as he thought the proposition through. 'Very well, Mr Barrett. I do not think five minutes is too great a price to pay for a new American ally to our cause. We are not murderers, you know. We have loved ones, too. That is the reason we have been forced to take this action.'

General Le Prince's usual equilibrium was being put to the test by the voice at the other end of the phone. 'I have eight hundred and twenty men at my command,' he shouted. 'They are answerable to me. Their safety and their lives are my responsibility. You have no right to suggest –' He stopped and listened. 'Yes . . . yes, of course . . . yes.'

A further pause, then he returned to the offensive. 'But it must clearly be understood throughout this operation that I remain answerable to the Commander-in-Chief and he, in turn, obeys only the President of the Republic.'

He nodded furiously as he listened further, anxious to get out his parting shot. 'I hear what you're saying but you must remember one thing: this is not just a matter of international politics but of life and death, *French* lives and *French* deaths.'

He put the phone down still trembling with indignation. 'It seems the Interior Ministry is going to make the British the scapegoats. We're getting visitors. A delegation is due here by midnight – a private plane from London. We are not to make any moves nor attempt any contact till then. Apparently the Governor of Hong Kong is currently in Whitehall. He will conduct the initial negotiations.'

Le Prince sat down and directed a half-amused frown at Renaud. 'An English gentleman against a bunch of butchers. Not an equation that I would like my life to depend on.'

The perspiring guard who had greeted Robert on arrival was deputed to escort him up to the third floor. They didn't take the lift – the terrorists had appraised the danger that the army might cut off the electricity supply and people could be trapped in it. Instead they trod silently up the thickly carpeted stairs, past the empty suite of DDA, the press relations company who handled most of the main stars at the Festival. Just a few, evanescent days ago Robert had joined the mass of other supplicant journalists, waiting hopefully to be granted a slot in the schedule of some visiting actor or actress. At the time it all seemed so vital and important. Now, as he surveyed the vacant desks with their unwanted piles of memoranda and publicity photographs and press kits, nothing could have mattered less. Passing interviews with transient celebrities, he thought, candy floss journalism and just as nutritious.

Unexpectedly a phone on one of the desks began to ring. The guard turned tensely towards the open office, covering it with his rifle as if he expected someone to come and answer it. His finger tightened on the trigger.

Robert doubted if the hotel's switchboard was working. 'It's probably a direct line,' he assured the man. But it was evident that the liberation fighter did not understand him. Instead he gave him a rough push, indicating that they should continue their journey upwards.

On the third floor landing they were confronted by a machine-gun on a tripod – an air-cooled M2 capable of firing 500 rounds a minute, if Madame Melville's photographs were anything to go by. Robert was surprised to see that the two Chinese men who sat at the table behind it, like babushkas in a Russian hotel, were not wearing masks. One was spindly with a goatee beard, his complexion as dark as peat. The other, muscled like a wrestler, had a round, smooth face with disproportionately tiny pin-prick eyes.

The sweating guard exchanged some explanatory words in Chinese with the burly one, who then rose and gestured to Robert to follow him along the corridor. They stopped at the sixth door on the right, a room, Robert calculated, that must look out directly towards the Palais des Festivals. The man unlocked the door and, without knocking, threw it open.

A tray of uneaten bread and salami lay in the middle of the floor, surrounded by a few books and screwed-up pieces of writing paper. Beyond them, by the window, Elizabeth was sitting at a dressing-table, writing in a black diary. She was wearing a long white dress, as if she were going to a party, and the setting sun haloed her hair a deeper shade of gold. Her face looked fresh and seraphic.

As she turned her head slowly towards the door, her haughty expression dissolved into one of transcendent delight.

'Robert,' was all she said.

He tried to speak but found only a vacuum in his throat where the words should have been.

'If you were Richard Gere,' she grinned, 'you'd be wearing a dashing white uniform.'

He struggled to find his voice. 'It's at the dry cleaners, I'm afraid. Will I do as I am?'

'You'll do.'

The guard eyed them with suspicion, as if they had been speaking in code.

'Can you leave us?' Elizabeth asked.

'No, this is not possible.'

'It's what I agreed with Kwang.' Even if the man bothered to check, Robert guessed, their time would be nearly over. But the mention of Kwang's name had the desired effect. The bulky figure backed reluctantly towards the door.

'You do nothing foolish. Five minutes. I will be listening

outside,' he shouted at them, emphasising his words with his gun and noisily locking the door behind him.

Robert remained just gazing at her. Instinctively he knew why she was dressed like that – it was the British way, putting on a good show right to the end. Yet she looked so young and fragile, like a little girl in a nursery in one of those English children's stories he had read with envy in his own childhood, the sort of girl who would have a nanny and a dog. Her eyes began to smile once more, the sapphire sparkle coming as unexpectedly out of the umber depths as it had that first day in Aspen. He wondered how the universe could be so compassionless as to offer him this precious treasure, only to threaten to remove it with such mindless barbarity.

'Are you going to spend the whole five minutes standing there?' she asked.

He emerged from his reverie. 'I was thinking.'

'What?'

'I wondered if you had a dog and a nanny?'

She laughed gently. 'Yes. Still do. One's in Surrey and the other's in Scotland.'

'After we're married,' he said, 'they could both come and live with us.'

'Oh Robert.' She stood up and stretched out her arms, her eyes full of tears.

He went across to the window, and held her tighter than he had ever held another human in his life.

'The best is yet to be,' she whispered, burying her face in his chest.

'The worst is nearly over,' he said, trying to comfort her.

'Pray for me, Robert. I'm sure an American God is likely to be much more powerful than mine.'

'Who's yours?' he asked.

She looked up at him and dashed away a tear with the sleeve of her dress. 'She lives in Hollywood – not your Hollywood, Hollywood Road. It's where I go to pray, the temple of the Dragon Mother. It must nearly be the eighth day of the fifth moon by now. You see, she's answered my prayers. But there's always a catch, isn't there?'

He was confused.

'The Dragon Mother of Yueh Cheng,' she explained. 'Thousands of years ago she discovered an egg that contained a dragon. So she reared it and it brought her luck. And now she helps unmarried girls to find good husbands. I prayed to her – it seems to have worked, doesn't it?' She gazed down from the window at the tank positioned at the end of the hotel drive. 'Or half worked.'

He drew her to him again. 'I'm going to ask to change places with you.'

'You're a lovely man, but they won't wear it. I think I'm the pick of the crop in here, after that French minister perhaps. Besides, what would it solve? We'd still be apart, one inside, one outside.'

'I think I could live more easily with myself.'

'I don't think there's going to be much more living inside here, not the way things look at the moment.'

'How do you know? Have they told you?'

'I've heard them talking in the corridor and when they've come with food. I've just got a smattering of Cantonese, although I haven't let them know that. They may be the sort of people who put bombs on aircraft or under schools but they're tremendously naïve. They expect to march out of here with their demands met. The only thing they're likely to meet is a blood-bath.'

'There'll be a compromise,' he insisted, desperately trying to reassure her. 'There always is.'

'Yes,' she agreed, lying bravely. 'I expect you're right.'

Both their bodies tautened as they heard the sound of the key in the lock. Elizabeth took a folded piece of notepaper she had been holding and slipped it into the breast pocket of his jacket. She drew his head down to hers and pressed her cheek against his.

'Be a god and hold me, work a charm,' she whispered.

'Now you must go. You have said goodbye.' The guard made as if to separate them.

Robert stepped back and reluctantly released her hand.

'Did you play Kim's game as a child?' he asked.

'All the time,' she replied. 'You've been taking some mental pictures, have you?'

'There's just one I want to keep. I thought that if we had a daughter we might call her Kim.'

'You come now,' demanded her gaoler, pulling him to the door.

'It's a boy's name in England,' said Elizabeth.

'Fine,' he replied, as the man turned the key in the lock. 'Let's make it a boy then.'

'Robert,' she called after him through the closed door. 'If anything should go wrong, have a drink at Ruthie's. Remember Porphyria – think of me.'

The luxury hotel had become a silent jail. Only one inmate had any measure of freedom. The moment the attack had taken place, Elvis Ho had scrambled up onto the roof and hidden behind a disused chimney. After the terrorists had flushed out the bedrooms, he had climbed back down to his, gathered up some pillows and sheets and now made a nest for himself in the small attic directly above it. From there he contemplated his plans for getting to Pornic.

The character of Cannes had changed dramatically in the course of the day. There had been talk of moving the Film Market to Monte Carlo but even the most cynical of salesmen balked at the idea of doing deals while the hostages were still in the hotel. So buyers, sellers, distributors, directors, producers, agents, actors, actresses, flacks and hacks had packed their belongings and made for the airport or crowded the trains to Paris and Milan, rich refugees seeking the security of their own hearths.

Besides, the Army had commandeered the Carlton Hotel, making it their emergency headquarters. As overweight exhibitors in Hawaiian shirts were ushering their overdressed wives, laden with designer bags from the Rue d'Antibes, into taxis to take them to the station, stern military men in jeeps were zipping up to the front door to replace them.

The previous year the obsolescent Cannes General Hospital had been moved from its location on the Avenue des Broussailles and amalgamated with the recently completed high-tech version in the new town of Antibes-les-Pins. But this was too far away. So, in ghoulish anticipation of the worst that might happen, the first two floors of the Carlton were turned into a temporary medical unit. The larger suites, which had provided luxury offices for Fox and Paramount and Universal and Sony and Warner Bros, were vacated and beds from the floors above were brought down and arranged in military rows. Most of the posters had been removed from the walls but the orderlies had left large portraits of Sylvester Stallone and Clint Eastwood and Bud Booker to gaze down incongrously on the anticipated victims.

A tart, antiseptic air of Dettol cleanliness spread through the hotel. Makeshift operating theatres were set up in the larger front bedrooms with extensive white sheets pinned over the windows to diffuse the strong Mediterranean light. At the end of the corridor, at the eastern extremity of the first floor, there lay the highly coveted tower suite. Now it had become considerably less coveted. Somebody had pinned a notice with the word 'Morgue' onto the door.

The upper floors of the hotel were given over to diplomatic delegations who were rapidly arriving from America, Britain, Australia and the United Nations, as well as a substantial civil service presence from Paris. Already the importation of computers, word processors, printers, photocopiers, extra telephones and fax machines betokened the fact that a bureaucracy was about to go to work, a bureaucracy that anticipated a long siege.

By early evening on a normal Festival day, the Carlton terrace would be bristling with people having a pre-dinner cocktail, the first drink of the day or maybe the forty-first. Deals would continue to be struck but in a more relaxed environment. Even if someone could only afford the price of a Perrier or a *pression*, it was an admission fee worth paying for a chance encounter with a good fairy who might give a financial kiss of life to a dying project. But on this sad Saturday, just a few tables were occupied by sombre men in sombre suits, speaking in tones many decibels lower than the required bonhomie of a Festival conversation. The underemployed waiters stood broodily under the canopy. Hardly any traffic moved along the once carefree Croisette. Even the palm trees looked mournful and the sea beyond appeared to be sleeping, cushioning the two vigilant warships that slowly rose and fell in its regular swell.

The atmosphere at the bar of the Martinez Hotel, just two blocks further to the east, was markedly different. While it would be incorrect to say the place was jumping, there were sounds of life and cheerfulness there not to be found anywhere else in the stricken city. Weather-worn and booze-hardened men, many of them dressed as if for the desert or the jungle, some with cameras hanging like precious pendants on their chests, greeted each other as if this were a class reunion which, in its way, it was. These were foreign correspondents and war reporters who, on hitting town, had headed unerringly for the Martinez as if summoned by some secret bell audible only to them. Most of the show-business journalists and film critics had been withdrawn from Cannes. Few newspapers had chosen to entrust the coverage of the siege to them, mindful perhaps of the renowned incident involving the drama critic who managed to review a play without mentioning the fact that the theatre caught fire shortly before the end. When his editor confronted him with the front pages of their rival papers and asked him about this blazing omission, the man replied defiantly: 'I'm a critic, not a reporter.'

Old hands from Latin America, the Middle East and Northern Ireland were used to covering catastrophes while distancing themselves emotionally from them and the traditional lukewarm jokes were already circulating the bar. 'What's the winner of this year's Palme d'Or? – *Kung Fu* at the Majestic.'

Madame Rivette found this new breed of reporter, over whom she failed to exercise her accustomed control with gilded passes to reward the obedient, very little to her taste. They kept demanding information and she had but a meagre trickle to dispense to them. A French government spokesman in a three-minute statement had given a literal interpretation to the word briefing. Yes, legations were arriving and would arrive from the relevant countries involved. No, he could not reveal the exact constitution of the consultative committee but, yes, there would *be* a consultative committee. No, the

Governor of Hong Kong would not be conducting direct negotations with the terrorists. Yes, he would be advising General Le Prince who remained in complete command. What about the seven o'clock deadline? Were there any plans to ask the terrorists to let the women and children go free? Were there, in fact, any children in the hotel? All such information was denied the press on security grounds.

Robert was constrained to appear before them for five minutes. He felt like a professional tennis player, bound by his contract to give an interview even after a match in which he had been shamefully defeated. At the debriefing with Colonel Bresson and Madame Melville he had been surprised that he could remember so many of the initial details. But he had no clear idea how he had left the hotel. Vik and Erik had been waiting at the foot of the stairs and they had just wandered out, with the omnipresent guards ushering them to the door. Robert's game, he thought, one in which the winner is the person who can erase everything painful from the memory.

He was impressed by Madame Melville's preparation. She had photographs of nearly all the hostages they suspected were in the hotel – this was easily done because the Festival office required delegates to lodge a second picture when applying for credentials – and he was able to identify most of those in the dining room. When they came to a picture of Elizabeth he froze. Yes, she was there, he said. In the dining room? Not exactly – he had to think quickly, she wouldn't be in the video – she was being led through the hall. There were probably many hostages in the bedrooms, he warned them, and in the event of an attack they would be the most vulnerable since they would be the last people the troops would reach.

Madame Melville sat beside him as he faced questions from the newly arrived reporters, vetoing most of them. It seemed farcical to Robert to hold a press conference in order not to tell anybody anything, but this was not unusual in government circles. He was able to say how he felt the hostages were which, with the three exceptions of the injured men whom Bresson had told him not to mention, they could have seen for themselves from the video which had already been broadcast.

No, he had no idea exactly who Kwang was. Yes, he thought the terrorists meant business, they gave every impression of being committed and ruthless. Here Madame Melville stopped him and sweetly assured the journalists that if they stayed close to the press room in the Martinez they would be the first to hear about any new developments. It was a method of keeping all but the most intrepid from trying to discover the progress of events by more adventurous means.

Sandra Lewis covered the event for *Arts Action*. The story, from her point of view, was less about what Robert had to say than the fact that one of their reporters was playing a crucial role in the siege. She was professionally jealous at his apparent luck in being in the right place the previous night and felt a competitive need to make a mark of her own. As a career girl, here was a chance to establish her name. Like the other remaining residents of the Carlton, she and Robert had been informed they would have to move out of the hotel. Alternative rooms had been found at the Montfleury, an annoying twenty-minute walk away at the top of the town. But Sandra had deliberately delayed checking out. Instead she went to a store in the Rue Hoche and bought a home video camera which she smuggled back into the Carlton in a Lacroix bag. As soon as she was out of sight of reception, she began to take pictures of the preparations under way to turn it into a hospital. No professional crews had been allowed into the hotel but Sandra put on the cheerful demeanour of an American tourist, smiled a lot, asked the orderlies to wave at the camera and managed to capture some exclusive footage, even a shot of the morgue, before a sergeant finally told her to stop.

Jim Hurley was delighted. Unlike Robert's hotel video, this was material that none of their rivals would have, keeping *Arts Action* ahead of the game. It was too risky to send it by satellite – that way all the receiving stations would see it and the more unscrupulous ones would lift it, their motto being transmit first and litigate over the rights later. So he instructed Sandra to go to Nice Airport, find some passenger who was embarking for New York and bribe them to take the cassette in their hand luggage.

'Dinner, then?' Robert came across to her as the less than

satisfied correspondents were filing out of the press conference.

She had decided not to tell him about her filming at the Carlton. 'No, I think I'll pass. No appetite.'

'Me neither,' he replied. 'I don't suppose you feel like getting extraordinarily drunk?'

'That's exactly how I feel,' she agreed, sensing that he still had the power to charm her but also acknowledging that their time had passed. 'Right now I have to get to the airport. There's fresh stock coming in from New York.'

'Can't the crew handle that? Vik knows the system.'

'Everything's changed with the new air schedules. Besides, they need a break. It's not just you who's been looking down gun barrels today.'

The remark was not meant to chastise him but it did. 'I know,' he said. 'They were great. They didn't get flustered or involved. They took it all so calmly.'

Then, without any warning, the flow of adrenalin that had been sustaining him over the past hours seemed to drain from his system. He clutched the back of a chair to support himself. 'Jesus Christ,' he groaned, 'I wish none of this had ever happened.'

Sandra put a consoling arm round his shoulder. 'You're crazy. You lucked out. If you don't get a job on the network news and a six-figure book advance, I'll – I'll marry Raymond Rainier.'

She kissed him on the cheek and gathered up her belongings. 'Ring you later.'

'He won't have you,' Robert shouted after her as she left. 'But have you got a little brother back home?'

Glancing round the room to make sure Madame Melville had gone, he decided he might as well have a few drinks at the bar on his own. It was doing a flourishing trade with journalists and television people but the barman was unusually quick in responding to his outstretched note.

'A whisky,' he ordered. '*Avec glace.*'

'With ice cream?' enquired the barman.

'No, on the rocks.' Robert realised, too late, that he was being sent up.

'For you, sir, on the house. A big one, I think, yes?'

Robert nodded gratefully. It seemed a lifetime ago that he had stood in P. J. Clark's and tasted a similar success. But then it had not been complicated by this emotional cataclysm, one he feared he would never recover from. The thought of Elizabeth made him realise he had forgotten about her note. He reached in his breast pocket and unfolded it. It was a poem.

'Be a god and hold me,
Work a charm.
Be a man and fold me
With thine arm.

That shall be tomorrow,
Not tonight.
I must bury sorrow
Out of sight.

Must a little weep, love,
(Foolish me!)
And so fall asleep, love.
Loved by thee.'

Underneath she had done a childish drawing of a heart with the letters E and R intertwined in the middle.

'Another whisky, sir?' asked the barman.

'Yes,' he said. 'And then another and another.'

'You television personalities – you go through life being spoilt like heathen idols.'

It was an American voice behind him. 'No,' Robert said, turning around, 'I just happened to –' Then he caught sight of the welcome and familiar face. 'Hutton – you're here!'

Hutton Craig held out his hand but Robert, in his euphoria, brushed it aside and embraced him.

'You seem to have picked up this French body language quicker than I have,' Hutton gasped, loosening himself from the hug.

'God, it's good to see you. Let me get you a drink.'

His old friend shook his head. 'I'm fine, thanks.'

'Well, let's find a table then and catch up on the news.' Robert thanked the barman for his fresh whisky and they made their way across to a less rowdy corner of the room.

'Why didn't you tell me you were coming?' Robert chastised him as they sat down.

'I hadn't really thought it through. I've been running the office on my own this month. In fact the foreign editor was on my back the next morning for not getting down here sooner. Congratulations, that was some scoop.'

'Beginner's luck,' Robert felt slightly embarrassed about it. 'How are Lynne and the kids? Well?'

'Yes, all well.' There was an unfamiliar dry note in Hutton's voice.

'Enjoying Paris?'

His friend averted his gaze. 'Actually they're not here. They decided to stay in New York.'

'Still looking for the right apartment.'

Hutton leant forward and took a sip of Robert's scotch. 'I'm not meant to have any of this but what the hell. Interferes with the pills they say. You may as well know, we've been on rocky ground for some time now. My fault to begin with, I suppose. A few feckless affairs, nothing serious, and not enough attention to Lynne. And then when I said we were going to France she said she wasn't. There had been a man for some years, apparently. A banker, would you believe? I just hope he's kind to the children.'

He looked at Robert as if to assess his reaction – which was more surprised than sympathetic. He had never seen his friend like this. Hutton was a man who had always appeared to have the perfect everything – perfect job, perfect home, perfect kids, perfect wife.

'What pills?' he enquired, searching for something to say.

'Sinequan. Anti-depressants. Short for *sine qua non*, I expect, since it's hard to exist without them. I've always suffered from depressions but never anything like this, especially in a foreign city. The good news is that you don't do away with yourself when you're in the middle of one, apparently your lassitude is so great that even suicide is too much of an effort. It's when you're picking yourself up and starting to come out of it that some people kill themselves. Ironic, isn't it?'

He gave a hollow laugh at the thought. As Hutton spoke, Robert could see for himself how inward-looking and tentative he had become. The laugh lines round his eyes had turned into creases of anxiety.

'Can you do the job? You were looking forward to it.'

'For a long while I couldn't. Not that I let the *Times* know. I suspect they made allowances for the fact that I was the new guy in town. Things are less easy now. I think the pressure's on for me to deliver on this one, otherwise I might be out on my ass. I should have levelled with them but I thought it would go on my record and harm my career with the paper. You know how people are.'

Robert swallowed the remainder of his scotch. 'Can I help? Anything. I'm sure there must be something.'

Hutton stretched across and lifted the empty glass. 'Let me get you another. Listen, it's good to see you again. I'm sorry to burden you with my problems. I'm really glad you're doing so well.'

'Hutton, I've never been doing worse in my life.'

'How so?'

'I've met a girl.'

'What happened to Tanya? I thought you were settled with her?'

'Unsettled, more like. It was never going to last. We both knew that.'

'Did *she*?' There was more than a hint of reprimand in Hutton's tone.

'She would have. In the long run. She's seeing some guy.' He paused, waiting for Hutton to speak, but he didn't. 'Okay, perhaps not. Perhaps I was exactly what she wanted, God knows why. Maybe I betrayed her. But that's life, a series of betrayals. Some we hand out, some we have to take.'

'I know,' said his friend, solemnly. 'So you met a girl.'

'It's more than that. Much more. I think I've met myself for the first time. She sort of explains . . . I don't know . . . It's complex. You've got to meet her. She's English.'

'So what's the problem?'

'She's in the Majestic.'

Hutton sat down again and put the empty glass back on the table. 'Sometimes I think I'm the only person in the world with problems. She's not dead yet, though. There could be a deal. They do those all the time in this town, I'm told.'

Robert was aware that these optimistic sentiments were only being offered to hearten him. 'What do you really think?' he asked.

Hutton scratched the side of his nose reflectively. 'The Brits aren't going to budge on this one. They've danced round the issue for too long to be seen to concede blanket nationality under pressure. Anyway it's against the British ethic to give way under duress. The French army's going in, sooner or later, that's for sure. The question is: are Mr Kwang and his friend bluffing or are they on a suicide mission? Our – the paper's–information suggests the latter. After Atlanta there's a feeling the Japanese Red Army's in on this and they don't deal in survivors. This operation smacks of their style. Did you see any Japs inside?'

'Not one.'

'See how professional they are.' Hutton was only half-joking. 'I don't know. But it seems unlikely these Hong Kong guys – what do they call themselves, the Popular Liberation Front? – are running this number on their own. If you ask me they've got some pretty heavy friends.'

As he spoke, he ceased to be an audience for his own thoughts. His attention was drawn to something at the entrance to the bar. 'Hey, look at that girl, over by the stairway. You can tell even at this distance she's French. You know how back home there are the girls you see in the glossy magazines, and then there are the ones you meet. Completely different. But have you noticed, over here, the ones you see in the street are the same as the ones in the magazines?'

Robert didn't bother to look but noted, with some relief, that not every spark of life had been extinguished by Hutton's black mood. 'There's something that keeps them fresh and groomed all day long,' he agreed, 'as if they had make-up and wardrobe just a few paces behind to prepare them for every entrance.'

'Wait a minute.' Hutton became unusually alert. 'She seems to be heading this way. Is it your animal magnetism or mine? I'll tell you what, I'll take a gamble: it's mine.'

Robert swivelled round to see the object of Hutton's transfixed desire. It was Chantal, trimly clad in a cream Festival T-shirt with its Phoenix emblem and a pair of navy shorts that allowed her deeply tanned legs plenty of scope for admiring glances as she threaded her way through the crowded tables towards them. Hutton rose to his feet with astonished delight as she arrived.

Chantal kissed Robert on both cheeks. 'I thought you'd be here. I needed to talk.'

He pulled across an empty chair from a neighbouring table. 'Sit down. Chantal, this is Hutton Craig from the *New York Times*, he's my best friend. Hutton, this is Chantal – I'm afraid I don't know your second name.'

'Coutard,' she said, taking Hutton's hand. 'But it doesn't matter. I'm pleased to meet you.'

'*Enchanté*,' he replied, breaking into a smile for the first time that evening.

But Chantal paid him scant attention, addressing herself earnestly to Robert. 'I've just come from the police. That Chinaman in the Majestic, he was the one who broke into our office in Paris, I'm sure. I saw him yesterday here in Cannes. And then I went to tell Raoul. But he was the wrong person. He had been working for them, the police say. He helped to plan this whole thing. And when they no longer needed him they killed him in this horrible way.'

A grimace flickered across her face at the thought of it. Robert took her hand. 'Why didn't you tell me *all* of this yesterday? Why didn't you tell the police then? Did you believe their threats?'

He could feel the icy shiver through her palm.

'If you had seen Raoul, you would have believed them. These men are worse than killers, Robert – there is too much pleasure in their killing.'

'Suicidal sadists,' Hutton observed.

'Tell me more.' Robert felt his chest tighten with anxiety. 'Were they masked? Did you see them?'

'Only one.' Chantal shook her head. 'A fat little Jap with arms like flippers, you must have seen him in there.'

'I didn't.' Robert was intrigued. 'Do you mean literally flippers?'

'No, he had fingers, but no wrists. His arms were wide from the shoulder to the hands.'

'With an American accent, deep, broken?'

She nodded.

'He *was* inside.' Robert turned to Hutton. 'He seemed to be number two to Kwang. But he was hidden behind an Arab head-dress.'

Hutton took over the questioning. 'Chantal, did you tell the police about him?'

'Sure.'

'And did they take down his description?'

'They did but they were not very interested. They say that now they have a picture of Kwang, that will tell them all they need to know. There was a man from Paris there I have spoken to before. They do not trust me, they think I am hysterical.'

'There was a break-in back in January in the Festival offices in the Faubourg St Honoré. They tied Chantal up,' Robert explained. 'They must have been planning this thing then. Everybody - the police included – thought they were after money but it looks like they wanted details of the Festival: schedules, plans, guest lists and, I suppose, credentials. Did anybody change the passes after the raid, Chantal?'

'No, why should they? Who needs passes to get into *le Majestic*?'

Robert was warming to his subject. 'I bet they never intended to go for the Majestic to begin with. They wanted to hit the Festival and get maximum media exposure and the most obvious plan would have been to infiltrate the *Palais des Festivals* and take that over. But they probably changed their minds when they found it was too unwieldy to hold.'

'Too unwieldy? I do not know this word. It is impossible to hijack *le Palais* – our security is too good,' she added with pride.

Robert gave Hutton an imperceptible wink. 'Chantal's in charge of the English-language press. She knows everything about us – every article we've written, every broadcast about the Festival, who we're sleeping with, whether we're gay or straight, the way we brush our teeth.'

Chantal blushed. 'We only file information for professional purposes. Nothing about the private life.'

'Wait a minute.' Hutton clicked his fingers like an engine stirring into life. 'You saw the Japanese guy, right? Rob, did you see any other faces?'

A light switched on in Robert's memory; nobody had called him Rob in ages. 'There were two Chinese guys, not very important though.'

Hutton was insistent. 'And did you tell the cops?'

'The security services, sure.'

'And what did they do?'

'They noted down details. But like Chantal, they're only interested in Kwang. They'll check him out.'

'Yes, and I bet you five hundred dollars he'll show up clean.' Hutton hammered a finger on the table to emphasise his point. 'Chantal, can we get access to your computer?'

'Not tonight. Le Palais is closed. There is total security.'

'But tomorrow. What about tomorrow?'

'Maybe in the afternoon. The Director is going to talk to the staff. But I do not think they will let you in.'

'They've got to. God knows, Rob, you've done enough for them. You can talk to this Director, Ronald whatever his name is.'

'Renaud,' Robert corrected him. 'I guess we could swing it. But I don't think you're going to find Kwang and his gang registered among the delegates.'

'Damn the delegates.' Hutton was on his feet, yelling. 'Let's get into the *Times* information system and find out who these motherfuckers really are.'

CHAPTER 23

Sunday 18th May 1997

Cannes

Summer presented its visiting card on the second Sunday of the Festival: it arrived by stealth during the night and the dawn was still and hot and glorious. The uncertainties of the spring weather were coming to an end. No clouds disturbed the contented sky and the Mediterranean beneath looked settled and wholesome.

This was the traditional day when the whole of the French Riviera would descend on the town for a final glimpse of the Festival. Cars from as far away as Saint-Raphaël, Saint-Maxime and Saint-Tropez, Cavalaire-sur-Mer and Bormes-les-Mimosas would jam the coast road from early in the morning for one last look at the stars and the star-makers. The Croisette was usually as crowded as Fifth Avenue on Saint Patrick's Day with a circulating parade of locals and delegates and tourists trying to catch the last tango in Cannes. The beaches would be bedecked with bodies anxious to pay the extravagant prices necessary to be thought a final part of this extravagant event.

But not today.

The roads had been closed. Only intermittent military vehicles and police motorcycles sped urgently back and forth. The wide pavement remained incongruously empty save for what looked like a sporadic journalist making his way from one point of information to another. The sun could have saved its rays, for the beach was all but deserted. Only a few small children paddled quietly in the shallow water.

It reminded Renaud of Arromanches-les-Bains. As a young man he had visited the film festival at Deauville, a commercial event that attempted to stretch the other end of the summer to give the local hotels an extra week's life in September and to promote American films that were due for release in France. He hadn't liked it – it had none of the class of Cannes. It seemed to be run by publicity people, not by anyone with a true passion for cinema. So he decided to leave and rented a car to visit some of the historic sights of D-Day. At Arromanches, where the first troops had landed on 6 June 1944, the remains of the cement-filled ships and barges sunk by the Allies to form a harbour were still there in a half crescent off the shore, like a ragged memorial of broken teeth. That September day had been just as clear and as warm as this one in May, yet no children played on the unspoiled sand, nor any adults swam in the brisk waters of the Channel, as if out of respect for those who had died there.

During his five years as Director he had always walked to work on the second Sunday. By this stage of the Festival, with only two days left, he had a sense of how well it had gone. There were rarely any bad years – the event was a self-propelling success – only good years and vintage years. Even the threats of the Libyan leader Muammar Gaddafi, which had kept the Americans away ten years previously, had not marred one of his predecessor's Festivals. To find a failure he had to cast his mind back nearly thirty years to les événements of 1968 when Jean-Luc Godard and François Truffaut and the rest of the French New Wave had brought the Festival crashing to a halt.

Renaud looked out across the bay. Normally, on such a Sunday, it would take on a vitality of its own, yachts with their multi-coloured spinnakers billowing on the horizon, water-skiers criss-crossing closer to the shore and motor boats carving furious furrows between the hotel piers and the larger vessels that lay at anchor. Today the sea was lightly flecked with a few curious craft that had risked coming to see any possible action, maintaining a cautious distance from the pair of frigates that continued to keep their guns steadfastly trained on the Majestic Hotel.

It seemed to Renaud that he had stepped into some hallucination born of his own anxiety, which would thankfully dissolve the moment he could clear it from his mind. But as he drew closer to the Majestic he could see the absurdly camouflaged tanks stationed in silent vigil and, high on the hotel roof nesting like carrion crows, a machine-gun post with two attendants silhouetted against the pure blue of the sky.

He knew it was the end of Cannes for him. He would have to resign whatever happened. He was partially relieved that his father was not alive to witness this fall from grace. And, if things went badly wrong, it could be the end of Cannes for everyone. It would be impossible for people to return next year to a place scarred by bloodshed and death. Maybe, he thought, this was part of some divine ordinance. Maybe, in some celestial blueprint unseen by man, it was decreed that there should only be fifty such saturnalia and no more.

Renaud glanced at his watch. He had intended to be early for the crisis meeting and now he was nearly late. He lowered his head and quickened his step.

'So, what did she say?'

'She said she thought we could start again and make a go of things.'

'And what did you say?'

'I said I thought we couldn't. I said we'd had a good time, and – you know, good times come to an end.'

Sandra closed the book she was reading. 'Why didn't you just tell her to fuck off? It strikes me her affections seem to be in exact proportion to your career prospects. As long as you're in the big time that's the only place she wants to be.'

Robert leant over the stone balcony and contemplated the two men looping a tennis ball backwards and forwards on the only Montfleury court that was occupied. 'That's not strictly true. I told her I was quitting when this was over and she still wanted to patch things up.'

Sandra pushed her sunglasses up onto her head. 'One day, Robert, you may begin to understand women. She knows you're not quitting. I know you're not quitting. Your career is just beginning.'

He turned to face her. 'I am, you know. There's something I've been meaning to tell you . . .'

But as he looked at Sandra, now every inch the war correspondent in the military grey shirt and slacks she had bought the previous day, raring to go to what she referred to as 'the party' at the Majestic that evening, he could hardly bring himself to explain.

'Yes?' she said expectantly.

'I – I need a breather, I want to get out for a while.' He studied her reaction. None was forthcoming. 'Besides, for some time now I've had an urge to write.'

'Your memoirs?'

He smiled. 'No. No more show-business, not for the moment. You're going to think this stupid but I've always wanted to write history books – sort of popular ones. Maybe for children.'

'You're right. I think it's stupid. What's wrong with reality, Robert?'

'History is real,' he countered defensively. 'Nothing could be more real. It's only when we fail to understand it that we find ourselves in fuck-ups like we're in today.'

'I know.' Sandra opened her book again.' We're all fucked up. If we read more books there wouldn't be any wars.' She snapped hers shut. 'Give us a break, kiddo. You're hiding from yourself. You've got the inside track on the hottest news story of the year and you stand here mouthing about books. This is history in the making – and if you don't want to be part of it you've got to be seriously disturbed.'

He had turned again to watch the men playing tennis. 'Maybe I am,' he replied, too softly for her to hear him.

He felt her arms come round his waist from behind. 'Here endeth the lesson. It's Sunday. I forgive you. But there's something I have to ask you.'

'Yes?' he enquired nervously.

'If you're really thinking of quitting, is it okay if I do some stuff to camera when the shit hits the fan? You could tell Hurley you were trying to get into the hotel ahead of the crew or something like that.'

The International Consultative Committee had been convened in the conference room on the floor above Renaud's office. His custom was to use it for the final meeting of the Festival jury to impress upon them the gravity of their decision making, but, prior to that, to have them gather in less formal surroundings, over a drink or a meal if possible.

Lord Brown either remembered Renaud or had been well briefed.

'Monsieur Callet, how nice to see you again. My wife sends her regards. She's been following your Festival with interest, even before these, er, these last days.'

Renaud scrutinised the Governor as closely as he could without seeming impolite. Behind the diplomatic breeziness, was there a sense of real tragedy? The man seemed to have aged twenty years since he had seen him in Hong Kong. His skin was grey and tired, his bearing weary, his eyes watery and lifeless. He could not have slept last night, a fact corroborated by his less than immaculate clothes.

'I remember her vividly,' Renaud acknowledged, shaking the Governor's hand. 'She seemed to be very upset and wistful about leaving Hong Kong.'

'That's the trouble with women. They tend to make everything so personal. You've got to keep an emotional distance from these things or else you'll never make the right decision. Never make any decision at all, probably.'

'Gentlemen, can I ask you to be seated?' General Le Prince assumed his position at the head of the table. 'We are under a certain amount of time pressure as you all know.'

Le Prince was flanked by the *Sous-Préfet des Alpes Maritimes* and the Commander of the CRS. Down the table on his right hand side sat the deputy French Foreign Minister, Joseph Doillon, then Rudolf Ruzicka, the assistant Secretary-General of the United Nations, and beside him Lord Brown. Facing them were Jules Marey, head of French Internal Security, Tait Brady, the Australian High Commissioner to London and, directly opposite Lord Brown, Defang Zhu, the Chinese Ambassador to France.

Writing pads, pencils and small bottles of Evian water had been laid out on the table in front of each place. The rest of the assembly – senior police officers, military men, civil servants and more junior aides – ranged themselves on the upright chairs along the walls. Renaud took up a position behind Defang Zhu where he could watch Lord Brown, who he sensed would be the key figure in the day's decision.

'In welcoming you to this tragic occasion,' began Le Prince, 'may I remind you that this committee, as is explicit from its name, has been convened for consultative purposes only. The final decision on our policy with regard to this siege remains solely with the President of the Republic or his officers acting on his orders.'

He cleared his throat to let the message sink in. 'Nevertheless we are in a position in this room to make recommendations. In the course of the night I have conducted bilateral discussions with all those here today. Now we have the opportunity to meet together to see if there are any options which we may have overlooked.'

He turned to the notes that lay before him on the table. 'I spoke to Mr Kwang again on the telephone just an hour ago. He declined once more our offer of fresh food for those inside the hotel. It would appear that they have sufficient supplies for a long siege, or at least they wish to give that impression. It is evident that he is in radio contact with other members of his organisation in various countries. In our previous conversation he was able to report details of the way his broadcast was presented in Holland, Australia and the United States. On investigation, these proved to be correct.'

'Which organisation?' It was Rudolf Ruzicka who put the question.

Le Prince looked at Lord Brown who bowed his head. 'There is no Hong Kong Liberation Front,' he said. 'At least, not until now. Kwang Lo has no sort of criminal record on our files. On the contrary he gives a lot of money to charity. Apparently he made a fortune in the export business, garments mainly.'

'Whatever his organisation,' Le Prince continued, 'I'm afraid I have little doubt of his intentions. This seems horribly like a suicide mission. He is awaiting our reply. If he does not get one, or it is one that does not accede to his conditions, he will, he says, begin to kill the hostages one by one. He informed me that the first execution will take place at seven o'clock this evening. When the clock in the church above the Old Port strikes seven, to be precise.'

'We should dismantle the clock.' The booming tones of Jules Marey rang through the room. 'It makes little sense to help his dramatic gestures.'

'I doubt if stopping the clock will stop the killings.' Henri Chaillot's deputy, Joseph Doillon, had a deliberate, academic voice. 'It will be a stain on the French nation if one single life is lost to these assassins. We must outmanoeuvre them strategically.'

'Yes?' General Le Prince waited for his solution.

'I speak for myself and my minister, Henri Chaillot, whose life is immediately in danger. It is essential that we offer some accommodating gesture to buy us more time.'

'Like what?' Marey eyed him over the top of his half-rimmed spectacles.

'That we will enter negotiations. That there is some chance that a form of agreement may be reached.'

Lord Brown inclined his head as if he were slightly hard of hearing. 'You mean that we should negotiate with these people simply because they are holding a gun at our head?'

'They're not holding one at your head,' countered Doillon. 'But at several of your countrymen and at one of France's most loyal servants.'

'There can be no question of any compromises.' The Chinese Ambassador, Defang Zhu, looked unfocusedly into the middle distance as he spoke, like a judge pronouncing sentence. 'These are vermin. They must be exterminated like vermin.'

Tait Brady was inflamed. 'Just wait a minute, Mr Ambassador, I may be wrong but I don't think Hong Kong is yours for another seven weeks.'

'Six,' Zhu corrected him, in the matter-of-fact way of someone telling the time.

'All right, try this one. Try Matsuyama. Just type in the letters MATSUYAMA – the computer should do the rest.'

'Is he a person or a movement?' Chantal asked.

'A bit of both. He took over from Junzo Okudaira. They're in cahoots with several Palestine splinter groups.' Hutton ticked off the man's achievements on his fingers. 'Lod Airport, the French Embassy in the Hague, our Embassy in Kuala Lumpur, the hijacking in Bangladesh and – we're pretty certain – the foiled attempt on the Olympics last year. This is Matsuyama's sort of town.'

'Nothing,' she said.

Hutton looked over her shoulder. 'No, you idiot, all one word.' He jabbed his finger impatiently at the screen where she had written MATSU YAMA.

Chantal stiffened. She didn't like to be treated in this fashion – after all it was she who was doing the Americans a favour. Robert sensed this.

'Go easy, Hutton,' he suggested. 'We're not likely to get there any more quickly by screaming at each other.'

His friend held up his hands in apology. 'I'm sorry. Sorry, Chantal. I didn't realise I was doing it. Boy, I could do with a drink.'

The atmosphere in Chantal's tiny office was vaporously hot and sticky. They had negotiated their way into the Palais with some difficulty. Security was now tighter than ever – a classic case of bolting the stable door in order to impress, Robert thought – but Chantal's credentials were in order for the staff meeting. Robert's accreditation card, even with its *presse soirée* and gold dot blessing from Madame Rivette, was useless. The first guard had levelled a gun at him before he had time to speak and, when he refused to go away, had looked intimidatingly like using it. Fortunately an officer came along at that moment and was quick to restrain him. He recognised Robert and put a phone call through to the head of security requesting admission. The answer was some time in coming but it appeared his name had now been put on the list. Hutton was another matter. As a journalist he was *persona non grata*. Chantal besought the officer to let him in, explaining that he was crucial in their search for information. Reluctantly exercising his own discretion, something quite rare in French bureaucracy, the lieutenant wrote out a temporary pass on condition that Monsieur Craig always remained in the company of the two and would leave the building by five p.m. at the latest.

Chantal had been amazed at the ease with which they crossed the Atlantic and entered the *New York Times* computer network. By simply typing in Hutton's codeword, MATELOT – a jokey epithet he had inherited from a previous Paris correspondent and had never been in the mood to change – she was able to access the newspaper's entire library.

A sheet of faces came up on the screen, some of them wearing Arab head gear.

'Let's call them up one by one,' Hutton suggested, calmer now. 'Robert, you'd better come and have a look.'

Robert stood directly behind Chantal. She dropped her hand from the keyboard and gave his knee a reassuring squeeze, a gesture that he reciprocated by laying a gentle palm on her shoulder. A series of unsmiling, unshaven faces paraded before them, changing as she clicked the return bar on her computer.

'Wonderful people to do business with,' Hutton observed drily, 'especially if you want a career in cement.'

'Why's that?' she queried.

'It's a tradition handed on from Abu Nidal. Whenever these guys put up a building, you can be sure there's a concrete foundation full of their opponents – other terrorist groups even.'

'Wait a minute, hold on.' Robert tightened his grip on Chantal's shoulder. 'The one we just pased – go back, I'm certain I've seen him before.'

'What do I do, Hutton?' she asked.

He leant forward and hit a rapid succession of keys that brought back the previous picture.

'That's him,' Robert exclaimed. 'Assam Abdul Jabbar al Baghdaddi. I could swear he was in the hotel, but I can't quite place him. Let me think. We're getting warm.'

'I know where you have seen him,' said Chantal.

'Where?' the two men yelled simultaneously in excitement.

'He was not in the hotel, I'm afraid. He was in the first file of the Red Army Faction. Do you not remember, near the very end?'

Robert stepped back and mopped his face with his handkerchief, embarrassed at his mistake.

'She's right,' Hutton agreed. 'Let's press on. Only twenty thousand more terrorist groups to go, each one prettier than the last.'

Chantal continued to press the return button, allowing about three seconds to scrutinise each photograph.

'Monsieur Craig,' she said, still looking at the screen.

'Hutton, please,' he insisted.

'Would I not be right in thinking you have a portable computer in your hotel room?'

'Yes,' he conceded sheepishly.

'And that it has a modem that will connect you on the phone line to the *New York Times*.'

'Right again.'

'So why are we doing it here, on my computer?'

'It's much bigger,' Hutton insisted sheepishly, 'and much faster. Besides, the lines out of Cannes are so bad – they have to be routed through Lyons or somewhere – I could never have held the connection.'

'But I am on the telephone line, also.' Chantal kept steadfastly clicking up the pictures.

'Much better circuit than you're likely to get in a hotel and –'

She finished his sentence for him. 'And you would not have been the only journalist to gain entrance to the Palais if we had gone to your room.'

'Bob's a journalist, too,' Hutton pointed out contritely.

'We have a government minister and an ambassador in there and the cream of our film industry. The Australian public does not want to see those people killed, nor anyone else.' Beads of perspiration were breaking out on Tait Brady's diplomatic brow. 'The British government must take action to avoid any tragedy and it they have to go as far as conceding nationality, so be it.'

Defang Zhu seemed to be in possession of an internal cooling system that made him impervious to the heat. It matched his character. 'There is no question of that. As soon as Hong Kong resumes its rightful position as part of the People's Republic of China we would revoke any such law. It is not possible for Chinese citizens to have British nationality, nor the nationality of any other country.'

'You can revoke what you like. That's the future. We're dealing with the present. We're dealing with people who may have no future. For Christ's sake,' – Brady turned to Jules Marey on his right – 'can't France offer them some form of temporary domicile? It's your problem.'

'It's not our problem,' Marey replied stonily. 'It remains for the present time, as it has for the past hundred years, the responsibility of the United Kingdom.'

All eyes now turned to Lord Brown, who had been making notes with a silver pen. Deliberately taking his time he screwed the cap back on and carefully placed it parallel to the pad in front of him. 'This is not an easy situation for us,' he said. 'We have not previously had any dealings with any Liberation Front. We've no reason to suppose that these terrorists represent anyone but themselves. We have gone as far as we intend to on the question of British nationality in the agreement of 1994. Her Majesty's Government cannot be blackmailed by these men. Whatever the price we may have to pay in the ensuing days, we do not intend to deviate from our stated policy and our solemn treaty obligations.'

He looked directly as Defang Zhu who nodded gravely. 'It is terrible thing that the government of another country must bear this burden,' Brown went on, 'but my advice to the General and his President is this, First, you must establish whether or not these men are bluffing. It seems to me there is a more than fair chance that they may be. If they are, you may freely arrest them. If they are not, then you must end this siege with military might and God bless those whose lives will be sacrificed in the preservation of international peace and justice.'

Robert stood for a moment with his forehead against the wall and closed his eyes. He couldn't get Elizabeth out of his thoughts, nor did he want to. He pictured her alone in her room and a surge of desperation came over him. Had she slept? Had they harmed her? Had they raped her? Was she still alive? He felt impotent and desolate. The clock in the Old Port struck five.

He could sense the eyes of the other two on the back of his neck and he feared that any words of comfort from Hutton might make him break down completely. 'We're wasting time with Japs and Arabs,' he said. 'Let's concentrate on mainland China.'

'All billion of them,' Hutton retorted. 'Footslogging work.'

'Fingerslogging, too,' Chantal observed.

'Why not start with the dissidents, the terrorist groups?'

'There is no terrorism in China,' Hutton pointed out with conviction. 'Remember Chairman Mao: "a terrorist is a fish in the waters of a liberal society." No revolutionaries lingering in jails waiting for their comrades to hijack an aircraft and barter their way out. Look at the way the Communist Chinese flushed out the Triads. There just aren't any there now. If they were caught, they were killed.'

Chantal looked up from the keyboard. 'What exactly are Triads?'

'Chinese mafia,' Hutton replied. 'They eat chop suey rather than spaghetti.'

'They are Chinese but not in China?'

'Not any more.'

'So where do they operate.'

'Everywhere. Every major city. Anywhere there's a Chinatown.'

She became more persistent. 'But you said Hong Kong.'

Hutton was flattered that she was regarding him as such a fount of knowledge. His thoughts lingered on her brown legs, neatly folded over each other.

'Are there any left in Hong Kong?' she repeated.

'I beg your pardon – any what?'

'Any Triads still there?'

He gave an ironic chuckle. 'Only about one in five of the entire population.'

Robert picked up her train of thought. 'So what's going to happen to them when the Chinese take over?'

'How should I know? They're not all criminals, you know. It used to be a noble thing to be a Triad.'

'But the ones that are dealing in organised crime,' – Robert snapped his fingers in satisfaction – 'they're going to have to get out, right?'

Chantal had already begun to attack the computer with renewed zest and the names and details of the foremost Triad groups rapidly came up in luminous green letters on the screen. 'San Yee On. Main Triad group behind gambling in Hong Kong. Renowned for their violence.'

She scrolled further down the file. There were photographs and sketches of suspected gang members. The information was less than complete. Unlike the terrorist dossiers the faces here looked eminently respectable. Only a propensity for wearing dark glasses suggested that anything might be amiss with these smart-suited businessmen.

'Those two men in the hotel,' she turned to Robert, 'anything like them?'

He shook his head.

She accelerated through the files, urged on by the conviction that they were going in the right direction. 'Wo Sing Wo, also known as Sing Wor, an offshoot of Wo Hop To, now believed to be based in Manchester, England. 14K, named after its original meeting place in 14 Po Wah Road, Canton. Offshoot of Hung Fat Shun. Infiltrated Holland and Britain in the 1970s, runs Chinatown in London's Soho. Tai Huen Chai, also known as the Big Circle. Active in Holland and Belgium. Known to have penetrated Britain and Australia in the mid 1990s. Ruthless and extremely brutal, its membership is believed to include many former Red Guards.'

'Look at this,' she murmured to the others. 'Red Guards.'

'They're different from the Red Army,' Hutton explained. 'Former Maoists. Bit old now. Carry on.' He read from the screen. 'Go Joey Tai, offshoot Triad group formed in New York's Chinatown around 1985. Run by Fred and Harry Yung – look at this – thought to have extensive membership in Hong Kong where drug –'

'Stop. Stop. Stop.' Robert was shaking Chantal's chair and screaming uncontrollably.

'I'm sorry –' Hutton began. But Robert cut him off.

'Not you. The picture. That group.' He gasped for breath. 'The two men on the extreme right. That's them. Can we go in on them?'

Chantal typed in the combination of letters so that the pair filled the screen, one corpulent, the other skinny, like Abbott and Costello. Abbott had the darker complexion with a goatee beard. Costello's eyes were mere pin-pricks in his porcine face.

'I'm sure of it.' Robert read out their names. 'Zhang Yi, 36, and Wang Feng, 37. Both born in Shanghai. Arrived in Hong Kong 1971. Both suspected of being active in the heroin trade in South East Asia.'

'Put that one in the memory and track the Jap,' Hutton found it impossible to contain his excitement.

He didn't have to wait long. 'There, look.' Chantal pointed to the stooped, almost shoulderless figure, with the misshapen billowing arms. 'Kenji Shindo,' she read, 'formerly active with the Japanese Red Army Faction, now in charge of security for Go Joey Tai. Further pictures files 237 and 238.'

She called up the numbers and there was the photograph they had all been waiting for. Shindo was pictured eating with a group of Chinese on the Jumbo Floating Restaurant in Aberdeen Harbour and seated beside him, smiling at the camera like an innocent tourist, was a man who, in the past twenty-four hours, had become one of the most famous faces in the world – Kwang Lo.

'Print them out,' pleaded Hutton. 'Print them, Chantal, three copies.'

He turned to Robert in exultation. 'It's a shared story. What do you want to do with it?'

Robert looked at the agitated features of his friend. 'It's yours,' he said. 'But you'd better be quick. We've got to tell the French.'

Hutton glanced at his watch. 'I can get this on the midday news as a *Times* exclusive. They'll promote my story in the first edition. It'll lead the paper, whatever happens.' He grabbed Robert by the shoulders. 'Thank you. I needed this one. You've no idea how much.'

He kissed Chantal on the cheeks. 'Lunch. In Paris. Right? On me. Le Pré Catelan.'

'D'accord, matelot,' she smiled.

'Great,' he responded delightedly, making for the door. 'I've got to go. Good luck.' Suddenly it dawned on him and he stopped. 'Jesus, Rob, I'd forgotten. Don't worry. She'll be all right.'

Robert managed a faint smile. 'Thanks. I guess we'll find out soon.'

As Hutton left, Chantal rested her brow on the keyboard in exhaustion. Robert knew it was his turn to explain.

'I have a friend. In there.'

'I think I sensed that. I'm sorry.'

He changed the subject. 'Listen, we'd better get this information up to the war council or whatever they call themselves.'

She lifted her head back slowly from the computer and rested it against the back of her chair. 'I will go and tell Renaud. Then I expect they will want to see you.'

She gathered up the two remaining photocopies and got up to leave.

'Don't be too long,' he begged her. 'I can't just stand here. I've got to *do* something.'

Chantal rested her cheek against his. 'Men should always be in love,' she said. 'That's the way women want them to be.'

Alone now, he sat down in her chair. He had nothing to do. After a while, he reached in his pocket and took out Elizabeth's poem and read it again. Chantal had left the computer switched on. To fill in the unforgiving minutes, he copied it out onto the screen.

'Must a little weep, love.
(Foolish me!)
And so fall asleep, love.
Loved by thee.'

He realised the machine was still connected to the *New York Times* archive so, following exactly the same method he had seen Chantal employ, he typed in the search and enquire code. The computer responded with its usual electronic hiccups followed by a humming pause. The screen went blank. He must have messed it up, he thought. But after thirty seconds the poem reappeared with two new lines flashing at the bottom. They gave the name of the author – Robert Browning 1812–1889 – and the title: – 'A Woman's Last Word'.

As he took in the information, a worry that had been nagging, unresolved, at the back of his mind came brutally to the fore and he realised the excruciating irony of what he had just done. They had found out who the terrorists were. Hutton had his scoop. Chantal would have told the committee by now, it was too late to stop her. But the fact that these men had no political following and were merely common criminals immediately ruled out any chance of a compromise. The British were hardly going to negotiate with a gang of Triads. It was now a question of total capitulation or total confrontation – most probably the latter. He had become the architect of Elizabeth's death. Porphyria, he thought, prophetic.

Elvis Ho knew that it was now or never. He had no idea what was going on inside the hotel but from the way the French army was manoeuvring at the gates to the Majestic he could tell that an attack was minutes away. It was too dangerous to remain in his attic room; he didn't like the look of the tank that was pointing directly at it. He had to get out fast once the bullets started flying. Just like the storming of the Summer Palace, he thought, as he ripped down the middle of another of his sheets.

'Well done.'

Robert took the Festival Director's proffered hand. 'It was as much Mademoiselle Coutard's work as mine.'

'I know,' the Frenchman replied, offering a wan smile, 'but you have done much for us and we are in your debt.'

From their vantage point of the roof of the Palais des Festivals, almost exactly where Robert had had his camera positioned two nights previously, they could see the vigorous troop movements below. Officers with mobile phones were guiding platoons of paratroopers and commandos into what looked like attack positions. The Croisette was now alive with a hectic traffic in jeeps and trucks carrying more soldiers. A row of ambulances had ominously drawn up in front of the Gray d'Albion Apartments.

Renaud read his mind. 'I expect you want to know what has been decided. It is confidential. You will not use it in a broadcast?'

'How can I?' shrugged Robert. 'No camera, no microphone.'

Renaud seemed reassured. 'In view of what you have done I think I can tell you. Sources in London have now confirmed that Kwang Lo is almost certainly one of the leaders of the Go Joey Tai Triad gang. There is no Hong Kong Liberation Front – the whole thing is a Triad operation. So on the advice of the Governor of Hong Kong, we have informed the terrorists that we know who they are and they have until their own deadline,' – Renaud glanced at his watch – 'which is in twelve minutes from now, to agree to our conditions for surrender. They will be given a fair trial and any terms of imprisonment will be served in European jails, at the end of which they will be free to remain in either Britain or France. This is a substantial concession – the idea came directly from the Elysée.'

'And if they don't?' asked Robert.

'It is thought they are bluffing on the question of executions. The odds against them are insuperable. They have forfeited any international support now their true *métier* has been discovered. Just one death would turn world opinion completely against them. But the only way to find out is to let the deadline pass. If we hear gunshots or see a body the troops will go in.'

Robert was incredulous. 'Why wait till then? Why sacrifice a single hostage's life?'

A voice behind him cut icily through the humid evening. 'It will be more than one if we have to go in. The General estimates seventy per cent civilian casualties. I'd put it closer to eighty.'

Robert swivelled round to observe a tall, balding man putting his pipe back into his mouth. 'I'm Brown of Hong Kong. No need to introduce yourself, I know who you are. Do you want a pair of binoculars?' He handed them to Robert. 'These are French army issue. Not much use, I prefer my own.'

Robert accepted the glasses from him and scanned the Majestic. The machine-gun post had been moved from the roof and there was no sign of life anywhere in the hotel.

'It's madness,' he found himself saying to Lord Brown. 'Why do they have to go in? Why can't they sit it out?'

'It's chaps like you who are largely to blame. If this thing hadn't been on every bloody television station in the world for the past two days, the French government could have held on for a bit. Now it's impossible. They have to clear this up. Quite apart from the national disgrace, it would be political suicide for the government if they're not seen to take decisive action. Look, something's stirring now. There, on the third floor, directly above the little garden. Can you see?'

Robert trained his binoculars on the movement. Indeed, something was happening. The balcony windows of one of the bedrooms had been opened. His hands began to tremble and the lenses of the glasses steamed up. He furiously wiped them on the front of his shirt. Bringing them back to his eyes, he witnessed a sight that sent a sickening shock through his system. A fragile figure in white was being pushed out onto the balcony. A violet blindfold covered her eyes and her arms were tied behind her back. She stood very still.

'Oh dear,' muttered Lord Brown, 'I rather feared this might happen.'

Robert felt paralysed, like a patient in an operating theatre who knows the anaesthetic hasn't worked but is prevented by the muscle relaxants from being able to tell anybody.

He opened his mouth to speak but the words would barely come out. 'You've got to stop this,' he eventually beseeched the man beside him. 'That girl. Don't you understand? She's mine.'

'Yours?' inquired the Governor.

'Mine,' he screamed, shaking with rage. 'I'm going to marry her. You've got to do something.'

Only a lifetime's diplomatic training prevented his companion from allowing himself to display his own emotion. 'She's mine, too,' he said very quietly.

'*Yours*? What do you mean?'

'My daughter,' the Governor responded. 'Beth. Or do you call her Lizzie?'

'My God.' Immediately it all came clear to Robert: the temple in Hollywood Road, Hong Kong, the smattering of Cantonese, her remark about being pick of the crop. The Triads knew exactly who they had on that balcony.

'You have the power. You've *got* to do something,' he implored.

'Beth's a good girl,' the Governor whispered. 'Whatever she faces she will meet with dignity.'

'Dignity!' screamed Robert. 'What's dignity got to do with it? Life is for living, not for handing over to history. I know all that shit about Scott of the Antarctic you fed her. You're a nation that thrives on a raft of dead failures. You have no conception of the present, just an out-moded value system that covers up the privileges of your mightily undignified past. Honour, dignity, the rule of law. What have you done to Hong Kong? Used it, thrived on it, then thrown it away and totally betrayed it. The greatest betrayal of this century. How can anyone do that? Christ, I cannot believe it. I'm looking at a father prepared to stand by and watch his own daughter's death, justifying it with pathetic platitudes. Well, they won't bring her back to life. Haven't you ever heard about sheer human compassion? Is it outlawed in the British Empire? Not in the rule book? Not part of the treaties? Dignity! You fucking English!'

He ran from the roof back into the Palais. It was nearly seven. He had to do something, at least create a diversion. He sped through the empty Moët et Chandon hospitality lounge into the vacant red-carpeted lobby outside the press conference room. The place was deserted except for a couple of soldiers smoking cigarettes. Robert had to stop himself from yelling at them to put them out and *do* something. Instead he headed into the museum-like atrium, past the giant photographs of Brigitte Bardot and Orson Welles and Grace Kelly. The escalator had been stopped so he charged down the marble stairs in the middle, three at a time.

There were no security men at the bottom to indicate which, if any, of the row of glass doors was open. He tried the metal bar on the nearest one. Useless, it was firmly locked. So was the second. And the third. And the fourth. In his desperation he rushed back up the last flight of stairs and grabbed a large white cylindrical stand with an ashtray on top. He ran back down again and flung it at the door as he reached the bottom step. To his amazement, the glass smashed into fragments.

He climbed through the jagged edges, dashing past the sandbags on the Esplanade Georges Pompidou, round to the right towards the Majestic. Two military policemen tried to stop him but, fuelled by some crazed energy, he circled past them and reached the detachment of paras who had formed up by the gates of the hotel.

Their commander was briefing the men. Clearly they would be the first to go in. Robert ran up to him, caught him by the arm and, exhausted, implored him: 'Don't wait. Go in now. They're not bluffing. Why lose an innocent life?'

'You must go back,' ordered the officer. 'It's dangerous.'

'I know it's dangerous,' Robert yelled. 'It's dangerous for her. You've got to help her. For God's sake, do something.'

Two corporals grabbed his arms and held him back, but even they slackened their grip in shock as the bell in the Saracen Tower struck the first note of seven o'clock.

Everyone's gaze fixed on the balcony. She was still standing there, rigid as a statue, but now the black barrel of a rifle emerged from the curtains behind her, trained on the back of her head.

At the very same moment a sturdy figure appeared on another balcony, four floors above where Elizabeth was standing. The man jumped onto the railing, balanced on it like a tightrope walker surveying the scene and then, with a terrifying howl, leapt off, seemingly bent on suicide. He appeared to be Chinese, one of the terrorists. But, as he fell, a trail of twisted white sheets billowed out behind him. He formed an arc in the air, swinging like a pendulum, and with one arm scooped Elizabeth off her balcony. All at once a rifle shot cracked out, and then another, as the two figures fell lifelessly to the ground, their landing masked from those watching by the bushes beneath them.

Someone shouted 'action' through a megaphone. On cue the paras flung open the gate of the Majestic and charged, hollering, up the drive, a network of smoke bombs and thunderflashes exploding ahead of them. Sheets of machine-gun fire swept across the drive from every conceivable direction. It looked as if a protective roof of bullets was sheltering the advance of the main assault force. Blazing flash bombs exploded, one after another along the walls of the hotel. At the same time every window in the lower storeys of the building was smashed by a series of explosions and the air seemed split by a terrifying noise as a direct hit from a tank blasted the plate-glass front doors out of existence.

Robert dashed forward in the wake of the advancing troops. The clamour assailed his senses and the pervasive smoke disorientated him. Blindly he ran on, crouching low as if this might protect him from the shrapnel. He veered to his right, scrambling over the fence that secluded the Majestic tea garden and pushed his way through the bushes, making for where he thought Elizabeth had fallen.

The core of the battle was now taking place inside the hotel and he found himself on his own as he approached the

Jacuzzi, a giant stain of blood spreading across its undulating surface. Two bodies lay inert in the middle, one on top of the other. Plunging into the pool he grabbed hold of the man and threw him to one side. Elizabeth lay motionless in the water. Her white dress was drenched in blood, her arms outstretched and her eyes closed. Robert lifted her up in his arms and put his lips to hers.

'Get your hands off me, you bastard,' she screamed.

He couldn't believe it. 'You're alive. Thank God.'

She opened her eyes at the sound of his voice. 'Robert, is it really you? I thought you were one of them.'

'You're alive,' was all he could say, 'you're alive.'

She held on to him, like a child, seeking comfort and protection. 'I thought it was all over. It was awful. They covered my eyes. I didn't want them to.'

'That man over there, Elvis Ho. It's his blood on you. He jumped from his balcony to save you.'

The mention of his name caused Elvis to stir. A patina of purple blood, still growing, extended across his stomach but he managed to open one of his eyes. He caught sight of Elizabeth's gold hair.

'Pornic . . . beautiful,' he mumbled.

His dying act had been his greatest stunt and his lifeless lips were now resolved into a crooked smile, as if he had finally found the escape he had been seeking.

'Elizabeth.' Robert tightened his grip on her soaking body.

'Yes?'

'I love you.'

'How much?' she asked.

He let her go and lay back in the bloodied waters, looking up at the sky, dark with smoke and bright with the cacophonous flashing of shells, and beyond the filtered blue of the dying day. The magic hour. It was an experience of extreme unction. Never in his life before had he felt so sheerly, purely, divinely content.

'Let me count the ways,' he said.

Elizabeth took his hand. 'If we were in a film,' she laughed, 'this is the moment where they would freeze the frame and roll the final credits.'

CHAPTER 24

Monday 30th June 1997

Cannes
The Mayor and City Council of Cannes decided that the Majestic Hotel should be pulled down and a permanent memorial be erected to the 172 people who died there. The Chinese-American architect, Ioh Ming Pei, was commissioned to design it.

No further film festivals would be permitted in the town. The event once known as the Cannes Film Festival would be amalgamated with the one held in Deauville.

Paris
Renaud Callet accepted the post of Director of the Musée d'Orsay, starting next January.

On the steps of Notre-Dame Cathedral, after the memorial service for Henri Chaillot, General Louis Le Prince informed waiting reporters that he would be taking early retirement from the Parachute Brigade.

Chantal Coutard planned to open a computer consultancy on the Rue Jacob. She was looking forward to her lunch that day with Hutton Craig. He had been slightly surprised that she had turned down Le Pré Catelan, suggesting instead that they go to the teashop above W. H. Smith.

Sydney
The Government's intention to announce The Don Lugg Memorial Prize and a bursary of fifty thousand dollars for the best film by a first-time director was thwarted by the Australian Film Board. The award was now to be called the Jenny Bates Memorial Prize and the bursary was increased to

two hundred and fifty thousand dollars.

Vincent Wall drove alone in his 1977 Holden out into the Blue Mountains beyond Sydney. He was looking for a small-holding which he could farm. He didn't want to make any more movies.

Vancouver

Elvis Ho's ashes were scattered in the Strait of Georgia in front of the Pornic Studios by his cousin and his aunt who were granted passports and domicile by the Canadian Government.

New York

Tanya Neris became a front-of-camera reporter for *Arts Action*, taking over the job from which Robert Barrett had resigned.

Hetty Berman signed a three-year contract with the French Tourist Board to help sell Americans 'safe holidays on the Riviera'.

Homer Mangold invited three fellow agents to lunch at '21' to hear about his experiences at the Majestic siege. When the bill came, there was an argument.

Burbank

Leland Walters steadfastly refused to let Warner Bros be associated with any film projects about the tragedy at the Fiftieth Cannes Film Festival.

This caused a rift with Bud Booker who was signed for a record thirty million dollars to play the lead in *Man of the Majestic*.

Barry Schenck, who put together the deal, was quoted in the *Hollywood Reporter* as saying that he didn't need Warners' backing – an Arab businessman had agreed to finance *Man of the Majestic*. Schenck offered Elizabeth Brown five million dollars to play herself in the film. She didn't return his calls.

Sandra Lewis was made senior West Coast producer of *Arts Action*.

Pinewood

Fyodor Lasky began pre-production on *Jupiter Landing II*, anxious to amortise the cost of the existing sets. He retained the same cast and crew, except for Howard and Elizabeth. He put his plans to film Dostoyevsky's *Notes from the Underground* on ice, indefinitely.

London

Robert and Elizabeth had rented an apartment in Wimpole Mews. He walked, as he did every day, to the London Library where he was researching a book on the Children's Crusade of 1212. This was thought by some historians to be the basis of the Pied Piper of Hamelin. He was going to have tea with Edgar Montillion at Fortnum and Mason. Elizabeth had a part in a production of *The Idiot* at the Royal Court. She thought she might be pregnant. Whether it was a boy or a girl, she and Robert had agreed to call it Kim.

Hong Kong

Lady Brown was not aware of her putative grandchild as she stood beside her husband, watching the British flag being lowered for the last time at Government House. Lord Brown had secretly agreed that the Communist Chinese could take over the Crown Colony twelve hours before the statutory time to minimise any demonstrations or risk of planned explosions. Forty thousand troops from the People's Liberation Army had landed at the Wanchai and Star Ferry Piers and now formed a solid brown river as they marched up to Government House. A news black-out had been imposed. Sheridan Kimber, like all other journalists, was under temporary arrest.

The new Governor, Defang Zhu, revealed that Kai Tak Airport was now under military control and no one, except the British, would be permitted to leave Hong Kong for the foreseeable future. This was the policy of the hard-line government of Premier O-Lan Wang. It was announced from Beijing that the Hong Kong Stock Exchange would be closed forthwith. Wang regarded it as a form of gambling and therefore immoral and illegal.

This had world-wide repercussions.